The Hand Life Dealt You

Additional books by author:

Firehouse Fraternity Oral History Series:
Volume I: Becoming a Firefighter
Volume II: Life Between Alarms
Volume III: Equipment
Volume IV: Responding
Volume V: Riots to Renaissance
Volume VI: Changing the NFD

The Newark Riots: A View from the Firehouse

An Eerie Silence: An Oral History of Newark
Firefighters at the WTC

Hervey's Boys: New Jersey's First Chinese Community
1870-1886 (And What Happened After That)

Fiction:
The Firebox Stalker
A-zou: A Woman Living in Interesting Times

Children's Fiction:
A Hundred Battles (YA)
A Broken Glass (YA)
Balancing Act (Middle Grade)

The Hand Life Dealt You

Neal Stoffers

Springfield and Hunterdon Publishing
Copyright 2018
www.newarkfireoralhistory.com

First Printing: 2018

ISBN 978-1-970034-02-8

Springfield and Hunterdon Publishing
East Brunswick, NJ 08816

Chapter One

Bob Brendler made his way to his Ford Thunderbird. Was this what life would be from now on? Going to retired Police and Fire picnics to reminisce about the past, talk about doctors, broken marriages, and discuss the future of others after driving a car meant for a younger man. He laughed to himself. It was a warm, sunny summer day and he had an hour's drive to think about it, no need for the radio today. Memories would keep him company on his trek. Leaning on his cane, he unlocked the car door, tossed his manmade appendage on to the passenger's seat, and eased behind the wheel. How had he come to this juncture of life? The time had flown past; the beginning now seemed so distant. God, he sounded old. It had all begun with a wedding, not his, Jack's.

****

Bob weaved through the reception hall looking at the name tags on each table. There were ten tables arranged around the dance floor with eight seats per table. Not that large a wedding reception. That is what happens when the bride and groom have known each other their entire lives; they tend to invite the same people. The band was setting up on a low stage at the far end of the dance floor to the left of the wedding party table. Servers were busy putting the final touches onto the hall. The smell of chicken marsala wafted through the air as guests streamed in from the church. Bob was one of the first to arrive, an advantage of traveling solo. He knew he would be seated with the guys from Six Engine. The name tag he was looking for belonged to

Kathy Stanley. With a quick scan of the room he picked out the old crew from Six. They waved to him and pointed to a chair at their table. The young Newark firefighter made his way toward them while continuing his search for Kathy's name tag. He had been introduced to her when she had stopped by the firehouse and saw her often when he worked part time driving a delivery van for the company owned by the bride's brother. But would she even remember him? Doubtful. Bob was determined to get to know her better and have at least one dance with the woman before the night was through. Knowing where she was seated would add to his chances of success.

The wedding of Jack Romanov to Gloria Helms was a major event around the firehouse. There had been wagers made about whether Gloria could cure Jack of his habitual meandering from one relationship to another. The ease with which she had tamed him had disappointed some of the guys, but Bob had expected it after the introduction to Gloria Jack had given him. At that time the two men had only known each other for a few months, but it was obvious to Bob that Jack had capitulated. Over the next three years, he had seen Jack commit himself to her and finally surrender to the holy state of matrimony.

Jack's best childhood friend had been Gloria's brother Frank. Gloria's best friend had been Jack's sister Stacey, who was the wife of one of the guys on his crew, Ray Frederick. There could be no secrets between the newlyweds because they had each seen the other through every step of life. Bob admitted to himself that he was a little jealous of such a comfortable relationship. He was an only child, so there had been no younger sister with a retinue of friends seeking his attention. He had to learn to fend for himself. The lessons he learned over the years would serve him well tonight.

Bob reached the table without seeing Kathy's name tag - a setback - but only a minor one. If he stayed attentive, he would spot her early. Then it would take a little aggression to keep other guys away and a little assertion to get her attention, both doable. His reputation around the firehouse was that of an aggressive young buck. These tendencies easily transferred from the fire ground to the dance floor, even if his dancing skills resembled a firefighter working. The guys around the table were from the firehouse on Springfield and Hunterdon, but all of them were now retired. From the name tags he could see that Six Engine's present crew was seated at the table next to this one, so Bob assumed he was sitting at that table. As he turned and moved in that direction Matt Richardson stopped him.

"You're sitting with the old guys tonight, Bob." Matt laughed. "Probably because Kathy Stanley is sitting here and she'll need some young blood to keep her awake."

Bob could not believe his luck. He should have known that Kathy would be seated with the old crew from Six. They were the ones she knew the best. She had been the reporter who had covered a sensational story centered on Six Engine just before Bob had been appointed to the job. These were the guys who were part of that story. The reporter spent the following year writing a book about those experiences which had required her to spend some time with them. Then one by one they had retired. Now Jack was the only one left from that crew. Gloria's brother Frank had been the man of the hour, but he had resigned from the job before Bob had been appointed. All of this meant that Bob had the best seat in the house. He wondered if Kathy would be happy with the arrangement. One of the guys suggested that they switch seats. This drew a swift response from his wife and laughter from everyone else.

The thought crossed the firefighter's mind that he was overreaching himself. Kathy was a beautiful, exotic bird. Why would she be interested in a simple firefighter? They did not match up well. She was a college graduate, a former television news reporter who had written and published a book. He was a vo-tech high school graduate. He did enjoy writing and took quiet pride in what he produced, but the products of his imagination were rarely shared with anyone. That only made the woman more intimidating. Compared to her experiences, his was a very provincial life. He was a Newark boy who rarely made it out of New Jersey, while she was an Amer-Asian girl from Rhode Island who had traveled the world. The realization that the best result would probably be her viewing him as a pleasant diversion brought a smile to his face. If it ever got that far, playing the part of a pleasant diversion would be fun while it lasted. The unpleasant part would come when she kicked his teeth in and threw him away. The ride would be worth it.

His seat allowed a full view of the hall, but put his back to the wedding table. The band was across the dance floor so they would not be too loud; an important point if he wanted to get to know Kathy better. As he sat, Bob looked at the entrance to the hall and saw Frank

4

and Chingli Helms walk in. Kathy Stanley was walking beside Chingli, chatting enthusiastically. They were both wearing Chinese silk dresses. If he remembered right, the dresses were called qipaos. The style they were wearing almost reached the floor and clung to the figures of both women, with a slit up the left leg that would distract every male in the hall. Chingli wore a dark green dress, while Kathy looked stunning in a sky blue one with a pheasant-like bird motif. Her brunette hair had red highlights and was pinned up in a tight bun on top of her head, exposing an elegant neck and dangling jade earring. What an exquisite picture; he found himself smiling in anticipation. Maybe he could draw some of her chatty enthusiasm toward himself.

Kathy began looking at the name tags on the tables. Matt stood up and waved to her, then pointed at the seat next to Bob. She smiled, waved back to Matt, and seemed to blush a little when she noticed Bob was sitting next to her seat. Bob found himself chuckling. A coy blush was a good sign. It looked like it would be a fun evening. Chingli walked with her friend to the table.

"Kathy Stanley, you remember Bob Brendler, don't you?" Chingli said with a mischievous smile. The way she spoke made Bob feel the seating arrangements were not surprising to her. With a gut feeling that Chingli had something to do with those arrangements, Bob stood up to shake Kathy's hand. The look on her face was one of complete surprise. Before reaching for his hand, she turned to speak with Chingli. They conversed in Mandarin Chinese.

Their short conversation was so melodious. Reminding him of why he had begun studying Mandarin, even if he had not understood a thing. The pink of her blush had deepened to a delicious tone of red which only made her that much more attractive. When she reached for his hand, its warm, soft suppleness sent a pleasant sensation coursing through his body. Not a good sign if he wanted to remain in control of the situation.

* * * * * * * * * * * * * * * *

Kathy had meant it when she told Chingli how embarrassing this was. Yes, she had mentioned that she wanted to chat with Bob, but not like this. Now she was a jumble of nerves. It was easy for Chingli to say not to worry. If he was as good a man as her friend claimed, talking and dancing would be fun, but that did not lessen the embarrassment. The entire situation was so disconcerting even if he did like her. Granted, she did want to get to know him, but now she was going to have to get to know him fast. At least she was with the old crew from Six Engine. If he turned out to be an insufferable bore, she could talk with them. She had found out the hard way that looks were not everything.

As she shook his hand, she apologized. "I'm sorry. That was impolite of me wasn't it?"

Matt couldn't resist teasing her. "That's the way she introduced herself to us too Bob. Don't take it personally."

"Oh, I didn't Matt." Bob said with a smile. "I enjoyed listening to it."

Kathy felt panic rising up inside her. "Enjoyed listening to it? You - - - -You understand Mandarin?

"No, no, not really. I've only been studying it for a couple of months. I just meant I enjoy the sound of it."

Kathy flashed a relieved smile as her heart rate slowed. If he had understood that little exchange between her and Chingli, she would have crawled under the table and died of embarrassment. "Did you begin studying Mandarin because of the sound or is there another reason?"

"Well, I don't want to mislead you. I'm not pulling a Frank Helms and majoring in the language. I study at a small language school in New York once a week. Just to occupy my mind. Although now that they called for a captain's test; I'll probably take some time off to study for that."

"You started studying Chinese for the fun of it?"

"You could say that."

She began to get a little nervous when she heard that. Tall, lean, handsome, and intellectually adventurous, here was a dangerous man. If he was being honest, this guy was just about everything she had dreamed of since high school. She would have to be very careful around him. It had been too long since she had been intimate in any way with a man. Experience told her she tended to make bad decisions after a prolonged dry spell. At least he did not appear to be a writer or a poet. What were the chances of that? About as good as being struck by lightning with a clear blue sky above you.

Even if he did write, a poet? Hardly likely, that was a trait that melted her heart. Even after all the writing and journalism courses she had taken in college, the art of poetry eluded her. Her lame

7

attempts at creating something profound in short verses were pathetic. It had always struck her as odd that she would find someone with the one skill she had never mastered attractive. Do people always seek out others with a trait they are missing? Is it an attempt to make themselves whole? Deciding she was getting too philosophical for the situation, Kathy pushed those thoughts to the back of her mind so she could concentrate on the task at hand. If she did not she would probably make a fool of herself or end up with a broken heart

"I've seen you at Six Engine and around Frank's office, so I don't have to ask you what you do for a living."

"And I've read your book, which is required reading in our firehouse, so we can move on from the preliminaries. Why don't we start with you sitting down?" He pulled out a chair for her. "Would the lady want something to drink?

"Thank you, a glass of white wine would be wonderful," she told him as she sat.

Dinner went smoothly, with small talk and banter around the table. Not exactly an opportunity to get to know Bob better, but sometimes small things can be revealed that raise a flag of caution. Nothing like that came out in the conversation. The band began to play after dinner. Bob turned to her with a smile.

"Would you care to dance?" he asked.

"I'd love to," Kathy responded enthusiastically. This would give her a chance to speak with him alone. Banter did not reveal much about a man other than his wit. Bob had held his own during dinner, now to see how he was one on one.

"I'll warn you," he said as they walked to the dance floor. "My dancing skills are limited. I don't usually step on my partner's feet, but I'm told my style is a little too robotic."

"Then you and I have something in common," Kathy answered reassuringly. "Writing is my forte, dancing is not."

The band began a slow song, forcing them into a more intimate dance style. The pleasure Kathy felt when Bob placed his hand on her back worried her. Easy, she thought as he looked down at her with a smile. The only trouble he seemed to be having was keeping his hand from slipping down the silk of her dress. She smiled to herself appreciating the seductive nature of a qipao.

"So, how do you know Jack or Gloria?" Bob began lamely as they moved around the dance floor.

Kathy chuckled before she answered. "Actually, I met them both at about the same time," she began. "Jack I met in the firehouse when I was working on a story. Then I met Gloria a few days later after Chingli introduced us. They weren't an item at the time. But Gloria changed that quickly."

"You give Gloria full credit?" Bob laughed.

"No, I wouldn't say full credit," she responded. "How does that expression go? He chased her until she caught him."

"Isn't that the way it usually happens?" Bob asked. "The male of the species is the aggressor and the female of the species attracts."

"Don't you think that's a little old fashioned?" Kathy parried. "Can't the female of the species be the aggressor and the male do the attracting now?"

"No doubt about it," Bob agreed. "From what I've seen both are equally aggressive and both are doing their best to attract."

"Is that how you view relationships?" Kathy asked with a smile; she had never been with a man who did not feel threatened by an intelligent, assertive woman. "As a meeting of equal partners?"

Bob laughed at her question. "I may be biased, having been on the receiving end of female aggression, but it seems the average modern woman sees what she wants and goes for it."

"And doesn't care who she steamrolls along the way?" she asked with a chuckle.

"No, no, I didn't say that," Bob quickly replied.

"But you meant it," Kathy observed.

"It looks like the bride and groom are beginning to make their rounds," Bob pointed out, strategically ending their little duel. Kathy looked up and saw that Gloria and Jack had stepped away from their table and were visiting the guest tables. The song came to an end, so they made their way back to their table.

Bob took out a card and quietly began to write something. He wrote on his lap and so intently that Kathy could not help but notice.

"You seem to be very busy. Are you writing some heartfelt words to Jack and Gloria?" Kathy asked with a smile.

Bob's face turned red, as if he had been caught doing something secret. "Oh, I just added a few words," Bob replied quietly.

"If it was just a few words then why are you turning red?" Kathy laughed lightly. "Come on, come clean."

"It's nothing really, just a few lines I write into all the cards I give at weddings. You'd probably find it silly."

"You should give a girl a chance," she said earnestly, "I don't think heartfelt wishes from a friend would be silly, no matter how they were expressed."

He was obviously thinking hard about whether or not to let her read the card.

"You have to admit, it's a little intimidating having something you wrote judged by a published author."

"Published author? Really Bob, I'm just Kathy, a fire captain's daughter. You run into burning buildings for a living. I shouldn't be intimidating to you at all." His hesitation made him seem so vulnerable and so irresistible.

"This is a hell of a lot harder than running into a burning building." He said after taking a deep breath. "It's a poem I wrote. I call it 'Love's Night' and jot it into all my wedding gift cards. It's nothing extraordinary really. I mean you must have studied and analyzed poems in college, so it won't be impressive. I don't know anything about poetic form; just kind of write what's in my head."

"I haven't had a poetry course since high school."

"I haven't had one since eighth grade." That brought laughter from both of them.

"Then we agree," Kathy suggested. "No judgments, only appreciation."

"Agreed."

He gingerly handed her the card. Kathy's heart skipped a beat as she read the poem. She now knew the young man sitting next to her was much more than he appeared. Her mind began to race. Was he for real? Had he actually written this poem? Many of the guys hitting on her turned out to be what her mother called paper tigers, a great façade, but after some probing not worth a second date. An advantage of being a reporter was learning to ask the right questions. Her probes of Bob had turned up nothing that suggested caution.

If he was genuine she would have to be move slowly and try to build something with him that could last more than a few months. She was not getting any younger. Thirty loomed just ahead and her mother was beginning to remind her of it. She still had time to move deliberately and Bob seemed more than worth the effort, at least right now. Time would tell if he was made of flesh or just paper. She was not foolish enough to throw herself at some guy because he wrote one poem, although his being tall, slim, and handsome made it tempting. But she was sidetracked again. He would get the impression she was an air head if she kept this up. This was worrisome to her because she had only begun to know him and was already flustered. She concentrated on the card and read:

Long is the night that love must pass through
Hard is the fight that must be fought
Dark are the times before the light turns true
When morning comes and love finds all it had sought

Bitter is the chill of nocturnal dreams
Whose images haunt our unconscious minds

12

Deep in the shadows our hearts are shaken by the screams
Of those who wait with despair for the true light of love to shine

Years sometimes pass before the horizon brightens
Bringing a promise of comfort and warmth
The hope of a new day dawning lightens
The burdens of dark inner battles that have been fought

Nothing worth having is won without a fight
Something worth keeping is made more precious that way
If love can survive the shadows before the light
We can be certain it will forever hold sway.

"Bob, that's beautiful," she said earnestly.

"No need to make me feel good," the firefighter replied quietly. His face was a little red again.

"I'm serious," Kathy continued. "You should submit it to a poetry competition or try to get it published."

He began to chuckle when she said this. "No, no. I'm not looking for recognition or anything," he said waving his hands in front of his face. "I just write for myself, kind of a release. I'm happy with that. It looks like the newlyweds are going to take their time getting here. Would the lady care for another dance?"

"I don't know," she said with a wide smile. "A firefighter, a dancer, and now a poet, that might be too much for a girl to handle in one night."

The band began a slow tune that allowed the conversation to continue.

"So, what do you do besides fight fires, work with Frank, and write poetry?" she asked.

13

"I study Chinese too, remember?"

"Yes, I do seem to remember something about that now that you mention it," she said looking up at him. Thank God he was tall. Her height had been a challenge for some of the guys she had dated. Seeing someone who was five six when you were five eight had led to awkward moments. It was one reason she avoided blind dates. "Any other secrets you want to reveal now or do you want to save them for another time?"

"Would the lady be interested in another time with me?" he said slyly.

"Yes, I think I would," she replied congratulating herself on the subtle manipulative question she had just posed.

"Well, when I want to relax I go to my guitar," he told her. "And when everything just gets to be too much, then I hit the road on my bike."

"Bike? What type of bike are you referring to?"

"A Harley Davidson hog," he said almost as a challenge. "Would you be interested in going on a little putt out to west Jersey?"

"I think I would," she said thoughtfully. "I'll warn you I've never been on one of those before, so you'll have to be gentle."

"No need to worry, I was raised to be a gentle man," he said with a sly smile.

The music seemed to carry her through the rest of the night. Kathy congratulated herself on a successful campaign, especially since it had been so spontaneous. She would have to speak with

Chingli to get a better handle on what she had started before too much was invested.

Chapter Two

Bob pulled up to the Port Authority office building on the black
Harley-Davidson that had been the unquestioned love of his life until
yesterday. Scenes from the day before swirled in his mind. The air
was crisp, yet warm enough for the denim jacket he wore; the sky was
blue; and his heart was full of hope. Kathy Stanley was amazing and
had agreed to go for a ride with him out to the woods of west Jersey.
He already had it planned out. There were country roads off Routes
202 and 206 in Morris and Sussex Counties that had spectacular
foliage this time of year. Granted she was from Rhode Island and
New England autumns were probably more picturesque, but he was
sure she would enjoy the ride. There was a particular diner out there
that served great meals and had a view. Conversations on bikes were
problematic, so the stops he picked out along the way were what
would make or break the outing. These were where he could get to
know her and introduce himself. Swinging his leg off the bike, Bob
took off his helmet and gloves, stashed the latter inside the former,
and strolled toward Frank's office.

The office was on the second story of a large rectangular building
off Calcutta Street. It was not exactly in a suburban office park. The
truck traffic was phenomenal. Riding a bike down here could be
intimidating. Parking around the building was limited compared to
office buildings outside the city, but Frank found it easier dealing
with shipping and trucking companies from the port. If pressed for a
quick description of the building he was walking towards, Bob would

call it non-descript. He knew the appearance of the building did not bother Frank. His business was done with Asia and purchasing agents, so not many customers passed through these doors. Those who did were interested in selling products in Asia or buying items imported from there.

The firefighter did not bother knocking when he reached the office door. He was here too frequently for that formality. When Frank needed a delivery driver, Bob often filled the position. That was one of the reasons for coming here today. If he was going to take the captain's test seriously, then part-time work would have to be cut back or even dropped. But Frank Helms was more than a part time job for Bob. The former firefighter was also a mentor, a good friend, and an excellent sounding board when questions of life and love came up. Whether that was from studying Asia, being married to Chingli, or having an old friend try to kill him was unclear. Whatever the reason for his clear mind and wise comments, Frank was a good source for advice, especially advice about studying or about one particular woman who had adopted his wife as a sister.

He pushed the door open quietly and poked his head in. Frank was behind his desk writing on a pad with his right hand while his left hand reached for the phone. His blue suit jacket had been shed, but his red tie was still dangling in front of a light blue shirt.

"Got a minute?" Bob asked quietly.

"Whoa, you know I always have a minute for you, Bob. What's up? Or should I guess?" he said with a wry smile. "Does it have something to do with your performance last night? You seemed to have had a great time."

"Did I have a good time? You don't know how good a time. I was trying to figure a way to get a dance and a few words with Kathy. Then I end up seated next to her. Now, what do you mean by 'performance'?" Bob responded with a proud grin. "I was the consummate gentleman."

"Hopefully that's what the lady wanted, right?"

"If you are interested in more than a one night relationship, you have to treat the lady like a lady."

"So Chingli was right?"

"Chingli?"

"Yeah, she made sure Gloria had you sit next to Kathy. She said it was because Kathy was at the old firefighters table and needed a young guy with her, but I know she was up to her usual manipulation."

"My interest is that obvious?"

"Only to my wife. She picks up on these things quicker than anyone else. Told me Gloria was after Jack before Jack knew Gloria had him in her sights."

"Did Kathy talk with Chingli last night?"

"Briefly, they were planning to get together today to review the situation. A war-room conference if you would," Frank said with a chuckle. "I'll warn you, my wife's involvement makes this a serious matter. If you don't believe me, talk to Ray and Jack."

"I am well aware of the legendary Chingli," Bob retorted. "But doesn't her magic require the lady to be interested in the gentleman?"

"If you were just a common gentleman, I'm sure there could be some doubt."

"I'm only a simple fireman, Frank, didn't think someone like her would find me interesting. She seems too cosmopolitan."

"You're underestimating yourself, Bob, especially with Kathy. She's been studying firemen for her entire life. She likes the breed. Remember her old man's on the job in Rhode Island."

"Her father's a fire captain, remember? But I'm only a blue shirt," Bob pointed out.

"Isn't there a captain's test coming up?" Frank asked.

"Actually, that's why I'm here," Bob confessed.

"Well. You can't stand there all day if we're going to discuss anything seriously," Frank said. Then he pointed to the chair in front of this desk. "Have a seat and I'll get you a cup of your favorite."

Bob sat as Frank stood up and turned to retrieve a coffee mug. After filling it with steaming water and adding some Jasmine tea leaves, he handed it to Bob. Gingerly sipping the hot liquid, Bob took a second to take in his surroundings. This office was as familiar to him as his apartment or the firehouse. The mixture of East and West permeated the space.

Frank swung back around to his chair behind the desk after pouring a cup for himself. The pleasant fragrance of jasmine seeped through the office air as they sipped tea and relaxed for a moment

"So, they called for a test," Frank began while placing his mug on the desk.

"Right and I'm looking for a little advice," Bob said hopefully.

"Advice on whether or not to take the test? Don't hesitate. You've fought more fires in the past three years than the average guy sees in a decade. Any veteran firefighter on your crew would know and respect that."

"That's not the reason I'm here," Bob said with a grin. "Although I appreciate the vote of confidence."

"I'm not blowing smoke up your ass," Frank said sincerely. "What else do you have on your mind?"

"Well, I figure you have a lot of experience studying. Maybe you could throw me some pointers."

Frank hesitated for a moment and then leaned back. The sound of the chair's creaking spring mixed with the roar of tractor trailers that came through the thin sheet metal walls. He reached for his mug and took a sip of tea. Bob shifted his weight nervously. Frank was trying to grow a business with very little help. Time was valuable to him. Bob remembered his friend had been reaching for the phone when he had poked his head into the room. There was a phone call that had to be made. It was ten in the morning here; that made it eleven at night in Taipei. He felt he was already asking too much, but needed this advice. The list from this test would be used to fill a lot of spots vacated by retirements. He needed to be on that list. Taking another sip of tea to calm himself, the firefighter waited.

"I'll do whatever I can for you Bob, but keep in mind I never really studied fire science. I was more of a meat and potatoes firefighter. The only subject I studied was Chinese, didn't have time for anything else."

Bob let out a quiet sigh of relief. "Chinese or fire science, it doesn't matter. Studying is studying. The principles are the same."

Frank chuckled at the comment, seeming to know it was correct. "I loved what I was studying," he replied as if testing Bob's resolve.

"I find fire science to be fascinating," Bob shot back.

"Do you have a study plan?"

"I'm trying to set one up, any suggestions?"

"Set aside time each day," Frank said, letting enthusiasm creep into his voice. "Establish a routine you can keep. If you get too ambitious you won't be able to stick to it and you'll get discouraged."

Bob wished he had brought a note pad to write it down. The advice was beginning to come at him quickly. He could only pray he would remember it, although what Frank had said so far was common sense.

"You need to set goals and objectives, you know, like read the Fire Chief's Handbook, a goal. Take notes on chapters one to three, an objective." Frank was becoming more enthusiastic with each sentence.

Bob was trying to soak it all in. Taking a shot and asking Frank for advice was turning out to be a good call. What his friend said next floored Bob.

"You could also enlist Kathy," he said with a mischievous smile.

"Kathy?" Bob shot back.

"Yes, and if you can prevent her from helping other guys, your chances are even better."

"I don't get it," Bob said in confusion. How could Kathy Stanley help him study for captain, unless Frank was referring to her helping with his writing?

"She helped her old man study for promotion. Said she had free time over a summer," Frank explained. "Bothered the hell out of Matt. Anyway, she's been through a lot of the text books; liked the Oklahoma State series the best. She's also interviewed some of the old chiefs and captains. One of the subjects she asks about is studying for promotion. She's a treasure trove of study techniques."

"Really?" Bob said sounding surprised. "I'm taking her out to west Jersey on my bike tomorrow. That's an ice breaker if ever there was one."

"Don't think you need an ice breaker anymore," Frank laughed. "Not from what I saw last night."

Now Bob's mind was racing. If he could talk Kathy into being a study partner, they could spend time together and he'd get his studying done. How sweet would that be? He got up from the chair with a huge grin plastered across his face.

"It's getting late in Asia. I've taken up enough of your time and I think you have overseas phone calls to make," he said apologetically.

"No," Frank reassured him. "I was only going to call Chingli before she went to lunch. The Asian calls are made before the sun comes up. Good luck Bob. See if you can inspire Jack to hit the books."

"Jack said he has too much on his plate right now adjusting to married life, maybe next time."

Frank shook his head. "Looks like this is going to be a good list to be on, the boy needs a shot of ambition."

"He's in love. Cut him a break," Bob chuckled. "The next few lists are going to be good. All the guys appointed when they went to four tours in fifty-nine are going to be easing out." He shook Frank's hand and headed for his bike.

Bob slid his helmet on, started the bike, and pulled in the clutch. It went into gear with a clunk. Easing out the clutch and accelerating, he pulled away briskly with a singing heart and a racing mind.

Chapter Three

Kathy strolled into the Rendezvous and scanned the tables to see if Chingli had arrived ahead of her. The small lunch crowd consisted mostly of business men. She felt under-dressed in her jeans and silk blouse. The students dressed like her would not claim the restaurant until dinner time. Nostalgic mementoes from the '50s lined the walls; everything from old car license plates to movie posters of the era created the theme. Lighting was brighter now than it would be later. Business men were interested in closing the deal or having something decent to eat while on the road. Subdued lighting was for the young romantics of the evening.

A hostess approached and asked how many would be in her party. Kathy smiled and held up two fingers, then asked for a booth instead of a table. Normally when she came here, Gloria would serve her at one of the tables in the center of the dining room. Today she wanted a little privacy so she could speak more openly with Chingli. Gloria had just begun her honeymoon, so they would have to settle for one of the other waitresses. The hostess picked up two menus from a pile next to her station and headed off to the dining area. Following close behind, Kathy stepped energetically into the dining room. Arriving at the booth, she shed her jacket and slid it across the bench seat, sitting on the side facing the entrance. Chingli walked in before the waitress had time to come over. Kathy waved to get her attention. The movement had the desired effect. Chingli smiled and walked to the booth.

"*Meimei,*" Chingli laughed as she sat down. "You did not regret sitting next to Bob yesterday?"

"You don't have to gloat," Kathy replied with a coy look. "But no, I don't regret anything about yesterday. It's tomorrow that concerns me."

Chingli wore a satisfied smirk on her face. Kathy could see the wheels were turning in her friend's head, which was good. She needed information about a certain firefighter and she needed it fast. Still in disbelief about how things unfolded at Gloria's wedding, the author was in research mode. Was the guy for real? Chingli was her only hope for answers before she climbed onto a Harley Davidson the next morning. The waitress pulled up before the conversation developed any further. They placed their orders after a quick glance at the menu and then took a moment to catch their breath.

"How well do you know Mr. Brendler?"

"I can tell you something about the way he is," Chingli started. "I guess you would call it personality. He is a lot like Frank, but he is different. Frank has two parts, one is a physical part. That is why he loved the fire department, must be something about men's chemicals. The other part is intellectual; that is why he loves Chinese. Both parts of him love a challenge."

Kathy listened intently. Chingli had never shared these observations with her, although the author had come to a similar conclusion long before. From her interviews and her experience with firefighters, Kathy knew that most guys were this way. It was the percentage of the split that divided them.

25

"What do you think the percentage of the split is for Frank?"

"What do you mean, 'percentage of split'?"

"You know, is Frank 50% physical, 50% intellectual or something else?"

"Oh, I see," Chingli laughed. "Frank is 51% intellectual and 49% physical. There is very little difference, just enough to put him in an office instead of on a fire truck."

"And Bob," Kathy asked. "What about Bob?"

"Bob is a lot like Frank," Chingli said thoughtfully. "But he is a little different. You can see it by how they use motorcycles. Frank had a motorcycle before the fire department. He went to South Dakota with it. Then he became a fireman and sold the motorcycle to buy a car. Bob still has a motorcycle and it is one of his loves. He will have a motorcycle until his body says no."

Kathy laughed at her friend's way of accessing the two men. Motorcycles were an indicator of the similarities and differences, but she wanted more than the impression created by Chingli's broad brush strokes. "So, Frank is 51% intellectual and 49% physical. What do you think Bob is?"

"Ah yo! That's what I have been trying to say," Chingli said in feigned exasperation. "Bob is like Frank, but he is more 51% physical and 49% intellectual. Bob will be on the fire truck until his body says no. He is like my father. Even when he became a general, he still tried to fly. It is the way they are. They cannot help themselves."

The waitress came with their meals, interrupting the conversation after Chingli's pronouncement. They began eating before moving on to the next stage of exploration.

"Your red gravy is much better than this, *Meimei*," Chingli pointed out.

"You think so?" Kathy replied between bites. "I guess if you're looking for something with a little more spice, this wouldn't do. When you run a place like this you have to cook for the average palate. Nini Anna's recipe was for family. She knew what she was doing. I just inherited the recipe." She reached for a piece of bread. "We have to get together and have a big Italian Sunday dinner."

"That would be nice. Maybe you could invite Bob," Chingli said nonchalantly.

Kathy almost choked on the bread she had just put in her mouth. After coughing and a mouth full of water, she recovered enough to say, "I think you're rushing things a bit. I haven't even been out on a date with him."

Chingli had what Kathy referred to as an all knowing smile of her face. "You are going to ride on his motorcycle tomorrow. That is Tuesday. You said Sunday dinner didn't you?"

"Not happening," Kathy said firmly. "Do you know how much work goes into one of those dinners? He's got a long wait before I do anything like that. I don't care how cute he is."

Chingli laughed and then turned serious again. "Bob is a good man. Do you want to get to know him better or do you think he will only be fun for a little while?"

Kathy felt the shift in the conversation and shifted into her research mode. "He strikes me as a great guy with a lot of potential. What I'm trying to come up with is how accurate the impression I have of him is?" She shifted in her seat, curling one leg up under her, and waited for Chingli's response.

"What is your impression?" Chingli asked quietly, then reached for her drink and took a sip, her eyes on Kathy the entire time.

Kathy had seen that look she was getting from her friend before. It was usually directed at Frank and was used to make him look inside himself for the answer to a question he had asked her. She would have more sympathy for Frank the next time it happened, but had known all along that she would have to come to her own conclusions. It seemed Chingli was not going to let her avoid the hard task of thinking. "My impression," she began after a deep breath, "can only be based on yesterday right now."

"Yes I know," Chingli smiled. "But you are not a woman who dives off a bridge before you know how deep the water is below you. Maybe I can help you with the water before the dive. Tell me what you think of him and how it makes you feel. Then we can plan from there."

Chingli always had an unusual way of putting things. Diving off a bridge seemed such an appropriate analogy. Kathy wanted more information so it would be less of a leap of faith and more of a calculated risk. Not the most romantic approach, but experience had taught her romance was an expensive luxury. What she knew of Bob so far told her to tread cautiously.

"I think he is so cute," she began with a laugh, "but you already know that. He seems to be an intelligent guy, but what shocked me most was that he likes to write. I think we could have some wonderful conversations about writing and books."

"So you have something to talk about," Chingli pointed out.

"I need more than that," Kathy sighed. "I have to delve into his mind."

"Do you think there can be more?"

"He showed me a poem he wrote on the inside of his card to Jack and Gloria," Kathy pushed on. "It was very touching and a little frightening to me. A poetic fireman could be irresistible. I'm afraid I'll make a fool of myself. If he's as sharp as he appeared yesterday, I might be in trouble."

"There are worse troubles."

The waitress appeared with the check, hinting they were overstaying their welcome. Kathy snapped up the check before Chingli could get hold of it. "My treat," she said. "I'm the one looking for advice." Chingli momentarily had a combative look on her face, but quickly acquiesced. Kathy handed the waitress a credit card and turned back to Chingli.

"I don't know how my mother would feel about it," she continued. "She always wanted me to see doctors or lawyers or some other type of professional."

"I understand your mother's desire," Chingli said. "But it is the modern world. A girl does not have to worry as much about her man's salary. You support yourself well. Your career looks promising, so it is only a matter of the heart. He loves his job. Can you accept him staying on the Fire Department?"

Kathy laughed. She had been weighing many factors, but Bob remaining on the Fire Department was not one of them. It was a non-issue to her. "I'm a fireman's daughter," she sighed. "I know you had a hard time with Frank and my mother has a hard time with my dad, but firefighters have always been a part of my life. The job doesn't bother me. He seems bright enough to make chief, but he also strikes me as a romantic which makes him doubly attractive."

Chingli smiled and reached over to touch Kathy's hand. "Then you should do your best to, as you said, delve into his mind. Peel back each layer of his mind like you would peel back the layers of an onion and see if what is there touches your heart. Frank always says the trick to life is finding happiness. Everything else is meaningless."

The waitress returned with Kathy's card and a receipt. Kathy signed the receipt and the two women slid out of the booth. She felt at peace. Following her heart would be frightening, but the potential rewards were worth it.

Chapter Four

It was a perfect fall day, with a hint of Indian summer to it. The sky was a brilliant blue; an occasional puffy cloud floated by. The air was still and carried a touch of summer humidity. What a day for a scenic ride through the northwestern part of the Garden State. Bob's mind was humming with the possibilities that stretched before him as he leaned his bike into the last turn before arriving at Kathy's address. He twisted the accelerator and shifted gears as the bike completed the turn and moved upright. Looking ahead, he saw Kathy standing in front of a building dressed in jeans that clung to her figure and a denim jacket. An involuntary smile grew under the face piece of his helmet. Just the sight of her was a pleasure. If he could get through the day without making a fool of himself, he would be happy.

Downshifting as he braked, Bob pulled the bike next to Kathy and shut it down. The rumble of a hog would drown out any conversation. He lifted his black helmet off, exposing his grin. Kathy returned the smile and asked, "Is this appropriate garb for a ride through the countryside or should I be wearing leather?"

"It's perfect," Bob laughed. "The weather is great and I promise not to drop the bike."

"That's reassuring," Kathy replied.

Bob swung his leg over the bike and unstrapped the white spare helmet. "Have you ever been on one of these?" he asked, then mentally kicked himself remembering her comment of the day before.

"No, the closest I come is a motor scooter in Taipei, but I'm an adventurous girl," she told him. "Not to worry."

"Since you did the scooter thing in Taipei, I can assume you have an idea about how to stay on one of these," he queried.

"Oh, yes," she laughed. "But this looks a little more substantial than that little scooter."

"Once it starts rolling the same principles apply," Bob began his standard introduction to motorcycles. "Just lean with the bike when I turn and you'll be fine. By the end of the day, you'll be laughing and asking for lower turns at higher speeds."

Kathy laughed. "I don't know about that."

"We'll see, now let me show you how to fasten the helmet."

"You can't have a real conversation with this on can you?" Kathy asked obviously disappointed.

"Well, we can shout at each other," Bob chuckled. "But we're going to stop along the way to enjoy the sights, get something to eat, and just talk. You know, enjoy each other's company." He felt very awkward saying it, especially since the thought had crossed his mind. Folding the passenger foot pegs down, he invited her to climb onto the bike. Once she was comfortably seated, he mounted the bike, started it, slid his helmet on, and pulled away.

After negotiating the S turns through South Mountain Reservation, the couple traveled up South Orange Avenue past Livingston Mall and turned toward Route Ten at a little red school house in Florham Park. Bob had taken the route for the sole purpose of measuring how Kathy would respond to the weaving required through the S turns. She reacted just as he suspected, with laughter. Miss Stanley was indeed a thrill seeker as he had hoped. This could be a fun relationship. They pulled into a diner on Route 15, just before Lake Hopatcong.

"Am I mistaken or are you enjoying yourself?" Bob asked with a smile after taking off his helmet and climbing off the bike. Kathy removed her helmet, shook her hair, and faced him. "It's pretty obvious isn't it?" she asked with a grin before getting off the bike.

"Let me guess," Bob teased. "You were a biker chick in your last life."

"No, I would have been a big hairy biker in my last life," she shot back. "But I am my father's daughter. Always loved the fast rides at the amusement parks, kind of a rollercoaster queen."

"Now we're getting at the truth," Bob laughed. "Is that why you like firemen?"

"No," she answered in a sassy tone. "That's why firemen like me." She climbed off the bike before Bob could respond. "Let's get something to eat and relax a little."

Bob found himself grabbing both helmets and catching up with her. She was proving to be everything he had hoped for, a smart, spunky woman with the nerve to challenge life. What more could a man ask for?

After being seated and ordering, Bob tried to direct the conversation toward Kathy's preferences and experiences. "How is it you got involved with journalism?" he started, after deciding that asking for help studying would be premature. It was not the best opener, but he found it hard to come up with something better while she was sitting across the table smiling at him. Besides he had begun to doubt the wisdom of asking for her help. What kind of impression would that make? Would he appear to be dependent or even worse to be taking advantage of her? It was more likely she would just laugh at him for being presumptuous. The waitress came with their drinks, interrupting the conversation. Bob hoped the flow would not be lost. Thankfully, Kathy picked up where they had left off avoiding an embarrassing pause and a restating of his question.

"Well, it started with a paper I wrote when I was twelve," Kathy began. "There was this history teacher in seventh grade that was a fire buff. We were talking about oral history in class and he thought I could write a paper, an oral history, on my father's job. To me interviewing my dad and his buddies was fun. Then I went to Taiwan with my mom and interviewed her grandmother. That was interesting, but I always loved writing, so it was natural for me to gravitate toward something that was fun and allowed me to do what I loved. That was the beginning. The whole 'change the world by informing people about the good, the bad, and the ugly' thing came later. That's the condensed version of how Kathy came to write. How about you?"

Bob hesitated for a moment, trying to get his bearings. How about me? It sounded like she was asking how he started his writing career. Putting it off to nerves, he interpreted the question to be one about his career. "Well, my dad was also a fire captain, so this type of career kind of runs in the family."

"No, no, no," Kathy interrupted then turned a little red. "I'm sorry, that was rude, but I was asking when you started writing."

"Started writing?" Bob asked with a chuckle. "I never really thought I had done that. I mean I do enjoy writing, but it's only an interest of mine, a hobby at best."

"When did you start writing poetry?" Kathy pushed on undeterred by his answer.

"Poetry?" he responded. Where this conversation was going was beyond him, but Bob was happy to play along, trusting she had no ill intent. "I've been playing guitar since I was sixteen. Always loved music and words. Never thought about it this way before, but I guess I started to write poetry when I started writing lyrics to songs." Bob surprised himself by making the admission. The guys he grew up with knew about the rock star dreams they had shared, but those dreams had died when the reality of life showed up. No extraordinary talent, no record contract; a bitter pill for a teenager but one that you easily got over. It was just part of growing up. However, the guys on the job knew nothing of his teenage fantasies. Not that he tried to hide them; it was just not a subject of firehouse conversations.

"You write songs?" Kathy asked.

"I wrote," Bob interrupted. "Or more accurately, I tried to write songs. That was a long time ago. It evolved into poetry which requires no musical talent, a trait I lack."

"But you still play guitar?"

"Yes, now that I'm not trying to imitate Duane Allman it relaxes me. What do you do to relax?" he asked trying to steer the conversation toward her interests. His was the boring tale of a Jersey boy.

"To relax? Besides going on motorcycle rides through the countryside?" she teased.

He chuckled and involuntarily looked down. "I'll take that as a compliment about my riding skills," he began, raising his head to look directly at her. "But yes besides enjoying the great outdoors on a motorcycle. What do you do to relax when you're alone?"

"I read," she replied looking him in the eye and smiling. It was almost as if she challenged him to remark on her habits.

"And what does the lady read?" Bob asked not the least bit intimidated by her tone.

"Oh, I enjoy good writing," she answered. "I don't limit myself. Literature, historical novels, history, I read a lot about Asia. And you, do you spend all your time reading fire service texts or can you pull yourself away to lighter fare?"

Bob laughed at her question. This was definitely proving to be the most interesting date he had been on. Not only was she beautiful, but she also had a sharp mind. Something in the back of his head was screaming caution. Before him sat the ultimate heartbreaker, but he could not help enjoying her company. "No, I have only begun perusing fire texts. My normal fare tends toward history and historical fiction. I just finished Clavell's Shogun. Have you read it?" he replied ending with his own challenge.

"Oh my God!" Kathy exclaimed. "Have you read his other books? I love Clavell. He is such an enjoyable way to learn about Asia."

Bob was astonished by the level of Kathy's enthusiasm. Fortunately he shared her view of James Clavell's work. This conversation was getting more interesting by the moment. "I haven't read King Rat yet. Taipan and Noble House were great. The characters were so well defined, the plots were convoluted, complex, and in the end satisfying. Good reads, all of them." Why did he feel like he was being interviewed?

The waitress came with their meals, momentarily interrupting the flow of the conversation. But Bob did not mind; unlike the conversations of so many other dates he had been on, this one had a life of its own. After a bite and sip of coffee, Kathy continued her questioning. "So, I have an excuse for being interested in Asia," Kathy said, the hint of a tease in her voice. "What about you?

"My interest in Asia began as a kid, reading about World War II," Bob replied seriously. "My father had served in the Pacific, so I was fascinated by the war with Japan. It just evolved from there. Of course, Clavell's writing helped."

As Kathy stirred her coffee, a mischievous look grew on her face. Bob found it unnerving that he could pick up on that look after spending only two afternoons with her. He braced himself and waited for whatever thought had planted itself in her mind to come to fruition.

"So, *Anjinsan*," she started, calling him a name of the protagonist in Clavell's Shogun. "Compose a spontaneous poem for me the way all good samurai do."

It took a moment to process this sentence. His first reaction was disbelief, Had he heard it right? Familiarity with the book reaffirmed he had heard correctly, but he still needed to confirm his understanding,

"You want me to compose a haiku now?"

"Not a haiku necessarily," she answered. "But a poem." A bold look of challenge was on her face.

"Really?" Bob asked almost to himself. The thought crossed his mind to just laugh off the challenge she had thrown at him, but he knew she was testing to see if he had the mettle to run with her. "Okay, any style of poem?" he asked trying to determine the exact nature of her request.

"Style is your choice," she said with a nonchalant look. "Impress a girl with your poetry. She might swoon here from the pure beauty of your verses." They both burst out laughing at the absurdity of their conversation.

"I'm sorry," Kathy chortled. "Ignore me; it was just a crazy thought that crossed my mind after thinking about Shogun."

Bob paused for a second and then rushed on, pushing way past his comfort zone, not really knowing why. "I'll tell you what, if you come up with a subject, I'll see if I can make you swoon."

A sparkle was in her eyes as she glanced around the diner for an appropriate subject. Her eyes settled on a Norman Rockwell style painting on the wall across from them. The painting depicted a father reading to his young son while a mother was brushing the little sister's hair in the background. "See that picture?" she said pointing at it. "Compose a poem based on that."

"Any style?"

"Any style."

"I don't really write haikus. My poems tend to be a few stanzas. Does the lady have a problem with me using a pen and paper?" Bob bargained.

"Not at all," Kathy chirped expectantly.

"You don't think I can do this do you?"

"Just the opposite," Kathy replied. "I think you don't believe you can do it, but I am sure you can."

"You're sure?" Bob asked. "And how have you come to that conclusion? Am I really that simple a book?"

"No, not at all simple," she said slyly. "But a girl can get a feel if someone is genuine quickly and the feeling I get is you can do it."

Bob studied the painting. It reminded him of his childhood with his father reading to him before bed. He had no sister, but the poem was not necessarily auto-biographical. After studying it for a moment, he collected his thoughts and began to write on a napkin.

The Quiet Time

The quiet time before I send you to bed
A time for sharing and books and tales
When we discuss some of the happenings of today and the hopes of tomorrow
This is our time to grow close before you become a man and leave

Lessons are sometimes taught in this time before your prayers
It is a time to wash and brush teeth, floss and change
We may read of Bilbo or Frodo or just a short, silly story
But it is our time to enjoy

39

Sometimes life is too rushed and we miss this stage of the day
Homework completed late or Tiger Cub meetings and then bed
We lose too much on days like these
This special period is shared by a father tired after a long day at
work and
his son who claims not to be sleepy after play and school

There are still tasks for me to do around our home
I must help your mother end her day
Your sister will need a cup of water and you will have a question
or two
before accepting your day's end
But the quiet time before you climb your ladder and say your
prayers should
be ours alone

It is a time for a father to be a father and a son to be himself

Kathy read the poem quietly. The smile went from her face, convincing Bob that she thought the poem a disaster and was trying to think of a polite way to tell him. He braced himself for the onslaught of criticism. His poetry was not meant for public consumption anyway. It was his own private release, so why did he care what she thought? The firefighter never worried about others opinions before, but he found himself expectantly awaiting Kathy's thoughts. That was bad.

"I don't know what to say," Kathy began. "You just wrote this now, honestly?"

"What do you mean?" Bob asked, confused. "Yes, I wrote it in front of you about that picture. That was your suggestion, wasn't it?"

"Yes. yes," she replied. "I'm sorry. It did sound like I doubted your integrity, didn't it? It's just that the poem is so moving." She seemed to be genuinely emotional, which caught Bob completely off guard. "I am so jealous of you." Kathy said emphatically and then laughed. "How did you write something like that by simply looking at that picture?"

It was Bob's turn to laugh. She appeared to really be impressed with his little creation. He realized that was what he wanted at the moment more than anything.

"How did I come up with that?" he began. "It was partly autobiographical. My dad insisted on reading to me. Of course, when he worked nights he couldn't, but if he was home he always did. I didn't see him much during the day because he always worked a part time job when he wasn't in the firehouse. So our only time together was in the evening. He used to say mom had me all day, so nights were his. It was time for us guys. He called my bedtime ritual our quiet time."

"Hence the theme of the poem," Kathy interjected.

"Hence the theme of the poem," Bob repeated. "Of course, I have no sister. There were several miscarriages after I was born. The doctor eventually told my mother any pregnancy would be high risk and advised her to settle for one son and not shorten her life. Dad agreed to that whole heartedly. They could have adopted, but apparently they didn't want to. Never really spoke with them about it. But now I'm off subject and getting boring." He chastised himself for getting too serious on a first date. They were out for fun, not reflections on the vagaries of life.

"No, not at all," Kathy said emphatically. "My folks had the same situation, so I grew up alone. Often wondered what it would have been like to have siblings. It probably made me more outgoing because I had no built in friends."

"Built in friends," Bob chuckled. "That's an unusual way to put it, but I can understand exactly what you mean. Anyway, back to the poem, it is only partially autobiographical. No sister, no bunk beds. Dad did read Tolkien to me as I got older."

"So you have many different influences on your composition," Kathy pointed out with a smile.

"Composition?" Bob laughed feeling better as the gray mood receded. "That sounds a bit pompous for a short poem written on a napkin."

"Can I keep the napkin?" Kathy asked.

"Of course you can," Bob replied. "Now we had better get back on the road. It gets chilly quickly out here after the sun goes down." He motioned to the waitress and asked for the check. They both got up and strolled to the bike. The sun was moving towards the western horizon. Bob calculated how long it would take to get back to South Orange. It would probably be dusk by then. Exposing the girl to the chill of an autumn dusk on the back of a bike was bad form. He wanted her to remember the day as a warm, fun ride, not a cold uncomfortable return. They had to hustle.

By the time they reached Florham Park the sun was approaching the horizon. There was still some humidity in the air, so the temperature was holding up. Bob turned onto Columbia Turnpike confident he could deliver his date home before she felt any chill. So far the day had gone better than he could have hoped. The two of them had worked out hand signals that allowed a rudimentary kind of communication that was not drowned out by the wind and the rumble of the Harley Davidson. A little while after they had passed Livingston Mall, Bob saw a driveway that gently curved into an office building and then swung back down to the road. Laughing to himself he leaned the bike up the driveway, eased through the loop, and returned to the road, all without slowing down. He heard Kathy squeal then he saw the cop.

The patrol car was on the opposite side of the road. Bob kept on eye on his rear view mirror as he slowed down. When he saw the patrol car make a U turn, he eased to the side of the road and waited. The car pulled behind him with its lights on. Bob shut the bike down and pulled out his wallet. The whole time Kathy was laughing.

The officer stepped out of his car and motioned for Bob to come to him. He stepped around to the curb side of the car and waited for Bob. "Good afternoon officer," Bob said politely.

The cop put up his hand to quiet Bob, then asked, "Are you a cop or a fireman?"

Bob hesitated for a moment, caught off guard by the question. "I'm a Newark firefighter."

"I thought as much," the cop said with a chuckle. "When I saw that move I knew you had to be either a cop or a fireman. Got any ID on you?"

Bob took out his department ID card and handed it to the officer. He turned to glance at Kathy. She had taken her helmet off and was standing next to the bike all smiles.

"You know Bob," the cop began. "When I went through the police academy an old captain gave a lecture on procedures and discretion. He told us if we could cut anyone a break then we should throw it to a police officer because he's a brother. Next he mentioned doctors and nurses because if you end up in some operating room you didn't want them thinking this is the guy who gave me that ticket. Then he said if you can, give a fireman a break because if you get in trouble they're the only ones crazy enough to help you. Now I know what he meant. That was the craziest stunt I've seen in a long time."

Bob could not help but laugh when he heard the comment about firefighters. Is that what cops actually think of us? Knowing it was not meant as a joke, he quickly controlled himself.

"Do you know you would have killed yourself and anyone who stepped out of that building and you would have taken the young lady with you?" the officer continued, ignoring Bob's chuckle. When he mentioned Kathy, the cop gestured in her direction and then paused a moment as if he recognized her. From the look on his face, Bob could see the patrolman was trying to place Kathy. Knowing cops, the first assessment was the wanted posters in the precinct. He needed to tell the guy why Kathy was familiar before she changed from a passenger into a suspect.

"Have you ever watched Eyewitness News officer?" Bob asked quickly.

"Yes, oh wait is that . . . she was a reporter wasn't she?" A look of recognition spread across his face, loosening its features.

"That's Kathy Stanley," Bob replied. "She was a reporter on Eyewitness News until a few months ago. Now she writes books and makes bad choices about who to date."

The cop tipped his hat in Kathy's direction then turned to Bob. Traffic continued to flow past their little drama as Bob awaited his fate. "So, do you know Ray Friedrick?"

The question surprised Bob. Cops and firemen, they all seemed to know each other. "Yes, officer, I work with him."

"Work with him, how's that?"

"He transferred to the fire department a couple of years ago. Something about guns and sheets," Bob immediately regretted his last quip.

"Sheets versus guns," the officer chuckled. "So, do you know the two professions that make their living lying in bed?"

Bob breathed a sigh of relief. The cop had not taken the remark the wrong way. "No officer, I don't."

"Prostitutes and firemen," he replied with a chuckle. "I went through the Newark Police Academy with Ray. Haven't spoken with him for a few years; not since that stalker thing, but back to business.

You've seen what speed and metal do to people haven't you?" the cop asked bluntly.

"Yes, unfortunately too often officer."

"Okay, do yourself and me a favor. Save the heroics and craziness for the firehouse. I really don't want to scrape you off the pavement or arrest you for running over some kid. And to hurt the sweet lady would be a sin. Safety first. Keep the bike on the road and within the speed limit. It'll make both our lives a lot easier."

"It won't happen again officer," Bob said contritely. "I don't think Miss Stanley was impressed. Hope I didn't ruin her day, I'd like to see her again."

"I can understand why," the cop said with a smile. "Good luck, stay safe, and tell Ray that Rich from Millburn said hello."

"Thank you officer," Bob said with relief. "I'll pass it on to Ray." Bob collected his ID and walked back to Kathy.

"You got away with it, didn't you?" she asked incredulously.

"He recognized you and gave me a break," Bob fibbed.

"It had nothing to do with being a firefighter?"

"You saw him tip his hat to you."

"Yes, but I know firemen."

"You doubt me?"

"Don't ask," she sighed. "Let's go."

The rest of the ride was thankfully uneventful. Traffic was beginning to build, but it was mainly traveling in the opposite direction. As they came down the hill into South Orange, the lights of the village had begun to come on. At the top of the hill, Newark's lights were visible, but gradually faded behind hills and trees until only the village lights could be seen. The bike rolled under the railroad station overpass and into the center of town. Kathy's place was a few lights beyond the town center.

When Bob pulled the bike over in front of her building, the thought of how to play out this final scene crossed his mind. He did not want to spook her by appearing too aggressive, but did not want her to feel he was not interested. Shutting down the bike and dismounting, Bob's mind was humming. Kathy got off the bike, removed her helmet, and put him at ease. "I hope you won't feel insulted or disappointed if I don't invite you in. I don't want to sound prudish, but I feel awkward and . . . "

"Not to worry, Kath," Bob reassured her. "I was raised to be a gentleman and had a great time just getting to know you better. Would you consider spending more time with this simple fireman?"

She relaxed and smiled. "No fireman is simple and, yes, I would definitely consider any offer seriously. I had a wonderful time. It was fun, even the encounter with the cop."

Bob laughed at her final remark. "Not my best moment, but you seemed to find it entertaining."

Kathy laughed. "It was different."

"Then I'll call you when I can come up with something interesting to do."

"It doesn't have to be that interesting. You're interesting enough for me." She leaned over and gave him a peck on the cheek, then walked to the front door of her apartment building and gave him a final wave before stepping into the building.

Bob laughed to himself, strapped the spare helmet to the back of the bike, put his helmet on, and started the bike. He put it in gear and pulled away feeling good about the possibilities.

Chapter Five

Bob pulled his car into the side lot at Six Engine. It had been an eventful seventy-two hours since he had left the firehouse. The weather had been perfect for his little foray into west Jersey and was holding up well today. Unseasonably warm with just a hint of a breeze. The law of average temperatures was going to make them suffer later in the winter. Just thinking of fighting fires in sub-zero temperatures made him shiver unconsciously. As he gathered his things, the thought came to him that the past three days were a short history of his time on the job. At Jack's wedding, he had sat at the table of his first crew. That appeared to be a set up on Chingli's part, so he and Kathy could spend a little time together. He owed Frank's wife a big thank you. Across from the old timers table sat the guys he worked with now.

They were a young crew. Captain Peter Schmidt had been promoted a year before. He was a converted truck man from Five Truck who always seemed to have a short hook in his hand. Old habits die hard. Then there was Ray, the former cop who decided to take the same path as his childhood buddy Frank Helms. He ended up at Six Engine because Frank and Jack had pushed him to ask for it. With the work Ray had done during the stalker murders, the mayor had given him carte blanche when he moved to the fire department; any firehouse, any tour he wanted. Jack had more time in Six than anyone on his tour. It had taken only three years for him to move from junior man to senior man in the company. Junior man was Hector

Perez. Hector had taken the same test as Bob, but since he had applied to the newly created position of bi-lingual firefighter and the city did not know what to do with the title, it had taken a court order to get him appointed. He and six other guys who had applied for that title were immediately dubbed the magnificent seven. If they had not checked the box for bi-lingual firefighter, all would have been appointed a couple of years before they were. This was a point that came up in the firehouse when the senior firefighters questioned Hector's decision making. Very little was sacred in that testosterone laced environment. All was meant and taken as good- natured ball busting. If it was not the Chief would not have tolerated it.

Chief Roy Simmons was a newly promoted Deputy Chief who had spent twenty years in the center of the city as the Fourth Battalion Chief. Bob could think of no Deputy he would rather work with. The experience the Chief had gained while a Battalion Chief could not be matched. It gave him the confidence to make quick calls on the fire ground, calls that kept firefighters safe and saved lives. The Chief was assisted by his longtime aide Hank Crane. Hank had worked with the Chief so long he could anticipate his instructions and give advice to young firefighters about how to interact with their Deputy. These guys were like family to Bob. This firehouse was like home. As he gathered his clean uniforms and bedding, Bob knew he was in for a rough ride. All had seen him with Kathy. Now he would have to account for what he did yesterday. It would be like blood in the water and the circling sharks would not be able to resist. He locked the car and went in to greet his fate.

"Here's lover boy now," Ray shouted when Bob opened the door.

"Yo, Bob, how is it Kathy didn't slap your face after she saw the way you looked at her in that dress?" Hector laughed.

"Is that what a Spanish girl would do?" Bob shot back.

"A Spanish girl would have teased you all night just for the fun of it," Hector responded. "Then she would rip your heart out in front of everyone, just to warn them that she deserves respect."

"I was very respectful of Miss Stanley the entire night," Bob pointed out.

Everyone was in the kitchen, waiting to pounce on him. Bob knew he should have pushed to get in earlier. Then he would have held the high ground. Instead he was at the bottom of the hill taking fire from all sides.

"It sure looked like you were trying, Bob," Captain Schmidt laughed. "You couldn't seem to find a comfortable place to put your hand when you were dancing."

"Cap, she wore that silk dress that just clung to her," Bob whined. "My hand kept slipping. It took effort to keep it in a polite position."

"You were struggling, that was obvious," the Captain said with a chuckle.

"Do you realize you were set up?" Ray asked.

"I got that feeling," Bob sighed.

The Chief and Hank were sitting quietly at the table nursing mugs of coffee while all this was going on. Bob noticed the smell of wet burnt wood permeated the room. It seemed to be coming from the apparatus floor. The third tour must have had at least one job last night. Finding out about that was for later. He could not spend time with questions about last night and certainly could not spend time parrying jabs in the kitchen. His gear was not on the rig and he was not in uniform. Polyester blend clothing was so much easier to clean than cotton, so it behooved them to avoid responding in street clothes.

"Set up?" Hank asked no longer content to simply listen. "Set up by who?"

"It's a long story Hank," Bob explained. "If you guys would let me get changed and put my gear on the rig, all will be made clear."

He walked to the back room and pulled his turnout gear from the first tour closet. The smell of a fire also filled this room. Turnout gear was hanging around the room turned inside out. The third tour had definitely had a job last night. He would have to read the company journal later. Right now getting his gear on the rig was most important. Fires were fought with street clothes under turnout gear all the time, but never without the gear. If the bell hit and his gear was not on the rig, he would miss the run and have a lot of explaining to do. Bob quickly went to the apparatus floor and threw his gear on a yellow fire truck covered in gray soot. "Must have been a good job," Bob thought as he went to check his air mask. The rig was an American LaFrance thousand gallon pumper. After making sure his SCBA was working properly and had a full air tank, Bob hustled up the stairs to change.

When he stepped back into the kitchen, the conversation had turned to washing the rig.

"Ray, I want you to pull out onto the apron," the Captain was saying. "Then put it into pump and use the booster line to hose it down thoroughly before you put hands on it."

Bob wondered why the Captain was giving special instructions on washing the rig. They washed it frequently, usually inside the firehouse with the hose on the apparatus floor. Why on the apron and why with the booster? He knew better than to interrupt. When the skipper noticed him, he would bring Bob up to speed.

"What was in that building?" Hector asked.

"Dioxin, Hector," the Chief answered. "They found barrels of dioxin in the basement of the exposure building. The barrels don't appear to have been compromised. Thank God they weren't in the fire building. That was vaporized. No one could tell me if there was anything in that building. Probably wasn't, but we want to play it safe. It's a warm day. I'm sure the EPA doesn't want us washing dioxin into the sewers, but I don't want you guys breathing it in on your next run."

"We'll just pull it out," the Captain added. "Use a little pressure to hose it down, then take out the brushes and clean it."

"There was dioxin at the fire last night?" Bob asked in disbelief. "I thought that stuff was banned? So, the fire was Downneck."

The Chief turned to Bob and laughed. "The fire was on Sixteenth Street, Bob," he said with an exasperated look on his face. "The State DEP and the EPA responded after they found out what was in the basement of the exposure. The guy from the EPA said it was the only place in the country with fifty-five gallon drums of dioxin exposed.

Go figure, on a residential street of the most densely populated city in the country. Can you imagine the press if people were exposed to that?"

Bob was taking all this in when he was blindsided by Ray. "So, how did yesterday go, Bob?" he asked nonchalantly. It was the proverbial pebble thrown into the pond.

"Don't we have to pull the rig out and clean it?" Bob asked dodging the question.

"I'll pull the rig out," Ray replied. "You can take a minute to tell everyone about yesterday."

"Okay," Hank said, obviously feeling uninformed. "You left saying you would explain about being set up and now there's yesterday. What gives?"

The house bell hit once, signifying it was eight o'clock and the tours had officially changed. Captain Schmidt stood up and walked to the watch room to write up the company journal.

"Don't hesitate because of me, Bob," the Captain laughed. "What I don't hear, I'll get from Ray later. He seems to be up on everything."

"It's all related, Hank," Ray said as he walked toward the apparatus floor doors. "And it involves a certain young lady who spent a few hours interviewing you." With that he pushed through the doors, leaving Bob to fend for himself with an expectant audience. The sound of the overhead door starting its ascent came from the apparatus floor as everyone waited for Bob to begin.

"Someone set you up with Kathy?" Hank laughed. "My boy, you owe big time."

Bob knew that would be Hank's reaction. He had been taken by Kathy from the day of his interview, muttering something about being thirty years younger. The girl had a way of charming firemen and squeezing information out of them. Then the poor bastards thanked her. The thought crossed his mind that maybe he should rethink this connection with her. She might just squeeze him and then discard him when she grew bored. As soon as that thought crossed his mind, he knew it was too late. He might end up with his teeth knocked down his throat, but he intended to enjoy the ride. The sound of the rig starting and pulling out came through the kitchen doors. Right now all he could think was that if anyone had set him up it was Ray.

"The setup, Hank," Bob began as the veteran firefighter walked to the sink and rinsed his coffee mug. "It's pure speculation right now, but it seems Frank Helm's wife Chingli insisted I be seated at Kathy's table. That's why I wasn't sitting with all of you at the wedding."

Hank took this with a smile and then waited for Bob to move on to the second part of the question. When Bob did not continue, Hank prodded him on, "What about yesterday?" he asked,

"Yesterday, yesterday," Bob muttered knowing it would come out sooner or later, but still feeling he was the victim of the firehouse grapevine, more specifically, the wives network. Ray's wife Stacey was behind this. "Well, I, ah, I took Kathy out for a ride on my bike. We spent the afternoon together taking in the autumn foliage and chatting."

Everyone around the kitchen responded with hoots and shouts. He was not going to hear the end of this, not for the rest of the day anyway. Kathy was too involved with the Fire Department for that to happen. Bob interpreted all the noise as encouragement. Ray walked back in with a sly smile on his face.

"So Stacey spoke with Kathy?" Bob asked trying to see how much Ray knew about yesterday.

"No, no," Ray replied. "She talked to Chingli. Chingli phoned Kathy."

"I thought it was something like that," Bob said under his breath. Then he remembered the cop from Millburn. "Ray, Rich from Millburn says hello."

"Rich from Millburn?" Ray asked sounding puzzled. "Oh, Rich from Millburn. He went through the police academy with me. Right, where'd you run into him?"

Bob regretted bringing the subject up immediately. How to explain where he met Rich without telling everyone about the boneheaded move that had predicated their meeting. "I had a little chat with him on South Orange Avenue," Bob said trying to weasel his way around telling the whole story. "He didn't know you had resigned from the Police Department, said he hadn't spoken with you since the stalker thing."

"On South Orange Avenue?" Ray asked suspiciously. "I thought he lived in Union."

Ray's expression changed as he began to see problems with what Bob had told him. Bob saw it coming. Never give a former detective more information than was necessary, not if you want to avoid being dragged through the firehouse mud.

"Where about on South Orange Avenue did you run into him?" Ray asked, honing in on the obvious half-truth of Bob's tale.

"Well, ah, yeah, it was ah, Old Short Hills Road and South Orange Avenue." Bob stammered.

By now everyone in the kitchen was listening. It was obvious that Ray had Bob on the run. They were all waiting patiently for the outcome, certain it would be worth it.

"And Rich was walking his dog or was he maybe on duty?" Ray asked, dragging it out and enjoying himself. With friends like him, who needed enemies?

"So, I was trying to entertain Kathy," Bob confessed with a grin. "And I just kind of swung the bike up this entrance to an office building and back out on to the street. That got the attention of your classmate who told me some story about cops not giving firemen tickets if they can help it because we're the only ones crazy enough to help them if they get into trouble."

The last part of his sentence had the desired effect of getting a loud laugh out of everybody, but did not put Ray off the trail. Former cop that he was, he knew there were details missing. No cop pulls over a bike because they went in an entrance and out an exit.

"You swung the bike into an entrance and then rolled out the exit. How fast were you going while you did this?" Ray pressed, quickly nailing down Bob's transgression.

"Well, I was under the speed limit," Bob answered.

"The speed limit of the parking lot or the speed limit of South Orange Avenue?"

"You know, that woman is a closet thrill seeker," Bob said going off subject. "I swung up that drive and she let out the cutest squeal. She was having a blast."

Before anyone could react to what he said, the phone from dispatch rang. Hector picked it up.

"Six. Full box for Sixteenth and Littleton Avenues, got it." He hung up the phone and said, "Everybody goes, telephone alarm, Sixteenth and Littleton."

The Chief and Hank went out through the watch room door followed by the Captain and Hector, all walking at a quickened pace. Bob and Ray exited the kitchen through the double doors at the other end of the room. Ray was driving, so he headed straight for the rig he had parked on the apron a few minutes before. The overhead door for the engine bay was still open. Hank had started the door in front of the chief's gig up when he had stepped out of the watch room. Bob walked to his boots, slid out of his shoes, reached down to his ankles to wrap his pants tightly around his leg, and slid his feet into the boots. This was done in one practiced fluid motion. The bells sounded ten times then there was a pause before they began again in a sequence, a group of four, a pause, a group of three, a pause, a group of one, a pause, and a group of six. The sequence was repeated one more time, station four-three-one-six, Sixteenth and Littleton Avenues. When he looked up at the rig, he saw smoke blowing past the firehouse. Jogging to the rig, he began to think of what was on that corner. He grabbed his coat and climbed into the bucket seat. Hector was already standing in the opposite bucket across the engine compartment from him. Ray had the rig started with the warning lights on. The radio came to life as Captain Schmidt climbed into the cab.

"Attention Engines Six, Twelve, Eighteen, and Seven. Trucks Five and Nine, Battalion Four, Deputy One. Respond on a telephone alarm, station four, three, one, six, Sixteenth and Littleton Avenues."

This message was repeated as the Captain turned on the siren and Ray pulled the rig out onto Springfield Avenue turning right. Smoke was rolling down the avenue; a column could be seen rising off to the right.

Bob heard the Captain call headquarters, "Engine Six to quarters, we have a heavy smoke condition."

"Received, Engine Six reporting a heavy smoke condition at oh-eight-sixteen hours."

Chapter Six

When Ray turned onto Sixteenth Avenue, Bob could see heavy smoke coming from a four story brick apartment building three blocks ahead of them. People were fleeing down fire escapes on the Sixteenth Avenue side of the building. Both he and Hector reached for the masks they had placed on the bucket seats in front of them. Bob slid his on quickly and reached behind him to turn on the air while looking over the cab roof sizing up the fire building. Brick, four stories, no exposures to the rear, he remembered a three story wooden frame building next to it on Littleton Avenue. There was a hydrant on the corner in front of the building. The smoke was changing from the gray of wood smoke to the black given off when petroleum based products were burning.

Ray pulled the rig up to the hydrant, leaving room for the truck companies to ladder the building. Bob looked at the windows facing Littleton Avenue and immediately picked out a woman on the third floor. The whooshing sound of pressurized air told Bob that Ray had switched the rig from road mode to pump mode. Jumping down to the sidewalk, Bob shouted up to the woman, "Stay there, we'll get to you!"

He hustled around to the other side of the rig where Hector was already unlocking the ladder. They quickly carried it to the building, threw it up, and helped the woman down. She was still in her night gown. That is one hell of a way to wake up, Bob thought as he scanned the rest of the windows. Seeing there were no more people at any of the windows facing him, he grabbed a few loops of the four lengths of inch and three quarter line. He twisted the hose and pulled it over his shoulder. The nozzle was dangling in front of his chest and the bottom loops of hose would peel off the top. He then stepped toward the front door. Hector pulled the rest of the line out of its bed, flaked it out along the sidewalk, and followed. Bob dropped the last loop of hose as he reached the doorway, straightened the line out, took his helmet off, and put his face piece on. Ray was waiting at the pump panel; as soon as the hose was stretched he opened the port and gave them water. Bob pulled the straps to his face piece tight and placed his helmet back on. The hose stiffened as water filled it.

The fire had control of the foyer of the building, so Bob quickly opened the line and knocked it down. He began moving into the building with the nozzle on straight stream. The Captain came out of the alley way between the fire building and the exposure as Bob entered the building. The sound of other companies responding could be heard in the distance. Their sirens receded into the background as he crossed the threshold and entered the quiet of a building abandoned to fire. Steam from his initial knock down shrouded the foyer. Before he had knocked the fire down, Bob had noticed the stairs were directly in front of him, rising to the left. He walked straight toward the stairs and ran into fire as soon as he cleared the entrance way. It crackled around him and up the stairs, but the initial knock down had cooled the air where he stood. Working the line off the ceiling and walls, Bob quickly advanced to the stairs. It appeared the fire on the first floor was restricted to the hallway. He heard Hector at the door behind him and so went to the stairs, playing the line into the second floor as he started up. So far, Hector had fed him line whenever he advanced. It had been a straight stretch. Now that the line had to advance up the stairs it was going to become more difficult.

"Hector," Bob shouted through his face piece. "Get to the bottom of the stairs!"

"I'm here," Hector shouted through the smoke and steam.

"I'm going up to the second floor," Bob shouted.

"Go," Hector replied. "I'll get line to you."

Bob could tell by the roar and crackle of the fire that it was burning freely on the floor above. He heard other companies coming into the building as he pushed up the stairs, opening the line to knock down more of the fire, then closing it to move in further. He knew to stay close to the wall in case the fire had already weakened the stairs. They seemed strong from the first to the second floor, but he was worried about the flight going from the second to the third.

When he reached the second floor hallway, the fire darkened down quickly. It still appeared to be surface fire here, so he pushed on to the next flight of stairs. Hector must have moved to the middle of the lower stairs because the line was still coming easily. The noise of another company advancing up toward him told Bob it was safe to continue his aggressive tactics. If he could contain the fire to the stairwell, they would make short work of this job. Captain Schmidt reached him as he hit the third floor.

"Bob," the Captain shouted, his words muffled by the face piece. "Twelve's coming right behind us. Keep pushing, they have us covered!"

"Okay!" Bob replied. The less he talked the better. He was getting winded, but he had no intention of giving the line up yet. There were at least two more floors to knock down and no time to switch positions on the line. Playing the line off the walls and ceiling, Bob kept pushing. The temperature of each floor was higher than the one below it. Time for a quick knock down was running out. It had taken one sweep of the line to extinguish the first floor fire. The second floor had taken a little more time to darken down. The third floor was proving to be stubborn. The glow in the hallway went out quickly, but there was obviously fire in one of the apartments. Twelve came up behind him and started to push into the apartment. Bob decided to gamble, hoping it had not extended in too far. He pushed on to the last flight of stairs and began working the line, quickly climbing the stairs. The flames could be seen through the swirl of thick grey smoke. When Bob hit the orange glow it subsided, but as soon as the line was moved the fire grew. It was in the fourth floor apartments. Before he could attempt to kick in a door and control the fire in one of the apartments, he heard the muffled shouts of his captain.

"Bob, back down!"

Knowing the Captain never ordered him to back down from a fire unless it was a safety issue; Bob made his way back to the stairs. When he started down them, the heat forced him to crouch and then crawl. The fight below was not going well. Hector and the Captain were waiting on the stairs just below the third floor ceiling line. As soon as he reached them, the heat let up. Bob lied on his belly just below the ceiling line and threw water into the fourth floor. The fire was growing quickly above him, but he could go no further. Waves of intense heat rolled over him, burning his neck and ears. The Captain saw how futile their attempt was and ordered Bob off the stairs. His air cylinder alarm began to sound, so the firefighter handed the line to Hector and started down the stairs. When he stepped outside and looked up the fourth floor was fully involved. Walking back towards the rig, he heard the Chief call for a third alarm and then order everyone off the third floor. Truck companies were setting up ladder pipes. It was going to an outside operation until the main body of fire was knocked down. Tired and frustrated, his ears and neck burning, Bob reached Six Engine and dropped his mask on the back step. Ray was going to need a hand stretching lines to feed the ladder pipes.

It took twenty minutes for the outside master streams to darken down the top floors. Hand lines had been backed down to the second floor and crews had come out to change air cylinders and regroup. Now they were going back in to finish the job. Bob climbed the stairs to the second floor. The air was relatively clear, so his face piece swung in front of his chest. The sound of water draining from the floors above filled the staircase. Captain Schimdt and Hector were ahead of him. They sorted through the lines lying in the hallway and pulled out Six's. The Captain took the nozzle and walked to the stairs leading to the third floor, squeezing past a group of truck men who

64

had just placed a ladder over the weakened stairs. The third floor hallway and the stairs leading up to the fourth floor were blackened; any wood was deeply charred. Bob fed the line to Hector who pushed it up to the Captain. Technically either Bob or Hector should have been on the ladder, but the Captain had insisted on taking the line up since both of them had been fighting the back pressure of the line all morning.

Bob positioned himself at the bottom of the ladder. The Captain crawled up the ladder with Hector on the bottom rung a few feet behind him. The ladder's rails rested on the edge of the upper landing. The stairs directly beneath the ladder were badly damaged by the fire and the thousands of gallons of water that had been thrown into the top floors. Sunlight showed through holes cut in the roof above, giving the entire scene a surreal feeling. Bob was watching his crew intently as they ascended the ladder. When the Captain reach the midpoint, Bob saw one of the ladder rails break through the edge of the upper landing. He instinctively reached for Hector, grabbing the air cylinder on his back, and pulling him back. The ladder twisted a moment then the second rail broke through the landing edge. The full weight of Captain Schmidt, the ladder, and the hose suddenly dropped on the stairs, collapsing them and hurling all down two stories with a crash. The empty space where they had been was filled with embers swirling in the air. A beam of sunlight illuminated the scene.

"Pete! Pete Schmidt!" guys began shouting.

The radio came alive with reports to the Deputy of a fireman down and calls for EMS. Bob turned to Hector to make sure he was alright.

"You okay?" he asked crouching down.

"Yeah, I think so," Hector gasped, "that was close."

"Pete rode the ladder down to the second floor," Bob told him. "Come on, we'll get past these guys and get down to him."

He helped Hector up then they both pushed through the crowd of firemen in the hall and at the top of the stairs. Bob knew the Battalion Chief must have ordered everyone off the stairs except for Rescue. He also knew everyone would turn a blind eye to him ignoring that order. It was his captain who was down. The two firefighters made their way past the crowd and navigated through the debris covering the stairs. When they reached the second floor Rescue was with the Captain and EMS was coming up from the first floor.

Captain Schmidt was conscious and answering questions put to him by Rescue. EMS had carried up a Stokes basket. The Captain was quickly placed in the basket. After a count of three, they lifted him and started down the hall for the stairs. With the patient out of the way, the ladder was extended to its full length and thrown up where the stairs had been. Water continued to cascade down the stairwell. Bob had positioned himself in the corner by the top of the stairs, ready to give a hand if there was a hang up. When the basket reached that point the EMTs had to spin it so they could move down the stairs. This left the Captain directly under a small waterfall from the upper floors. Water and debris were splashing off his chest and he could do

66

nothing to divert it because he was securely strapped in. Bob saw what was happening and quickly stepped in. Leaning over his captain, he used his back to protect him from the torrent that had been splashing off his chest. The EMTs turned the basket and carried their patient down and out to their rig. Bob climbed up the ladder ahead of Hector to finish up.

When Six returned to quarters it was past lunch time. Ray backed the rig into quarters after Hector and Bob had stopped traffic. They were all thinking of their skipper. Bob looked at the rig as it was backing in and remembered they were supposed to wash it. Ray had apparently hosed it down at some point during the fire, as it was no longer covered with gray soot. They would probably wash it anyway because there were pieces of charred wood and soot from this fire all over it. The two firefighters waved to the cars stopped in front of the firehouse and walked into quarters, squeezing past the front of the rig. The sound of pressurized air being released filled the apparatus floor as Ray put the parking brake on. The chief's gig was not in quarters. Knowing Chief Simmons, Bob figured he was at the hospital with Captain Schmidt. He walked through the kitchen door and almost ran into the Chief who was just sitting down with a cup of coffee.

"Chief," Bob said almost as a reflex reaction. "Sorry, I thought you'd be with the gig. Something happen to it?"

"No, no," the Chief said with a chuckle. "Hank went to pick up Captain Schmidt. No room in the gig for all three of us, so I had to hang back."

"How is he, Chief?" Bob asked not waiting for Hector and Ray.

"No breaks," the Chief started. "Only soft tissue injuries. He's going to be sore for a few days. I don't expect him back tomorrow, so I guess that puts you in the seat. You'll get a detail tomorrow. I really haven't decided about the rest of the day. Don't like you oh and three, but Hank can help out if we get something. Don't rush getting back in service. There are plenty of companies looking for a piece of a fire. Get cleaned up and catch your breath."

"Okay Chief," Bob replied, relieved that Captain Pete was okay.

Hector walked in, clearly unhappy about something. He had been brooding since the two of them had gone back into the fire building after the Captain was taken to the hospital. Bob was waiting patiently for the questions to boil over. That's the way Hector was and there was no changing him.

"Chief," Hector blurted out, unable to contain himself any longer. "I should have been on the top. Why did the Captain insist on going up the ladder first?"

The Chief had an understanding look on his face. He took a moment before answering.

"Hector, sometimes it's hard to make a call like that. Bob was beaten up from the initial attack. It was obviously risky and required a little more experience. Remember if that ladder had held, he would have been alone on the fire floor until he had control of the hallway. Probably felt he should take the risk himself."

"But how am I ever going to get the experience if I'm not given the chance?"

Bob grabbed Hector's shoulder. "Slow down cowboy, you have plenty of time to get experience. It was his call and he didn't want to get one of us hurt. Now let's get dry gear on the rig and take showers."

With that Hector took a deep breath and turned towards the back room. The gig siren sounded before he reached the doorway to the back. Sounds of the overhead door starting up and the gig backing in told everyone that Hank was back with the Captain. A door slammed. Ray and Hank could be heard talking to the Captain, who limped through the kitchen door with a grin on his face. His bravado fooled no one.

"Look at you," he said with a forced chuckle. "I leave you alone for a few hours and you fall apart, can't even take showers or offer your gimpy captain a cup of coffee."

"We try Cap," Bob said as Hector walked over to the stove and filled a mug for his skipper. "But you're a hard act to follow." Then he became serious. "How are you feeling?"

"Been better, but I'll recover," he replied, continuing his bravado.

"We haven't called your wife yet, Pete," the Chief said. "Since you're going to make it home for dinner, I thought it best to leave that up to you."

"Thanks Chief," he replied with a sigh. "It sounds better when I say I'm alright instead of you saying he's alright."

"Use the phone in my room," the Chief suggested.

Hector passed the mug of coffee to Captain Schmidt, who limped out of the kitchen while he and Bob went to get dry gear. Bob reached up to touch his ears as he walked to the back room. They were definitely sore, but it didn't feel like there were any blisters. There was an odd sensation running up his right calf, but it did not seem worth mentioning it to anyone. He probably should record his sore ears in the company journal and fill out compensation papers, but as long as there were no blisters he would forego that tedious bit of paper shuffling. Besides he had an appointment to see a new doctor. He had changed medical insurance to something new called a health maintenance organization and wanted to check out one of the doctors on a list they had sent him. The thought crossed his mind that there would not be any more ball busting about Kathy today. The Captain was banged up and Hector was having a hard time of it. He would have much preferred the ball busting.

Chapter Seven

Kathy stood outside the Shanghai restaurant on South Orange Avenue, a jumble of conflicting emotions. The weather had turned more seasonal, so she was wearing a long gray woolen coat over her jeans and blouse. There was a little bit of a breeze and the sun was dancing in and out of the clouds. She was shocked at herself for the reaction she had when Stacey told her Pete Schmidt had ridden a staircase down two floors at a fire the day before. Was it because she knew Pete? He was not seriously hurt. When Kathy had spoken to his wife Laura, she had taken it in stride. Pete had called her to say he was alright. That was better than the Chief calling and certainly better than the Fire Chaplin knocking on her door. "If Laura could take it in stride, why is it bothering me?" Kathy thought as she started to pace slowly in front of the tiny eatery. There was something else going on in her psyche. She was certain that something was Bob Brendler and it bothered her. When she was in such a state Kathy fell back on comfort food, which translated into Chinese or Italian cuisine. The little restaurant she was marching in front of was a gem that had opened recently. The food was great; it was inexpensive, but it just did not have the ambience some people find so important. It was all about the food to her, especially when seeking comfort.

Chingli strolled around the corner, apparently parking in the municipal lot behind town hall. Kathy felt a wave of relief pass over her, but this only lasted a moment. Her friend had been through hell before Frank had resigned. That experience may have given Chingli some insight into how to deal with the emotions roiling inside the writer, but it was her romantic experience Kathy needed now more than anything. The cockiness she had exhibited the last time the two had spoken about falling for a fireman had evaporated. It was one thing to grow up with a father who fought fires. That had been part of the world she was born into. It was quite another to feel herself falling too quickly for a guy who did it. That was purely voluntary.

"*Meimei*," Chingli greeted her. "You look troubled."

"I'm confused, conflicted," Kathy confessed. "My mind is spinning and I don't believe what's happening and my reaction and . . . oh, I don't know!"

Chingli reached for her hands with a smile and said, "Maybe we should go inside out of the wind, have a cup of tea, something to eat, and chat. Everything is so much clearer when you aren't hungry." With that she turned, stepped to the door, and pulled it open.

The smell of Chinese cuisine drifted across the room as they stepped in. The narrow space was occupied by square tables covered in red that marched down both side walls. There was no receptionist. Customers had to make their way to the rear of the dining area and place their order at a counter along the back wall. Then the waitress, who was the owner/chef's wife, would bring their meal to them. Unless you spoke Mandarin there was little small talk between the owners and the customers. The young couple was "F.O.P.", fresh off the plane. Kathy had only been here a few times, so she did not know much more than that. Chingli would probably get the whole story in the first ten minutes.

They stopped at a table about midway between the entrance and the rear counter. There were no other customers, but it was only eleven thirty. Both removed their coats before Chingli made her way to the back. Kathy dropped into a chair and tried to stop her mind from spinning. The irony of Chingli ordering when Kathy was the one who recommended the place was not lost on the author. She acquiesced out of sheer emotional exhaustion.

Her friend came back and sat across from Kathy. She had an empathetic look on her face as she asked, "What is confusing you?"

"Six Engine had a fire yesterday," Kathy began to explain.

"I know," Chingli interrupted "Pete was hurt in a fall, Bob's ears were burned a little, and Hector feels bad because he thinks he should have been on the . . . how do you call the end of the hose with the nozzle?"

"The tip," Kathy answered the question and then asked. "Bob's ears? What . . . what happened to Bob's ears?"

"Didn't Stacy tell you about the burns on Bob's ears?" Chingli asked. "I wonder, did Ray tell her? Firemen have a way of not saying things they don't want their wives to hear. Frank calls it lying by omission. He did it to me a lot, especially with all those shootings. But Frank talked with Bob and his ears were burned a little at that fire. He didn't go to the hospital, but they are uncomfortable."

"Well, that doesn't make things any easier," Kathy sighed. "I am having a hard time with this. It's a surprise. I mean I grew up with my father doing it."

"But your father is not the same as a - - -," Chingli thought for a moment. "How do you say it? A romantic interest."

Kathy chuckled for the first time since dealing with the fluster of the day's emotions. "A romantic interest seems to require more from me," she admitted. "I don't understand. We have been on one date; we danced at a wedding. I hardly know this man. Why does it bother me?"

Before Chingli could respond the waitress brought a hot pot of tea. Uncharacteristically, Chingli only passed pleasantries. This warmed Kathy's heart. She knew her friend was there for her.

"Do you believe in what Americans call love at first seeing?"

"Love at first sight," Kathy muttered. "No, and I didn't say I was in love, let alone that it was love at first sight. There is an attraction to him, but he's an attractive guy. Getting to know him a little just made him that much more attractive."

"Attractive enough to move your heart?" Chingli probed.

Kathy felt a little embarrassed to acknowledge she was smitten so quickly. She did not want to admit it to herself. How could her friend pick up on it that quickly? "I didn't mention my heart at all," she said defensively. "Just don't know why I feel so discombobulated . . . so flustered . . . so confused." She knew she was in trouble when she had to ratchet back her English. After years of experience speaking with her mother, Kathy naturally adjusted her vocabulary to match her audience. When this reflex failed, it was a sign that her emotions were struggling.

"Did your mother ever teach you anything about Buddhism?" Chingli asked.

Kathy shook her head no. Her mother had become a good Catholic girl when she married. *Jia ji sui ji, jia gou sui gou*, is what she had said. When you marry a chicken, you follow a chicken. When you marry a dog, you follow a dog.

"*Qian shi de guan xi*, is how the Chinese would explain this. It is a relationship from a previous life," Chingli explained.

"Did you feel like this when you first met Frank?"

Chingli smiled and looked off into the distance. "I met Frank in Hong Kong and just needed someone to try on a jacket. His classmate started us off. She and I spoke in French, so Frank didn't understand. Seton Hall was one of the schools I was thinking about and he seemed special even though we didn't say much to each other. He just encouraged me to attend Seton Hall. We both agreed it was a *qian shi de guan xi* moment. He was the type of man I like. What type of man do you like?"

Their meals came as Chingli asked this question. She had ordered a spicy chicken dish and a spicy shrimp dish. They both smelled delicious. The respite provided by their meal allowed Kathy to think. They ate family style taking a little from each dish and commenting on the flavors. What kind of man do I like? Kathy thought. She knew when it felt right, but to put it into words was proving illusive. Chingli did not push for an answer while they ate, giving Kathy time to mull it over. They were sipping tea after their meal when Chingli pushed for an answer. By then the lunch crowd had begun to pile in, quickly filling the small space with conversations and laughter. It was a young crowd, mostly college students. This was not a restaurant for a quiet business lunch.

"What kind of man do I like?" Kathy repeated. "It's a dichotomy . . . it's split into two parts," catching her nervous slip to improper vocabulary again. "When I was a freshman I dated a really poetic type of guy. That's one type I like. Only problem was when he heard what my dad did for a living he made it clear that he thought firemen had to be crazy to do their job. After that he lost his luster. He was a poetic coward as far as I was concerned." She giggled after hearing herself admit that. "Another part of me likes the manly, strong fireman type. Not the macho kind of guy, but one who is sure of himself and has a little nerve."

"Bob wrote a beautiful poem for Gloria and Jack," Chingli mentioned offhandedly.

Kathy now felt completely exposed. Chingli had all her weaknesses when it came to men.

Her friend smiled reassuringly. "You don't have to worry, *Meimei*. I will keep your secrets. Is it *qian shi de guan xi* or love at first seeing?"

Kathy laughed and then blurted out, "It's neither. I told you that already. I just have to figure out how to handle Mr. Brendler. Didn't think I would ever meet a guy who could satisfy both parts of what I look for. If he's for real, he might just do it. What to do?"

Chingli took a moment to think then reached across the table to touch her friend's hand. "If you want to know, you are going to have to risk something," she reminded Kathy. "Go slowly if you can and see if he is for real."

Kathy smiled and said "thank you." Then she went to the register and paid their bill. Chingli had told her what she knew had to be done all along. She would have to build slowly, but knew the greater the risk, the greater the reward.

Chapter Eight

Bob put groceries for the night's meal on the firehouse kitchen counter. He had made a point of coming in early just to avoid getting jumped as soon as he walked in the door. The guys from the second tour had made some comments about Kathy, but after a day in the firehouse they were more interested in going home. Hector and Ray had come in shortly after him, placed their gear on the rig, and had gone directly upstairs to change. He took the skirt steaks out of the bag and placed them in the refrigerator. Makings for the salad followed. The egg noodles remained on the counter as did the jars of beef gravy. Steaks with noodles smothered in gravy and a tossed salad. It was not gourmet food, but it filled a man up. The gourmet flavors had retired from this firehouse, at least until his crew could develop their culinary skills. That was a process that would probably take a few years. The crews in some companies around the city had been together for decades. Even if they had not been assigned to the company they now called home, they had often worked together in busy companies and then transferred. The meals in these companies were for gourmets.

Jack and Gloria had returned from their honeymoon the night before. It had only been a four day, three night escape to Disney World, then back to reality. Jack was acting captain tonight, if he ever got his newly wed self in. Captain Schmidt had injured his back in the fall the other day. The Chief suggested he nurse it instead of pushing to come back and really doing some damage. Bob had tried to get

Jack up to speed earlier in the day, but he had conveniently left out any reference to Kathy. Hopefully that would give him some peace until Ray or Hector said something. This would all run its course by the time the Captain returned to duty. Bob just had to ride out the next couple of nights. The sound of the rear door opening told Bob that Jack was finally in. He poked his head around the corner to make sure.

"You made it before the time blow," Bob shouted. "Good to see the Florida sun didn't broil your brains." Jack looked a little sunburned, but other than that no worse for the wear. He dropped his bedding and uniforms on one chair and dropped himself in another.

"Is there any coffee?" he asked weakly. "I need a little something to kick start my engine."

Bob laughed as he pulled down a mug and filled it with coffee. "What's the matter? Spend too much time wrestling with Mickey?" Bob poked. No sympathy was given around the firehouse for someone who partied until he dropped.

"I don't expect understanding from you, just a cup of coffee," Jack muttered.

Bob handed him the mug of Joe. After taking a swig, he began to brighten up. "So, I hear you made a move on one of our wedding guests. Gloria saw it coming, insisted on Kathy sitting with you. I think Chingli came up with the idea. There was something about her helping get things started."

Bob was not surprised that Jack knew something about what had transpired while he was in Florida. The girls network would have kept Gloria informed about the basics. Whether Jack knew about the traffic stop was the question. That would probably be where the ball busting would start tonight since it was where it had ended the other day. "I was set up. That's the consensus around here," Bob informed him. "Chingli started the snowball down the hill and waited to see if it would grow. You better go up and get changed. You have to write up the book at the time blow, remember?"

"Yeah, yeah," Jack said as he finished his coffee. "For pennies an hour, I get to pull the air horn and write stories."

"Stories?" Bob laughed. "You're getting jaded in your old age."

Jack stood up and walked to the back room for his gear without responding. Bob reached into the cabinet and grabbed a pot to boil water for the noodles. Then he walked to the back for his gear. He could hear Hector and Ray coming down the stairs. It was time for him to change into his uniform. As he picked up his boots, Bob touched his leg and remembered what the doctor had said. The boots probably bruised a nerve in his leg. It must have happened when the stairs collapsed and everything went crazy. The doctor said it would take a few weeks to heal, but there were no signs of weakness in the leg. He put it behind him and carried his gear to the rig. After checking his mask, he went upstairs to change.

When Bob returned to the kitchen, the room was humming with culinary activity. Hector had the steaks on the grill while Ray was working on the salad with Hank. Bob headed for the counter to retrieve the pot for the noodles. As he stepped to the sink to fill it, Hank asked, "So, Bob you said our little Kathy is a closet thrill seeker? Maybe she should take the test for the job."

Bob thought for a moment before replying. The absurdity of calling Kathy little was obvious to everyone. She stood a couple inches above Hector. Not that she was interested, but the chances of her passing the entrance test high enough to get on the job were remote. The changes in testing procedures ordered because of the consent decree effectively put the job out of reach for women unless they had some sort of veteran preference. Only healthy young bucks passed high enough to be appointed. Bob turned on the water and turned to Hank.

"I don't think she's interested in coming on the job," Bob replied. "She likes to write about us, but she didn't say anything about wanting to do our job."

"I heard her say she thought firemen had the best job in the word," Jack chimed in.

"When did she say that?" Bob asked

"She was covering that story and Frank was acting like a bad boy because he had stopped to talk to Mr. Detective over here," Jack said pointing at Ray. "She was trying to break the ice, so she said that. Frank could never keep his mouth shut so he did the next best thing and said something in Chinese. The two of them started having a conversation in Chinese and we were all sitting there saying 'what?' But anyway, she said she always thought firemen have the best job in the world."

Bob chuckled at that little morsel of information and stored it away. You never know, he thought, it might come in handy someday. "She might have said it, but I still don't think she wants to do our job.

She's more than content playing the supporting role, not interested in being the star."

"But she likes thrills?" Hank interjected.

"Safe thrills, like roller coasters," Bob replied.

"Or sitting on the back of a motorcycle with someone who wants to show off?" Ray poked.

"I wasn't trying to show off," Bob parried. "I was trying to entertain."

The phone from dispatch rang before Ray could reply.

Hank picked up. "Six. Signal Nine two forty two West Kinney."

The guys from Six walked out of the kitchen to the rig as the joker circuit on the alarm console clicked indicating an alarm was about to come over the system. Hank started the overhead door up as Ray and Jack slammed the cab doors. Bob and Hector climbed into the bucket seats; Hank would close the overhead door. The bells started as Ray pulled out of quarters, one sequence of nine, one of four, one of seven, one of five, and one of two, station four seven five two. Two forty two West Kinney Street was one of ten high rise buildings that made up the Hayes Homes, the public housing project that rose up across from Six Engine's quarters. The operator had said nothing about what they were responding to. With the projects it could be anything from a fire to a woman in labor to people trapped in an elevator. They would not know until they arrived on the scene.

It was a short ride to the building. Bob looked at the old incinerator chimney first. EPA regulations had put a stop to burning garbage by the project janitors. Instead trash compactors were installed at the bottom of the garbage chutes. But this did not stop the burning of garbage. The chutes jammed up continually; then the residents either accidentally or out of frustration set the garbage on fire. It did not appear to be the case this time because Bob's scan of the roof revealed no smoke. Ray parked the rig at the curb by two forty two. A young woman ran up to Jack as he opened the cab door.

"There's a brother on the fourth floor. He's hurt. He's hurt bad and EMS ain't come yet. You gotta help him."

Jack reassured her; then picked up the radio mike.

"Engine Six to quarters."

"Engine Six."

"We have a report of a seriously injured man on the fourth floor of two forty two West Kinney, Inform EMS."

'Inform EMS, received Six. Eighteen thirty two hours."

Bob walked to the rear side compartment, opened it, and pulled out the oxygen. Hector came around and grabbed the first aid kit. They headed for the entrance of two forty two. Jack was a few paces ahead of them.

The entrance to the building was wide open, the doors having been ripped off their frame months before. No one was standing around the opening. The three firefighters quickly passed through, climbed the short flight of concrete stairs to the first floor, and stepped to the elevator. Jack pushed the button, but there was no familiar clank from the shaft telling them it was working. They moved to the stairwell and began climbing to the fourth floor. It was a dark ascent because the lights had been ripped out of the wall. The stairwell was permeated with the mixed stench of urine and smoke which made breathing unfriendly. By the time they reached the landing, Bob felt his legs were unusually fatigued. The odd sensation in his right leg also seemed more pronounced. The doctor had not said the bruised nerve would affect his stamina, but apparently it did. Not that it was anything other than a minor annoyance. Since he was told it would clear up in a few weeks, he chose to ignore it.

As they stepped through the doorway into the fourth floor hall, they saw a young man lying on the floor in front of an apartment door. He was cursing and moaning, but had no obvious injuries.

"Sir, what's your name?" Jack asked as he crouched down.

"I'm Mr. Brown," the young man replied. "They stabbed me and left me to die!" His words reverberated off the dirty yellow glazed brick walls.

Bob touched Jack on the shoulder. As acting captain Jack had to communicate with headquarters. Bob and Hector would take over the care of Mr. Brown. Bob crouched down and asked, "Mr. Brown, where did they stab you?"

"Right in my chest," he answered angrily. "I'm gonna die and nobody cares!"

"We care and we're not going to let you die," Bob reassured him. "Can I have a look at where they stabbed you?" He was very concerned. There was no blood around the patient, who was in obvious pain and convinced he would die of his wound. If he suffered the kind of wound Bob suspected, they would have to hurry.

"Yeah, you go and look," Mr. Brown replied. "They stuck me right here!" He was pointing to the left side of his chest.

Bob carefully unbuttoned the young man's shirt and gently pulled it aside. The blade had penetrated the upper chest wall between two ribs in the area of the aorta artery. There was not a drop of blood on his skin, just a cut less than an inch in length. The young man suffered another spasm of pain, curling his legs up and cursing.

Jack was standing a few feet away, talking to headquarters.

"Six to quarters."

"Six."

"Could you give me an ETA on EMS?"

"They can't give us one."

"Let them know we have a young man on the ground with a stab wound to the upper chest. We need a bus ASAP."

"Received Six. Eighteen thirty seven."

Hector had opened the first aid kit and taken out gauze bandages. There was a look of bewilderment on his face. Bob could see the junior firefighter had not grasped how serious the situation was. This was not the time or place to bring him up to speed. Hector offered a package of gauze which Bob took even though it was useless.

"I'm dying and nobody cares!" Mr. Brown repeated.

"We're getting an ambulance for you," Bob reassured him. "They'll be here in a minute."

"I ain't got no minute. Ain't no ambulance coming for me," the young man muttered, showing signs of losing strength. "I'm gonna die in this dark, smelly hall in front of my door. For what? I ain't got no money to give the bastards. Why'd they have to go and do this?"

They could all see that time was running out. The most frustrating part for Bob was that there was nothing they could do. The man was bleeding internally. He needed a surgeon, not a firefighter.

"Headquarters to Engine Six."

"Engine Six," Jack responded hopefully.

"EMS says they have a bus enroute."

"Six received."

"Just hold on a little longer, Mr. Brown," Bob encouraged the young man. "The ambulance will be here in a minute."

"I'm trying," he replied weakly.

They could hear EMS climbing the stairs. Hector ran over to the door and waited for them. The EMTs had a gurney and their medical kit with them. They leaned over to exam the patient, who had become silent. Bob told them what he knew then everyone worked to get him on the gurney and down the stairs. They could see the young man's eyes roll back while they raced across the concrete to the ambulance. As the bus pulled away, Bob knew they had not made it. The man died because he had no money. The thought sickened him. Hector looked confused.

"Do you remember all that first aid they taught you at the Academy?" Bob asked Hector.

"Yeah, but they didn't teach me anything like this," Hector said sounding confused. "He only had a little cut. I thought he was faking it until his eyes rolled back. What happened?"

"He was bleeding internally," Bob told him. "They stuck that knife in up to the hilt, but it was like a puncture wound. No external blood and nothing we could do but wait for EMS. He needed a surgeon to open his chest and repair his aorta." The last sentence was spit out in frustration. He cursed to himself and climbed on the rig. Jack called headquarters to go back in service. It was a quiet ride back to quarters.

Bob was sitting on the front bumper of the rig after dinner reviewing what had happened. The situation had been beyond their capacities or training. The blade of the knife had probably cut a vein or artery feeding the heart. The man had bled to death in front of them and they could do nothing but ask EMS to hurry. Even if that bus had arrived quickly, what would have been the chances of Mr. Brown surviving the ride to the ER? This realization did not help. The frustration continued eating away. Jack came around the rig and stood next to him.

"Don't let it eat away at you," Jack counseled. "We did all we could. Beating yourself up won't help."

"You're right," Bob admitted. "Just seems so evil. The bastards who stuck him didn't have any money, yet stabbed him because he had no money."

"You're going to give everybody around here ten bucks so they can give it to thieves and avoid getting stabbed?" Jack asked. "I know that sounds cold, but that's the logic you're using. We're just little firemen. If the country's leaders are having a hard time with these problems, how are we going to solve them?"

"Yeah, you're right. I said you were right," Bob replied. "I'll just hide that memory away in my little dark locker in the back of my mind."

"So, tell me about Kathy," Jack said, changing the subject and hopefully the mood.

"Tell you about Kathy?" Bob muttered, allowing himself to switch gears. If he was to survive emotionally on this job, he knew he had to do a better job of that. "Well, so far she's everything I had hoped she would be and since I have a pretty good imagination, that's frightening.

"Doesn't sound good," Jack quipped.

"No, it doesn't," Bob replied. "I still don't see what she sees in me. She seems to like the way I use words."

"Use words?" Jack asked. "How's that?"

Bob rarely spoke about poetry around the firehouse and then only to Jack. He felt even more reserved about that subject tonight. "My poetry," he laughed. "She likes my poetry."

Jack chuckled. "She must have met a dozen bona fide poets, there's more at work here than your poems. Maybe a little animal magic?"

"Kathy and animal magic?" Bob chuckled. "She seems too smart for animal magic, if I have any."

"It's all part of the stew that keeps the human race going," Jack pointed out. "A little musk, a little poetry, a little conversation, and you have animal magic."

"Don't women call that romance?" Bob quizzed.

"That's just a polite way of saying it," Jack answered. "Seriously, how did it feel over the past few days? I get the impression things have started to develop pretty quickly."

Bob thought for a second about the past week, what a start! But was there enough energy to keep the ball rolling or would it be slowed to a halt by the inertia of doubts and fears? The doubts would probably be hers. He thought he had the fears cornered.

"I have tried to slow it down a bit," Bob confessed. "Have not been the least bit aggressive or suggestive. Just trying to get a feel for where she's coming from. If anyone's going to get their teeth kicked in it's me. So I have my foot on the brake. Besides I have a promotional test to worry about."

"She's got you running does she?" Jack asked ignoring the test comment. An omission Bob noticed immediately, but chose not to include in the conversation. The two had spoken often about taking the test. Jack did not think he was ready for the responsibility of worrying about other firefighters. Bob was of the opinion that his friend would make an excellent captain. That was where the matter stood and now was not the time to go into it again.

"I'm fighting it," Bob sighed "But I think it's a losing battle. Just going to enjoy the ride and see where we end up."

"Sounds like a plan, not a good one, but a plan," Jack laughed. Bob stood up and they both walked to the kitchen. This was the second time the ball busting had ended prematurely because of what had happened at an alarm.

Chapter Nine

Kathy looked for any signs of buds on the bushes that guarded the entrance to Frank and Chingli's building. There was a hint of spring in the air. The winter had been mild. Not mild enough for another ride on Bob's bike, but very little snow had fallen and what little snow there was had quickly turned dirty and melted. She had to return to Rhode Island to see any white flakes. More than one of the old timers she had interviewed in Newark's firehouses had commented about the weather. This winter had not convinced any of them to throw in the towel. If next winter were the same, none intended to go anywhere.

She climbed the stonework steps to the glass entrance door and rang the Helms' bell. Chingli's invitation had been welcomed. Kathy needed some advice on how to get her relationship with Bob to the next level. The man spent so much of his time studying, there was little time left for her. She understood the commitment needed for a promotional exam, but he should come up for air occasionally. Kathy had mentioned that she had helped her father study for promotion. These not so subtle hints had been ignored or gone completely over his head. The door buzzer sounded, signaling the door latch was opened. Kathy pulled the door and stepped into the foyer.

Chingli stood at the entrance to her small apartment. Why she and Frank still lived here was beyond Kathy. Their business had been growing steadily. They could afford better digs than this. Not that the apartment was substandard. It was not. It was just small. Frank and

Chingli were obviously not a pretentious couple. It was wonderful to see two people who were so in tune with each other. They had not always been in sync. The first time Kathy had visited this apartment, Frank had wanted her to somehow\persuade Chingli that he should stay on the job instead of taking an offer from her uncle to start a business. How an intelligent man could harbor such ridiculous thoughts still amazed her. They had weathered that storm, although Kathy thought Frank never really got over resigning from the job. He accepted it, but he was not happy about it. She was certain if Bob were forced into the same situation he would die. He and her father had a lot in common that way. The past months had taught her about the tolerance and the concerns her mother had faced all those years. She was surprised at how her slowly deepening relationship with Bob had given her new admiration and respect for her mother. That was for another time. Her relationship may be deepening, but it was doing so at a snail's pace. How to move it from friendly phone conversations and occasional dinners to something more intimate, something with a little more commitment? Chingli had said that Gloria and Stacey would be here. Her intent was to turn the evening into a war council.

She stepped into the dining area of Chingli's little empire. Gloria and Stacey were seated on the living room couch a few paces from the door. Kathy removed her coat, draped it over the back of one of the kitchen chairs, and dropped her purse in front of it before walking into the living room. The decor of the room had not changed much since the first time she was here. It was a mix of the East and West. A handmade rug with the Chinese character for happiness covered the wooden floor. The white of the walls was broken up by lithographs of the French countryside. A Chinese silk painting adorned another part of the wall and books in Chinese, English, French, and Japanese were displayed on shelves. The couch and love seat were standard earth tone units, but in a corner of the room stood an unusual silk screen. The central focus of the room was the scrolls of Chinese calligraphy hanging on the wall. Kathy could not read them, having forgotten years before what she had learned in Chinese school as a child, but they added a certain elegance.

Gloria and Stacey stood up and hugged her. The four shared a special bond from the stalker experience a few years before. That bond was only deepened by the help with and advice about their men they had given each other. Kathy had been giving the whole time. Her friends were eager to lend a hand now. Even though there was no overt plea from the author, all knew the time had come for Kathy to vent and ask advice. Maybe they could help her deal with the frustration and contradictions of her heart.

"You look great!" Gloria said.

"No she doesn't," Stacey disagreed. "She looks worried."

"She's young, accomplished, and beautiful," Gloria pointed out. "What's to worry about?"

"Bob," Chingli said flatly.

Leave it to Chingli to lay it all out on the table. Less than a minute into their little conspiratorial gathering and the agenda was already established.

"How are things going with him?" Stacey asked.

Kathy sighed before she answered. "At times I feel things are not going at all," she replied. "Not that I'm looking for some kind of whirlwind romance, but he's so focused on studying for the captain's test, there's not much time left for anything else."

It felt good to finally verbalize her frustrations. Her friends were listening intently, letting her vent. "He's so much more than that. I try to get him to realize it, but it seems the only way for him to prove himself is by doing well on this test."

"Who is he trying to prove himself to?" Chingli asked.

Kathy paused for a moment. She had never really thought about that, just assumed he wanted to show the world. "Do you think he wants to show me?" she wondered out loud.

"That's possible," Gloria said. "From what little I can pry out of Jack, Bob isn't sure you really take him seriously. He knows your father made captain. Maybe he feels if he does the same, you'll think more of him."

Kathy let out a sarcastic chuckle. "Think more of him? Where would he ever get the idea that I don't think enough of him? All I do is encourage him to write and think about going to college. He knows I think he has a lot of talent. Where do men get ideas like that?"

"Slow it down Kath," Gloria chortled. "That was my thought, not his words, just something to consider."

Kathy laughed at herself. Verbalizing her feelings was showing her that she was more interested in this relationship than she wanted to admit. From Chingli's next question, it was apparent that she understood how vulnerable Kathy felt.

"You said so much about him that we didn't know," Chingli pointed out. "Tell us about him. After so many months you must have, as you once said, delved into his brain. What is Bob Brendler really like?"

"Yes, please," Stacey added enthusiastically. "We knew our guys for a long time. They were the three stooges when Gloria and I were growing up. Bob is an unknown entity. Introduce us so we better understand, then we can come up with a plan that will deliver him to your doorstep neatly wrapped and ready for grooming."

They all laughed at Stacey's way of putting it. With those remarks, Kathy was sure the four had crossed the legal threshold from casual conversation to conspiracy.

"Okay, I'll lay Mr. Brendler bare for you," Kathy began. "As I said I'm trying to talk him into going back to school although he insists he's not the college type of guy. His mind is sharp enough, but he doesn't tolerate fools or useless information well. So studying biology when he's a history major would drive him nuts."

Her three friends were focused on her every word. That attention warmed Kathy's heart. Something told her she would need their support and they were obviously willing to give it. But that is what friendship is for.

"He's still studying Chinese in New York," she said chuckling to herself. She had to somehow convince him that the time would be better spent with her. "He writes poetry, not just poetry, he writes profound poetry off the top of his head. It's amazing to see, but he is unimpressed with himself. The one thing that defines him is his job. He really does love fighting fires, which makes sense because he's an outdoor type of guy, a physical kind of guy. In the end, and I hate to admit this, but he reminds me of my dad."

Chingli, Gloria, and Stacey sat quietly for a moment. Then Gloria sighed and said, "He's inside your mind now, isn't he?"

Kathy felt tears well up in her eyes as she shook her head yes. She felt an amazing bond with these three women who were now working so hard for her. The thought crossed her mind that it was the shared experiences of the past few tumultuous years that had solidified that bond. That thought suddenly opened her mind. She had unwittingly just stumbled upon the answer to her relationship problem. This realization hit her like a freight train. It was so obvious now. After all the interviews she had conducted with firefighters she had learned that what held a company together, what made firemen feel like brothers was the shared experience of fighting fires. "Shared experiences," she muttered to herself without thought of her friends understanding.

"Shared experiences?" Gloria asked.

"Yes," Kathy answered energetically. "It's what holds fire companies together; makes the guys feel like brothers, shared experiences, shared hardships. It's what binds a lonely girl from Rhode Island to a couple of Jersey girls and a woman from Taiwan." She smiled at her friends. "I think if I can convince him to let me help him with his studies, we'll add that missing ingredient; that shared hardship, to take everything to the next level."

"So, then we have to come up with a way to convince him you can help him study," Stacey chirped. "I seem to remember something about you helping your father study, right?"

"Yes, but I've mentioned it to him several times and he doesn't pick up on it," Kathy said in frustration.

"You just don't present it right," Gloria said. "A man would hesitate because he's afraid you'll be a distraction." The she leaned forward and asked, "Can you act like a strict nun when you're around him?"

Kathy laughed, "Of course I can."

"Then become Sister Mary Elephant. You don't ask him," Stacey said. "You tell him. You lay down the law. He has no options. If he wants to do well, you'll show him how. If he refuses, he will weep with frustration after he fails."

They all moaned. A plan was beginning to take shape and Kathy felt a weight lift off of her.

"Who is Sister Mary Elephant?" Chingli asked.

Kathy, Gloria, and Stacey laughed. Then Gloria explained Cheech and Chong and Sister Mary Elephant.

****

Kathy turned onto Prospect Street in Nutley determined to become Bob's study partner. Her epiphany the previous night had solidified the plan. The knowledge that she now had an answer to her stalled relationship problem gave her renewed purpose. She parked the car across the street from the three story frame Bob called home, making sure she parked in a legal space. They were particular about that around here. It was funny how he wound up renting the top floor of the only building in this quiet suburb that resembled an inner city apartment building like those around Six Engine. It towered over the small ranches that dominated the neighborhood. The elderly couple who owned the building lived on the second floor. According to them, the building once stood alone surrounded by trees and fields until the building boom of the '50s. A throwback to another era when Newark was the economic engine of the region and people lived along bus routes and train lines leading into the city.

Marching up to the front door, she pressed the doorbell long and hard. The building predated the whole ring the bell, buzz in routine used in larger, more recent apartment buildings. Bob came down the stairs, saw her through the door window, and opened it with obvious reluctance. Kathy pushed right past him before he could voice a protest. The stairs leading to the upper stories were directly in front of her. Four quick steps carried her past the first floor apartment door. The stairway was dim, what light there was came in through a window on the right at the landing to the second floor. A smell unique to old, dry wooden framed buildings permeated the air. It was not the smell of dust and certainly not a mildew odor, more like the smell of carefully aged wood. Linoleum covered the trends of the creaky stairs she was making her way up. An Italian grandmother kept the stairs and halls impeccably clean. She knew that type of woman well, having grown up with one.

"Kath," he whined. "Please, I have to study."

"I know," she snapped back as she climbed the stairs. From the sounds behind her, she knew Bob was following. "What are you studying today? Have you put a system together or are you just randomly reading text books?"

"I've got a system," Bob protested defensively. That was good, she thought, a man trying to defend himself had doubts. Those doubts were her ticket to what she wanted.

"I haven't even made my bed," Bob continued to protest. "You should at least give a guy some warning before you invade his privacy."

"I'm not interested in your privacy," Kathy laughed coolly. "Only your study methods." Bob's apartment was at the top of the stairs. He had left the door open a crack. As she stepped on to the third floor landing, she noticed a vertical metal ladder ascended the wall in front of a blocked door to her left. From Bob's descriptions, she knew the door would have opened into his bedroom, but had been nailed shut long ago. The ladder vanished into the ceiling and led to a scuttle that opened onto the roof. According to him this was the standard arrangement in most of the buildings in which he fought fires. He felt right at home which seemed a little odd to her. She could understand feeling familiar, but at home? Fire buildings did not strike her as homey. Some parts of a firefighter's mentality remained incomprehensible to her.

She reached the door to his apartment and stepped into the kitchen. This was her first time in his place. That was a sad statement after close to six months of dating. The room was in the rear of the building. Two large windows let in an abundance of sunlight. There were simple white curtains on these, but no blinds. She could see Bob's car parked beneath two trees in the backyard. There was a small lawn on either side of his parking space. Hedges demarcating the property line were a few feet in front of his car. The kitchen itself had an old style white gas range on one wall; cabinets built into the wall were next to the range. The sink with its cabinet lined another wall. A small square table surrounded by chairs with foam cushioning covered in green plastic sat in the center of the room and a refrigerator occupied an enclave next to the windows. The room amazingly had three doors and an open doorway which led to the front of the apartment. She was not interested in what was behind the doors or through the doorway. Her focus was on the table and the surrounding chairs. It took her a moment to take all this in and decide on her plan of attack. Sister Mary Elephant it would be. He could throw all the knives he wanted, she was determined not to be distracted.

Turning to face him, she snapped, "Let's see what you're studying today. Show me your work."

Bob walked over to the table and presented a book to her. She took one look and bristled. "No, no. no!" she exclaimed. "You don't highlight anything. Highlighting is just a way of putting off studying. Do you have a notebook around here? A legal pad? Index cards?"

Bob looked shocked at first and then began to chuckle. "So, you've decided to help me study?"

"I decided to help you study ages ago," she snapped back. "You just couldn't pick up on my hints and suggestions, so I'm going to impose myself upon you. I've done this before, remember? Now, notebook or at least something to write on?"

He produced a legal pad, but from the look on his face he was not sure why.

"See all the highlighted passages," she instructed. "Write the information out. It would be even better if you read them out loud as you wrote. The more senses you use, the more you'll remember. Do you have a tape recorder?"

"In the other room," he replied. "Should I go get it?"

"Not right now," she answered sternly. "Too much to do now. You have to write out. Later we'll put what you write on index cards so you can study on the run. When you're in the car, you play back the tapes you'll record."

His stern, worried expression had been replaced with a grin. "So, what inspired you to make my studying for promotion you're next project?"

"Well, for purely selfish reasons. That's the only way I'm going to see you, isn't it?" she said flatly. "A couple of warnings, first I give tough quizzes and second I don't study and kiss, so don't get any ideas. Think of me as a nun."

"Kathy Stanley, you're such a romantic."

"No time for romance right now, we have to get you rolling. As I understand it, they've changed the format of the test. You have to write essays, time to start writing." With that she handed him the legal pad and picked up the text book he was studying. "Chapter one," she began. When he hesitated, she pointed at the pad. He picked up a pen and began to write.

Chapter Ten

"Bob, I think you're getting a little carried away," Jack laughed. "The Chief of the Department is not going to get down on his hands and knees to inspect under the oven."

Bob laughed at himself. It was his first inspection and he did not want to let Chief Simmons or Captain Schmidt down. "Been on the job three years, Jack," he explained. "Never been through an annual inspection. Just don't want the Chief or Captain Pete to be embarrassed."

"How about we go upstairs and change into our dress uniforms now," Jack suggested. "We're not going to get a lot of warning from Hank. They'll inspect Seven Engine before us. Even in heavy traffic, it won't take more than ten minutes for them to get here."

Bob stood up and looked down at his knees. No need to brush them off, there was not a speck of dust on them. He glanced around the kitchen one last time. The floor was thoroughly scrubbed and waxed thanks to one of the guys on the fourth tour who had a business on the side that did just that. Everything in the house was cleaned, waxed, polished, and stored neatly. Just because they were busy did not mean they got a pass on the Fire Chief's annual inspection. All four tours had made the place shine. Of course, it helped that the house had been remodeled a decade before. Some of the houses in the city had not seen even a paint brush in 25 years. The guys in those houses could be forgiven if their quarters were dulled by wear. They only had to clean them. There was little money in the city for Fire

Department capital improvements and what little there was went towards new rigs and modernizing equipment. He walked out of the kitchen onto the apparatus floor, continuing to look for any detail that might have been missed then climbed the stairs to change his uniform.

It was a warm spring day with a gentle breeze. The members of Six Engine were standing on the firehouse apron watching traffic go by as they waited for the Chief of the Department to arrive. The Captain, Ray, and Hector were standing as a group in the sun, talking. Bob went to the edge of the apron to look up Springfield Avenue for the Chief's car. Jack was the last one down. He walked over to Bob, stood in front of him, and asked, "Is this tie on right?"

Bob adjusted the tie a little. "You said I was too worried," he teased. "Then you spend an inordinate amount of time going over the bunkroom."

"Don't want the skipper or Chief to loss face," Jack replied.

"That sounds familiar," Bob said. "Like something I said a few minutes ago."

"Yeah, well we're all in the same boat aren't we?" Jack retorted. "How's studying with Kathy going?"

Bob thought for a moment. Studying with Kathy? He did not study with her. When they studied she transformed herself into a strict, no nonsense nun, cold, heartless, to the point, and always focused on the test. The quizzes she gave and the essays he had to write were brutal. "I don't study with Kathy," Bob laughed. "She calls herself Sister Mary Elephant and nothing I do will draw even an ounce of pity from that cruel heart. With everything she puts me through, if I don't ace this test I should go find another job."

Jack was smiling at the obvious discomfort his friend felt. Bob knew he was being melodramatic and was certain Jack knew it as well. The girl drew the best out of him. His study skills had improved profoundly and with them his chances of promotion. The only wild card was the State Department of Personnel's revamping the test. Multiple choice questions were out; essays on fighting fires were in. Those who passed the essay portion moved on to a verbal dealing with a disciplinary problem and then a group problem solving session. No one had done this type of test before, so no one knew exactly how to study. Maybe that was why Jack was not even bothering. Before Bob could bring up the question, Jack threw another at him.

"How do your legs and arms feel today?" he asked.

The strange sensation that had first appeared after the fire on Sixteenth and Littleton had come and gone over the past months. Today was not a good day. He had spoken with Jack about it before briefly, telling him it was probably caused by stress.

"Today's not a good day," Bob began. "One arm feels like it's on fire, the other feels like it's ice and the legs are still strange. Between work and studying six to eight hours a day the stress is brutal. Sister Mary Elephant doesn't let up. At least she doesn't walk in dressed like a tease. I'd probably go crazy if she did that."

"You're a stronger man than I am," Jack chuckled. "To have a woman like that next to me while I was trying to study would be a study in futility not fire science."

Bob laughed at his friend's take on the situation. He glanced up Springfield Avenue to see if the Chief's gig had reached Bergen Street then turned to Jack again. "It's funny, but studying with her," Bob confessed. "It's changed how we related to each other or at least how I related to her. She's more than a girlfriend now. She's also a friend. I really like being around her. She changed the way I learn and has really shown me I can do this." He had never said this to anyone else, but knew Jack would treat the information discretely. Bells began to sound in the firehouse before Jack could respond. The conversations on the apron fell silent as everyone listened. A group of ten bells told them it was a full assignment. This was followed by a group of five bells. The box was for the East Ward. Six would not respond until at least the second alarm. Hector started to walk into the firehouse to record the alarm in the company journal. Conversations quickly picked up where they had left off.

"It sounds like she's getting to you," Jack said only half in jest.

"Oh, she is," Bob sighed "I still think I'm too provincial for her, but we've been through that already. Just going to enjoy the ride, might get a promotion out of it too. I'll owe her that even if she gets bored with me and leaves."

"I know Frank told you this," Jack chuckled. "And I certainly have, probably Ray did too. She likes firefighters, especially tall, young firefighters. If you're interested, I'm sure she is."

"Those not at risk are always confident," Bob muttered. The radio in the background came alive, but he could not make out what was said. Glancing east down Springfield Avenue, Bob saw a pillar of smoke rising off to the right. "Looks like they've got a job." Everyone looked east.

"That was a fifty-eight box," Captain Schmidt said. "It has to be a school in that area. Why don't you guys take your jackets and ties off and put them in the kitchen."

Hector came out as they started in. "We're last due on the second, Cap," he said. "They've got a roof fire in Oliver Street School. It doesn't sound good."

"Okay, Hector," the Captain responded. "Take your jacket and tie off and do me a favor and take these in to the kitchen with you." With that he removed his jacket and tie and handed them to the junior firefighter.

Bob glanced up the avenue as he walked in. He could see the front of the Chief's car at the light on Bergen Street. Before he could point this out to the Captain, the radio came alive again.

"Deputy Two to quarters, emergency."

"Deputy Two."

"Second alarm."

Bob trotted to the kitchen, threw his jacket and tie on a bench, and shot back out to the rig. The Chief of Department gig rolled past quarters with lights and siren on. Hector was already behind the wheel of the rig starting the engine. Bob kicked his shoes off, slid into his boots, and moved to the overhead door buttons at the front of the house. The captain's door slammed and Hector rolled the rig out. Bob hit the button to start the door down and jogged to the bucket seat behind Hector. As soon as he was on board, the Captain hit the siren and Hector pulled out into Springfield Avenue. Ray was sitting in the jump seat across from Bob with his turnout coat on. Jack was standing in front of him. Rolling down the hill, they could see the column of smoke had grown and darkened. Bob threw his coat on and sat in the seat. He felt no need to look at the fire from this far away. He would size it up when he could see the area and the building. The thought crossed his mind that they were going to be fighting a fire in their dress uniforms. The dry cleaner was not going to appreciate the odor.

When Six arrived on the scene, Ray took a hydrant up the block from the school and Hector stretched in. Bob could see this was going to be a different kind of operation than they were accustomed to. It was not your typical three story frame. Teachers had children corralled up the street. Parents were rushing toward them. Police squad cars had the area around the school blocked off. There were multiple hose lines going into the main entrance of the building and a few aerials ladders were raised to the roof. Thick smoke was pushing out of the cockloft. There was no sign of truck men on the roof, but three columns of smoke rising directly from the top of the building showed it had been vented. A roofing company truck was parked beside the school. Bob wondered if this company used union workers. So many firefighters had part time jobs in the roofers local. He doubted any of those guys were working this job. By the looks of it, the fire started on the roof where they were working. On duty or not, firefighters were firefighters and knew how to avoid setting a roof ablaze. Hector pulled the rig up to the edge of the fire scene and parked it. As Bob climbed off he scanned the crowd very quickly remembering that Kathy said she would be in the Ironbound doing an interview today. He thought he caught a glimpse of her, but did not have the time to confirm it. This school was an ordinary constructed building with brick walls and wooden floors, from its age the ceilings would almost certainly be metal. The only way to get at this fire was to pull the ceilings down and hit the fire from below. The roof was vented so now the real work of pulling metal ceilings and dousing the fire would begin. The thought crossed Bob's mind that they needed more truck companies.

The Captain turned to Bob and Jack. "Stretch a two and a half to the door on the west side of the building and wye it off."

They pulled their boots up, put their gloves on, and walked to the back of the rig. Jack climbed onto the back step and pulled the two and a half down. Bob grabbed the hose, draped it over his shoulder, and began dragging it to the side door of the school as Captain Schmidt had ordered. He dropped the hose in front of the door and hustled back to help Jack break it down and connect it to an outlet on the rig. Ray was helping Hector with the supply line from the hydrant. Captain Schmidt was busy retrieving a two and a half to inch and a half wye from the rear side compartment. He had a couple of hooks leaning against the rig next to him. When Bob noticed that he knew they would be doing truck work when they got inside. That solved the problem of not enough truck men. By the time Hector had water from the hydrant, everyone had masks on and there were two inch and three quarter lines attached to the wye waiting to move into the building.

"We'll move one line in at a time," the Captain told them. "Get as much as you can onto the floor below the fire before the lines are wet. We're going to be pulling ceilings and then hitting the fire. Are you ready for a workout guys? "

He asked the question with a smile, allowing the old truck man to show through for a moment. If the ceiling turned out to be metal, they were going to get a real workout. Bob had not pulled a metal ceiling since the academy, but the memory of how difficult it was had not faded. They started stretching one of the lines up the stairwell. It took a few minutes to get situated on the top floor. Lines from the companies that had stretched in through the main entrance were working their way down the hallway one room at a time. Six had the only lines coming in from the west side of the building. Bob and Jack went into a classroom to the right. The Captain and Ray went to a room across the hall. Bob had the hook and Jack had the line. They would switch between the two to try and evenly distribute the anticipated exhaustion. The smoke was more a haze since the fire was above them and the roof had been vented, but they still needed the masks. Bob scanned the room. Desks were lined in neat rows and still had math books opened on top of them. The chalk board had an incomplete problem written on it, the lesson interrupted by the fire alarm. A modern hanging ceiling hid the original ceiling. Bob quickly pulled this down to reveal what he knew would be there, an ornate metal ceiling. He scanned the edge molding to find a seam. Once he picked one out, he drove the point of the hook into it, crushing the molding and creating an opening. Wedging the hook into the opening, he pulled the tin down. This exposed the edge of the ceiling panel. He slid the hook under the edge of the panel and pulled down vigorously. The panel peeled away from the lathe and plaster above it. The firefighter then drove the hook through the lathe and pulled, creating a hole which revealed an inferno in the cockloft above them. Jack hit the fire to darken it down before Bob enlarged the hole. After the initial knockdown, they continued to pull the tin, lathe, and plaster down until the debris from the entire ceiling covered the children's desks and books. They did this for three more classrooms before meeting crews coming from the other direction. By the time the last room was darkened down their arms were hanging and their dress uniforms were drenched with sweat.

After the Chief ordered them out of the building to rest, Bob and Jack met up with the Captain and Ray at the Bell and Siren canteen truck. It was at jobs like this that the coffee and cookies this volunteer organization provided firefighters was really appreciated. As they stood sipping their steaming cups of Joe, Kathy walked up.

"And why are you now chasing fire engines Miss Stanley?" Captain Schmidt teased.

"I chase firemen, Cap, not fire engines," she replied. Her response produced hoots and hollers from the guys around the canteen truck. Bob felt his face redden a little, but doubted anyone would notice since his face was covered with soot.

"You boys all have dirty minds," Kathy admonished. "I was conducting an interview with one of the guys at Eight Engine when this alarm came in." Her response caused more laughter. Then she turned to Bob. His turnout coat was open so she could see his dress uniform beneath it.

"Oh, your uniform!" she exclaimed.

"Yeah, the Chief was about to pull in for the inspection when they banged the second," Bob laughed "So, I'm going to need a good dry cleaner."

"Don't worry," she reassured him with a smile. "I know a good place. You can tell them I sent you."

"Is this place in Jersey, Kathy?" Ray asked. "Or up in Rhode Island?"

"A girl always has to know a good dry cleaner, Ray," she shot back. "Stacey must have taught you that. It's right on South Orange Avenue, in the village."

"Finish up boys," Captain Schmidt said. "Got to get back in. Kathy can give Bob the info and we'll see if we can get a fireman's discount." With that he finished his coffee and started back into the building. His crew threw down the last of their drinks and followed. Before Bob was out of ear shot Kathy shouted, "We're still on for tonight?" Bob shook his head yes and waved good bye. Kathy sighed and turned away.   From here

I can still smell the smoke, Kathy thought as she opened her apartment door. Bob would be here in a couple of hours. She had to shower, come up with something special to wear, and wanted to call her mother to discuss her dilemma. The strategy session at Chingli's had not advanced far enough to guide her tonight. Not if the plan brewing in her mind came to fruition. She glanced around her living room to make sure nothing was out of place. Bob had his annual inspection today; she might have to pass muster tonight.

Her living room walls were decorated with pictures of family and home. She had picked up one lithograph after being inspired by Frank and Chingli. Frank called lithographs the poor man's fine art. It did add a nice touch, depicting the Rhode Island shore after the summer season. The empty beach and lonely waves crashing ashore gave her a melancholy feeling at times, but most often the scene gave her comfort. She chuckled to herself when she realized that Bob would think its subject was the Jersey shore. She had to get him up to Rhode Island someday.

Kathy carried the bag containing her recording equipment, writing material, and assorted other necessities for interviewing firefighters to her back office. She hurriedly took out the tapes she had produced today, labeled and filed them, and stored her equipment. This room would probably be the children's bedroom if a family lived here, but that was not the stage her life was in at the moment. Her mother was accepting of this although a little disappointed. Dad was just accepting and proud of her. Instead of a bedroom, the room served as an ideal repository for the oral history project. She kept one desk for writing and cataloging her work. On another sat a transcribing machine and a typewriter. She was thinking of getting some sort of word processing machine or personal computer, but the cost was a little high right now. Maybe in a year or two the price would drop. From what she had heard about them, a word processor would make her task infinitely easier. She finished her oral history tasks and scooted back out to the living room.

After hanging her coat in the closet, Kathy began to go over the room to make sure it was in presentable condition. She puffed up the pillows on her coach, a comfortable, single purpose seat. She found dual purpose hide a bed type sofas hideous. What was the point of having an uncomfortable bed hidden inside an uncomfortable couch? Assessing herself while she stirred the potpourri in a glass bowl to freshen the air, she decided her status at the moment was vulnerable. Likely to make emotional mistakes was more accurate. She had started birth control again knowing from past experience that things can develop very quickly with little control. Recalling Bob's response to her comment about chasing firemen gave her encouragement. Men did not blush unless something was true. All these thoughts and emotions were leading down a path that she had wanted to go down for months, yet fear had held her back. Bob had not pushed her. He had always been very polite, very gentlemanly, and very cautious. Call mama, she thought. Someone had to help her through this jumble of contradictory emotions. Resolution hardened in her heart, so she went to the kitchen and picked up the phone.

"Mama," Kathy said quietly. "Got a minute to talk?"

"Of course I have a minute," her mother replied. "I have hours and hours for you. You don't sound good."

It was always unsettling to Kathy that her mother could pick out the tiniest nuance in her tone and know how she felt. "I have something on my mind," Kathy began. "That I'd like to run past you."

"It's about that boy you told me about," her mother stated.

"Yes," Kathy replied. "I'm confused. I don't understand my reactions to some things. I guess I just need to talk to you."

"That is good," Mama said. "That is what mothers are for. What are these things you want to talk about?"

Kathy began to explain her conflicts and her fears as she paced in the kitchen, three steps this way, three steps that way. Going to the limit of the phone wire as she nervously twirled it in her fingers. In the back of her mind she knew she was confessing and hoping for absolution.

"He sounds like a wonderful young man," her mother sighed. "I had always hoped you would find a doctor or a college professor, but you love a fireman. It is difficult when you give your heart to someone like that. Not like having a father who fights fires. Now you must choose to put your heart in danger. That is how I felt all these years. You will begin to understand now."

"I have already begun to understand, Mama," Kathy said. "I now see how much you love dad. It's something I just took for granted all my life."

"A-yo, stop," her mother exclaimed. "We Chinese don't have to say such things. It is the way of the world. You must follow your heart. At least you have removed one worry from me."

"Removed a worry?" Kathy asked, puzzled.

"Yes. How your father would react to a college professor. I know how he will react to a fireman," her mother laughed.

As Kathy hung up the phone, she sprang into action. How to set the trap so she would be in control? First, draw the blinds then rearrange the pillows. Next shower and change into something suitable for greeting her prey. She dashed into the bedroom, her heart pounding with new found determination and anticipation. After her shower, she would pick out clothes for the beginning of the night and something sultry for when she sprang her trap. She knew she had his mind. Tonight she would claim his body. Then she would have his soul. She had always hoped to find a soulmate and was now sure one would walk through door in about an hour. All would be risked on this chance.

Kathy stood looking at the red kimono laid out on the bed. Deciding it was perfect she went to the kitchen and looked in the refrigerator. Was it to be Chinese or Italian? Chinese would be best. The ingredients were already cut up, and stir frying would take no time at all. Next back to the living room to adjust the pillows again, this time so there was more room on the couch. Then a last minute glance into the bedroom to make sure nothing embarrassing was visible. The doorbell rang just as she completed her inspection.

One last look in the mirror and then a stroll to the door, she did not want to appear out of breathe. When she opened the door Bob was standing there in a leather coat and jeans with his arms hanging in front of him and his hands together. He was rocking back and forth on his heels and glancing at the flow of traffic on South Orange Avenue, appearing as relaxed as he could be. Totally oblivious to what awaited him.

"I've decided it's time we skipped restaurant food," she began innocently. "And I prepared you something special."

The expression on Bob's face changed from one of relaxed and accepting to curious and adventurous. "You really want to go through that trouble?" he asked.

"Yes, it'll be fun," Kathy replied.

"Cooking will be fun?" he asked as he stepped in. She noticed his quick glance around the living room. It was good she had set it up to make the impression she wanted.

"It depends on what you cook. Let me take your coat," Kathy insisted. She did not want it taking up space that might be needed for the evening activities. Lying on a leather coat was not romantic. "I have to change. I can't cook in these clothes," she said setting the trap. "Sit down. Make yourself comfy. I'll only be a minute."

She walked to the bedroom hoping he did not pick up on her anticipation. Quickly shedding her clothes like a serpent that had out grown its skin, she slipped into the kimono and glanced in the mirror to see the effect. The silk hung on her breasts just right, giving a subtle, seductive hint of what was hidden just beneath. Her heart was pounding; her hands were moist; and her smile was both wide and genuine. It was time to spring the trap and claim her prize. Men were so easy.

When she strolled back into the living room Bob rose from his seat slowly. His eyes were consuming her while his mouth hung open in surprise. The reaction told her she was in control of the night.

"Do you always cook in a kimono?" he asked with a sly smile.

She walked up to him and whispered "It depends on what I plan to cook."

"What do you plan to cook tonight?" he asked quietly. His breathing had picked up noticeably.

"Tonight the first thing I plan to cook is fireman." She stretched up and kissed him gently. He returned the kiss with a little more energy, telling Kathy his body now belonged to her.

"Fireman is it?" he asked with a smile.

"Yes, can you give me a size up of the situation Mr. Brendler?" she asked as she slowly unbuttoned his shirt.

"I'd say I have a working fire in a five foot eight beauty," he replied while loosening the knot of her kimono belt.

"And can you put out that fire?" she asked while unbuckling his belt eagerly as he kicked off his shoes.

"Miss Stanley, the only fire I can't put out is the one inside me." He slipped the kimono off her shoulders and let it fall to the floor.

She unbuttoned his pants, pulled the zipper down, and gave them a sharp yank. They dropped to the floor and Bob quickly kicked them to the side. The last barrier to her desire was removed while she kissed his body from the chest down to the legs. As she stood up she felt his arms lift her gently and place her on the couch. All had gone according to her plan. Now he was hers, even if he did not know it yet. Between kisses she whispered, "I hope you did your studying for the day. Tonight is for us alone." Then she let everything go and gave herself to the love of the moment.

* * * * * * * * * * * * * * * * * *

Kathy hustled to her office for paper. She was still floating from the previous night, wrapped in her kimono, slippers slapping the floor of the hall, and face aglow but eyes tired, joyously tired. Instead of rummaging around the room, the author swooped down on her interview kit and retrieved a legal pad. Bob would be very familiar with this type of paper since he wrote his study notes on one every day. Swiping a pen from the desk, she scooted back to the living room where her beau waited. He had been on the way out when a "thought" had crossed his mind and he asked for pen and paper. Kathy had no idea what it was about, but he was due in the firehouse after his unscheduled sleep over so there was no time to waste.

The unscheduled sleep over had been one of the most memorable nights of her life. They had slept at times, but their sleep was broken by bouts of passion and hunger for each other. She was not the most experienced lover, but she had never imagined two people could meld the way they had over the course of the night. He seemed to have an unquenchable desire for her and her for him. Neither had meant for their little tete-a-tete to last the entire night. The built up tensions that had been put off or denied for all these months had demanded release. There was no thought involved beyond her scheming. There had been little they could control. Passion had demanded restitution for their denial and restitution had been given. Now he had to work. When she reached him he was waiting by the door with his coat on.

"Here you go," she said giving him the pad with one hand and the pen with the other. This opened the front of her kimono enough for him to see beneath it.

"Beautiful," he sighed.

"Bob, stop," she chided him. "You have to go to work."

"I've been working all night," he responded with a mischievous smile.

"I know, naughty boy," she parried. "But the Chief still needs firefighters on rigs, so write your thought and get to work."

He sighed and began to write. Watching Bob write fascinated Kathy. He wrote with the same energy and passion he exhibited throughout the night before. It seemed the entire world was tuned out. The pen moved in spurts as if he considered many options and then had to quickly record the thought he had settled on. She knew he was in a creative flow, so her silence was needed. Make a sound to interrupt him and she would interfere with his mind's flow. Kathy had experienced this sensation when she wrote, although she doubted it had reached the obvious intensity Bob was experiencing. This lasted for a few minutes before he seemed to have spent his creative energy. Then he looked up.

"That's a thought?" Kathy teased.

"Sorry, thoughts are not controllable," Bob said with embarrassment. "They just flow until exhausted." He read over his "thoughts" one more time and seemed satisfied. "My lady, consider this my thank you note for what we shared last night. It was a unique night filled with warmth and love."

Did his speech always become poetic when he wrote poetry, Kathy mused. She accepted the legal pad and read his thoughts:

A Part of Me

Take a part of me
The part that has been empty for so long
Keep it forever and fill it with what you choose
I no longer have need of its questions or pain

Give me a part of you
So I may be made whole and be changed
I want only the empty part
The one you have been trying to give me all along

Forgive me my resistance and fear of change
I did not know I had to lose myself before I could be found
The two of us could help each other in life's search
And perhaps find happiness and ourselves along the way

So take this part of me
I no longer have need of it
Foolishly, I thought it important
But have now found it only keeps me from finding myself

Kathy struggled to hold her composure as she read the verses. By the time she finished the poem, tears were flowing quietly down her cheeks. "I love you Bob Brendler."

"I love you Miss Stanley," he responded with a whisper. "Bu yao shang wo de xin."

Kathy chuckled through her tears at his attempt, not perfect, but understandable. "Your tones are horrible," she said smiling up at him. "But I won't break your heart, I promise."

He leaned over and gave her a peck on the forehead, turned, opened the door, and left. Her heart was ready to burst into song.

Chapter Twelve

Bob dashed out of Kathy's, bolted down the shrub lined walkway, hopped down the brick steps leading up from the street, and jogged to his car. His head was literally spinning, as if he had just been on a high speed ride in an amusement park. A large cup of black coffee was needed to jump start his day, although some food would probably help the spinning more. No time for food, but plenty of coffee at the firehouse. There had not been much sleep to be had the previous night. His trot slowed as he approached his car. Stepping into the street, he walked to the driver's door, but pulled up short when he noticed something on the windshield. Reaching over he pulled a parking ticket from under the wiper blade. It was only then that the firefighter noticed a street sign prohibiting overnight parking. Not that he could have done anything with the knowledge. The way the night unfolded did not allow for time to move his car. A Newark firefighter decal on the rear window did not deter the cop who issued the summons. Millburn cops might give the crazies a break, but South Orange cops apparently did not. Stuffing the ticket above his sun visor and slamming the door, Bob chalked it up to the price of love, started the car, and headed for Springfield and Hunterdon.

As he navigated his way to Six Engine, Bob made an attempt to understand what had happened the night before. He was seduced, but more than that had occurred. They had crossed into new territory. The incipient physical relationship was already rich, but also fraught with questions. The most pressing one as far as he was concerned involved his own experience. How could they have made love five times and yet he have had only one climax? That was supposed to be a female problem. Stress caused impotency in men, but "super potency?" Bob had never heard of it. Granted if you had to have one or the other, this was the way to go. Better to have your lady scream in ecstasy than cry in frustration. Figuring it was a combination of the stress from studying and exhaustion from pulling metal ceilings, he put that part of his assessment aside.

Weaving through early rush hour traffic, Bob thought of his relationship with Kathy and the new level it had reached. She was ready for something more than a tutoring position, but how far was she willing to take him? There was nothing he had ever looked for in a woman that she did not have. But did he have all the attributes such an exotic creature needed for fulfillment? Frank and Jack both assured him the author found young firefighters attractive and she was plainly infatuated. What happened when the attraction and subsequent infatuation wore off? Did he have other traits that would take their place and solidify her affection or was he headed for a fall? He had to find time to talk with Jack. Just verbalizing his thoughts would make things clearer. Pulling into the side lot of Six Engine, he hopped out of the car and stumbled through the rear door. His crew was sitting around the kitchen table.

"Last man in again," Hector admonished him. "God, you look beat. Out partying again last night or were you being good and studying so you can lord it over us?"

"Never made it home last night," Bob confessed. "Didn't get a lot of sleep either; need some coffee for a jump start."

"Fresh pot coming down now," Ray said. "Out on the town all night?"

"No, he went out to dinner with Kathy," Jack informed them.

"Not exactly," Bob muttered as he poured a mug of steaming black caffeine laced coffee. Just the scent gave him energy. "She cooked me dinner."

"Did you say she cooked you?" Hector laughed.

"No, I said she cooked dinner for me," Bob replied.

"Let me get this straight," the Captain interjected. "You didn't make it back to your place last night and Kathy cooked dinner for you."

"Yeah, a nice Chinese dish," Bob answered, knowing he was going to be a target for the rest of the day, but too tired to be evasive.

"The noose is slowly tightening," Ray chided. "And he doesn't even know it."

"Maybe I'm a willing victim," Bob parried, deciding complete capitulation was his best defense.

"Don't tell Hank," Jack warned. "It'll break his heart knowing his little Kathy seduced you."

"Who said anything about seduction?" Bob shot back.

They all laughed at Bob's attempt not to kiss and tell. A burst of the Chief's siren interrupted the conversation. Hector stepped out to open the overhead door.

"They had a forty-five box a few minutes ago," Jack said, responding to Bob's puzzled look. "Twenty-nine had a brush fire."

With that Bob finished his brew of wakefulness and went to get his gear. It was going to be a long day for him. Maybe he could get a little rest in the afternoon. Getting through the morning was going to be tough.

Jack and Bob drew the second floor for the daily housework. After sweeping and mopping the bunkroom, both were working in the back. Jack mopped the locker room while Bob scrubbed the bathroom that was off of it. The two had been working quietly, but curiosity got the better of Jack. He walked over to the bathroom door and leaned against the doorframe, the handle of the mop resting against his chest. The smell of disinfectant permeated the air, but went unnoticed by both men. Some things you just have to get used to.

"So, how did last night go?" Jack asked.

"Last night?" Bob sighed. "It was interesting."

"Interesting?" Jack chuckled.

"Yes, interesting, and completely spontaneous," Bob said.

"Spontaneous sounds better than interesting," Jack pointed out.

"We planned to go out for dinner," Bob said opening up a little. "But when I got to her place she said she's going to cook dinner. Goes to get changed, supposedly into cooking clothes and comes out with a red silk kimono on and things developed from there."

Jack was chuckling at Bob's account. It seemed he was not particularly surprised. Bob debated speaking with his friend about his stress concerns. He decided he needed another opinion.

"It was a special night," he began. "But not everything went as expected, at least not for me."

Jack's expression turned serious. "She didn't give you the old 'It was a special gift, but don't take it too far.' Did she?"

"No, no, no," Bob laughed. "She set me up, seduced me, and then cried with joy when I wrote her a poem."

"You wrote her a poem," Jack said shaking his head in disbelief. "You are a diehard romantic. Who would have thought? So, what went wrong?"

Bob was still hesitant and a little embarrassed. Remembering what he told himself about ecstasy versus frustration gave him the gumption to push on. "Well, I think the stress is really taking over my life," he began. "All that built up pressure must have gotten to me because I, ah, I - - - well you see, we were intimate five times over the course of the night."

Jack had a look of amazement on his face which quickly changed into a sly smile. "You afraid she'll expect that every night and you won't be able to deliver?"

"No," Bob sighed. "The problem was I didn't pop off until the last time."

"Pop off?" Jack asked, puzzled. "You mean you didn't climax until the fifth time? Where did you learn that skill? You must have driven her crazy."

"That's not it, Jack," Bob said in frustration. "I didn't do it on purpose, believe me. It's not that I controlled myself. I just couldn't, not until I got some sleep. Then things were closer to normal." Jack appeared at a loss for words so Bob continued. "She's everything I could ask for and she was a real temptress last night. Everything reacted the way you would expect except for the finale. My back got tired, that's what stopped me."

"And you think it's the stress?" Jack asked.

"What else?" Bob replied.

"How long until this test?" Jack sounded worried. "If you keep this up, it's going to kill you."

The two firefighters finished up and made their way down to the apparatus floor, where Captain Pete met them.

"I want to take a look at a building on Tenth Street the third tour said was abandoned last week," Captain Pete told them. "We can pick up lunch at Red Star if you want. Ray, Hector, and Hank were talking about sandwiches."

Bob dozed on the rig as it made its way up to Tenth Street. The hiss of the parking brake alerted him to their arrival at the building. He realized this was an opportunity to conduct a size up of a building while he was exhausted, something he would certainly have to do if he were promoted. Jumping down from the bucket seat that had served as a cot for ten minutes, Bob gave the building a quick once over. Three story frame, asphalt shingle siding, one pillar missing from the small roof over the front door placing a torsion load on that part of the building. There were no glass panes in any of the windows that he could see, so horizontal ventilation was pretty much complete. One hydrant was on the corner about two hundred feet behind him. Another was mid-block about two hundred feet ahead. Debris were scattered along the four foot wide alley way between the building and its immediate neighbor to the south. A vacant lot stretched out from the north side.

This building had been occupied last week. Looking in the front door, he could see a bathtub had crashed through the stairs leading to the second floor. A closer inspection revealed the stairs from the second to the third floor were nonexistent. The wind was calm; the temperature was in the sixties; and the sun was shining brightly. Experience told him that scavengers had already pulled the wires and piping out, leaving gaping holes in the walls and floors. Apparently they had wanted to take the tub for scrap metal, but the stairs could not take the weight.

"Bob," Captain Pete called. "Come here." Bob walked over to the Captain wondering what was up.

"You've been hitting the books," the Captain began. "Tell me how you would size up the situation you see here."

Bob smiled to himself remembering his answer to a similar question the night before. "Three story frame, asphalt siding, torsion load on the roof above the front door, horizontal ventilation complete, access limited until a truck company arrives because the stairs have collapsed. We have hydrants on the corner and in the middle of the block. One exposure on the south side of the building, none on the north."

"Okay, okay," the Captain interrupted. "That's a pretty complete textbook size-up, but I'm looking for something a little more practical.

You have fire showing form the top floor, how would you fight the fire?"

"I'd stretch in from the corner past the building," Bob said thoughtfully. "Then stretch four lengths to the rear."

"Why to the rear?"

"The stairs have collapsed in the front."

"Before you commit to stretching that far, let's confirm the rear stairs are intact," the Captain said as he began walking toward the back. Jack and Ray joined in, stepping over the castoffs of urban life that were scattered about. They climbed the rear stairs and went through each floor, looking for holes in the floor and anything out of the ordinary. It was better to see obstacles in the clear daylight than fall over them in the dark, smoky atmosphere of a working fire. It was lucky they did; most of the rooms had broken furniture and garbage strewn about. The furniture let off a mildew smell that they knew would get much worse before the building was knocked down. This odor was mixed with the scent of plaster, wet wood, and rotting garbage. If this building was still standing in July, the rancid odors would have become unbearable.

"Jack, why don't you go down and watch the rig for a minute?" the Captain asked. "Hector should come in and have a look. These places tend to spontaneously ignite in this neighborhood." They laughed at the Captain's observation.

After noting all the holes and preplanning a fire in the building, they stopped at the Red Star Meat Market to pick up cold cuts and bread then returned to quarters. Bob was famished. Black coffee had zero calories, not much for a man to run on. Deciding the lack of food had been the cause of his vertigo; Bob was looking forward to lunch to get his balance back. A couple of sandwiches should put him right.

As he and Ray prepared lunch, Jack's voice drifted in from the apparatus floor. They placed a platter of sandwiches on the corner of the table and listened to Jack's conversation.

"Janet Banks," he shouted with laughter. "Haven't seen you in a few years. What brings you here?"

"That's Mrs. Banks to you, fireman," a craggy voice responded. "I come to see my old friends."

"You're going to be disappointed, Mrs. Banks," Jack informed her. "Everyone retired or left the job. I'm the only one left."

"That's okay, I always thought you was the cutest one," the voice replied with a loud laugh.

"Where have you been?" Jack continued.

"Oh, I went to see my people in South Carolina," she told him. "I'm hungry. What's for lunch?" With that the door from the apparatus floor was pushed open and an African woman in her sixties walked in. Jack came in behind her.

"Janet, you're not supposed to be back here," Jack scolded lightly.

"I told you young man, I'm Mrs. Banks to you," she said ignoring his point.

"Okay, Mrs. Banks," he laughed. "Say, where is Mr. Banks? You never brought him around."

Bob and Ray were smiling at the character who had come in with Jack. She had obviously been around the block a few times, but it did not seem to bother her. Too busy talking to Jack to pay attention to her surroundings, Mrs. Banks had not noticed them yet. She was dressed in a coat that was too heavy for the day's temperature. Her clothes were worn, but clean. From what Bob could see, she was missing a couple of her front teeth. A black imitation fur hat covered her head, but strands of gray hair had found their way out from under it. Even though her clothes were plain, she was colorful.

"Mr. Banks," she snapped. "I ain't seen him in eleven years," clearly not pining for her estranged husband.

"Eleven years?" Jack asked sounding surprised. "What happened?"

She had a smile on her face as she recounted her story. "He come home drunk one night," she said flatly. "Started hittin' me, knocked my front teeth out, so I left."

"That's the last you saw him?"

"No, I waited for his sorry, drunk ass to go to sleep," she said with a chuckle. "Then I went back with a bat. That's the last I saw him." She finished her story with a loud laugh, turned, and noticed Bob and Ray. Seeing Ray brought out another shout of recognition. "What's you doing here?" she shouted. "Wasn't you a cop? Oh, you don't remember me do you?"

Ray had a bewildered look in his eyes even while a broad smile creased his face. Bob could tell there was something familiar about Mrs. Banks to Ray, but his buddy was having a hard time placing her.

"You was a cop," she insisted. "I remember you. You arrested me for being naked."

A light came on in Ray's eyes when she said that. "Yeah, I remember you now, Mrs. Banks." he said. "That was a cold night."

"And you rescued me," she said. "I was drinking that night; don't know what happened to my clothes. You was real nice, put a blanket over me before you put me in the back of the car and took me in. Woke up in the West Precinct next morning. Them boys gave me some clothes and I just scooted out of there. Never been back. Stopped drinking after that. Now what's for lunch?"

She began looking around the room. When her gaze fell on Bob, she smiled broadly. "Oh, I like him," she gushed. "He's cuter than you."

Bob laughed, "And I'm single," he told her with a grin.

"You mean you got married?" she asked Jack. "My heart is broken and I'm still hungry."

"You're not supposed to be back here, Mrs. Banks," Jack tried again. "What if we had to go out?"

"Then I'd have lunch," she said having noticed the platter of sandwiches. She began to walk toward the end of the table with the platter on it. "Okay, I'll leave, but first I'm gonna take some of these." With that she lunged at the platter, scooped it up, and ran to the other end of the table. Jack and Ray chased her while Bob just laughed. When she reached the end of the table, she placed the platter down, grabbed a sandwich, and slid out the door laughing. "Thank you firemans," she shouted. "I ain't gonna be hungry now."

"Well, we're short one sandwich," Bob said, "But it was worth it for the entertainment value alone."

"She's a character," Jack agreed. "Life's dealt her a bad hand, but she kept her sense of humor."

"We better eat before she comes back for more," Ray laughed. He went to hit the house gong to tell everyone lunch was ready.

* * * * * * * * * * * * * * * * * *

Bob sat in his kitchen waiting for Kathy, unsure how the evening was going to turn out. He had to study. Last night's little foray had cost him his normal study time in the firehouse. He had spoken with Captain Pete about truck work and picking through the building had given him the opportunity to size up a real structure, but that was far from enough. He had given up the futile attempt to hit the books when he found himself dozing instead of reading. An afternoon nap was necessary to save tonight's study session. The snooze had also solved the vertigo problem which had persisted even after eating. Jack was right; the stress was going to kill him. Now a woman who had suddenly become a lover was going to walk through his door and he knew he did not have the strength to resist her. You are screwed was all he could think.

The sound of someone coming up the stairs told Bob she had arrived. He steeled himself for the discussion that they were about to have. Studying was paramount he would tell her. What they had given each other last night was the ultimate gift, but they could not let it derail his efforts for promotion. There would be other dates set aside for romance, but tonight they had too much material to cover. If she found that hard to accept, then he would politely, lovingly ask her to leave so he could study. All of this swept through his mind as he watched the door open. Maybe it had not been a good idea to give her a key.

Kathy stepped into the kitchen with a stern look on her face. Her clothes were unusually modest and she wore no makeup. Before he could say a word she was laying down the law to him. "Let's get one thing straight," she snapped. "What happened last night stays there. The woman you were with is not here, understand?" He shook his head lamely, partly out of shock and partly out of relief.

"A nun just stepped through your door," she barked. "The kind of nun who if you so much as write the number eight the wrong way, will drive your head into the blackboard and make you stay after school to practice the correct way of writing that number. Am I clear?"

He shook his head yes as a smile eased its way across his face.

"Don't you smile at me young man!" she scolded. "I'm here for study purposes only. Don't try to get around me or tempt me." She then marched to the table and picked up a chair. This she put in the doorway from the kitchen to the rest of the apartment. To do this she had to close the apartment door which had remained open the entire time. Apparently as an escape route. With the doorway blocked, she turned to face him.

"No one goes past that chair until I leave," she stated. "And you're not getting me to lie on a cold kitchen floor so wipe those thoughts out of your mind and that smile off your face. We planned to go over truck work tonight, salvage, overhaul, ladders, and ventilation. Did you study at all today? Never mind, I don't want to hear your excuses. I spent the whole day transcribing interviews. At least you were moving around and talking with people."

With that she sat across the table from him and started throwing questions his way. "What is the ideal angle for a ladder?" It looked like it was going to be a productive night.

Chapter Thirteen

It was a beautiful early summer evening, a little warm and humid, but nothing unusual for New Jersey. The dog days of summer were still a month away. Kathy was walking with Bob through Vailsburg Park toward a large field on the northern edge of the park that contained four baseball diamonds. The play area of the park was crowded with children on the swings or the see-saws. Older boys were playing ball on one of the diamonds at the near end of the park. She could see a group of men at the far end of the field. As they drew closer, the familiar faces of men she had interviewed became recognizable.

Bob was carrying a large cooler full of assorted non-alcoholic drinks since alcohol was prohibited in the park. She carried his glove and bat. They both wore plain dark blue baseball caps, tee shirts, and jeans. Kathy wore the jeans in case she had to sit on the grass; Bob in case he had to slide into second base, something Kathy was not sure she wanted to watch. Eighteen was not too long ago for him. Firemen seemed to fixate on that particular age and think their bodies remained there forever. She had witnessed more than one "age denial" injury while watching her father and his buddies. The extra pounds around some of the guts served as evidence that young bodies change. The presence of those bodies on a baseball diamond showed that the psychology of firefighters had not.

"Some of those guys don't look like they belong on a baseball field," she commented to Bob.

"We're playing softball," Bob laughed. "Their bellies won't get in the way. Where are you going to sit?"

"Don't worry," Kathy reassured him. "Gloria is coming with folding chairs. If not I can just plop myself on the grass."

"Hey, here's Bob," Ray called from across the field. "He's got a cooler full of drink and a sports reporter to record our exploits."

"The beer's welcome," one of the older men shouted. "But there's no need to report anything. Some of the guys may not have been totally honest with their old ladies about what they were doing tonight."

"Sorry, no beer guys," Bob shouted back. "That's for later." His news was greeted with groans.

Kathy laughed. "Don't worry guys. I won't write anything. I'm here for the fun of it only." She spotted Gloria on the first base side of the field. Bob's tour must have set up over there. Glancing at the third base side, she recognized guys from the second tour, confirming her supposition.

"I played high school ball on this field," Bob told her. "Had my best game and my most memorable game here."

"They weren't the same?" Kathy asked.

"No," Bob continued. "My best game or at least the game that felt best to me was against Edison Tech. I went three for four, with a double that felt so natural when I hit the ball I can't forget it."

"That sounds like your best," Kathy commented. "What was your most memorable?"

"That was against Passaic Tech," Bob informed her. "I got hit by a fast ball in my left elbow. My arm swelled up and there was no one to substitute for me, so I played the rest of the game in a fog. The coach moved me to right field. In the bottom of the ninth with two out, a fly ball goes to right field and I don't have the wits about me to catch it. Normally it would have been an easy catch, but I barely knew where I was so we lost."

"Ouch," Kathy moaned. "That must have hurt both your elbow and your pride."

"Not important now," Bob laughed. "We weren't playing for the state championship and even if we were, a year later it was just a memory. What counts is putting food on the table and contributing to something worthwhile."

"Were you such as sage in high school?" she asked with a hint of sarcasm as they crossed the infield.

"I told you," Bob replied. "I was in a fog. My dad took me to the emergency room to get the elbow x-rayed after my mother saw the size of it. But whatever damage that was done to my pride quickly healed. Now it's just a memory connected to this field."

The story only made her less enthusiastic about watching him slide into second base. After all he was about eighteen when that fast ball collided with his elbow. They reached Gloria and dropped their freight next to her chair. Captain Pate was organizing the squad, so Bob went over to him leaving Kathy with the wives.

"Where's Stacey?" Kathy asked Gloria after noticing she had not accompanied her husband.

"Oh, she has something at school," Gloria informed her.

"Have summer classes started already?" Kathy wondered.

"Apparently for the Nursing School they have," Gloria returned. "Now, have a seat."

They were about twenty feet from the first base foul line. Kathy noticed they had actual bases, so it appeared the game was to be played somewhere above the sand lot level. From her interviews Kathy knew the NFD had a proud history of softball, fielding teams that had competed on the national level. That was twenty years before. The play tonight was not going to be anything nearly as high powered as those teams. Some of the guys were young and athletic like Bob, but others were too fond of beer and carried fifteen or twenty extra pounds around the middle. Gloria had made the same observation. She chuckled and leaned toward Kathy. "I don't know if I'd be comfortable with Jack playing if he had a gut like some of these guys," she quipped.

"Shh," Kathy admonished her. "They fight fires don't they?"

"I guess you're right," Gloria replied. "Most of them are in decent shape, but some of them still make me nervous. I'd feel better if Stacey were here, just in case."

"Don't worry," Kathy laughed. "They all have extensive experience in first aid."

The guys came back to their rooting section one more time before the game started. Jack reached into the cooler for a drink and offered one to Bob who declined. The two walked over to Kathy and Gloria, laughing.

"That doesn't sound good at all," Jack was saying. "I don't remember you having a hard time holding your beer."

"I can hold my beer just fine," Bob snipped back. "It's the byproducts of drinking too much fluid that are a problem. If I start drinking now, I'll spend half the game running to the men's room."

"I don't remember you doing that before," Jack pointed out. "When did that start?"

"Haven't really thought about it," Bob admitted. "Just gradually happened, I guess. Must be the stress."

"The stress," Jack muttered. "Okay, let's forget about stress tonight and just have a little fun."

"Sounds like a good deal," Bob laughed.

Kathy and Gloria overheard their conversation, but kept quiet. Kathy had noticed that Bob had to interrupt their study sessions to "hit the head" as he put it, but had not thought much of it. Maybe she should talk with him, but that was not for tonight. The first tour trotted out onto the field with her and Gloria shouting encouragement. Tonight was for relaxation, not worries.

As the team threw the ball around, Gloria turned to Kathy. "So, how are the studies going?" she asked with a smile.

"You mean how are things going between Bob and me?" Kathy asked in return.

"You've been hanging around Chingli too much," Gloria chuckled. "But yes, it's been a few months since our little strategy session. Are you happy with the progress?"

Kathy thought about the months since her epiphany at Chingli's and subsequent seduction of Bob. Their relationship had moved to a higher plain that night, but it was the following night that had solidified everything. They now had an established routine. Study dates were study dates and other dates were more romantic. Bob was an exceptional student and a tender, considerate lover.

"Am I happy with the progress?" she repeated as the first pitch of the game was thrown. "I am content. We have a routine that allows for study and romance, just not on the same night."

"A routine?" Gloria asked. "Girl, you sound like an old married couple."

"Believe me, he doesn't perform like an old man," Kathy blurted out, regretting it immediately.

"And what is that supposed to mean Miss Stanley?" Gloria laughed in feinted shock.

Kathy could feel her face turn red. Her mouth had trapped her. Now she was going to have to explain or everything would get blown way out of proportion.

"Well, Bob's a very athletic, physical kind of guy," she started, but then stalled out not sure how to put it.

"And?" Gloria asked, waiting for the full statement.

"And he has a lot of stamina," Kathy said with an embarrassed chuckle.

"Stamina?" Gloria laughed quietly. "Could you make yourself clearer?"

"I don't know how much clearer I can be Gloria," Kathy said in exasperation. "I'm never - -- - physically frustrated. There is nothing pre-mature in our relationship."

The two women laughed loudly, drawing some puzzled looks from the other wives. Kathy was not comfortable discussing the topic on the sidelines of a softball game. She looked out at the men playing and was inspired.

"You see that pitcher?" she asked Gloria who looked toward the field to see a middle aged man winding up.

"Yes," she answered with a look of curiosity.

"His first assignment was down neck," Kathy began. "First day in the firehouse, he's putting the garbage out behind the firehouse and a citizen walks up and asks for directions to a certain street. He's from Vailsburg and so he hasn't a clue. Goes to get his captain who hears the question and says, 'You're standing on it.''

"No, really?" Gloria asked laughing.

"Really," Kathy answered chuckling. "After that he started studying the map."

"How many of these guys have you interviewed?" Gloria asked with genuine interest.

Kathy looked over the opposing bench and the men from the first tour. "Eight," she answered.

"And how many stories like that have they given you?" Gloria continued.

"Like what?" Kathy asked thoughtfully. "If you mean exactly like that, only one other. If you mean ridiculous stories that show the funny side of a crazy job, plenty."

"Someone else had the same experience?" Gloria asked in surprise.

The batter hit a fly ball to left field which was caught bringing the first tour in. The girls cheered before Kathy responded. "Very similar to that," she began. "See the third baseman? He was asked by a truck driver where Belmont and Waverly was. This was right after they changed the name of Belmont Avenue to Irvine Turner Boulevard and Waverly Avenue to Mohammed Ali Avenue, which is what the signs above their heads said."

The first batter for the first tour was one of the young guys. He drove the ball into shallow left field and ran like a deer, stretching what should have been a single into a double. Bob was the next batter up. Jack was first base coach. Before Bob stepped up to the plant, Jack called him over for a quick conference.

"Now what do you think those two are talking about?" Gloria wondered.

"I couldn't guess, but we'll find out in a minute," Kathy said. "I don't think they were chatting about where they're going after the game."

Bob shook his head yes and walked to the batter's box. The pitcher wound up and threw the ball down the center of the plate. At the last minute, Bob squared for a bunt, laid the ball down the third base line, and dashed for first. He did not get more than three steps before the protests from the opposing team drowned out the spectators' cheers.

"No, no, no," the pitcher shouted. "No bunting or someone's going to get hurt."

Jack and Bob were laughing. Bob went to pick up his bat and set himself for the next pitch.

"I knew they were up to something," Gloria laughed. "Jack is a frustrated baseball strategist. He's going to tell us that would have been the perfect play, you watch."

Kathy laughed and leaned forward to see how her man was going to do his second time at his first at bat. The pitcher delivered the ball and Bob jumped all over it, driving it high toward left center field over everyone's head. Kathy could tell he knew how far he had driven the ball. She looked at him running and was shocked to see he was laughing as he ran. It was not a little chuckle with a smile on his face. He was plainly having a belly laugh as he scooted around the bases. The girls stood up and cheered.

"Will you look at him," Gloria said between cheers as she clapped. "He's laughing so hard he might not make it around the bases."

Kathy attributed her next comment to having fun and dropping her guard. "No, he won't run out of gas, believe me. I know from experience; the man can go a long time before he gets winded." As soon as she realized what she said, her hand went up to cover her mouth. Any hope of Gloria not noticing was quickly lost. Her friend was in stitches, with an exaggerated look of shock on her face.

"Kathy," she whispered between spurts of laughter. "You've ruined my image of you. I always thought you were so sweet and innocent."

Kathy knew she looked as flustered as she felt; her face reddened for the second time in the evening. "What makes you think I meant that the way you took it?" she asked in a futile attempt at innocence.

"Your face is bright red, Kath," Gloria pointed out while continuing to clap. Bob reached home plate and jumped on it with both feet. The ball had just made it to the infield. Kathy wished she had inherited a little more of her mother's color. A shout from the field thankfully shifted their attention.

"How about we say bunting is okay?" the pitcher suggested. The infielders voiced their strong support, but the first tour was not going for it. Everyone laughed as the next batter stepped up to the plate.

* * * * * * * * * * * * * * * * * * * *

"We want a rematch!" one of the guys from the second tour shouted. "But first we're gonna have to bust Bob's legs. Sorry Bobbo, it just has to be."

"You go near him," Kathy jumped in. "And I'll tell everyone all your secrets."

A howl went up from the crowd at McGovern's Tavern when they heard that. Bob was making his way through the crowd of firemen with mugs of beer in his hands.

"What a woman, Bob," someone else shouted. "You don't have to defend yourself. She does it for you."

Not everyone looked at it that way. There were howls of protest, especially from the men Kathy had interviewed. "Kathy, you should be careful. Those guys from Springfield Avenue can't be trusted." Bob wondered, did the intensity of the protests come from his hit or from her interviews? He reached the table where Kathy, Gloria, and Jack waited without spilling any beer; having already run the gauntlet for the girls' drinks, he sat down to relax.

Kathy was telling stories from her interviews. Gloria seemed very interested. "You keep telling us funny stories," Gloria pointed out. "But I know you have dark ones also. How do you get these crusty, scarred old firemen to open up?"

"I don't start by asking hard questions," Kathy explained. "That would be rude. Each interview begins with the same question. 'Why did you become a fireman?' I build from there. We talk about the city, about equipment, just about a lot of things I think people would find interesting. My purpose is to give John Q. Public an opportunity to know the fire department and understand firemen."

"So, you put them at ease," Gloria observed. "Then you drop the heavy stuff."

Kathy chuckled at her friend's take on her interviewing style.

"I think you're being a little dramatic," she said. "It's not a confrontational interview with some politician who was just indicted. It's a friendly casual conversation. If they don't want to answer a question, we move on. No one has ever backed down from my questions. They enjoy sharing their experiences."

Jack had been sitting quietly listening, but could not restrain himself any longer. "Firefighters like to tell stories," he quipped. "Especially to pretty ladies."

"You are a cynic, Jack," Gloria snapped. "What are you going to tell Miss Stanley if she interviews you?"

"The truth of course," he answered his wife.

"Oh, I'll get to Jack," Kathy assured Gloria. "Just not right away. I'm interviewing according to seniority, so I get the past before the present."

The air was beginning to get a little smoky from the cigarettes. Bob had always found the way firemen smoke comical. How many times had he seen guys come out of buildings coughing and spitting out black mucus, only to reach inside their turnout coats for a cigarette. Smoking was one habit he did not regret avoiding. Of course, he could say he smoked buildings, but that would be an exaggeration. If you did not wear a mask in Six Engine, you were left behind. Jack had made that clear. Left behind meant eventually transferred out, not something Bob wanted. He often wondered how he would react if he were promoted and transferred out of Six.

"You're very quiet," Kathy said interrupting his thoughts. "A loud, smoky pub doesn't seem to be the ideal place to contemplate anything. What's on your mind?"

Bob snapped back and chuckled. "Just thinking about the changes if I get promoted."

"A twenty percent raise," Jack laughed.

"And a lot of responsibility," Kathy reminded. "That's one of my questions. 'How did you adjust to promotion?' I get some interesting answers."

Bob let it go. He did not want to bring up the negatives that would come with a promotion when Kathy was working so hard to help him. He was flexing his hand unconsciously while reaching for his beer.

"Something wrong with your hand?" Kathy asked casually.

"They have a little buzzing sensation," Bob answered.

"From the bat vibration?" Jack asked.

"No," Bob laughed. "That was the cleanest hit you could ask for. God, it felt good. I didn't notice it at the time. It'll go away, always does." He regretted the last few words immediately.

"What do you mean it always does?" Kathy perked up and asked.

"Sensations come and go," he reassured her. "Just my body's way of handling stress." From the look on Kathy's face, Bob could see that explanation was not going to fly.

"That doesn't sound normal," she began. "Maybe you should see someone."

Bob picked up on a change in her voice that said this could blow up. The nun was about to subsume the lover and begin demanding action. How to change the subject? A little humor might do it.

"I am seeing someone," he chirped. "And all these guys are jealous."

She slapped him lightly on his forearm, accepting the compliment reluctantly. "That's the poet coming out in you again," she said.

The noise from the crowd kept their conversation private. Bob did not want any attention brought to his use of poetry as a release. Jack and he had already discussed how a rough crowd like the one surrounding them would react to his poetry. They both concluded there would not be a large audience for romantic poetry on the Fire Department. Firefighters tended to be a rough and ready lot. There were plenty of exceptions, but not enough to make him feel comfortable. Just when he thought the subject had been put to rest, Gloria became inquisitive.

"Maybe you should try to get some of your poetry published under a pseudonym," she suggested.

"That's the coward's way out," Jack observed.

"So he hides all his work?" Gloria asked. "Just keep it to himself? People with talent have a responsibility to share it with others. It will enrich their lives. Maybe it will inspire or comfort someone."

Bob could not believe how bad his luck was tonight. Every topic of conversation seemed to turn serious and turn against him. Whatever happened to casual conversation and banter? "I think you're getting carried away," he responded hoping that would put it to rest.

Kathy jumped in to keep his torment alive. "I'll speak with my publisher," she told him. "A poetic big city firefighter, that's an interesting twist don't you think?" Her ambition for him reared its ugly head again. They had had this conversation before. He wanted a simple life with a purpose. That was what the Fire Department gave him. She wanted to develop what she called his talent.

"Poetry doesn't sell," he interjected in an attempt to stop the runaway train this conversation was becoming. "Besides I don't want to be famous."

Shouts from the direction of the entrance drew everyone's attention and broke the flow of the conversation. By the sound of it Frank and Chingli had stepped into the pub.

"Frank," someone shouted. "When you coming back? We miss you."

"Don't give him ideas," Chingli warned. "If he tried that, I would make his life, how would you say, miserable."

Laughter followed the comment. As far as Bob was concerned, the cavalry had just arrived. Now Kathy would have Chingli to chat with and maybe forget the topics they had been discussing. Chingli saw them and quickly walked over.

"*Meimei, nimen hen keai. Haizimen hui hen piaoliang,*" Chingli bubbled seemingly without thought to Bob's study interests.

"*Jiejie,*" Kathy exclaimed in panic. She had turned beet red as soon as she heard it. Bob understood a couple of words, but nothing more. Chingli was apparently talking about them and there may have been something about pretty, but that was all he could pick out. It was the color of Kathy's face that let him know she found it embarrassing. He remembered that Kathy had blushed when she was speaking with Gloria before the game. It seemed to be a tough night for her with her friends.

Kathy turned to Bob while these thoughts were running through his mind and hurled a question at him. "Did you understand that?"

"I'm still in book one," Bob laughed. "Checking baggage at the airport."

She spun around and confronted Frank. "Frank Helms, don't you dare translate that!"

Frank held his hands up in feinted fear. "I would never compromise a lady's secrets," he laughed. "I hear you're the hero of the game, Bob. Let me get a beer and you can give me the blow by blow."

Chingli sat with Kathy and Gloria. She turned to Kathy with a big smile and said, "Don't be so nervous. I know he could not understand. You don't like my joke? Frank says I should learn to joke like an American."

Kathy chuckled at her over reaction, then noticed someone had just walked in. "Oh, that's Chief Covey from Training," she told Chingli and Gloria. "Excuse me; I want to talk with him." She got up and scooted across the floor. Bob would have felt marginalized, but he and Jack had been enjoying the female drama unfold. Why Kathy wanted to speak with Chief Covey was beyond him. If he remembered right, she had already interviewed him. Everything comes to he who waits, he told himself. Frank came back with his beer and sat next to Bob.

"So, what did Chingli say?" Bob asked quietly leaning in toward Frank.

Frank leaned back and glanced around to make sure the girls would not hear, then leaned forward and put his elbows on the table.

"She said you two are a cute couple and your kids would be beautiful," Frank replied in a conspirator like tone.

Bob laughed quietly. That explained why she had turned red instantly. Why did women always jump so far ahead? If Kathy did not get tired of him and they actually stayed together, children would be a long way off if they came at all. Putting those thoughts aside, Bob contemplated how he could add color to his tale about the game. Frank said he wanted a blow by blow, but he had mentioned nothing about accuracy.

"Okay, Mr. Homerun king," Frank began. "Tell me about your exploits tonight and feel free to embellish. I'm looking for a good story and Kathy swears you're the next Hemingway." Bob laughed and proceeded to give an account that was loosely based on what had actually happened.

* * * * * * * * * * * * * * * * * * *

Bob pulled his car out of the parking lot and turned west. Kathy was sitting quietly next to him. It had been an enjoyable evening and a welcomed respite from the grind of work and study. After weaving through the streets, he turned onto Market Street and headed toward South Orange Avenue. It was a clear shot up that road to Kathy's apartment. Granted they would pass through some of the toughest neighborhoods in the city, but those neighborhoods were his first due district. He knew them well.

"Why did you want to speak with Chief Covey?" he asked having wondered all night about it.

"There's a class starting at the Academy in a few weeks," she informed him. "I was thinking of writing a piece for the Star Ledger about their experiences in training. It'll help with the oral history too."

"You think the Ledger would be interested in something like that?" Bob asked, doubt dripping from his voice.

"First I have to find out if the department will go for it," Kathy said. "Then I'll run it past the Ledger. Before I speak with headquarters, I wanted to speak with Chief Covey to make sure he was okay with it."

"And is he?" Bob asked.

"He's all for it," she replied. "Even gave me hints on how to approach headquarters and who to contact at the Ledger, although I already knew that."

The neighborhoods had gradually begun to improve with more buildings and fewer vacant lots. When they passed beneath the Parkway there was a sudden marked difference in their surroundings. The Parkway had always been the demarcation line in this part of the city. When Bob was a boy, he was allowed to play ball in Vailsburg Park just to the west of the Parkway. Westside Park which was located to the east, was out of bounds. The area west of the Parkway was Vailsburg. The area to the east was simply the West Ward.

Kathy had been sitting quietly as if reviewing the happenings of the night. Bob had not let on that Frank had translated Chingli's cheerful encouragement. He was smarter than that. From what he knew of the woman in his passenger's seat, she was building up to a verbal tsunami. The firefighter braced himself and waited. It would not take much longer.

"You said the buzzing sensation in your hands come and goes," she began. "How long has that been going on?"

"Oh, for a little while," Bob answered evasively. "It's just my body's reaction to stress, been working and studying too hard. It'll go away. I'll take a deep breath, get a little sleep, and it's gone."

"Just like that it's gone?" She said sarcastically. "Bob, that's not normal. My father worked and studied and nothing like that happened."

"That's why I said it's my body's reaction to stress," he countered.

"You have the same kind of body as everyone else," Kathy reminded him.

"No I don't, you tell me I have a cuter body than everyone else," he joked trying to change the subject.

"Not funny," she snapped. "I think you should see a doctor, get an evaluation. Something is not right. Better to get it early before it gets worse."

He did not want to tell her it had been getting gradually worse over the past few months. That would serve no purpose other than make her worry. "I don't have time now," Bob asserted. "After the test, if it doesn't go away on its own."

"But the test is months away," Kathy pleaded.

Bob appreciated her concern, but there was no time and he had been through this before. "Don't worry, I know my body," he said confidently. "This will go away." He regretted the way he spoke as soon as it came out, realizing his tone sounded condescending.

"Well, excuse me for caring!" Kathy snapped angrily.

"Sorry," Bob apologized. "That didn't sound the way I meant it. If it will make you feel better, I'll see if I can't shake loose a couple of hours and get to the doctor's."

"If it will make me feel better?" Kathy answered in disbelief. "You men are all so pig headed! How about if it will make you feel better? Personally, I feel fine except for the pain driving this car."

Bob took a deep breath and smiled at her. "If I can shake some time loose, I'll go see a doctor for my sake."

She sighed and looked away from him. "It's not just for your sake," she whispered. "It's for ours."

They did not speak again until Kathy got out of the car and said a frigid good night. He waited for her to get inside her building before driving away. His head was spinning from the conversation. Bob had a feeling that this issue was not going to go away any time soon. The night had begun so well. Now it looked like Kathy was going to transform herself from a lover into a nurse. That was not good. What to do? What to do? Maybe I should run it past Frank, Bob thought. He has more experience dealing with an unreasonable woman.

Chapter Fourteen

Much like the night before, the air Kathy stepped out into was comfortably warm with a hint of humidity. Patches of sunlight broke through the canopy formed by the shade trees along South Orange Avenue. The sounds of early evening traffic greeted her. She had questions humming through her mind to which she had no answers. How can men so easily ignore their body's signals that something was not right? They were all so focused on making their mark in the world, as if what they did would make everything right. How can she convince the fool who dropped her off last night that there was something besides stress contributing to his symptoms? Symptoms! He would protest loudly to her calling what he was experiencing symptoms.

As she walked past the small municipal park that occupied the space across the street from her building, Kathy could not help but note the difference between it and the county park of the previous night. This was a public park for promenades. There were no ball fields or play areas. Paths wound through its well-tended grass fields. Stalwart oak and maple trees stood guard over the walkways like sentinels. A breeze rippled through the tree tops and the subtle fragrance of flowers from someone's garden floated through the air to her. What a wonderful day to be alive, except for that stubborn, pigheaded, cava tos, that is what Nini Anna would call him, a stone head.

Stacey and Gloria should have some thoughts on how to solve the riddle of the stone headed fireman. They were each married to one of their own and had been more than happy to meet with her for dinner to discuss their three men. Maybe she should just give him an ultimatum; go to a doctor or do not bother calling me again! As soon as the thought crossed her mind she knew she could not do it. What if he said no? Then he would not see a doctor and she would not be with him. That was a lose/lose situation if ever there was one. She swore under her breath in Taiwanese. He was too much a part of her now. Manipulation was the only solution. She was counting on her two coaches to help her choose the right form for the occasion.

She reached the Shanghai restaurant where Chingli had advised her those months before. They would not be a foursome tonight because Frank's office was too busy. That was a shame; Chingli was such a good manipulator. Kathy would have to present any plans to her before implementation. It was the perfect evening for their little pow-wow. The guys were in the firehouse, so it would be dinner with the ladies' auxiliary. Firehouse wives and a girlfriend scheming against their men; what a wonderful way to spend the night.

Kathy pulled the door open and saw Gloria and Stacey waiting for her. A knot in her stomach had made lunch undesirable, so the aromas that greeted her were enticing. The restaurant had a good sized crowd. Business had improved enough for the owner to hire a few college girls as waitresses. Apparently, the red table clothes had brought the good luck Chinese tradition felt that color would bring. His wife now greeted patrons as they came in. It would be a little more difficult to have a private conversation, but she was sure they would manage. The owner's wife gave an enthusiastic greeting. Kathy pointed to her friends and walked over to their table. The two women already had appetizers and tea on the table. They stood up with understanding smiles.

"What does Chingli call you?" Gloria asked. "*Jiejie*?"

Kathy smiled at her friend's attempt to comfort her. "No, *jiejie* is older sister," she explained as they embraced. "She would call me *meimei* which means younger sister. I call her *jiejie*."

Stacey laughed at the two of them then hugged Kathy. "I'm not even attempting to get those terms straight," she surrendered. "You look worried."

"Did you order dinner yet?" Kathy asked as they sat down. "Chingli insists everything looks better after you eat."

"No, we were waiting for your expertise before ordering," Gloria answered. "And I agree with her, everything looks a little better after you eat, provided the food is enjoyable."

"Don't worry, your taste buds will be titillated," Kathy laughed as she waved to one of the waitresses. She was an overseas Chinese student from mainland studying at Seton Hall. They had chatted on earlier visits about adjusting to American life and the vagaries of American English. Kathy always felt there was something deeper that the girl was reluctant to discuss. She was of the generation that would have experienced the chaos of the Cultural Revolution, so Kathy was sure there were scars hidden just beneath the surface. This tiny restaurant was not the place to bring up such topics, so they were left buried under a thin layer of politeness that neither of them wanted to disturb. When the waitress offered a menu, Kathy declined and immediately began reciting the dishes she wanted to order. The waitress quickly placed the order and returned with a tea cup which Kathy filled. After a sip to calm herself she turned to her friends and asked, "How can I get a pigheaded fireman who thinks he is his own best doctor to actually see someone who went through medical school?"

Stacey looked a little blanched upon hearing the question. Gloria picked up on her hesitancy and jump into the void. "It looks like we're going to spend a lot of time talking about med school tonight."

"Medical school?" Kathy asked puzzled.

"That's for later," Stacey insisted, recovering from her momentary reticence. "Right now it sounds like the problem is a stubborn man."

Kathy decided to let the med school question go for now and instead launched into her rendition of the stubborn fireman blues. When she finished her tale, she pleaded, "How can I get him to a doctor for an evaluation?"

"Well, the first thing you don't do," Stacey said. "Is demand he go or else. That just makes him defensive and stubborn. There's something in the male psyche that prevents them from admitting weakness. They seem to think no woman will stay with a man who shows any sign of it. Seeing a doctor says he admits he is weak and not in control of his life."

Gloria shook her head in agreement. The two of them confirmed Kathy's suspicions. She knew instinctively that the issue was not really time taken away from study. If that were true, they would still be plutonic friends. Stacey had stated what not to do, but that left her in the middle of a wilderness without a compass or map. The question remained; what to do? Gloria spoke up and moved the conversation up a notch. "So you have to lead him to the realization that it would be best for him to see a doctor," she said. "What matters to him most?"

"The captain's test," Kathy answered without hesitation. "His life revolves around work and study. I'm just a pleasant respite when we're not studying together."

"Studying," Gloria muttered. "Don't they have to write an essay on the exam?"

"Yes," Kathy replied, wondering where her friend was going.

"He mentioned a buzzing sensation in his hands. If it affects his writing somehow," Gloria said thoughtfully. "You could use that. How's his penmanship?"

"He writes like a guy," Kathy informed her. "His penmanship is legible and it hasn't changed since I first saw it." Kathy thought she could see where Gloria was going with her questions. Maybe they could shake something loose tonight and formulate a plan.

"Any complaints about his eyes?" Gloria continued. "With all the reading he does, his eyes are his most important asset."

Kathy thought for a moment. She could picture Bob frequently rubbing his eyes. He never said a word about it and she never pointed it out to him, but it was there.

"Maybe his eyes could work," she said slowly. "He never complains about them, but he does rub them an inordinate number of times when we study. I read as much as he does and I don't think I rub my eyes even once."

"Sounds like we might have something," Gloria exclaimed.

Stacey had been listening intently. Since she had missed last night's game and subsequent pub conversation, this was the first she had heard of Bob's complaints. Before she could jump into the conversation, the waitress returned with their meals. Kathy had ordered three different dishes, a shrimp dish with vegetables in a red sauce, a chicken dish with peppers and onions, and a beef dish with broccoli. A large bowl of steaming rice was placed in the middle of the table. Kathy immediately reached for the rice scoop and started serving her friends. Stacey and Gloria served the entrées themselves. The table became quiet as they tasted their meals. Moans of pleasure accompanied the first taste of each offering. "At the end of the night, I want an opinion from each of you," Kathy said between bites. "Which is the tastiest meal? And no copping out by saying they're all great." Her friends were too busy sampling the cuisine on the table to protest.

After they had consumed enough to take the edge off their appetites, Stacey resumed the conversation. "Bob has buzzing hands and is rubbing his eyes," she started. "Any other complaints?"

"Well, there's one other unusual thing," Gloria said with a mischievous smile.

"Is there?" Kathy asked sounding puzzled.

"It seems Bob has unusual staying power." Gloria finished.

"Gloria!" Kathy whispered emphatically. "That's not a symptom!"

The conversations around them seemed loud enough to mask anything they said, but Kathy still did not want this topic discussed. Bob's prowess as a lover had nothing to do with his problems. Gloria was just trying to have a little fun to lighten the mood which would have been fine if they were not in such a public place. There was no way to avoid talking about the subject with Stacey now. How to minimize the embarrassment was the question. She took a bite of the shrimp and waited for Stacey's response.

Stacey looked confused. "Staying power?" she asked.

"You're blowing it totally out of proportion," Kathy insisted.

"What is she blowing out of proportion?" Stacey asked.

"Kathy put it best last night," Gloria hinted while reaching for the chicken. "She said there was nothing premature about their relationship."

"Premature?" Stacey mused. You mean like premature ej - - - ?"

Kathy desperately interrupted her. No matter how much chatter there might be from the tables around them, there were still too many people in too small a space for this conversation. "Yes, yes, yes," she interjected hastily. "I am completely satisfied with our physical relationship, but that's not a symptom. That's just a strange sense of humor."

"Strange sense of humor?" Gloria laughed. "You laughed harder than I did last night and don't try to deny it."

"Maybe I did, but that was out of embarrassment," Kathy claimed.

"And maybe I laughed out of envy," Gloria replied, causing all three to burst into laughter.

When they calmed down, Stacey became serious. "You said it's not a symptom, but it could be," she insisted. "Let me ask around school, but remember I'm not in med school. Don't expect a diagnosis of some kind."

Kathy now wanted the conversation to move off the subject of Bob for a while. School seemed the perfect diversion. "How is school going, Stace?" she asked. "I was surprised they started summer classes already."

Stacey had a smile that said she understood Kathy's desire to change subjects. "It really hasn't started," she explained. "I'm working with a professor, she's a medical doctor, and she asked to see me last night. You see she wants me to go to medical school."

Kathy instantly made the connection with Gloria's comment when she first arrived. Her reaction at first blush was excitement for her friend. This was tempered when her mind flashed to the commitment of time, energy, and money that would be involved. A professor's enthusiasm does not pay the bills or mollify a husband. This was not going to be an easy decision. She took a sip of tea and asked, "How did Ray react to the proposal?"

163

"Girl," Gloria admired. "You are so in tune with others feelings."

Kathy laughed. "Isn't that the first thing that crossed your mind?"

"It might have been the second or third that crossed my mind," Gloria laughed. "It was the first out of my mouth, but I've known Miss Brainy for a long time. You have a way of understanding people and their feelings so quickly. I guess that's why you're such a good reporter."

"I think you're embarrassing her, Glor," Stacey interposed. "Ray, he hasn't heard the proposal yet. I wanted to get opinions from my girls first. Now, let me explain the whole deal. There's a scholarship that was set up for nursing students or nurses who show promise. It was established when there weren't a lot of women doctors, so its purpose is to encourage women to become physicians."

"And your professor thinks you might be able to win the scholarship?" Kathy asked.

"My professor said the scholarship is mine if I am willing to make the commitment."

"Wow, that is wonderful," Kathy exclaimed, although she could still see something was weighing on her friend.

"Yes, but there's so much going on right now," Stacey sighed. "Ray wants to start a private investigation company and I have commitments at the lab. Med school will be a full time grind, no more night classes. So, I'd have to leave my job. We've been trying to save for a house and the years it would take to graduate med school and then the residency and specializing. What about having children? It's so complicated because it's such a long process and such a commitment of time and energy."

Stacey's torment was obvious. She was overwhelmed with the possibilities and complexities of the situation. To have an opportunity like this suddenly thrust into your life would challenge anyone. Kathy looked to Gloria for some guidance, but she seemed as overwhelmed as Stacey. They were too close for the emotions to be separated from the rational. She thought for a moment and then jumped in with both feet. "The first thing we have to do is divide the problem into manageable pieces. You have to take the MCAT right?"

"Not according to my professor," Stacey said. "As she explained it, the faculty of the school chooses the scholarship recipient. Their opinions take the place of the tests that predict how well the recipient will do. I just have to make the decision."

It struck Kathy as very ironic that getting a pass on the medical school admission test would strike her as a negative, but she was confident Stacey would do well and taking the exam would slow the process down. That would give Stacey more time to adjust to her new circumstances. Now it was full steam ahead. "The next consideration and probably the most important question to ask yourself is do you want to be a physician?"

"I always have," Stacey confessed. "To help cure diseases and relieve suffering would be the ultimate high."

With that admission, Kathy realized that this was literally a dream come true. If Stacey were to pass up this opportunity, she would regret it for the rest of her life. "That brings us to your hubby," Kathy sighed. "How do you think he will react?"

"He's my biggest backer when it comes to my studies," Stacey said.

"But he's never experienced the demands that med school will put on both of you," Gloria interrupted.

"Exactly," Stacey agreed. "I think he'll be thrilled and proud at first, but when the sacrifices involved become clear, he may balk. I just don't know." A dejected expression took control of her as she reached for a dumpling and slumped in her chair.

Kathy was wracking her brain trying to come up with some way to ease Ray into the situation and produce the results they wanted. Could they play on his ego? That would only be a short term solution. They needed something else, something that would draw his soul into a commitment to medical school. What that might be, she still did not know. "The only way to find out is to tell him," she concluded. "Just put the whole thing in the best light you can. You said he wants to start a private investigation firm? Does he regret leaving the police department?"

"No, not at all!" Stacey insisted. "And I regret it even less. After what happened with that nut case, I wanted nothing to do with guns. It's only been in the past year that I could tolerate even seeing one. But he misses the intellectual challenge of investigations. I think he's been thinking about it for a while, but had to let me get over the gun thing."

Kathy knew Stacey was referring to the psychotic young man who had been convinced that she was the Tsar's daughter and needed to be rescued from the Bolsheviks. That was a bizarre side show of the stalker serial killings three years before. It had taken a lot of hard work on Stacey's part to overcome that trauma. The girl had resilience if nothing else. How could they use Ray's desire to become a P.I. to advance Stacey's desire to become a physician?

"You said Ray missed the challenge, right?" Kathy confirmed. "Then if he asks why you want to do this, say you need the intellectual challenge. That should make him more receptive. Does he know you always wanted to be a doctor?"

"He used to laugh at me when we were kids," Stacey admitted. "He'd tease me. Say I'm too pretty to be a doctor. None of the doctors we saw were women, so we just assumed doctors had to be men."

Gloria laughed at the old memories. "Jack and Frank used to take red crayons and put marks on their fingers so Stacey could heal them."

Kathy had a warm feeling listening to these memories of her friends. She felt so fortunate to have become part of this group. These thoughts made her want to help Stacey with her quandary that much more. "Then this isn't something coming out of the blue," Kathy stated, becoming more optimistic as they worked through the problem. "Maybe you're just worrying about something that will fall into place. Take the first step and tell him. He knows it's a lifelong dream and now it's being offered to you on a silver platter. He does love you. I think he'll go for it."

Stacey and Gloria seemed to relax as if her assessment had removed lingering doubts and reaffirmed their own take. Stacey took a sip of tea and smiled. "How about your problem?" she asked bringing the conversation full circle.

"You mean my stubborn, invincible firefighter?" Kathy quipped.

"Are you ready to commit to the fight with his pride and denial?" Stacey asked.

"His pride?" she responded. "I'm the one who tries to show him how much talent he has, how well he can write. He denies everything I've told him. I've been dealing with his pride and denial all along. But now it's serious. It involves his health." She picked up her cup of tea and sipped it, wondering if she would ever understand how anyone could think stress caused the constellation of symptoms Bob was trivializing.

"If you're going to try to get him to move, you'll need patience," Stacey pointed out.

"Patience? But what if it's something serious?" Kathy protested.

Stacey put up her hand to calm Kathy. "I didn't say the patience of Job," she assured her. "Just a little patience. Pay attention to him rubbing his eyes and ask how he's feeling. Sooner or later he'll admit his eyes are bothering him. Get him to an eye doctor. See if they find something. When you're there, mention his other stress symptoms. The doctor will recommend he see another specialist. Step by step he'll work his way through the specialists he should see for each symptom."

"All because he might need glasses!" Kathy exclaimed. "Doctor, you're brilliant."

"Oh, make sure you get him to an ophthalmologist, not an optometrist," Stacey warned. "You'll need an MD to assess him."

Kathy went to get the check from the waitress before it was brought to their table. The advice Stacey gave her was invaluable. The cost of dinner was a small price to pay for it.

Chapter Fifteen

Bob put the last of the dishes into the sink. Dinner had gone well with no interruptions for the first time in months. Ray had picked up half of dinner. Hector had brought in the other half. Jack had cooked, which left clean up to him, even if he was acting captain. He grabbed the steel wool pad and began soaping down the plates in the sink. The thought of how his mother would react to this firehouse style of clean up made him smile. Steel wool on plates was just not an acceptable option when he was growing up. The only one in the kitchen with him was the Chief, who was waiting for his Battalion Chiefs to report to him with the day's paperwork.

The discussion he had with Kathy the night before was playing through Bob's mind one more time, filling him with doubts. Not about the relationship. He realized all relationships go through rough patches as adjustments are made to each other. It was the effect a rough patch could have on his test preparation that bothered him. Somehow, somewhere along the way he had become too dependent on Kathy's guidance. He was unsure if she was even speaking to him. In the firehouse it did not matter, but what if they had a study date? After finishing the cleanup Bob turned to the Chief. One advantage of being in a chief's house was the readily available advice.

"Chief, could I run a question past you?" Bob asked.

"Sure Bob," the Chief responded with a smile. "What's on your mind?"

Bob sat on the bench across from Chief Simmons, laid his arms on the table, and asked earnestly, "Do you think I should be in a study group?"

The Chief looked a little surprised at the question. Everyone in the house knew Bob was studying under the tutelage of Kathy. What he asked was unexpected.

"Aren't you studying with Kathy?" he asked.

"Yes, but I thought maybe working with other guys would bring different perspectives," Bob posited. "Bring different approaches to solving the problems they throw at us."

"You know, on previous tests that would have worked," the Chief started. "Because some of the guys would probably have taken a test or two. Problem now is no one has taken this type of test. I really don't see a large benefit to going with a group on the written portion. When they go to the oral, you might get something from being able to practice with guys in the group. Of course you might also end up coaching your competition, especially if Kathy teaches the tricks of her trade."

"The tricks of her trade?" Bob asked confused. The Chief did not look surprised at Bob's response; he seemed to be expecting it.

"Bob, see if you can take a step back and analyze this," the Chief suggested. "The girl was a reporter in the New York media market. That's the toughest market in the country. She did her job well. The station was disappointed when she left and would probably take her back in a heartbeat. It's possible a national station would eventually pick her up."

Bob listened to the Chief's analysis, having never really thought about that aspect of Kathy. It now struck him as ironic that he missed such an important part of her talent. The author she was had been intimidating enough. To think she was also a talented television reporter would have been frightening. It was good he had not looked beyond her writing talent. If that had happened, he doubted they would be where they were today.

"You're scaring me Chief," Bob laughed. "What's a woman like her doing with a guy like me?"

"Don't try to understand the ways of the heart," the Chief laughed. "She has her reasons, they all do. Acceptance is the beginning of wisdom."

Bob shook his head at the unlikely match he had made. How long it would last was anyone's guess. He had definitely not held on to his heart. She was in complete control of the situation and there was nothing short of suicide he could do to extricate himself from it. Trying to take the Chief's advice on acceptance, he pushed those thoughts to the side and focused on Kathy's skills and the promotional exam. "How would interviewing skills help on the test?" he wondered out loud.

"It's not her interviewing skills, Bob," he pointed out. "It's her presentation skills. Every night when she stood in front of that camera, she had to make a coherent presentation including all the relevant facts in as concise a manner as possible. That's what they'll be looking for. Whether it's the instructional portion or the group problem solving portion you'll have to be coherent, factual, and concise."

He had not thought of it from that angle. The study techniques Kathy had taught gave him an advantage, if only because they had worked for her both in college and with her father's test prep. Knowing the success rate of a study system gave him a little extra confidence. That was what made good firefighters, the confidence that what they were doing had been tried before and had worked. The oral was virgin territory. No one had experience with that type of testing. The guys assigned to Training might have an advantage because of their instructional experience, but the presentation techniques Kathy had mastered as a reporter would be invaluable. With this realization came the thought that she might actually think he was using her to get promoted which was laughable as far as he was concerned. How could he reassure her if she began to entertain the same thoughts? That was another quandary he would have to put off facing until it came up, if it ever did. His plate was already too full to add another worry.

"Thanks Chief," Bob said earnestly. "Now all I have to do is get her to speak to me again."

His last wry remark brought an understanding look from the Chief's eyes and a knowing comment. "I thought you might have had a few unpleasant words with her," he guessed with a smile. "That's where the study group question came from, isn't it?"

Bob shook his head yes and rubbed his eyes. They were bothering him a bit more than usual tonight. He figured it was to be expected when relationship stress was dropped on top of study and work stress.

"Are your eyes bothering you?" the Chief asked.

"It's nothing, Chief," Bob told him. "Just too much reading in too short a period of time. After I rest up, it'll go away."

"Careful, Bob," the Chief advised. "Too much reading without taking a break and you can read yourself into needing glasses. My doctor calls it West Point myopia. Supposedly, it was named after a study of West Point cadets who studied so hard they became near sighted."

"It's not that my vision is bleary, Chief," Bob explained. "It's ambiguous, off in my peripheral vision. I've just learned to live with it." The hot line rang as he said this. Chief Simmons picked it up and handed it to Bob.

"Six. South Orange and Springfield, on a signal five, van fire, got it."

Bob hung up the phone then walked to the alarm console and pressed the button for the house gong. He pushed the door to the apparatus floor open and walked to the captain's side of the rig. Captain Pete had taken a personal day to attend his son's high school graduation. Jack, Ray, and Hector came in from the apron where they had been enjoying the comfortable temperatures while they watched the neighborhood stroll past the firehouse.

"Signal five to South Orange and Springfield," Bob shouted. "Reported as a van fire."

Jack hopped into the driver's seat and started the rig. Everyone else put on their boots and climbed aboard. Ray and Hector went to the extra effort of donning their helmets, but Bob did not bother because he was in the cab. Jack rolled the rig out onto Springfield Avenue and turned left. Traffic was light so he could pull out and turn onto the avenue without stopping. Bob turned on the siren as they descended the hill heading east toward the South Orange Avenue intersection.

The van was parked on the opposite side of the road, just west of the intersection where South Orange Avenue veered off following the direction of the deer path it originally was. It was a Volkswagon van with an engine compartment fire in the rear. Jack pulled the rig across Springfield Avenue and parked in front of the van leaving plenty of room for the crew to operate. Hose can be stretched, but if something unusual happened it would be difficult to move the rig quickly. Bob called on the scene and went to size up the van while Ray and Hector went to stretch the booster line from the back of the rig. Smoke was pouring out of the opened rear compartment, but there was also something else happening. As he walked, the curb behind the van came into view. Bob saw flames flowing down the street. He turned and shouted with a smile, "Hold up on the booster, it looks like we have a flammable liquid fire. Come over here and have a look at this."

The guys looked puzzled, but dropped the booster and walked down to Bob. The owner of the van came over at the same time. He was a middle aged man with blond hair who did not fit into the neighborhood at all. Not that this was much of a neighborhood;

vacant lots strewn with glass and the remains of foundations surrounded them. The twelve story Stella Wright projects rose up a few blocks to the south and some businesses still eked out a living across South Orange Avenue, but that was about it. Pedestrian traffic ended a couple of blocks to the east at the Essex County Courthouse.

"Is this your van?" Bob asked.

"Yes, I don't understand what happened," the owner said nervously. "It backfired down by the courthouse and then just seemed to run out of gas. When I got out to check it, there was smoke coming from the engine."

"Did you get it tuned up recently?" Bob queried.

"Yes, as a matter of fact I did," the owner replied.

Jack, Ray, and Hector walked up in time to hear this exchange. "You got to get another mechanic," Hector commented.

"I did it myself," the owner confessed.

"The backfire probably set your air filter on fire," Bob informed him. Then he turned to his crew. "Looks like it's leaking gas. We have a flammable liquid fire flowing down the street," he chuckled when he heard himself say it. This was not exactly a major incident, but it was an accurate description of the situation. "Get the dry chemical extinguisher," he told Hector. "And hit the engine compartment. Then we'll have to deal with the mess in the curb before it goes down the sewer."

While Hector got the extinguisher, Jack and Ray discussed how to deal with the burning gas at the curb. Bob thought for a moment and then joined the conversation. The absurdity of how things were unfolding was not lost on him. Having a conference to discuss how to extinguish a fire was not what the public expected from firefighters. Thankfully there was no danger of it spreading, so they could afford to determine the best way to deal with it. Hector came down with the extinguisher and gave the compartment a quick shot eliminating that variable from the equation.

"I never saw anything like this," Jack said. "How did that happen?"

Hector had leaned down to look at the engine compartment, now he was standing quietly thinking. He had been a mechanic in his previous life, so Bob knew he was looking for an answer to Jack's question. "These vans have a short rubber hose that feeds gas to the fuel pump," Hector explained. "My guess is the thing backfired, started to burn, and melted that hose. The gas is just dripping down to the pavement and flowing down the street."

His explanation did not solve the problem of the burning gas flow. They could hang around for fifteen or twenty minutes for it to burn off. That would be ideal except for the worry about it going into the sewer system. There was not enough dry chemical left to cover it and a CO2 would leave unburned gas on the ground. Bob turned to Jack and said, "Looks like it's time for a foam drill."

"I was thinking the same thing," Jack agreed. "I think that's what Pete would do."

Hector and Ray looked confused, so Bob explained. "We can't wash this down with water; it'll just float the burning gas down the sewer. I don't know what's down there. If there's some sort of volatile gas from God knows what in this neighborhood, it might cause an embarrassing boom. Best way to handle a flammable liquid fire is with foam. In this case only a little foam, but it'll be a good drill. I mean, when's the last time we used foam?"

They laid down a nice blanket of foam along the curb, then loaded up and called back in service. Bob felt for the poor guy whose van had burned. All he could do was direct him to a pay phone down by the courthouse. Jack turned the rig up South Orange Avenue and headed back to quarters. Bob looked across the vacant lot and watched the owner walk toward the phones, leaving behind the remains of his only form of transportation.

Jack turned onto Jones Street and headed for Springfield Avenue. The rig pulled up to quarters. As Jack slowed, Ray and Hector got ready to step down and stop traffic. Before Jack came to a complete halt, Bob thought he saw something to their left. It looked like smoke. "Hold on," he said loudly. "Jack, pull up to Bergen Street."

Jack looked up the avenue. "I think we have something," he muttered and pulled back out onto the road. Bob threw on the lights and siren. The sounds behind him said that Ray and Hector were putting their masks on. Bob reached for the mike as the rig rolled to the intersection. A quick glance revealed smoke coming from the second floor of a three story frame. Two little girls were standing on the sidewalk in their night gowns and an agitated crowd was forming.

"Engine Six to quarters, emergency," Bob said into the mike.

"Engine Six."

"Give me the box for Springfield and Bergen, we have a smoke condition in a three story frame."

Jack pulled the rig past the building and quickly threw it into pump. Bob jumped out of the cab, pulled his mask out of the side compartment, and looked at the building. Three story frame, smoke coming from the second floor, some visible fire in a window, but the glass was intact. There was a hydrant on the corner that Jack could easily stretch to on his own. Hector and Ray were already stretching the three lengths into the building. A man in the crowd ran up to Bob as he stepped on the sidewalk.

"The girls say their little brother is in there," he told Bob.

Bob quickly stepped over to the girls, squatted down to their level, and asked gently, "I want to help your brother. Can you tell me which floor he's on?"

The poor girl was so terrified she could not speak. All she could do was point at the building. Her finger was pointed at the upper floors, so Bob at least knew the boy was not on the first floor. "How old is he?" he asked in a last attempt to get useful information from the little girl. She held up two fingers.

Bob sprang up from his crouch and headed into the building. Hector had the tip at the top of the stairs leading to the second floor. Ray was calling for water. Jack wet the line from the booster tank and revved the engine up to provide pressure. Then he ran to the back of the rig to begin stretching three inch hose to the corner hydrant.

"There's a two year old boy on the second or third floor," Bob shouted before donning his face piece. "Push in on the fire. I'll go above and search there."

He passed Hector as water surged into the hose and began climbing the stairs to the third floor. Heat had begun to build, but it was not too hot yet. Bob turned his back to the locked door and gave it a quick mule like kick. The door crashed in easily. He then began a systematic search keeping the wall on his right. Visibility was good. The fire had apparently not had a lot of time to build. Bob doubted the boy was up here since the door was locked. Frightened children fleeing a fire do not lock doors on their way out. That did not mean no one was in the apartment, only that a two year old boy probably was not. A quick preliminary search turned up nothing, so Bob made his way to the door. The sounds of other companies arriving came up from the front door below. When he reached the landing he heard Hector shouting, "He's still breathing! He's still breathing!"

He flew down the stairs and saw Hector rushing down the flight to the first floor. Ray was in the doorway with the line in his hand and his face piece dangling in front of him. Bob took his face piece off and asked, "Hector found the kid?"

"Yeah," Ray replied. "He was tangled in some bedding, looked like at the base of the fire. He was still alive, but barely, Hector grabbed him and ran. He's taking it hard."

Bob cursed under his breath and hustled down the stairs. What did Ray mean by "taking it hard"? He made his way down the stairs going against the flow of firefighters coming in. Ray and Hector had the fire knocked down. They would just have to check for extension. This was a little piss ass fire, but a toddler's life appeared to be on the line. When Bob stepped out of the building, Hector was on the rear step of the rig broken up. He looked at Bob and apologized. Bob just put his hand up to reassure him.

"Just stay there," Bob told him. Then he walked over to the Chief.

"Chief, did they take the boy to University?" Bob asked.

"Hank took him in the gig," the Chief said.

"Was he still breathing?" Bob continued.

The Chief shook his head no. "One of the guys from Eighteen was doing CPR on him when Hank took off. We'll have to see what they can do in the ER."

Bob swore under his breath again. Jack walked over. "I talked with Community Relations," he started. "They have the girls in their car right now. The story they got was the three of them were playing with a candle. They dropped the candle behind the bed. The sisters ran out of the room. The brother tried to get the candle. Mom? They didn't know where mom was. She showed up and the neighbors got really pissed. She went to the Howard Bar for a drink and some socializing, left the kids alone. The Chief called for a squad car and the Red Cross."

Bob took all this in. It added to everything else that was going through his mind. He knew this was going to be one of those jobs that stayed with him. Taking a deep breath, he started back to the rig with Jack. Mr. Acting Captain had to drop his mask, talk to one of his guys, and get back into the building to finish up. He said a prayer for the toddler in the emergency room and put his mind back on the task at hand. A distracted firefighter became an injured firefighter far too often for him to lose focus.

Chapter Sixteen

Why had he not called? Kathy asked herself. She was the one who was annoyed, not him. Over the past months they had fallen into a pattern whenever there was a disagreement. She would ignore him; he would apologize; and they would move on. He worked the firehouse last night and Bob always called her before he left the firehouse. It was not something that she demanded or even requested. It was something that he did because he knew it put her at ease; just to tell her everything was all right. He still had ten fingers and ten toes and no broken bones. As far as she was concerned, more than anything else it said he loved her. Maybe she pushed a little too hard about the doctor, but that was out of love and Bob should realize that. So, why had he not called?

Kathy decided sitting wondering would not relieve her anxiety, so she picked up the phone and called him even though she was unsure of what to say. When he did not pick up, she swore under her breathe in Taiwanese. Well, there is more than one way to skin a cat, she thought and dialed Gloria. As soon as Gloria picked up, Kathy began questioning, no hello, no good morning. She needed answers quickly before her imagination ran away with her.

"Did Jack say anything about Bob?" Kathy shot out, twirling the phone cord nervously with her fingers.

"Good morning, Kath," Gloria countered sweetly. "Yes, as a matter of fact he did. You haven't talked with Bob yet, have you?"

Kathy felt some of the worry lift. At least he could talk. Gloria would have told her immediately if something had happened, right? She was sure her friend would not keep bad news to herself, so Kathy brought it down one notch. Have I spoken with him?

"No, we haven't spoken since he dropped me off after the game," she admitted as she paced the kitchen floor.

"Bob is working for Frank today," Gloria informed her. "It was a last minute favor. Doesn't he usually call you when he gets out of work?"

Kathy began to feel herself get more emotional. Why had he not called? He still worked for Frank occasionally and always called before he left the firehouse. Had he ever worked for Frank after a night in the firehouse? Maybe he had not and that was why there had been no phone call. Yes, but he could have asked Frank to call!

"He always calls me when he gets off," Kathy snapped. "Why didn't he call me this morning?" She knew Gloria could not answer, but she just needed to vent.

"Jack said they had a fire last night," Gloria told her. "A two year old boy died. Bob was acting captain. That might have something to do with it."

Kathy stopped pacing abruptly as she took in the information. Her anxiety melted away. She remembered how her father had reacted to the death of a child at fires. There was always an extra hug from dad when that happened. From her interviews she knew a child's death was one of the most difficult aspects of the job. The only thing worse was the death of a brother firefighter.

"Did Jack say how Bob was after the fire?" Kathy asked.

"Jack didn't say. Maybe he's thinking about it," Gloria speculated. "Hector took it hard. He has a two year old nephew he's close to, so that's understandable. Bob does have to write a report and they were first due, so I'm sure he has a lot on his mind."

Kathy knew Bob was going over the fire in his mind. He had told her more than once about his efforts to control the "what ifs". She was sure he was wrestling with questions about what had happened. He would need time and brother firefighters to talk with. It was good he went to Frank's today, she thought. Frank had a good ear and was a fountain of sensible advice.

"Are you okay?" Gloria asked, bring Kathy back to reality.

"Me? Yes, why do you ask?" Kathy lied even though she knew Gloria would see right through her.

"Because you sound worried," she answered. "You don't have to confess that your imagination took you for a ride, but just remember you can call anytime you need to."

"I know," Kathy answered. "Thanks for listening." She hung up the phone and laughed at her panic attack. If anything had happened half the fire department would be at her door to help. That was just the way they were. It was no secret that she and Bob were an item. Get hold of yourself, girl, she thought. Your biggest worry is getting him to a doctor. Stay focused.

* * * * * * * * * * * * * * * *

Bob parked the delivery van and walked up to Frank's office. He did not mind doing his friend the favor of running a delivery up to Short Hills Mall; he just wished the timing had been better. A little extra sleep would have helped him after last night. Now his study routine was totally disrupted. Not that a lot of studying got done on the day between his nights in the firehouse. If he got to review the topics he had worked on last with Kathy, it was considered a good day. Although the last topics she had thrown at him had more to do with her worries about his health; with a heavy dose of diplomacy thrown in. They had not spoken since he had dropped her off after the game. That was thirty-six hours before, a long time for her to go without talking to him. He should have called her before he left the firehouse, but it had been such a bad night and Frank had called. The woman who had stepped out of his car two nights before would not cut him any slack, probably an unconscious reason why he had not called.

Frank was working on his new toy when Bob opened the door to his office. A brand new Apple IIe computer sat on the desk Chingli used. It had dual disk drives and 128 kilobytes of desktop memory. Frank used it for inventory control and word processing. He swore it would save him a mountain of paper storage. Instead everything would be stored on five and a quarter inch floppy disks. Now the little guy can store information like the multi-national companies, or so Frank claimed. When Bob had pointed out that Frank's little firm was a "multi-national" company, Frank laughed and changed his description to huge conglomerates. Whatever the description of companies with large mainframe computers; this little Apple was supposed to make Frank's life easier.

Bob closing the office door pulled Frank's attention away from the computer screen. "Dropped it off without a hitch," Bob informed him. "They were very grateful for the extra effort."

Frank stood up and stretched. "I've been battling with this machine all morning," he complained. "Thank you for your extra effort. I heard you had a bad night. I really appreciate you going the extra mile for us."

"No big deal, Frank," Bob laughed. "I'll be looking for advice or a sympathetic ear sooner or later."

Frank shook his head knowingly and walked toward the coffee mugs. He grabbed two and looked at Bob with raised eyebrows. Bob knew what his friend meant. A cup of hot tea always helped the conversation and Bob intended to cash in on his extra effort. What to bring up first? Before he said anything, Frank threw a question his way.

"How are you handling what happened last night?" he asked while making the tea. Frank did not pull punches. Bob wondered, did he pick up his directness from Chingli, did Chingli pick it up from him, or was it a mutual attraction type of trait? Where ever Frank got it from, his question left no doubt about what topic to bring up first. His friend walked over and handed the steaming mug to Bob.

"I think I'm handling it okay," Bob said as he accepted the mug. "Hector had a rough time of it at first. The boy was the same age as his sister's son and they're close. I had my doubts about what we did, but in the end there wasn't anything we could have done to change what happened. I called the fire in. We were on the scene before anyone could pull a box or call it in. The fire was a little piss ass, nickel and dime, one room job. We didn't need the full assignment. By the time the last companies arrived, the fire was out and the boy was on the way to the ER. Yet the little guy died." Frank listened while sipping his tea. It felt good to verbalize the frustration, especially to someone who understood so well.

"Jack said the neighbors freaked when they found out where the mother was," Frank said quietly.

"Yeah, Jack witnessed the whole show," Bob sighed. "I think the Chief called for police backup to protect her as much as have her arrested."

"That's hard to watch," Frank said. "She's hysterical because her son was taken to the hospital and she's arrested for child endangerment."

"My old man always told me," Bob said thoughtfully. "When you become a parent, you're not allowed one mistake. You make a million of them and get away with it, but you're not allowed one because that one could cost you your child."

Each man took a sip of tea and sat quietly for a moment. "Now I have to write a report on our actions at the fire," Bob continued. Before he could beg off another cup of tea and say he had to leave, Frank made a suggestion.

"You know, Jack was here earlier and left some department report paper. Why don't you write the report on the computer?"

Bob thought about it. He had never worked on a computer before. Did it take some special skills? What was the learning curve like? He was about to decline when Frank jumped up and walked over to the machine. "You look intimidated," he chuckled. "Don't be. It's like a typewriter except you can change what you write and then print it out. Come on."

Bob smiled, finished his tea, and walked over to have a look. He unconsciously rubbed his eyes before leaning over to see.

"Did you get something in your eye last night?" Frank asked.

"No, no," Bob replied. "My eye's just tired. It's from the stress, studying, working, dealing with women."

Bob was unsure where he came up with that last remark. He was dealing with one woman only and she was proving to be more than enough. Frank laughed at his explanation than turned more serious.

"Didn't I hear something about buzzing hands the other night?" he asked.

"I thought your arrival put an end to that part of the conversation, at least until I got in the car," Bob answered. "But I'm sure the girls discussed it with Chingli." He was tired of talking about it. The subject may be new to his friends, but it was very old for him. He chided himself on mentioning it in front of Kathy. Now everything was getting blown out of proportion. "It's just my body's reaction to stress," he repeated for the umpteenth time. "It comes and goes depending on how my days go."

"Stress is insidious," Frank commented with understanding. "They don't know a lot about its effects. I'd say you should go relax

189

with Kathy, but that doesn't sound like a viable option at the moment."

Bob chuckled ironically. "No, we've been having words or more accurately we had words. She is apparently not speaking with me right now."

Frank got up to pour another mug of tea while he was talking. It appeared to Bob that his friend was preparing for an extended counseling session. Should he impose on Frank even more? They still had a report to write and Bob had an idea floating in his head he wanted to write down before it floated away.

"And your words were about what subject?" Frank prodded.

"About me seeing a doctor," Bob answered.

"Let me pass on a bit of wisdom one of my chiefs gave to me," Frank offered. "I call it the possibility probability dichotomy. Women fear what is possible. Men fear what is probable." Bob shook his head energetically in agreement when he heard this. How true it was, he thought. There was probably nothing wrong with him that could not be straightened out by a quiet vacation, but the possibilities were endless.

"A little advice from somebody who has been there, give the girl a call. She is concerned more than angry," Frank counseled. "Then placate her right now. Tell her you'll see a doctor if things don't improve, something like that. She'll calm down."

"I told her that the other night as she got out of the car," Bob admitted. "It didn't seem to work."

"My boy," Frank laughed. "You can't expect a woman to calm down instantly. Call her. I think she's waiting for your call."

"You're probably right," Bob sighed. "I'll call her before I go to work, but I have a report to write first."

"Come on," Frank insisted. "I'll introduce you to my new playmate."

Bob sat down in front of the computer with Frank standing next to him. The ease of writing on a word processor was surprising, even if he only pecked at it with two fingers. This was a typewriter on steroids. After the report was printed out, Bob had a request. "Do you mind if I type in some thoughts I've had in my head since I woke up?"

Frank simply gestured toward the computer with a smile. Bob began to type. After finishing, he printed it out and then thought to impose on Frank one last time for an opinion. It surprised him that he had the need and the nerve to share a poem with another firefighter, but this poem was different from anything he had previously written. It had a purpose, to be cathartic.

"If it's not asking too much, could you give me your opinion," Bob asked. Frank was the perfect person to critique his little creation.

Waiting: A Fireman's Poem

Waiting as I lie in bed
Staring at the paint peeling from the metal ceiling
Waiting to be called to tragedy
I earn my living waiting and hoping

Hoping that the call will not come
That my services will not be needed

191

Hoping that the dilapidated buildings that surround me will survive
  another night
Fearing that a bell will call me to action

Fearing that a small life will need me
And that I will arrive too late
Fearing a young mother will be lost in panic
Rushing to escape the flames of revenge

Rushing down a brass pole
The heat of friction burning my hands
Rushing up the avenue toward a cloud of smoke
Reaching for a hose to try and save a life

Reaching for the last ounce of strength and courage
As I darken the bright glow of the fire on the third floor
Reaching for a small hand; rushing to find a pulse; fearing none will be found;
  hoping beyond hope for a small life; waiting, waiting . . . .

Frank read through the piece, dropped his hand with the paper to his side, and looked up at the ceiling for a moment as if he were organizing his thoughts. "You just wrote this?" he asked.

Bob had a feeling of déjà vu. Kathy had asked him the same question in the diner. He felt like he was going to develop a complex of doubting himself or at least what he wrote. It seemed every time he asked for an opinion, the first response was to ask if he really wrote it.

"Well, some of the ideas have been in my head since a job we had last year," Bob explained. "There were no flames of revenge last night, but the feeling I walked away with, the frustration, that solidified last night."

Frank sighed, held up the poem with his right hand, and pointed at it with his left. "This is why Kathy can't get enough of you," he told Bob. "You used what, a couple of hundred words, and captured the heart of a big city firefighter."

Bob laughed at Frank's dramatic assessment. "I think you're getting a little carried away," he said. "But do you think it will calm her down?"

"Definitely," Frank assured him.

With the report out of the way and a pacifier for Kathy written, Bob felt pretty comfortable. That was until he remembered the Chief's take on Kathy's value as a study partner. Frank might be able to help there also, he thought. If Chingli had said something or if he had overheard something, then his friend's opinion would be priceless.

"Can I ask you something that is totally off the subject?" Bob started, playing with the empty mug beside the computer.

"Shoot," Frank answered.

"The Chief and I had a little chat last night about studying and how Kathy is helping me," he explained. "And he gave this analysis about how Kathy is my ace in the hole because she was a television reporter and so gave presentations every night, not just any presentations, but concise, pertinent, coherent presentations, just like they'll want on the exam."

Frank shook his head in agreement. "I never really thought about it, but I agree with him. She's one hell of a woman, Bob."

That was not what he wanted to hear. That nagging question of "What is a woman like her doing with a man like me?" kept cropping

193

up. "I never thought of it either," he confessed. "But as soon as the Chief said it, it made sense and scared the hell out of me."

Frank looked surprised. "Why would it scare you?"

Bob took a deep breath and then took the plunge. He had never opened up like this to anyone except maybe Jack and even Jack had not heard this part of it yet.

"I can't figure out what a woman like Kathy sees in a man like me," Bob started. Frank attempted to interject a protest, but Bob held up his finger to stop him. "I need to get this out now or it might never come out. It'll just eat away at me. Now, when the Chief said that last night, the first thing that passed through my mind after 'wow' was 'Could she think I was using her to get promoted?' The next thing was if she did think that, how could I convince her otherwise? That's the part that scared me. I don't know how anyone can defend themselves against an accusation like that."

Frank stood there looking at Bob and shaking his head. "You know the two of you are the perfect couple," he laughed. "She talks to Chingli about how you're the perfect guy for her and how she's nervous about it. You're talking to me about how she's this exceptional woman, the perfect match for you and you're nervous about it. Are the two of you trying to drive yourselves crazy over your perfect match? Can't you just accept the fact that the girl is crazy about you?"

Bob felt a little like he was being admonished by a favorite teacher. The way Frank put it made him feel foolish. The advice he was getting was the advice Chief Simmons had given him last night verbatim.

"The Chief told me last night that acceptance is the beginning of wisdom," Bob chuckled.

"That's why he's a Deputy Chief, because he's so damn smart," Frank pointed out. "The best advice I can give you right now is call the girl; give her a good excuse about why you didn't call this morning, and then accept the way she feels about you. There are a lot worse things in the world." With that Frank walked over to his desk, picked up the phone, and held it out to Bob.

Chapter Seventeen

Kathy turned her car onto Franklin Avenue in Nutley, content with the results of her work. Bob sat quietly beside her. It had been a little more complicated than first anticipated because of his health insurance. Since he belonged to a health maintenance organization, it was necessary to jump through a few hoops to get what she wanted. Now it was game on, or as the announcer at the Olympics said, "Let the Games begin." She had the advantage. He did not know the ball was in play. With the coaching Stacey had given her on how to guide the conversation in a doctor's office, Kathy was certain she could get a referral to another doctor. Maybe he just needed a nutritionist to correct a vitamin deficiency. Would his insurance cover something like that she wondered.

Why Bob had chosen an HMO was beyond her. It was too new an idea. How could he know it would work the way the salesman claimed it would? In theory the concept sounded great and reinforced what she had been saying all long. Take care of problems when they are small and avoid the expense of something major. One large disadvantage was you had to see doctors who participated in the plan. If your doctor did not, you had to find another doctor who did. Thankfully, the ophthalmologist Stacey had suggested was a participant in Bob's HMO. There had been no need to persuade Bob to see an ophthalmologist instead of an optometrist. His primary doctor had referred him to one.

They passed through the business center of Nutley quietly. She could tell Bob was not happy with the situation he found himself in. His insistence that there was nothing wrong with him had fallen flat with the doctor. Now he would have a thorough eye exam, which included dilating his pupils, thank God. That gave her the perfect excuse to accompany him. He would not be able to drive home. The businesses along the street gave way to an expansive lawn that swept down from a geriatric center. Branch Brook Park appeared off to their left, its springtime cherry blossoms having given way to the heat of a Jersey summer. Clara Maas Hospital stood on a hill across from the park. They had an appointment in the professional building next to the hospital.

"I still don't know why I should see an eye doctor," Bob said breaking the silence at last. "My eye sight is 20/20."

"And we want to keep it that way," Kathy reminded him. "It's a lot easier to study when you can see, don't you think?" She hoped it did not appear that she was gloating, but she was. It had taken weeks to reach this jump off point. Did he realize this might just be the beginning of their search? Whether or not his eye symptoms were related to his other problems, an eye doctor was not going to tell him why his hands felt strange. That would take another referral to another specialist. They would have to chip away at the problem, but she would make certain he found an answer. It did not matter if he wanted one or not. He was going to get one. She was intent on that.

Kathy turned at the entrance to the medical center and guided the car through the short winding road up a hill. After parking in the lot next to the building, the couple walked to the concrete stairs leading up to the side entrance and climbed to the doors. She had a pair of his sunglasses in her purse for him to wear when they left. The office had told her the doctor would probably dilate his eyes, so he would need some protection when he stepped back out into the sunlight. Bob opened the door and invited her to step in with a gentle wave of his arm. Reluctance was written on his face. She knew he had been placating her these past weeks, but it did not matter. Just avoid any victory dances, she told herself. This is the beginning, not the end.

After filling out the requisite forms and waiting for twenty minutes, the two found themselves in an exam room with Doctor Erhler and his assortment of examination machines.

"Tell me what brings you here today?" the doctor asked while glancing at the forms Bob had filled out. Before Bob could answer the doctor threw another question his way. "You're a Newark firefighter? Do you know Hank Crane?"

"Yes," Bob smiled. "I work with him."

"Really," the doctor chuckled. "His son has been a patient of mine since I started. Hank told me quite a few stories."

Bob seemed to relax a little after hearing that. Kathy could not believe how lucky she was. Maybe he would be more forthcoming because there was a fire department connection.

"So, Bob," Doctor Erhler asked in a lighter, friendlier tone. "What ails you?"

"I have this, I really don't know how to describe it, doc," Bob explained. "There's a blurry spot in my peripheral vision out here somewhere." He reached out to his right indicating a position above his head.

"Okay, let me have a look at you," the doctor said more seriously.

After completing the exam, he asked Bob if he had anything else unusual. It looked to Kathy like Bob was about to answer no, so she stepped in.

"His hands have a buzzing sensation, doctor," she interjected. Bob was none too pleased.

"I don't think that has anything to do with why we're here," Bob said impatiently.

"Buzzing sensation?" Doctor Erhler inquired. "Anything else? Other strange sensations? Sometimes we can put it all together in one diagnosis."

Bob looked a little taken aback. "I just put it off to stress," he admitted. "Those sensations are in my legs and feet at times, but they all just come and go."

The doctor suddenly appeared very interested. "Did you say all of this comes and goes?" he asked.

"Yes, it depends on how stressful life gets," Bob answered.

"How about when the weather gets hot and humid, do the symptoms worsen?" the doctor probed.

Kathy could see Bob did not like the words symptoms at all.

"I wouldn't call them symptoms," he insisted.

"Let's call them sensations then," the doctor compromised. "Do the sensations grow stronger in hot, humid weather?"

Kathy was now purely a spectator and she knew it. It was obvious the doctor had something in mind and he appeared to be concerned about whatever it was. She could not guess how Bob would answer the question. He had never mentioned anything like that. Her beau was sitting quietly. Hopefully he was thinking about the doctor's question and not about how she had brought him to this office.

"Now that you mention it, doc," Bob confessed. "I think they might or at least they seem to persist in hot weather."

"Persist meaning they don't go away?" was the doctor's next question.

"Yes," Bob answered. "You think it's more than stress?"

"I'm an ophthalmologist, Bob," the doctor said. "Your retina, optic nerve, and cornea all appear normal. But you apparently have a floater. Not unheard of at your age, but usually reserved for people who have a few more years under their belts. I can't say why right now. It would be better to speak with someone who might be able to put the pieces of the puzzle together."

"Could this be serious, doctor?" Kathy asked unable to accept the role of spectator any longer.

Doctor Erhler turned to her and gave an understanding smile. He must have dealt with hundreds even thousands of women worried about their men, she thought. Why was it that women felt the need to ask the obvious questions while men just listened to what doctors said and sometimes, not always, but sometimes followed their advice? "As far as I'm concerned," the doctor said patiently. "He appears to have a floater in the peripheral vision of his right eye. Could it be an indication of something more serious? Maybe. It might also just be stress, I can't say right now."

Bob gave Kathy a look that said, "Now look what you've done." Then turned to the doctor and asked in a resigned tone, "Do you have someone you work with?"

As they walked back to the car, Bob was deep in thought. Kathy's heart was racing. He clearly was not happy. She wondered if he would take it out on her. She was the one who had insisted he see a doctor. Their relationship had never faced anything like the uncertainty just given to them. This "it might be nothing but then again it might be something" pronouncement left them in limbo. The thought of his complaints evolving into a serious condition had not crossed her mind. Vitamin deficiency was the worst she had considered. Now he suddenly needed an appointment with a neurologist. Was Bob going to accept the necessity of this or was he going to jump down her throat? He was wearing his sunglasses as the doctor had suggested. That was a good sign. At least he was listening to advice. Since she was at a loss on how to start a conversation in this situation, she decided to fall back on firehouse like humor.

"Those glasses really make you look sexy," she tried, praying he would react well.

"Careful little girl," Bob came back with a smile. "If you tempt this old man with statements like that, he might offer you some candy and suggest a play date."

Kathy felt a wave of relief flow through her. Tears began to well up in her eyes, so she glanced at the park across Franklin Avenue to give herself a second to rein in her emotions. Then she went back at him.

"Do you realize you are my prisoner?" she asked as they reached the car.

"Your prisoner?" he asked snidely. "How's that?"

She unlocked the passenger side door and turned to him, her face almost against his chest. Looking up at his face, she said, "You are totally dependent on me because you can't drive with your eyes like that. I can take you anywhere and have my way with you."

He looked down at her, bent over, and kissed her gently. "Do with me what you will," he whispered into her ear. "I surrender." Then he slid into the seat. She jumped around to the driver's side and hopped in behind the wheel. It was only fifteen minutes to Bob's apartment and he could not study for at least another hour.

Chapter Eighteen

The air was sweltering. It was the dog days of summer and Jersey was in the midst of a hot, hazy, and humid heat wave. A calm wind and cloudless sky made the temperature hotter than the ninety-four degrees in the shade reported on the radio when Bob parked his car. He was standing on the PATH train platform in Harrison waiting for the World Trade Center train into New York. It had been a couple of months since he had made this trek into the city. Focusing on the promotional exam left little time for Chinese, but he could not resist the one day class being offered today at the Chinese Language Study Institute. How to convert complex Chinese characters into simplified characters was worth the trip. The sun was still to the east so he could stand in the shade thrown by the station building. In an hour it would be unbearable where he stood.

Bob was perspiring freely just standing watching for the train to leave Newark's Penn Station. The high rise office buildings of New Jersey's largest city dominated the skyline looking west. If he had the inclination and the fortitude to tolerate the heat, a few steps beyond the shade of the station house would have revealed the New York skyline looming through the haze to the east. Looking south down the tracks, he would be able to see the train depart. It was well under a mile between the two stations, but the Passaic River lie between them. While waiting in the heat, he could not help assessing himself. Were the sensations he spoke with Doctor Erhler about yesterday worsened by the heat? In the sauna that engulfed him everything seemed accentuated. Was that the power of suggestion or was he acknowledging changes that had been ignore before?

The small briefcase he was carrying looked out of place with his shorts and tee shirt. The case contained his textbook and a Chinese to English dictionary. He had just begun to learn how to use the dictionary when the exam was announced, so his skills were rudimentary at best. Since the class was about converting complex to simplified characters and the dictionary was for the latter, Bob doubted it would be useful. Better to have it with him just in case it would help to get more out of the class.

Looking across the river, Bob saw a train leave the station and so stepped out into the sunlight. It arrived quickly, minimizing his time in Hades. The chime of the doors opening followed by the announcement "World Trade Center train, next stop Journal Square" gave him a feeling of familiarity. For the past year, he had ridden the train to Jersey City and then switch to the 33rd Street train. At 23rd Street, he switched again to the F Train of the New York subway which took him to 42nd Street. The Institute was a short walk from the subway stop. It was the best five bucks he could spend. The entertainment was phenomenal, that is if you enjoyed watching people. New Jersey was about as diverse a place as you could wish for and New York City was New York City.

Bob had no trouble finding a seat, there were few people riding the tubes this time of day on a Saturday. Setting down in a seat at the center of the car, he opened his case and retrieved both the textbook and the dictionary. These he opened on his lap and began to practice looking up characters. His tee shirt was damp with sweat from his time on the platform, making it cling to his back. When he leaned back on the cushion of the seat, his body felt a momentary shock from the chill of the plastic. The air conditioning kept the temperature in the train well below the furnace on the station platform. He would not fall asleep on the ride into the city. When they stopped at the Journal Square station, Bob picked up his books and case and hopped across the platform to the 33rd Street train that was waiting there. This train was a little more crowded, but he still had no trouble finding a seat. The firefighter dropped down next to a young man who had the appearance of a college student.

He went back to his dictionary work, but quickly discovered the guy beside him was not shy and was very opinionated.

"Is that Chinese you're studying?" the young man asked.

"Yes," Bob answered simply, unsure what else to say to a question with such an obvious answer. The chimes announcing the closing of the doors sounded followed by the announcement that this was the 33rd Street train and the next stop was Grove Street. The rattle of the train passing over the rails filled the background as he waited for the young man to set the direction of the conversation.

"Why would you want to study Chinese?" was his next question. "I mean everybody speaks English, don't they?"

Bob was not sure how to respond. He now doubted his first impression of this guy being a college student. Was his last question born out of ignorance or arrogant chauvinism? Curious, Bob decided to probe a little and see what his fellow passenger thought would be useful.

"What would you suggest people study?" he asked as the train passed into the tunnel leading under Jersey City and then under the Hudson River. The windows became black as the sunlight vanished and the sounds of metal on metal grew more pronounced. The volume of their conversation instinctively rose a level.

"You mean what language?" the young man asked.

Bob shook his head yes, not knowing what to expect.

"Latin, people should study Latin," he responded confidently.

Bob almost dropped his books. He could not believe what he had just heard. As far as he knew, there were no native speakers of Latin left on earth. Could the guy have meant Romance languages? "Do you mean Latin dialects?" Bob quizzed, giving the kid a way out.

"No," was the confident reply. "People should study Latin. You see, if you know Latin then you can recognize the roots of thousands of English words."

With that answer, Bob knew he was dealing with someone who had spent too much time in class and not enough time among people. The train was winding and squeaking its way under the Hudson as he thought of a way to convince the guy next to him that foreign language study was not a waste of time.

"So, you really think that Latin would be useful in today's world?" Bob began.

"Yes, don't you see?" was the reply. "It gives you the key to so many words. It's also used in medicine and law."

"I see your point, but don't you think it's a little short sighted?" Bob asked and then pushed on without getting an answer. "I really only study Chinese as a hobby. A friend of mine majored in it. He got me interested. His wife is from Taiwan and assures me, even though English is a required subject in their schools, very few can actually communicate in it."

The train had wound through the trans-Hudson tubes and was pulling into the Christopher Street station. The young man stood up to disembark with an apologetic smile. "Really, that's interesting," he replied. "I guess what I mean is the political and business leaders of the world all speak English. Why go through the trouble of studying a foreign language? Can't we use our study time for more important topics?"

With that the train doors opened and Bob's entertainment walked off. The only word he could use to describe the conversation was surreal, although it did hit on a particle of truth in his case. He had stopped his foreign language study in order to prepare for the promotional exam. But then he studied for enrichment only. God help America if the attitude that had just stepped off the train became widespread.

As the train rushed through the stations, Bob gathered his things and stood up. When he stood there was an uncomfortable feeling in his stomach and his head was spinning a little. Putting it off to the effects of standing too quickly, he exited the train and made his way to the city subway. It felt like a blast furnace in the subway tunnel which did not help his spinning head or queasy stomach. By the time he stepped off the small elevator into the Language Institute he felt nauseous. Taking a moment to sit on a chair and attempt to calm his stomach did not help. His breakfast was churning. The cool air inside the building had no effect. There was a burp to warn him and send him scurrying to the men's room where he lost his breakfast in one violent eruption. Bob knew he could not sit through a class no matter how interesting its content, so he excused himself after picking up the class material and began the long journey home. He could only pray his stomach had emptied itself.

* * * * * * * * * * * * * * * * * * * *

Kathy picked up the phone and poked in Bob's number. He should have been back from New York an hour ago, but he had not bothered to call her. A little annoyed at his newly developed habit of forgetting to call when he said he would, she put it off to preoccupation with what the doctor had said. Doctor Erhler had asked if his symptoms or should she say his sensations were affected by the heat. Today would be the litmus test. This heat and humidity would beat down the hardiest of souls. If his symptoms worsened as the temperature rose, he would be absolutely wretched today.

He picked up the phone on the fifth ring. As soon as she heard his voice, Kathy knew something was wrong.

"I made it to school and then promptly vomited in the men's room," Bob moaned weakly, then put down the phone. She heard what sounded like dry heaves in the background.

"Bob?" she called into the phone.

"Yes, I'm here," he said weakly. "I guess I caught a stomach virus. I'm gonna lie down with a bowl next to me and see if I can't sleep it off."

"I'm on my way over," Kathy told him.

"No, no," he replied with some energy. "I don't want you catching this."

Kathy was already resigned to catching whatever he had. She had been with him every step of the way yesterday. If he had a bug, she had it too.

"Bob, think of what happened yesterday," she reminded him. "I appreciate your chivalry, but you're a day late. Do you think you have a fever?"

He put the phone down once more. This was followed by the sound of him retching again. When he recovered, he picked up the phone and answered hoarsely, "No, don't think I have a fever. At least not right now, but the room is spinning."

"Do you have any crackers or cola?" she asked remembering her mother's remedies when she was growing up.

"I don't think so," Bob muttered.

It did not surprise Kathy in the least. He never had a lot of food or drink in his apartment. The refrigerator was empty for the most part, maybe a six pack of beer, grape jelly, and a half gallon of milk. If he cooked a meal for himself the ingredients were purchased and immediately prepared. The freezer contained ice and that was about it. An occasional loaf of rye bread and some peanut butter rounded out the culinary ingredients in his neat little bachelor's world. There was a paucity of junk food, although when she dropped things in his kitchen garbage can, she had seen Burger King containers and pizza boxes. His nutritional intake was better than the average single male, but he was not a saint.

"I'll stop and pick some things up," Kathy asserted. "You rest, no need to get out of bed when I get there."

She hung up the phone then quickly picked it up again. Stacey was not a doctor yet, but she was far enough along in nursing school to be a good source of reliable information. They had not had a chance to talk since Stacey had told her about the possibility of attending medical school. Had she discussed it with Ray yet? Kathy felt guilty about the sudden intrusion without a word in between, but she felt desperate. Home remedies and old wives tales were all she had to go by. Was there some significance to him not having a fever? What about the room spinning? She did not remember any spinning rooms when she had an upset stomach as a child. Punching in Stacey's number, she hoped her friend would not take offense to her "silence until needed" recent history.

Stacey answered the phone with her usual energetic hello. Hopefully she would remain cheerful when she learned who was calling.

"Stace, Bob's sick," Kathy blurted out, not knowing how else to begin.

"What happened?" was the response.

"I'm not sure," Kathy began to explain. "He went into New York and then he didn't call when he got back, so I called him and he sounded absolutely wretched when he picked up the phone. He didn't say that much. Just that he had a stomach virus. Then he put the phone down to vomit, came back and told me I shouldn't go over to help."

"Stomach viruses are very contagious," Stacey warned her.

"We spent the whole day together yesterday," Kathy replied. "I already have whatever he has. It's just taking longer to come out. I want to get him set up before I get knocked down. He doesn't have a thing in his place to eat or drink. I remember crackers and cola when I was a kid, but I don't know if that's really appropriate." Kathy was breathless when she finished, shocked at herself for becoming flustered at a common stomach virus, but he sounded so needy.

"Okay, Kath, slow down," Stacey reassured her. "He's not three years old. It's probably a roto-virus, so he'll get over it in a day or two. The most important thing is to keep him hydrated. Cola might calm his stomach a little, but that bit of wisdom is from the same place you got it. They just tell us to pay attention to hydration."

Kathy felt a little calmer. He was a grown man after all, she told herself. Why the over reaction? She decided it was probably the worries about his health over the past few days that had tipped the scales to the irrational. Spending time in doctors' offices make one aware of all that can go wrong with the human body.

"Sorry Stace," Kathy said. "We went to the doctor's yesterday. I guess it made me oversensitive."

"What did the doctor say?" Stacey asked.

"What did Ray say?" Kathy countered.

"You first, we can talk about Ray later," Stacey insisted.

"All he would say is Bob has a floater in his right eye," Kathy sighed. "When he heard about the buzzing sensation in Bob's hands, he became more interested and suggested he see a neurologist."

Kathy found herself hoping Stacey could shed a little more light on what the doctor suspected. She realized that was asking too much of a nursing student and so moved on to the question she had already asked Stacey.

"So what did Ray say?" she persisted.

"Oh, he was thrilled, then conflicted, then proud, then nervous," Stacey answered. "In the end proud ruled the day. I'm sure everyone in the firehouse will hear about it. Everyone, that is, except Bob. He should stay home for a day or two and recover."

"They're not due back until Monday," Kathy said after working through their schedule in her head. "It's a shame. He's off for the weekend and he's sick, but I have to get going or he's going to die from dehydration or hunger."

Stacey laughed at Kathy's sarcastic self-criticism. "Don't be so hard on yourself," she counseled. "We all flip out occasionally when life blindsides us. But don't hesitate to call if things get worse."

"I won't," Kathy promised. "And Stace, thanks for the help in getting him to a doctor. Everything is going the way we hoped it would." Kathy hung up the phone; gathered everything she thought might be useful; and dashed out the door.

When she arrived at Bob's, it was already late afternoon. The air remained stagnant, waves of heat could be seen shimmering up from the black top, and the street was unusually quiet for a summer weekend afternoon. The only sounds were shouts of children coming from a neighbor's pool. This was not a day for bicycles and baseball. The quiet hum of air conditioners working hard came to her as she crossed the street and unlocked the building door. Kathy stepped into the small foyer with a bag of groceries in one hand and her purse in the other. The temperature dropped dramatically as soon as she crossed the threshold. Even silk blouses were unbearably hot in this weather. At least Bob had an air conditioner in his bedroom. She anticipated the rest of the apartment would be uncomfortable, but nothing could be done about it.

When she opened the apartment door, the sound of dry heaves coming from Bob's bathroom greeted her. She closed the door and looked into the closet like room that contained the sink and toilet. Bob was on his knees saying his prayers to the porcelain god. If this were from a hangover, it would be comical. Instead it renewed her concern. Why do things like this always happen on weekends when you cannot get hold of a doctor?

"Hello, babe," Kathy said quietly. "Can I help you?"

"Yeah," Bob said weakly. "If you have a gun, shoot me and put me out of my misery." He stood up, supporting himself with one hand on either wall and staggered out of the narrow room.

Kathy braced him up by sliding under his arm and led him to the bedroom. He was drenched with sweat and appeared to have no equilibrium to speak of. After helping him lie down in the air conditioning, she got a towel and wiped his face and chest. No need for a chill from lying covered with sweat in an air conditioned room.

"You look great," he said.

"You look horrible," she replied. "When did you drink something last?"

"Please don't talk about food or drink," he moaned.

"Bob, you have to drink," she insisted. "Dehydration is your biggest worry."

"Yes Doctor Stanley," he teased.

"Not funny," she snapped. "That's from Stacey not me. Where is your doctor's number? I don't like the way you look." She realized that his appearance made it impossible for her to sit quietly and watch him retch. After a quick check of his forehead to see if he was feverish, she retrieved the doctor's number from the drawer Bob had pointed to. A message was left with the answering service before she went to the kitchen to pour a glass of cola. Stirring it vigorously to remove the carbonation, Kathy offered the flat result to Bob and prayed it would calm his stomach. It did not. The cola was promptly deposited into the bowl Bob had taken into the bedroom in case this happened. She took it to the bathroom to empty, cleaned it in the kitchen sink, and carried it back to the bedroom. When she stepped back into the cool air, Bob was lying with his hands on the sides of his head.

"Everything is spinning," he complained. "I can't stop it. Even with my eyes closed I feel like I'm spinning."

Kathy had been there an hour and had only seen Bob's condition worsen. Was the doctor going to return her call? She had been putting off calling Stacey so the doctor could get through, but now she was at her wits end. Scolding herself internally for being so weak, she went to the kitchen and picked up the phone.

"Stace, it's me," Kathy said trying not to sound desperate. "He looks completely washed out, white as a ghost. I can't get any fluids in him. What should I do?"

"Have you called his doctor?" Stacey asked calmly.

"Yes, no answer yet," Kathy told her. "He says the room is spinning. He was lying in bed holding his head between his hands, trying to stop it from spinning."

"He has vertigo?" Stacey asked. "When did that begin?"

"I guess I left that out before," Kathy confessed. Stacey was quiet for a moment

"You're down the street from Clara Maas, right?" she asked.

"About ten minutes away," Kathy replied.

"There's something else going on here," Stacey told her. "A stomach virus doesn't give you vertigo. Maybe you should get him to the emergency room and have a doctor look him over. They might be able to give him something for the vertigo."

With that Kathy became a creature in perpetual motion. Dress Bob, grab purse, keys, bowl in case he vomits, down the stairs supporting him so he does not lose his balance, dance across the street, into the car, and dash to the ER.

When Kathy called Stacey again it was after nine o'clock. Bob was resting in bed, his stomach calmed by an anti-vertigo medication. He was also on antibiotics only because the ER doctor could not find anything obviously wrong with him. By the process of elimination he settled on a diagnosis and sent them on their way. Whatever caused Bob's symptoms, the medication was working making Kathy glad they lived in the twentieth century.

"Stace, it's Kathy," she whispered into the phone even though Bob's door was closed.

"What did the doctor say?" Stacey asked.

Kathy took a deep breathe before telling the story. She had an explanation, so the pressure was off. Just had to take a second to calm myself, she thought. She exhaled and answered Stacey. "After a lot of questions, taking his temperature and blood pressure," Kathy started, then immediately got sidetracked. "His blood pressure was eighty over fifty-nine. I couldn't believe it. Anyway the doctor decided he must have a middle ear infection. He prescribed an antibiotic and a medication for vertigo."

"A middle ear infection?" Stacey sounded suspicious. "But he had no fever. That's unusual."

"I pointed that out to the doctor," Kathy said. "He said that happens sometimes."

"Okay, I'll take his word for it," Stacey said. "He's resting now?"

Kathy let out an audible sigh before answering. "Yes, thank God. He's sleeping. The doctor said to stay in bed for a few days until the medication does its work. His equilibrium should return quickly."

216

"So, you're going to camp out there," Stacey guessed.

"Well, at least until he can stand on his own," Kathy replied.

"And his apartment has no food and you have nothing prepared for even one night. How are you going to survive?" Stacey asked rhetorically. "Ray and I will be there in a little bit. We'll keep Bob company while you go home and get your stuff and don't give me an argument!"

Kathy felt tears well up in her eyes. It had been a long day; without Stacey's help she did not know how she would have made it through. All she could do was whisper an emotional thank you into the phone.

Chapter Nineteen

"You sure you're okay?" Jack asked Bob. They were in the upstairs locker room throwing on their uniforms. They were both wearing shorts. Pulling turnout boots over bare legs was not comfortable and so was to be avoided whenever possible.

"I'll be fine," Bob assured him as he buttoned his shirt. "The head's not a hundred percent, but it's in the high nineties, kind of like the weather." He had been out of work for a week and could not take it anymore. The vertigo had subsided slowly. Reading had been impossible for the first few days. Kathy had ended up reading out loud to him and quizzing him on the material they had covered. He had found it very difficult to write, so he had to tell her responses to fire scenarios which he found incredibly hard to do. It was so easy for him with a pen and paper. Ideas seemed to flow from the pen out of their own volition. Saying them out loud stymied the creative process.

The whole affair had shown him how important equilibrium is to so many of life's everyday tasks. Now that everything was approaching normal, there was no way he was staying home another day. Kathy had not been encouraging, but she had no way of knowing his status now. As soon as standing and walking without losing his balance were possible, she became dependent on him giving an honest assessment to know his condition. His honest assessment was that the downtime was driving him crazy. He could not tell her that, so he had given her an overly optimistic picture and she had relented. Bob never told Kathy about the thoughts he had when he was lying in bed before they went to the ER. "I will never be the same." Looking back, he realized it was a melodramatic idea of the moment that was quickly pushed to the back of his mind after seeing a doctor.

The two firefighters made their way down to the kitchen. Bob had not really spoken to the Chief or Captain Pete, so he expected them to throw questions his way. Ray had seen him at the worst point and Bob was sure he had informed everyone in the detailed manner a former detective would. As long as no one asked him to do a pirouette, he could fudge his way through the coming inquisition. When they hit the kitchen, it was the usual morning scene; a bunch of firefighters nursing coffee around the table. The crowd was short one man because Hector was on vacation. Bob went for the coffee then sat down at the table as if nothing had happened. The Captain and Chief jumped on him immediately.

"How are you feeling?" Captain Pete asked.

"Back to normal, Cap," Bob lied.

"From what Ray said," the Chief piped in. "You were in pretty bad shape."

Bob looked at Ray, who smiled at him. "Mr. Former Detective may have given a pessimistic assessment, Chief," Bob joked. "What did the future doctor have to say?" Hopefully, the last question would move the focus off his illness and onto Stacey's opportunity.

"The present nursing student thought you looked horrible," Ray interjected. "And I agreed. You were totally wiped out, but you look like your normal ugly self now."

"I'll take that as an acknowledgement that I look better," Bob chuckled.

"Okay," Captain Pete sighed. "But no ladders today, Bob."

"I agree," the Chief said. "And no driving. Come back slowly. I don't want to have to explain to your old man how I let you get banged up."

"Agreed Chief," Bob said hoping the examination was complete. "So Ray tell me about the scholarship and what you think."

Laughter from around the table greeted Bob's question. It must have been a popular topic of conversation while he was out. Ray put his elbows on the table, dropped his head into his hands, and moaned. "You know," he began raising his head up to reveal a seemingly bewildered face. "It must have been so much easier in the last century. You married a smart woman so she could help you out and you'd have smart kids. Now, you marry a smart woman and she just makes you look dumb by getting scholarships and having dreams of becoming a doctor."

That brought another round of laughter from everyone. Bob could see the pride in Ray even as he bemoaned his new situation. It dawned on him that Ray was now facing the same challenge he had been dealing with since Kathy entered his life. How to have a relationship with an exceptional woman and not lose yourself? Ray's next comment confirmed this.

"I can understand how Bob feels now," he sighed. "I always knew how smart she was, but now the world has discovered it."

Bob empathized with his buddy. It had taken him months to come to terms with dating someone like Kathy and he still was not sure she shared the depth of his feelings. At least Ray was married to his goddess. Having known her throughout his life was an advantage, but that could also complicate things. Ray had been the one Stacey looked up to; now she was going to take off and he might feel marginalized. It could change the whole dynamic of their relationship. That was tougher than anything Bob had faced. He had walked into his relationship with Kathy knowing what he was buying into. Ray was going to have to change.

"That's what happens when you give women the right to vote," Hank laughed.

That brought hoots from the assemblage. Jack moved down the bench away from Hank as if to avoid being contaminated by the comment. The Chief put his mug on the table and without taking his eyes off the coffee commented, "Think of all the wasted talent a hundred years ago."

"My wife uses all her talent to raise the next generation of talent," Captain Pete commented. "Now we have to use our talent to give the city a day's worth of work." A mixture of moans and laughter followed this as they stood up to begin the day's routine.

Bob sat at the watch room desk studying after lunch. The morning had gone smoothly. A couple of false alarms and a run to the projects had broken up the housework and in-service inspections. Now the afternoon would be his to do some catch up studying. The test would be at the end of the month. By that time he had to have absorbed the information in over a dozen textbooks and become proficient at writing essays that demonstrated he had converted that information into knowledge. If he passed it, it would be off to the races again to prep for the oral. Looking at the company journal, he saw the past week had been very slow. The first tour had not caught a working fire for two weeks. Hopefully, that trend would continue and he could put a dent in the material he needed to study.

After two hours of hitting the books, Bob got up to pour a cup of coffee. His eyes were getting heavy as the mid-afternoon crash crept up on him. He had to move around a little or he would not retain anything. Jack and Ray were in the basement working on an antique dresser Jack had picked up in an abandoned building. He wanted to surprise Gloria with it. The workmanship on the piece was impressive, solid oak all around, dovetailed drawers, dado-rabbit joints holding the top on. If Jack could do a decent job of stripping off the old paint and staining the wood to bring out its natural beauty, Gloria would be thrilled. The Captain and Chief were doing their daily paper work in their rooms and Hank was probably reading in the bunkroom. That left Bob as the only soul on the first floor. He poured the coffee and went back to study. As he sat down the hot line rang then the joker circuit on the alarm console clicked.

"Six," Bob barked into the phone.

"Six, on the box to Dassing Avenue and Whitney Street, we have several reports of fire."

"Dassing and Whitney, got it." Bob hung up the phone and pushed the button on the alarm console for the house gong. Then he stepped out onto the apparatus floor and shouted, "Everybody goes! Several reports of fire on Dassing and Whitney."

He could hear the sound of Jack and Ray coming up the stairs from the basement. After pushing the buttons to start the overhead doors up, the clunk of Hank coming down the stairs joined the cacophony. The Captain and Chief would not be far behind

Bob walked over to his boots, kicked off his shoes and slid his feet in. Ray opened the driver's door and turned on the battery so they could hear the coming radio transmission over the growing noise. A round of ten bells came over the circuit as the rig started. Chief Simmons had positioned himself between the rig and his gig at the front of the apparatus floor and waited to close the doors. Ray pulled out while the bells counted out the box location.

A cloud of gray wood smoke was hovering lazily over the street in front of the fire building when Ray turned onto Whitney Street. The humidity held the smoke to the ground like a wet blanket. He stopped at a hydrant on the corner of Dassing and Whitney. Captain Pete leaned out the window and shouted "Two lines!" Bob and Jack wrapped the three inch and two and a half inch hoses around the hydrant barrel and then jumped onto the back step. Bob push the signal button and Ray rolled down the street. The rig stopped just before the building which had smoke pushing out around the edges of the first floor doors and windows. Quickly throwing on their masks, the two firefighters went for the three lengths. Captain Pete, trusting his crew, went to help Ray hook up. Jack pulled the first few layers of hose out of the bed and began walking toward the building. Bob pulled out the rest and followed. As he crossed the sidewalk he noticed a distraught woman being comforted by others.

Jack hit the front door and halted immediately as if considering something. He threw his face piece on and rushed into the building. Bob flaked the excess hose out on the sidewalk and dove in after his friend. When he reached the front door the reason for Jack's momentary stop became evident. The smoke was down to the floor. They had a basement fire. Jack had to choose in an instant whether to attack the fire down the interior stairs or stretch to the basement door which was probably in the backyard. He had chosen the interior stairs. It was no doubt the quickest way, but also the most dangerous. Until they fought past the level of the basement ceiling, they would be in a chimney.

Bob donned his mask while feeding line into the building. He heard Jack's muffled shouts for water, stepped out of the smoke, and signaled Ray to wet the line. The hose came to life as water flowed down its length, surging past Bob into the gray cloud ahead of him. He stepped into that cloud and instantly lost all visual contact with the world. His field of vision was now a complete impenetrable gray. The instant he lost visual reference points his head began to spin. Three steps into the building and Bob found himself on the floor. He fought his way back up and fed line to Jack then fell hard. It was obvious that his equilibrium was not up to the task of working blind, so he began to crawl. When Jack pulled for more line, Bob stood up, pushed hose forward, and promptly fell again.

The sound of other companies arriving and that of the Captain moving toward him came through the smoke. Bob continued his dance with the floor until stopping at the stairs. He could hear Jack working the line in the basement and knew his buddy needed help down those stairs, but also knew there was a good chance of his falling down them. There was really no option. If he fell, he fell. It was part of the job. Jack pulled for more line and Bob pushed it down to him. Then he stepped into the chimney and hoped for the best.

"Bob, you okay?" the Chief asked. He had expected questions because he was limping a little. His act in the first floor hallway was hidden and did not seem to have done much damage. Maybe a few bruises, but nothing that would show right away. The fall down the stairs was harder to conceal and his knee had taken a shot. The Captain and Jack would both probably have questions about the noise on the stairs. Questions Bob was not sure he had answers to.

"Just banged my knee , Chief," Bob answered.

"Do you need to go to the ER?" the Chief continued his check.

"No, I don't think so," he replied. He had enough of emergency rooms over the past few weeks and had no intention of setting foot into another one any time soon. "I'll be okay after I walk it off."

"Okay, make sure you book it," the Chief relented.

"Will do Chief," Bob assured him before going to drop his tank. Ray stepped behind him when he reached the rig and grabbed the air cylinder. Bob released the harness and Ray took the mask off his back and placed it on the back step of the rig.

"Did you see that woman when we pulled up?" Bob asked over the hum of the engine pumping.

"You mean the hysterical one?" Ray asked.

Bob shook his head yes while he shed his turnout coat and helmet. He could feel the heat lift off his body even though the air around him was sweltering. His clothes and the inside lining of his coat were all drenched with sweat. Everything is relative, he thought. The diesel fume laced air felt fresh compared to the atmosphere inside the fire building.

"She's the owner of the building," Ray said with a pained look. "Going crazy because she had to cancel her home owners insurance yesterday. That kind of frustration is hard to watch."

"Canceled it yesterday?" Bob asked shaking his head in disbelief. She must have made the choice between insurance and food which meant she did not have the resources to repair the damage done by the fire. It was a small fire brought under control quickly as far as the Fire Department was concerned. It was a life altering event to the owner who must have worked a lifetime to buy this property.

"God that hurts," he muttered.

"Damn straight," Ray agreed. "You okay? You don't look good."

Bob figured he must look pretty spent because everyone was asking how he felt. Realizing he would have to swear Jack and Ray to secrecy before he admitted anything, he only muttered that he was fine then went to change his air tank. Ray motioned for him to rest and began changing it for him. Bob tried his best to appear normal, but the heat had worsened all the sensations he had discussed with the doctor. Those coupled with his still screwed up equilibrium, meant he did not feel the least bit normal. The only sensations that would pass for normal were the aches from his falling act inside the building. He knew there would be pain and bruising tomorrow. How to hide it or at least explain it to Kathy was his concern. Ray finished changing his tank, so Bob threw his turnout gear on, picked up his mask, and headed back into the building to finish up.

Chapter Twenty

Kathy stirred the contents of a large pot on her stove then adjusted the flame under it just enough to keep it simmering. The tantalizing scent of freshly made Italian red gravy filled her apartment. The average person would have been surprised that a single woman would have the size pot that sat on the front burner of her range. It was not a stereotypical piece of cookware for an unattached female. This type and size belonged in the kitchen of an experienced cook who had a hungry family to feed. Not that she was an inexperienced cook. She had been making red gravy with her mother and grandmother all her life. It was the volume of gravy simmering in front of her that did not fit with the single lifestyle. Of course, she had not purchased the pot. It had been a going away present from her mother. The not so veiled hint had been that she should maintain her cooking skills for when the right man came along. She placed the wooden spoon used to stir the tomato puree, tomato paste, water, and assorted seasoning on the spoon rest. The mixture would have to be kept at a slow boil for a while longer before it was transformed into Nini Anna's gravy. The author was hoping she had not lost her touch. It had been so long since she had prepared a large pot of her heritage meal.

Why was he doing this? Her conversation with Chingli months before crossed her mind. An old fashioned Sunday meal like her grandmother made to impress a man was out of the question. She could still hear herself ask, "Do you know how much work goes into one of those meals?" Now she was planning to cook one for Bob and was preparing one for the girls as practice. Insanity was the only word to describe it. Her publisher was asking questions about the oral history and here she was cooking. Why practice on the girls? She had told her mother cooking to prove herself was an outdated notion, but Kathy just could not shake the feeling that she had to display her culinary skills to be taken seriously by any man. That feeling obviously came from a lifetime of listening to her mother. Chingli had once warned her that women never really get away from their mothers, especially Chinese mothers.

To call the dinner a practice run for Bob was really a stretch, she consoled herself. After all the love and support Chingli, Gloria, and Stacey had given her over the past months, Kathy felt a need to thank them. Since she was half Italian and half Chinese, there was no way to avoid showing thanks with good food. So she was going to treat them to a meal like Nina Anna made on Sundays. It would be the four of them at the beginning. Frank was coming in later, a concession to Chingli since she did not want to simply abandon her husband and leave him to his own devices for dinner. The girl talk would have to be completed before he arrived. Maybe she could get an honest male perspective from Frank. The men in everyone else's lives were in the firehouse today, so Chingli's other half would have to sink or swim in a sea of estrogen.

Kathy added the meatballs she had cooked earlier. After stirring the contents one more time, she began preparing the ante pasta. Another pot filled with water sat on the rear burner awaiting everyone's arrival. The spaghetti would be the last thing prepared. She checked the roast beef, confirmed everything was safe, and went to change out of her cooking clothes. This was a dress rehearsal after all.

Stacey and Gloria arrived together with a bottle of wine and a lot of questions. Kathy put the wine aside and held off the questions because Chingli was walking up the front path. After they had all settled in the living room and Kathy checked dinner one more time, the questions resumed.

"How did he look the last time you saw him?" Stacey asked.

Kathy tried to put her feelings aside and give an honest, objective answer. "He looked like he was normal, but having a bad day."

"Normal, but having a bad day?" Gloria asked. "How often does he have a bad day?"

The question brought Kathy up short. She had not given the answer a lot of thought. It had come out naturally. Only with Gloria's question had the absurdity of it occurred to her. Had she become so accustomed to Bob's seemingly ever changing condition that another category of describing his health had emerged? Her stunned silence must have been plainly evident to the three women on her couch. Chingli gently prodded her out of shock. "Meimei, does Bob have many of these normal but bad days?"

"I . . . I don't know," Kathy stuttered. "Until Gloria asked the question, I hadn't thought about it. I just accepted it. Now that I think about it, that way of describing him evolved over the past months.

When he's feeling stressed out, he mentions his eyes and hands or whatever. That's become a bad day."

Stacey had a concerned look on her face. "When I asked around school, most people had no idea what it could be. A few have said it might be in his head, which would support his stress theory," Stacey reported. "But I had an opportunity to discuss it with one of my professors. He's a neurologist and thought it was an interesting case. His advice was to see a neurologist, so he agreed with the eye doctor."

"Meaning it could be a neurological problem?" Kathy asked.

"No one will say," Stacey replied.

She was not looking for answers to Bob's mysterious health issues, so Kathy was surprised by the sudden disappointment she felt. At least a consensus seemed to be building. "I'm going to make an appointment with a neurologist whether he likes it or not," she said vehemently. This declaration caused a pause in the conversation which allowed Chingli to subtly change the subject.

"So, how do you feel about Bob?" Chingli asked.

"Worried," Kathy confessed. Her friends shook their heads emphatically. She knew all they could do was give support. Whatever Bob's problems might be, they were beyond anyone in the room

"We're all worried," Chingli reassured her. "Besides worried, how does your heart feel? Has his illness given you doubts?"

"Doubts?" Kathy asked with surprise. "No, there are no doubts in my heart."

"He is no longer a super man," Chingli pointed out.

Kathy laughed at the description her friend used. She had never thought of Bob as a super man. That may be an image that young firefighters have of themselves, but she had not held that view since she was old enough to know what her father actually did for a living.

"Firefighters may think they're indestructible," Kathy mused. "But I know they're not."

"So, how do you feel?" Chingli persisted. "Is the magic . . . how does Frank say it . . . wearing thin?"

Kathy laughed and bowed her head. Leave it to Chingli to call her on the carpet and demand an answer. "You don't pull any punches, do you jiejie?" she observed.

"Pull punches? *Shi shenme yisi?*" Chingli asked.

"You don't hesitate to ask hard questions," Kathy explained.

"Why should I? You are my meimei," Chingli stated.

Kathy thought about how to answer. Had Bob's troubles made him damaged goods or was she too involved for that to happen. It took only an instant to consider the question. The answer sat lightly on her heart and was felt by every fiber in her being.

"You can't change love the way you change clothes, can you?" she asked with a laugh. "His illness, whatever it is, only made him more human and so more lovable." Suddenly she found herself confessing, "Sometimes, I just lie there with him beside me and watch his chest rise and fall and I feel so full, so complete. I know it's infatuation and hormones and all that other science, but I just feel love and I feel so vulnerable that I pray, pray he feels the same way. Then I lean my head on his chest and fall asleep listening to his heart, satisfied, fulfilled, feeling like my life has purpose."

The room became silent for a minute. Then Gloria said softly, "Kathy, listen to yourself. You're living a poem." Kathy shook her head, too full of emotions to speak.

"Do you think your prays have been answered?" Stacey asked.

"If they haven't, I'm in trouble," Kathy sighed. She felt the magic of the moment melt away when the reality of what she might be facing over the next few weeks returned. "When will Frank get here?" she asked, not sure she wanted him in on the conversation.

"Frank went to the gym," Chingli informed them. "He should be here in twenty minutes or so."

"Okay, so where do you stand with doctors and getting him evaluated?" Stacey asked.

"You know, sometimes I hate him or his stubborn streak," she complained. "I have to work so hard just to get him to think of his health. I make the appointments and I drag him to the doctor's office. Then he sits there and denies anything is wrong."

Stacey listened patiently while Kathy vented then asked, "Do you have a neurologist picked out yet?"

Kathy appreciated the opportunity to release a little steam. Even with all the support of her friends, there were times she felt so alone. As if she were the only one who saw Bob was in trouble. He would not admit it; that was certain. What was it about men that made them deny what was obvious to everyone else? But Stacey had asked a question and she had let her mind start to brood instead of answering.

"No, no neurologist yet," she replied. "The ophthalmologist gave Bob a few names, but we haven't picked one out yet. He seems to be avoiding talking about it. Do you know of any? They'd have to be in his insurance plan."

"I'll see if I can collect a list from around school," Stacey told her. "Then you can choose."

"Okay," Kathy said. Then she stood up. "You girls chat. I have a pot of gravy to look after." She walked to the kitchen to make sure everything was as it should be. After her apron created a protective barrier between her clothes and any wayward splashing of tomatoes, she stirred the contents of the pot, then turned on the flame under the water and began removing the meatballs from the gravy. The doorbell rang before she completed the job. That must be Frank, she thought. Could he provide the male point of view that would make Bob's reluctance seem more reasonable? The conversation in the living room came to a momentary halt. Gloria shouted she would get the door, so Kathy began to move the food to the dining table. The only hold up was the spaghetti which would be done in ten minutes. In the meantime, they could enjoy the ante pasta. Stacey and Chingli came into the kitchen while Gloria greeted her brother. Dinner was ready just as the man walked through the door, how 1950ish, how nauseating. She chuckled to herself as she finished retrieving the meatballs.

"Now whose recipe is this?" Gloria asked as she used bread to soak up the last bit of gravy from her plate.

"My grandmother's," Kathy told her.

"You should bottle this and sell it as gourmet spaghetti sauce," Gloria suggested. "You'd make a million."

"The meatballs were the best part of the meal," Frank asserted.

"Typical male," Gloria teased her brother. "Always looking for something to sink your teeth into. You have to learn to enjoy the subtle flavors of life, big brother."

Kathy sat contently listening to the sibling banter. The meal had been a success. The girls complimented everything and Frank had moaned with pleasure. Nini Anna had made the day. Now how to steer the conversation with Frank so she could get information from him? A full stomach always caused a man to drop his guard. Chingli had promised to help, but how to start?

She decided her usual frontal assault would be appropriate in his unsuspecting state. "So, Frank," Kathy began. "We girls were discussing Bob's troubles before you arrived and none of us can truly understand his male psyche. We were hoping you could enlighten us."

Frank reacted with a laugh. "That's a very complex subject made more so by a language divide," Frank asserted.

"A language divide?" Gloria asked, not letting her brother get away with dodging a difficult question by using levity.

"Yes, we don't use words the same way," Frank answered. "Guys want a quick answer to their questions which women consider to be curt and insensitive. They use humor to get a point across. Women say there is a time and place for levity."

"Well, you were a language major," Gloria pointed out. "So help us bridge the divide."

"I can only try," Frank promised, seemingly amused by the proposition.

Kathy saw the other women were waiting for her to set the tone. Once a frontal assault has begun, it would be disastrous to change course; so she dove in. "Why is he so reluctant to admit there is something wrong with him?" Kathy began. "What is it about men that make them hesitant to see a doctor?"

Frank sat quietly for a moment considering the questions. "I'll try to answer the second question first," he began. "I don't know how many guys I've talked with after something went wrong with their health . . . I mean guys who should have a cardiologist as their primary physician because of family history. When I ask them why they didn't see a doctor sooner, they usually reply, 'Because I was afraid they might find something.'"

"That makes no sense," Stacey blurted out.

"Didn't say it made sense," Frank admitted. "And I wouldn't go that route. I haven't heard that denial of a health issue cures it."

"Then why do men deny there's a problem?" Kathy asked in exasperation.

Frank looked a little uncomfortable, Kathy could see that. He knew she was referring to Bob. Loyalty made him reluctant to answer. He looked at her directly and answered seriously. "Because men know that admitting they are not healthy is a sign of weakness and a weak man is a lonely man," Frank informed her.

This brought a chorus of protest from all four women in the room. Frank held up his hand to quiet them. "You ladies asked for an honest answer," he reminded them after they quieted down. "I'm trying to give you one. I didn't set up the system. Mother Nature did that. In the dating mating game the healthy male is considered the best choice. Don't you think so? I've seen no rush of women to find sickly guys they'll have to nurse for the rest of their lives."

Kathy listened. On the face of it, what he said was right. But it was more complex than that. What of love? What of the strong mind in the weak body? She would not let Frank get away with such a simple answer.

"How can guys boil relationships down to something so simple?" she asked. "What of the strong mind inside the weak body?"

"How does a man prove he has a strong mind?" Frank asked. "And I'm assuming you mean a smart man not a stubborn one."

"He does it through conversation and innovative thinking," she insisted, realizing she was now having a debate with him.

"Does conversation and innovative thinking prove he can provide for her?" Frank asked. "Because in the final analysis, isn't that the male's role, to provide resources?"

Kathy relented on the resource assertion. No matter how romantic a woman might be, she needed to know her mate could provide support for her and any children they might have. That was true in every society on the face of the earth. What bothered her was Frank's assertion that a strong mind could not prove the ability to provide.

"Yes, communication and innovation can prove the ability to provide," she insisted.

"But doesn't it take a much longer time to prove?" Frank asked. "That requires a proven track record where a healthy body signals that he can dig ditches if necessary to support her. All he has to do is pledge that he will provide for her some way, somehow."

This brought Kathy up short. She could continue the debate by denying the validity of his argument, but it would be untrue. In the end a man with a weak body would have to prove he could provide. A man with a healthy body need only assure that he would provide.

"So you're saying that the male of the species is predisposed to self-denial?" Gloria interjected.

"I'm saying that from the time we are toddlers, we know that it is our job to provide for and protect the females in our lives," Frank answered.

This brought a pause in the conversation. Stacey and Chingli appeared shell shocked by the exchange. Kathy felt a new understanding of why Bob acted the way he did. She may not agree with it, but the thought process was clearer.

"So, this world view of men," Gloria continued to push. "It's not something they are conscious of?"

Frank shook his head yes. Kathy wondered if this is how the siblings had grown up, constantly debating issues. She knew from conversations with both of them that any physical aggression on Frank's part was strictly forbidden. There was no way to gain acquiescence from his strong minded little sister. They must have had to discuss disagreements and negotiate a settlement. Was that the secret to their close relationship?

"I find it's rare for any guy to be conscious of why he reacts to women the way he does," Frank admitted. "Sometimes I don't know why I react the way I do. Do you ladies know where your reactions come from?"

Once Frank admitted that he could not explain there was no sense pursuing the subject further. It had been fully explored. Kathy wanted answers to other questions that had been perplexing her and felt this was a unique opportunity. To pull one of these guys away from his buddies and have him answer her questions was impossible. She had not even interviewed them for the oral history. If she had to choose one for an interview, Frank would be the one. God give me the insight to take advantage of the opportunity, she prayed before pushing forward.

"You guys talk among yourselves," Kathy began the next subject. "Can you explain to me why Bob seems hesitant to fully accept me?"

Frank appeared stunned by her blunt question. She knew she was pressing her luck and he might just laugh it off, refusing to answer. There was a silent moment of contemplation then he opened up. His first salvo was the request for an oath. Demands of fealty and confidence, so important to men she thought, laughing internally. She had not even needed Chingli's manipulative ploys; Frank was ready to try for an explanation.

"None of this gets out of this room?" he asked them.

They all agreed. "Good because the boy needs some encouragement. All three of us have been trying, but sometimes he's thick. Bob is not the least bit hesitant to accept you," Frank explained.

"He is intimidated by you, but intends to enjoy your company until you get tired of him."

Kathy was dumbfounded and sat for a moment trying to comprehend what Frank had just said. Tired of him? How could she ever tire of him? Intimidating? Her?

"I'm intimidating?" she asked incredulously. "He's six foot two and a hundred and eighty-five pounds and I'm intimidating?"

The girls all laughed. Frank just smiled and commented, "You just supported my point about what makes men valuable."

Kathy had to take a mental step back. That thought had to be compartmentalized for now. They were on a separate subject at the moment. "But it's not his body that has me, it's his mind."

"You have to admit, the initial attraction was his body," Frank pointed out.

Even if she was to admit that, it was not the entire story, but she wanted to avoid a philosophical debate. They had just completed one and she was not sure she had prevailed. "That may have been part of the initial attraction," she conceded. "But it was far more complicated than that."

"Look, he is head over heels for you," Frank continued. "He just has doubts about an Ivy League graduate and then author finding him, a vo-tech high school graduate and lowly fireman, anything but a pleasant distraction."

"Ivy League . . . " Kathy stammered. How was she supposed to respond to that? It was not like she asked for his resume. The guys she met in college were boorish idiots even if they were academically brilliant.

"How can he not know how I feel?" she demanded. "I've done everything I can to get that point across to him."

"Have you told him?" Frank asked.

"Told him?" she muttered.

"Tell him," Frank advised. "Young guys are like young women. They're focused on the physical aspects. It's the old bastards who understand the mind thing."

Kathy smiled at Frank's observation. Maybe she was spending too much time interviewing older firefighters and so lost touch with the mindset of the younger variety. She had a lot to think about and wanted to talk with the girls about it to get their take. There was only one other question for him before she ceased her inquisition, "So, Frank, do you think my Nini Anna's recipe will impress Bob?"

Frank laughed with her. "Kathy, that meal will make him putty in your hands."

Chapter Twenty-one

Someone pounding on the overhead door pulled Bob out of the chair in the watch room. The aluminum and thin fiberglass doors that kept the outside world at bay could produce a tremendous racket when struck. Those sounds reverberating off the apparatus floor walls were usually a sign of trouble in the immediate neighborhood. No corner of the firehouse could provide refuge from the rattle. He stepped through the door and walked to the side wall with the overhead doors buttons. The sun was still strong, highlighting the silhouette of a woman on the light green door panels. She hit the door in front of the chief's gig again. Her shadow moved in a very agitated manner, implying she was in immediate trouble. Bob hit the button to start the door up. Sounds from the kitchen and stairs told him the guys were coming.

In the two weeks since his equilibrium had gone south, Bob's balance had returned to normal. It had been necessary to embellish his explanation of the bruises from the last fire they had fought when he spoke with Kathy. She gave no indication that his story was doubted, so that episode seemed to be closed. As the door creaked and rattled its way toward the ceiling, a woman with blood running down her face was exposed. Bob grabbed a wooden chair that was under the first aid box hanging on the back wall and then opened the box for supplies. As he placed the supplies on the chair, Jack stepped out onto the floor from the kitchen.

"What do we have?" he asked walking over to Bob.

"We'll be right with you ma'am," Bob assured the woman before turning to Jack. "Looks like some sort of head trauma."

Jack picked up the chair while Bob carried the supplies to the front. Hector and Ray had walked around the other side of the rig and were talking with the woman. Captain Pete came around behind them and started the door in front of the rig up.

"Why don't you have a seat here?" Jack suggested when he arrived with the chair.

"No, no," she refused. "I ain't sitting down. Can't run from him if I sit down."

When Captain Pete heard this he immediately sent Hector to the watch room for the portable radio.

"What happened ma'am?" the Captain asked.

"My husband beat me on the head with a stick," she told them. "I ain't sitting cause he might come and hit me again."

Bob opened gauze pads and began to work on her wounds. There was a nasty gash on top of her head and a small cut on her left cheek. The profusion of blood from her scalp wound made her injuries appear worse than they were, but he knew any head trauma could be serious. The firefighter paid close attention to her eye pupils while he placed the bandages. They appeared normal, but she would still need an evaluation by a doctor. Hector came back with the portable as Bob and Jack began wrapping cling bandages around her head. Traffic on Springfield Avenue continued to flow past the firehouse while this scene played out.

"Engine Six to quarters," the Captain called.

"Engine Six."

"Put us out on a signal five for first aid and have EMS respond to our quarters."

"Received Six."

As the Captain lowered the radio, a man carrying a three foot long stick with nails protruding from the top rushed up to them and began swinging it at the woman. Ray saw him coming and quickly stepped between them. The woman screamed and ran behind the Captain.

"Whoa, my man," Ray shouted. "What are you doing?" He quickly disarmed the man and moved him away from the woman. "You can't go around hitting her with a stick," Ray told him in an attempt to calm him down. "You want to end up in jail?"

The man cursed and began shouting at the woman. Bob went over to back up Ray because this guy was well over six feet tall and carried some weight on him. "Why are you hitting her?" Bob asked. "What did she do to make you want to hit her with that?" he asked pointing at the stick.

"She stabbed me!" he shouted and pointed at his upper chest just below the collar bone.

When Bob saw the wound his mind immediately flashed back to Mr. Brown lying on the floor in the projects. "Cap," he called. "I think you should come here." Captain Pete walked over with a quizzical look on his face.

"We're going to need another bus," Ray told the Captain quietly.

"Another bus? What's going on?" the Captain asked.

Bob explained very quickly as he monitored his charge.

"Engine Six to quarters," Captain Pete called.

"Engine Six."

"Inform EMS we need a second unit and have the police respond also."

"A second EMS unit and have the police respond, received."

"Hector," the Captain called. "Bring that chair over here, please."

Hector carried the chair over with a smirk on his face while Jack stayed with the woman. When he saw the wound on the man's chest, the smile vanished. His look told Bob he had the same flashback. Hector put the chair down and the man dropped into it. Captain Pete leaned over to examine the wound. "Are you having trouble breathing?" he asked.

"No, I'm breathing okay," was the response. "She stuck me good; it hurts like hell."

"I can imagine," the Captain told him. "Do you feel like your belly is swollen or your head is spinning?"

"No, just hurts where she stuck me," the man told them, the last words were shouted toward the woman.

"Easy my man, easy," Ray counseled. "She's your wife?"

"Yeah, she's my wife." he replied.

"That's right and he was with some young thing!" she shouted back. "Got what he deserved."

"She's my cousin's daughter woman!" he shouted back. "We was just talking. Why'd you have to go and do this?"

The sounds of sirens coming from different directions told Bob their part in this little drama would be over shortly. He placed a bandage over the wound lightly knowing EMS would have to assess the victim before they transported. The Captain told them the husband would go in the first ambulance. It appeared he was one lucky bastard to have sustained a knife wound to the upper chest and still talk about it.

While the Captain wrote up the book, Bob waited in the kitchen and talked with everyone.

"That's a loving, caring relationship," Jack quipped.

"Be careful about crossing women in this neighborhood," Hector added. "They defend their turf."

"Sometimes I think all women are capable of that kind of reaction," Bob said with a laugh. "I don't care what anyone says, there's nothing more frightening than an angry woman."

"Hell hath no fury," Ray agreed.

"So, why do we chase after them?" Bob asked. No one tried to answer.

"You trying to tell us that sweet woman you're with can do something like that?" Hector asked.

"You doubt her?" Bob shot back with a laugh. "Believe me, she has her own agenda and if I don't agree, watch out. She already took me to the emergency room once."

"She took you," Hector pointed out. "That dude's old lady sent him to the ER."

As the banter died down, Bob wondered if Kathy would send him to the ER if he did not follow through on his promise to see other doctors. Now that the vertigo was gone, he did not feel as urgent a need to be evaluated. Why spend time and money for someone to tell him he should take it easy? Any thoughts along those lines would meet with vehement resistance on her part. God, she was acting like a wife. The thought brought an unexpected smile to his face. He could envision a lifelong relationship with her and Chingli was of the opinion that any children who might result from such a union would be gorgeous. The fantasy passed quickly when he reminded himself he was over reaching. Ivy League authors do not commit to vo-tech firefighters. Enjoy the ride, he told himself, when she wakes up it is going to be one hell of a drop.

The Captain finished and went back upstairs. The guys settled in the kitchen to watch a ball game and Bob went back to his book. There would be no questions about domestic violence and stab wounds to the chest. He picked up his fire tactics book and continued his review. A click from the joker told him the attempt might be in vain. The hot line rang confirming it. Hector picked up the phone before Bob had a chance.

"Six, Fifteenth Avenue and Seventeenth Street; got it." He hung up the phone while they all began moving toward the apparatus floor. Bob hit the house gong to alter the Captain and then followed.

"On a signal nine to Fifteenth Ave and Seventeenth Street," Hector shouted as he cleared the kitchen door. Hank came down the stairs after the Captain to take care of the door and man the first floor.

Bob was driving, so he pulled himself up into the seat, started the rig, and turn on the lights. After confirming everyone was on board, he pulled onto the apron while the Captain turned on the siren. The rig paused momentarily on the apron waiting for the traffic to clear then pulled out onto Springfield Avenue. Bob turned onto Bergen Street heading for Fifteenth Avenue. It was two short blocks on Bergen Street then a left onto Fifteenth Avenue for a seventeen block run. Traffic was light two hours after rush hour, so it was easy.

"Engine Six on the scene."

"Six on the scene."

"Six to quarters, signal three hundred."

"Received Six, attention all units, Engine Six reporting a signal three hundred."

Bob turned the rig down Seventeenth Street and headed back to quarters. Before they could reach Sixteenth Avenue, the operator called.

"Quarters to Engine Six."

"Six."

"Check the box at Sixteenth and Thirteenth."

"Six received and responding."

For the next twenty minutes, they zigzagged their way east, responding to false alarms. Whoever was pulling the boxes apparently arrived at their destination because the alarms finally ceased. Bob began heading back to quarters when headquarters called again.

"Headquarters to Engine Six."

"Engine Six."

"Six, on a signal five. Check the box at Bergen and Fourteenth Avenue."

"Six, received and responding."

The Captain put the mic back in its holder and switched on the lights and siren one more time. "Do you think this one is connected to the other alarms, Cap?" Bob asked as he turned east on Fifteenth Avenue.

"Maybe not," Pete sighed. "It's a little off the path of the others."

When Bob turned onto Bergen Street, they could see a man standing by the box on the corner of Fourteenth Avenue. Bob pulled onto Fourteenth. The hiss of the parking brake told everyone the rig was parked. The guys jumped down from their seats and the Captain slid out his. Bob stepped out and walked around to the sidewalk side of the rig to see if he might be able to assist.

"There's a woman in the restroom in there," the man who stood by the box said pointing to the bar entrance. "I think she overdosed on some shit."

The Captain called headquarters to report the situation as he and Jack walked into the bar. The latter carried the port-a-lite just in case. Ray and Hector made their way to the back of the rig for the first aid supplies and the oxygen. The guy who pulled the box stood outside as if he were waiting to go in. Bob must have unconsciously had a questioning look on his face because the guy walked over to him.

"She just staggered in," he explained. "Didn't order nothing. Walked over to the restroom. I told her it was for paying customers only. She says, 'I'm in trouble. You better call somebody.' Before I could do anything she goes in. Then I hear a bang, like she fell over. I go open the door, sure enough, she's out on the floor. Shit all over herself. The smell drove me out of there, so I called you guys. That's a powerful odor. Nobody can stay in that little room with that for long."

Bob listened patiently, trying to get any information from this man's story that might help care for the victim. He could hear the Captain call for EMS in the background.

"You said she staggered in and said she was in trouble. Any sign of what that trouble was?" Bob asked.

The man shook his head and answered adamantly. "Oh, yeah. She didn't say nothing, but you only have to look at her arms to see she's a junkie. Must have shot up too much dope."

"She didn't say what kind of dope?" Bob continued his probe.

"Nah, she just came in to use the bathroom," the man answered. "Junkies, they don't know nothing when they high."

Hector came out, leaned over the curb, and vomited. This set Bob in motion. He jogged over to Hector to see if he was all right. "What happened?" he asked.

"Man, you can't stay in that room with her too long. I tried, but the odor was too much. You can't breathe. The Captain wants you to go in with a couple of masks. I'll keep an eye on the rig."

"Okay," Bob replied. "Just relax and stay in the fresh air." Then he hopped over to the rig, grabbed two masks, and went into the building. Jack and the Captain were at the far end of an elongated room dominated by a bar. Apparently, the man Bob had been talking to was the bartender since there was no one else in the place. He threw on one of the masks as he walked to the back. When he reached Jack, he handed the other off. The door to a tiny room in front of them was ajar. A woman's foot extended out of the room and a thick, unforgettable stench was coming from it.

"What happened?" Bob asked as he pulled his face piece on.

"Hector got cocky and crawled in there," the Captain told him. "He was trying to lift her up, but she's wedge in between the toilet and the sink. She weighs more than he does, for Christ's sake. I told him to get out, but it was too late so he lost his dinner. Enough talk let's get her out of there so we can work on her. EMS is backed up."

Bob stepped into the closet that passed for a rest room. She was a heavy set woman. It looked like she weighed over two hundred pounds. He had to place his feet very carefully because the only clear space was between the woman's body parts. Her head was wedged up against the back wall of the room. A large gash was open on her forehead. It looked fresh so it was probably produced when she collapsed. Cautiously placing his feet on either side of her head then bracing his back against the wall, Bob was able to get a hold of her shoulders and lift her up. Human excrement saturated her clothes. Jack had hold of her legs. Together they squeezed her out of the room and placed her on the floor. All of them could immediately see she was in critical shape. Jack and Bob took off their face pieces while the Captain conducted an assessment and Ray bandaged her forehead. Her breathing was erratic and shallow. When a light was passed over her eyes they remained dilated.

"Engine Six to quarters."

"Engine Six."

"Any word on EMS?"

"We'll try again, cap."

"Six received."

"She's not going to make it if EMS doesn't get here pronto," the Captain told them. "It's only two blocks to College Hospital, she's not dying here if we can help it."

Bob, Ray, and Jack all shook their heads in agreement.

"Headquarters to Engine Six."

"Engine Six."

"EMS says they can't give an ETA right now."

Without uttering a word, the four men began to move the woman out of the building.

"Get her up in the bucket," Captain Pete ordered. Jack, Ray keep her wedged in there. See if you can't get that seat belt on her. Hector get the oxygen and the supplies then see if you can get some O two into her. Bob no speed records just get us to the ER without her falling off the rig."

The entire crew began moving while the Captain called headquarters.

"Engine Six to quarters."

"Engine Six."

"Inform College Hospital we're coming in with an overdose victim, female, approximately thirty years of age, dilated pupils and shallow breathing. We're a few minutes away."

252

"Received Six."

By now Hector had retrieved the equipment. Bob, Jack, and Ray had wrestled the woman into the bucket seat behind the Captain and strapped the seat belt around her. Bob had said a short prayer of thanks when the buckle had snapped shut. It had probably been months since anyone had checked to see if the seat belt actually worked. He jumped down and hopped around to the driver's seat. The drive to the hospital was quick but controlled. No one trusted that seat belt.

The woman was still breathing when they pulled into the ER entrance. A team from the ER was waiting as they arrived. Jack and Ray unbuckled her and slid her out of the seat and onto a gurney. After they had all climbed back into their seats, Bob pulled the rig out onto Bergen Street. Hopefully the woman would pull through. It had been a night for first aid and that was no longer on the promotional exam. With a little luck, he could finally get back to his review.

As they approached Bergen and Sixteenth Avenue, a young girl began waving her arms and calling. Bob pulled over, resigning himself to the fact that he would not be able to study tonight. Captain Pete leaned out the window to listen.

"My friend fell through the grate on Sixteenth Avenue."

"Fell through the grate?" was the perplexed question she received back from the Captain.

"The one in the sidewalk on the side of the school," she explained.

Bob could picture the series of grates on the Sixteenth Avenue side of Camden Middle School. Each had to weigh hundreds of pounds. The slight girl in front of them certainly could not move any of them. How could her friend fall through one? Captain Pete directed him to pull the rig around the corner. When he parked, they could see that one of the grates had indeed fallen into the cavity in the sidewalk it was meant to cover. They all walked over to the large gap in the grates, unsure what they would see. Bob expected a limp body with broken bones, but the girl who had waved them down did not seem to be upset. Looking down into the opening, they saw a teenage girl standing about ten feet below them looking up.

"That's what I need," she called up. "Could you get one of your ladder trucks and get me out of here?"

"How did you get down there?" Jack asked in amazement.

"I don't know," she told them. "I was just walking with my friend and then I was falling."

"Are you hurt?" the Captain asked.

"No, I don't think so," she replied. "I just slid down that and landed on my feet."

Bob could not believe what he had just heard. She was one lucky girl. Captain Pete turned to them with a smile. "How about we drop a ladder down to her and get the young lady out?"

"You got it, Cap," Jack answered.

"We'll have you out of there in a second," the Captain told her before he called headquarters and requested they be put out of service.

"Thank you," she shouted up.

What a screwed up night, Bob thought as he rolled out of the watch room cot. No fires, but some blood and a lot of running. He had not gotten much sleep. The guys from the third tour would be arriving shortly, so he went to start the coffee machine. That done, Bob stepped over to the small bathroom off the kitchen to empty his bladder, but found he could not. It was as if something was blocking his urethra, no pee came out even when he pushed. Perplexed but not worried, he went out to the kitchen and made sure it was clean for the incoming tour. The bladder would work itself out, he was sure.

By the time he got home, Bob was worried. Jack was of the opinion that he had a kidney stone and assured him it would hurt like hell when it finally came out. Whatever was causing it, his bladder was getting increasingly uncomfortable. He placed his dirty uniforms in the bedroom hamper and went to the phone. If he failed to call Kathy, she would be worried and then ticked off. Start to call just to be nice and it becomes an obligation. That was a lesson to be remembered. He picked up the phone while debating about mentioning his overly full bladder. How many hours since he had peed? It had to be fourteen, sixteen. How many hours' worth of urine can a bladder store? Bob punched in Kathy's number still undecided about mentioning his latest problem. Could a recalcitrant bladder be caused by stress?

"Good morning," Kathy answered after one ring, a bad sign as far as Bob was concerned. She had been waiting. Granted the call was a little late since he usually called before he left the firehouse, but it was not that late. Why had he not called from the firehouse? Was he too preoccupied with his possible kidney stone or did he just not want to hear her gloat about how he could not deny he had to see a doctor?

"Hello babe," he replied in a voice that sounded as tired as he felt.

"Sounds like you had a bad night," Kathy judged from his tone. "Do you think you'll be able to study today? The test is in three weeks."

"I don't know," he answered, trying to get his groggy mind to make a decision. He finally came down on the side of informing her since this problem really could not be hidden anyway. "Right now my main problem is I can't seem to pee."

"What do you mean 'can't seem to pee'?" Kathy demanded. "Why wouldn't you be able to pee?"

Bob's first inclination was to say if he knew he would have figured out a way to rectify the situation. That thought quickly receded. He was getting bitchy from his engorged bladder. Not a good sign, but the discomfort was becoming pain. "Jack thought it might be a kidney stone plugging up the piping," Bob told her.

"A kidney stone?" Kathy shot back. "I'm on my way over. Do you want to meet me at the ER or should I drive you?"

Bob felt the pain in his bladder. He wanted quick relief. "I'll meet you at the ER," he told her, giving up all hope of a quiet solution.

"You can drive okay?" she asked.

"I can drive," was his reply.

Bob was pacing the ER waiting room floor like an expectant father when Kathy walked in. Sitting down was now out of the question. First his equilibrium, now this, he was beginning to appreciate the simple things in life that most people took for granted.

"You registered with the nurse, right?" Kathy asked.

"Yes, I called ahead but they don't take reservations," he said lightly. "So I gave them my name as soon as I walked in."

"Men and their warped sense of humor," she scolded. "This could be serious. Has anyone said what it might be?"

She was showing signs of racketing up, Bob thought. Humor was not going to calm her. Just the facts, like Sergeant Friday wanted. "I have to be seen by a doctor," he informed her. The nurse called his name in time to keep a lid on her worries.

"You have to be a family member to accompany him into the exam room," the nurse informed Kathy when she started following Bob. He knew that would not sit well with her.

"We were here recently," Kathy pleaded. "There was no problem with me accompanying him."

"I'm sorry," the nurse countered sympathetically. "It's a new policy."

By the looks of it, Kathy was about to explode and the nurse who was limiting her was going to take the brunt of her frustration. Bob touched her lightly on the arm to forestall any outburst and asked, "Can she accompany me if she's my fiancé?" He was not sure where the question had come from. His thought at work or the mention of a family member, both could have been the seed. It had the desired effect on the nurse.

"She's your fiancé?" she asked skeptically. "I don't see a ring."

"It just happened," Bob insisted. He glanced at Kathy while waiting for the nurse to respond. She had a smile on her face and tears in her eyes. He was not sure what had just happened, but Kathy was content for the moment.

Kathy's reaction was not lost on the nurse, who gushed, "Did it just happen?"

"Yes," Kathy answered with a tearful laugh. "It just happened."

"Well then I guess it's all right," the nurse decided. "Come on, the doctor will see you in room two."

Bob hoped they would not take his blood pressure because it would be through the roof. His mind had just accelerated to a mile a minute. He had apparently just asked Kathy to marry him and she had not slapped him for being presumptuous. The doctor came in before they could even acknowledge what had happened.

"Hi, I'm Doctor Radon," the doctor introduced himself.

"Bob Brendler," Bob said. When the doctor looked at Kathy, Bob felt obliged to continue. "And this is my fiancé, Kathy Stanley."

"Kathy Stanley," the doctor repeated. "Are you the news reporter?"

"I was," Kathy chirped. Bob had not seen her this bubbly in months. "I stepped back from that to write."

"Yes," Doctor Radon smiled. "I read your book, fascinating."

Bob was thrilled that Kathy accepted her role as fiancé. Either she was enjoying the fun of beating the system or she was genuinely happy with the title. Whichever it turned out to be, he had a problem that needed attention. Before the conversation could progress any further, he cleared his throat.

"What's the problem?" Doctor Radon asked.

"I can't empty my bladder," Bob told him.

"Why don't you lie back on the table," he suggested. "And I'll have a look." He began to palpate Bob's abdomen around the bladder. Bob winced involuntarily, causing the doctor to stop.

"When was the last time you voided?" he asked next.

Voided? That was a new term for Bob. He assumed that in medical parlance when you pee you void your bladder.

"Seventeen, eighteen hours ago," Bob informed him.

"Your bladder is very full," the doctor told him. "I'll get you some relief. Unbuckle your pants please."

Bob was so miserable by now he would do anything the doctor requested. Pride or modesty was long gone. Relief was all he wanted. The doctor put on latex gloves while Bob unbuckled his pants. Kathy moved to his side at the top of the exam table and placed her hand on his shoulder for moral support. The doctor inserted a catheter and drained his bladder giving him a wave of relief that masked any discomfort.

"You'll need an appointment with a urologist," the doctor informed them.

"First a neurologist, now a urologist, it doesn't end," Bob sighed.

Doctor Radon looked concerned. "Did you say an appointment with a neurologist?" he asked.

"Yes doctor," Kathy interjected. "He's already been told he should see a neurologist. Can you recommend a urologist?"

Kathy walked out of the emergency room like a triumphant warrior. In her hand was the phone number of a urologist, in her ears rang the last comment of the doctor. "You have a sharp woman, Bob. Count yourself lucky." Bob had acknowledged the truth of his statement, but was still uncertain how Kathy was going to play out the fiancé role he had thrust upon her. He may have backed into a marriage proposal. Either that or she would deflate his ego with a flippant comment about how clever he was to come up with a quick ploy that allowed her to accompany him.

"I'll call the urologist," Kathy turned to him and announced. "Maybe we can get an appointment the same day as the neurologist. With the test coming soon, you'll have more free time so it won't matter will it? I'll just call to see what I can get. We're going to have to find out what's going on. Don't you think? So, I'll look over your work schedule and call. If that's okay and, and, . . . "

Bob stood beside her and listened to the torrent of words. He had never seen her as flustered as she was now. She was building up to something and did not appear angry. Either she was finding it hard to tell him how silly he was to even think she would take his ploy seriously or she was waiting for him to get up the nerve to admit he was serious. Bob was about to tell her how serious he was when she started to cry.

"I need to know," she sobbed. "How serious are you? Did you say that so I could stay or did you mean it?"

Bob reached for her and gave her a hug. "Why are you crying?" he asked. "Do you want to take it seriously? You're the woman. It's your prerogative to say yes or no."

"Then I say yes, Mr, Brendler," Kathy laughed through her tears. "I've been searching for you my entire life."

It had not happened the way he had imagined it would. No flowers, no romantic dinner, no ring, not even a poem, but he had made a commitment he had every intention of keeping. Why was she crying? He prayed they were tears of joy. Now he needed some sleep, then they could go to lunch and celebrate. He was supposed to be in the firehouse tonight.

Chapter Twenty-two

The creaking stairs leading up to Bob's apartment seemed earsplitting to Kathy. She knew Bob should still be sleeping. At least that was the plan when she left him. They had both come here from the emergency room. He had crawled into bed while she had rummaged through his kitchen for something that might be made to resemble breakfast. The refrigerator had yielded bread and eggs which she transformed into egg sandwiches. Only an hour into her engagement and she was serving him breakfast in bed. Not a good precedent, but she did not think him foolish enough to expect a repeat any time soon.

Opening the apartment door quietly, Kathy slipped into the kitchen and eased the door shut. It was warm in the room, but not unbearable. She dropped her purse on a chair at the kitchen table. The table top had three piles of books resting on it. A small stack of legal pads filled with notes rested in front of the books; beside the pads was a tape recorder. From what she could piece together between the scene in front of her and Bob's comments, he had taken to eating standing up while listening to tapes of recorded notes. It was no wonder he was always tired.

After her little foray into domestic servitude, Kathy had returned home and gone to work. The urologist had been contacted and the situation explained. She had requested an appointment as soon as possible. When told her they had a cancellation which opened up a time slot that afternoon, she had jumped on it. Expecting a vigorous protest from Bob because he was scheduled to work tonight, Kathy had called Pete and explained the situation. The captain had assured her Bob would be covered and to tell him not to worry if he was a little late. She made no mention of the change in their relationship feeling it was Bob who should tell the guys about it. She would inform the girls.

Stacey and Gloria were at work, so she was not able to call them. Chingli had a doctor's appointment and probably would not be back for another half hour. She had been unusually closed mouth about the reason for her doctor's visit. Kathy knew she would hear about it eventually, but right now she was ready to burst with joy and could not share her news. She stepped quietly to Bob's bedroom to check on him. He was still sleeping soundly, so she eased the bedroom door closed and made her way back to the kitchen. No longer able to contain herself, Kathy picked up the phone and called Chingli. The phone was answered on the second ring.

"*Jiejie*," Kathy whispered. "What did the doctor say?"

"The doctor said I have either swallowed a softball or I am pregnant," Chingli announced with obvious satisfaction.

"Pregnant!" Kathy squealed quietly. "Oh, jiejie I am so happy for you. This is really a special day. I have news for you also."

Kathy told the story of her experience in the Clara Maas emergency room. It was Chingli's turn to squeal with delight. The two women chatted about Kathy's engagement and Chingli's condition. Then Chingli shifted off the happy subjects.

"What did the doctor say about Bob?" she asked.

263

"He really didn't say much," Kathy admitted. "Just that he should see a urologist, so I managed to get an appointment with one this afternoon. They'll find the problem and fix it."

"If they can't find the problem or they can't fix it, what do you plan to do?" Chingli asked, insisting on confronting the hard questions up front.

Why must she ask that on a day like today? "My heart hasn't changed," Kathy stated. "The body only holds the man I love."

"Why do you love him?" Chingli continued.

"Why?" Kathy asked quietly and then took a moment to collect her thoughts. "He is far from perfect, but he is so deliciously full of potential. Just needs the right woman to realize it."

"And you are that woman," Chingli stated.

"I know I am that woman," Kathy agreed. She heard the sound of Bob getting up. "He's awake, jiejie, got to go."

She hung up the phone and headed toward the bedroom, her reaffirmation to Chingli of the love she felt reverberating in her mind. The task facing her right now was getting him to the doctor's office. With all her chicks in a row, Kathy was reasonably sure she could deflect his doubts and manipulate him into going.

* * * * * * * * * * *

Bob could not believe she had talked him into this. He had to be in the firehouse in three hours at the latest. Why was he going to see a doctor now? He had "voided" his bladder when he got up. It was uncomfortable after the catheter, but he was sure the burning sensation would go away on its own. They were not riding up this elevator because of a burning sensation. The firefighter had to admit that his experience that morning may not be tied to stress, although he had not admitted that to Kathy. When he exhibited some reluctance, a flood of words had assaulted his ears. He had to admit it was not normal. The doctor will find out what it is and treat it. Then whatever it was would go away. If they do not treat it, it will get worse. Bob had learned early in life not to stand in front of a runaway train and the woman standing beside him was definitely out of control. Hopefully this doctor would give him a simple explanation for his recalcitrant bladder, have him pop a pill, and he would go on his merry way.

They stepped into the doctor's office and were immediately given a clipboard with forms to fill out. He started to write then Kathy stepped in.

"Here, I'll write, you talk," she ordered. "My handwriting is easier to read."

"I can write legibly," Bob protested.

"And I can open jars with stubborn caps," she countered. "But you do it so much easier."

Their relationship had obviously moved to a higher plane. That did not bother him, but it would take some getting used to. He had never shared the parts of his life that Kathy was now melding into with anyone. The lyrics to a song by The Band came to his mind, "If I spring a leak, she mends me. I don't have to speak, she defends me. A drunkard's dream if I ever did see one." The only problem was he was not a drunkard. The rarified atmosphere on this higher plane was getting him dizzy. Probably should talk to Frank or Jack or Ray, someone who had a woman looking into every corner of his life. He needed pointers to help navigate through this transition period. They were not uncharted waters, just new to him.

They finished the forms and were directed into an exam room. Bob could not help but look at his watch.

"Don't worry about the time," Kathy reassured him. "We didn't have to wait long and besides, Pete said it's okay if you're a little late."

"That's easy for you to say," Bob told her. "I'm going to spend half my night explaining being late and the other half describing exactly how it is I came to be engaged to the famous and well sought after Kathy Stanley."

She smiled at him with sparkling eyes and laughed. "Are you going to tell them the God's honest truth or are you going to embellish?"

"I might have to change parts of the story because they won't believe it," Bob chuckled. "Ray is going to be particularly difficult. He put himself through hell with his doubts. Stacey finally settled it by demanding a ring. I spontaneously told you, you were my fiancé."

"Are you happy with the results of your spontaneity?" she asked quietly.

"More than you can imagine," he told her. "My only regret is there was no romance to it. We should have flown to Paris. I should have given you flowers with a ring, at least written you a poem. You deserved better than me proclaiming you my fiancé and then waiting for your reaction."

"You are a romantic at heart, Bob Brendler," Kathy said with a beaming smile. "We can do all those other things later. It's the love of the moment that counts." Their conversation came to an abrupt end when the doctor walked in.

"What can I do for you?" Doctor LaConti asked after looking over the forms they had filled out.

"I woke up this morning unable to void," Bob told him, making full use of his limited medical lexicon.

"Have you had trouble before?"

"No, this was the first time."

"How strong is your stream when you void?"

Bob had to stop and think about this. It was not something he had ever put thought into before. After considering the past few months, he had to acknowledge that his "stream" was weaker than it had been.

"Now that I think about it, doc," Bob replied slowly. "I remember it being stronger in the past."

"How far in the past are you referring to?"

"I'd say it changed gradually over the past maybe year," Bob guessed.

"Any other symptoms?" was the next question.

"No, none to do with this issue," Bob assured him.

Kathy had obviously been chomping at the bit the whole time. With his insistence that there were no other symptoms, she jumped in like a race horse out of the gate.

"He has had a number of issues over the past six months or so," she began. "His hands feel a little numb; he has a floater in his right eye; and when we are . . . " Here Kathy hesitated and began to blush. Then she dove in with both feet. "When we are intimate, he, he takes a longer time to finish." Her voice trailed off after saying this.

The doctor listened to her quietly. Bob knew she wanted everything on the table, but he had to get to work and the excess information was just wasting theirs and the doctor's time.

"Kath, that has nothing to do with why we are here," he insisted.

"No, no," the doctor interjected. "Sometimes we can put all of these symptoms into one diagnosis. I'd like to set you up for some tests. Can you get a day off during the week? It's an outpatient procedure. I'd like to have a look at your bladder."

"I'm a Newark firefighter, doc," Bob told him. "So I work nights and days. A day during the week shouldn't be a problem." He did not like the sound of "look at your bladder." Unless it was an x-ray or an ultrasound, there was only one way into the bladder and he knew from this morning that was not comfortable.

"You're a Newark fireman?" the doctor asked. "My father was a big fire buff back in the day. He used to ride with the Rescue Squad a couple of times a month. Drove my mother crazy."

This was the second doctor to have a fire department connection since his ordeal began. Bob could not believe his luck. He had heard the older guys talk about old Doc LaConti. From everything they had said, he was a fireman's friend. Hopefully, the connection would translate into a better doctor patient relationship. That would put

Kathy at ease. They set the date for the test, made an appointment to discuss the results, and picked up instructions from the front desk. Apparently, this was more involved than an x-ray and required anesthesia. Kathy scooped up the appointment cards and the instructions, dropped them in her purse then looked at the time.

"There's a wonderful restaurant in Branch Brook Park," she hinted. "I'm sure there won't be a wait at this time of day."

"I don't think we have time for a sit down lunch," he answered. "Do you have the energy for a walk in the park instead?"

"I think I can handle that," Kathy relented. "If I pass out, you can rescue me."

"That would be a pleasure," Bob assured her.

As they walked out to the parking lot, she turned to him and asked, "You didn't think I'd let you get away with that did you?"

Her question took Bob by surprised, so he decided to plead ignorance. "Get away with what?" he asked innocently.

"No other symptoms," Kathy laughed. "After all those months of strange sensations and spinning rooms."

"I keep telling you the sensations are from stress," Bob said defensively. "And the spinning rooms were from an inner ear infection." She acquiesced on those points and moved on to what seemed to be her main bone of contention. "You really enjoyed me trying to verbalize our love life didn't you?" she accused him.

Bob laughed just remembering her embarrassed, halting attempt to explain their intimate relations. She smacked his arm when she saw this.

"It's not funny," she insisted. "Do you know how embarrassing that was? I may not be the most experienced woman, but even I know men have a limit and it's not twenty minutes and their back gives out."

Bob smiled, but inside he knew he had been caught. They had never spoken about the times there was no climax for him. He had hoped she would not notice or would just think of him as a disciplined lover. Even though there had been no tears of frustration, Kathy apparently wanted him to experience something more than an aerobic workout. Deciding the best way to parry her attack was by using humor, he pointed out, "That only happens occasionally. Maybe it's my way of showing you how much I love you."

"Bob Brendler, you are so full of it," she snapped back. "It's not normal."

They arrived at their cars as she proclaimed this. Bob did not want this conversation to spill into a romantic walk so he attempted a little more humor to see if that would put it to bed. "You're right," he conceded. "It's not normal, but then I'm not normal. I enjoy the challenge of fighting fires. Doesn't that make me a little crazy?"

She looked up at him, stretched to give him a kiss, and then whispered in his ear, "Sometimes you are the most romantic man I ever met, but right now you're an insensitive prick."

Bob burst out laughing. Kathy joined him, signaling his tactic had worked. "Spoken like a true firefighter," he told her. "You should keep better company."

"There is no better company," she replied. "Now do we have to drive or can we just cross the street? You only have an hour if you want to make it in before the time blow."

"Follow me my lady," Bob invited her as he offered his arm for her to hold.

They walked down a fairly steep hill and crossed Franklin Avenue. The sounds of the street faded as they walked into Branch Brook Park. Fields of grass and cherry trees stretched out in front of them. The couple walked quietly for a few minutes, each lost in their own thoughts while enjoying the other's company. It was a day when everything seemed possible. She wanted to hold onto that feeling, but knew she could not. Kathy knew that there might be an internal battle being waged in Bob's body that would rob her of possibilities, but not of her love for him. She glanced up at him and knew he was the one she had been waiting for.

Their pace slowed as they meandered across the field. It did not appear that they had a particular destination to Kathy. It was a stroll to enjoy the warm weather, the sunshine, and each other's company, a time to communicate.

Bob chuckled and confessed. "You know, I think my parents are going to love you. They may not believe me when I tell them, but once it sinks in you will become the daughter they never had."

Kathy thought for a moment then asked him, "Did you tell them about me yet?"

Bob looked surprised at her question. "Of course I spoke with them about you," he protested. "Mom calls once a week and wants to know all about my love life. Well, not the gritty details, but if I'm seeing anyone and what kind of girl is she, that sort of thing."

Kathy smiled thinking about the conversations with her mother. She did not want to tell Bob that mama really wanted her to marry a professional. Then her mother's remark about her father came to mind. "My dad is going to love you," she said. "A firefighter and a carpenter, you're made to order for him."

"Made to order?" Bob asked. "I guess if I do well on the test and get promoted."

Kathy gave him a knowing look. "Is that why you're so determined to make captain?"

"Well I figure if a captain's salary could afford Columbia," Bob reasoned. "Then he would feel I could provide for you if I were a captain."

Kathy smiled and shook her head. "A captain's salary did not pay for Columbia," she informed him. "I attended on a scholarship."

"Oh, God," Bob muttered.

"Oh, God?" Kathy asked. "Oh, God what?"

Bob laughed and shook his head. "I'm glad you didn't tell me that until now. It was frightening enough dating an Ivy League girl. If I knew you were that smart, it would have scared me off."

It was Kathy's turn to laugh. "You have a very high opinion of my schooling," she said. "Maybe too high?"

He thought for a moment before answering. "It's not your schooling," he said. "If you learn calculus at Columbia or at a county college, it's the same course. Calculus is calculus. It's winning the competition to gain entrance that's impressive."

"I see," she said. "You know the only competition I'm interested in winning is the one for you." She stopped and put her arms around his neck. "That's the most important victory of my life."

He leaned over and kissed her lightly. "That doesn't change my desire to do well. I can't sit on my laurels after all," he told her. "Trophies can be forgotten and pushed to the back of the shelf."

She looked him in the eye and asked, "So you want to do well simply to impress me?"

"Not entirely," he answered. "Remember my father was a captain, so family pride is involved."

"Pride?" she snapped as she pulled her arms down. "Men are all so concerned about their pride." She shook her head and decided to get the conversation back to where it began.

"I'll warn you," she said. "Both my parents wanted to have a large family. They will put not so subtle pressure on me to fulfill their dream."

Bob looked shocked at first, which was the purpose. Shock him and you immediately move him off the undesired topic. He chuckled as they continued their stroll across the field. "A large family," he muttered. "How about we pick out an engagement ring first? Then we can talk about a family, although the consensus is our children will be beautiful."

Kathy stopped short as soon as she heard this last comment. She felt her face turning red. "He translated that didn't he?" she demanded.

Bob appeared to be a little confused at first then he seemed to make the connection. As she expected, he tried to protect his friend. "Who translated what?" he asked.

"Don't try to play ignorant with me, Bob," she warned him. "You know exactly what I'm talking about. Who said our children would be beautiful?"

Bob made some unintelligible sounds as he struggled to answer the question.

She resigned herself to not getting a straight answer from him and pushed on. "Okay," she said. "I'll answer for you. Frank translated Chingli's comments after the softball game. No need to cover for him. I should have expected that." Kathy laughed at herself for reacting to a predictable male behavior. But he had brought up an important topic, the engagement ring. She intended to gain complete control of that matter. They were not going into debt for his male ego, especially since she did not give a hoot about how impressive an engagement ring they purchased. Her mother had never even had one and her parents got through just fine.

"You may have already forgotten since you were trying to cover for Frank," she said in an accusatory tone. "But you mentioned an engagement ring. I don't want you trying to be romantic and running off to buy some super expensive diamond. Promise me, we'll pick out a ring together."

Bob looked relieved; although she could not be sure it was from the change in subject or her demand about buying a ring. "I promise," he assured her. "Now I have to think about getting you to your car and me to work."

They turned around and headed back to the parking lot. Kathy was happy with the conversation. She could not have planned it better. They had not covered a lot of ground walking through the park, but they had covered quite a bit in their talk. On the way back, she told him the news from Chingli and watched his reaction, anxious that she might have spooked him with her comment about her parents wanting her to have a large family. She had no intention of fulfilling her mother's dream. This was not the sixties and she had to worry about a career. Bob appeared happy for Frank and Chingli, but not overly enthusiastic about quickly joining them on the road to parenthood. As he said, let's worry about the engagement ring first. What a day it had been, eventful, informative, almost surreal, but one of the happiest of her   life.

Chapter Twenty-three

Traffic was working against him. Thank God he had thought to put his clean uniforms in the car before he left for the doctor's office. Bob swung the car around someone making a left turn and gunned the engine. As he crossed West Market Street, a column of black smoke became visible ahead and to the right. He swore to himself. At least he knew where Six Engine was. With no turnout gear, Bob could only take over the driver's job. That would free up an extra hand to help out inside the building. He covered Bergen Street from West Market to South Orange Avenue as quickly as possible without crossing the safety threshold. It was better to arrive a minute later, than not to arrive at all. Crossing South Orange Avenue, it became clear the fire was off Fourteenth Avenue around Camden Street or Fairmont Avenue. A quick right onto Fourteenth and then a left onto Camden put him on the scene.

There was a group of young men in front of the fire building pointing and yelling. Bob was the first on the scene. He pulled his car to the curb on the opposite side of the street away from the area companies would need to operate. The fire had hold of the back porch of a three story wooden framed building. All three floors appeared to be involved. The firefighter jumped out of his car, remembering to lock the door and take the keys. He hustled over to the group of men who had continued to rant and asked, "Has anyone called the Fire Department?"

The group immediately fell silent, looked at each other, and then ran as one toward the corner firebox. Bob was shocked. He was standing in front of a working fire in shorts with no radio, no water, and no ladder. This was why the Chief insisted the engine leave quarters first. The first question that needed to be answered was, "Is there anyone in the building?" A teenage girl ran up to him to give an answer.

"My uncle is in there!" she cried.

Bob made his way to the front door. When he found it was locked, he turned his back to it and gave a powerful mule like kick. The door crashed in easily. Looking into the hallway, Bob saw the layout of the stairs was similar to his apartment. There was a haze of smoke floating through the air. Realizing he made a mistake by not asking what floor the girl's uncle was on, Bob glanced back to see if she was close enough to throw the question at her. The girl had moved across the street where neighbors were giving comfort. He was on his own. Knowing how rapidly the fire was growing, he headed for the top floor. There was a small window of opportunity before the flames took over that floor. Start from the top and work your way down, he told himself. The smoke gradually thickened with each step he climbed. Quickly passing the second floor door, Bob ascended to the third floor. He was now coughing and his eyes were burning from the smoke. Upon reaching the third floor landing, he immediately began bounding on the door, staying as low as he could.

"What's you want?" a male voice called from behind the door.

"The building's on fire!" Bob yelled. "You have to get out!"

"Go away, leave me alone," the voice responded.

Go away? Leave me alone? This was insanity. Something was definitely not right. He stood up, gave the door a hard kick, and stepped into the apartment.

The girl's uncle was sitting on the edge of a beat up couch talking to himself.

"I said leave me alone. Why don't nobody listen to me?"

This guy was either drunk or mentally unstable. Bob hoped it was the former.

"My man," Bob shouted between coughs. "The building's on fire! You've got to get out!"

The smoke continued to thicken rapidly; the sound of the fire's crackle came from the rear of the apartment. He looked to see if there was a door that could be closed to buy a few extra seconds, but there was none, just the glow of the fire. This guy had to move fast.

"Got to get out? Fire?" the man muttered. "I got to get my shit." He stood up, coughed, and began to stagger towards the back.

"Yo!" Bob shouted. "You go back there and you die! Understand?"

"I got to get my shit!" the man shouted. "Leave me alone!"

Bob was now desperate. In another half minute they would be dead. Either he abandoned this guy, dragged him out, or they both died. He knew he was not dying or abandoning anyone, instead he grabbed for him. The man resisted, so Bob did the only thing he could think of and punched him in the face. The blow brought this guy down to his knees. Bob quickly grabbed him and dragged the man to the hallway. By the time they reached the stairs, the firefighter was retching and coughing. Thank God he had not eaten lunch with Kathy. It would have ended up on this landing. He hoisted his moaning, semi-conscious charge onto his shoulders and began the descent through the smoke, coughing and retching down to the street.

When he stepped out into the sunlight, Six Engine was just pulling up. Bob could see Hector and the Captain in the cab through his smoke induced tears. The Captain was on the radio. Two lines snaked down the street behind the rig. Jack jumped off and ran to help Bob who eased his burden down to the ground. The chief's gig was coming down the street and sirens in the distance announced more help would arrive shortly. What a way to start a night!

* * * * * * * * * * * * * * * * * * *

"I really don't think you should write for this one," Bob told the Chief. "I had to sucker this guy to get him out. That wouldn't read well."

He had finished a shower and was making his bunk when the Chief asked to speak with him. They were standing in the chief's room off the front of the bunk room. Chief Simmons had requested Bob explain what had happened. No one knew that he had proposed to Kathy. There had been no time to pass on that news. The Chief wanted to hear Bob's version because the man he had rescued had told anyone who would listen that the fireman had sucker punched him. After he told his story, the Chief had commented that it sounded like a commendable act. What if this guy decided to get a lawyer and try to sue or have him arrested? Bob wanted no official papers floating around detailing his assault to save a life.

"How about we let the Captain put it in the company journal?" the Chief suggested. "He can mention the rescue, but he didn't see how you subdued the person you rescued. That part can be left to the imagination of the reader. If this guy doesn't mention anything then we can go from there. You're not the first firefighter to knock someone out so they could be rescued. Don't let it worry you."

Bob thanked the Chief then went down to help with dinner. He knew he was going to have to fess up before Jack or Ray spoke with their wives. If the news entered the firehouse via the wives' network, he would never live it down. When he stepped into the kitchen, Jack glanced up from chopping garlic and gave him an odd, questioning look. He was unsure what it meant. Was it about his problem this morning, about the doctor's visit, about Kathy, or about the fire? It had been an unusual day. Which part of the day was on his friend's mind?

"What happened after you left this morning?" Jack asked while continuing his chopping.

"I got home and still couldn't pee or void as the doctor put it," Bob said, choosing to go with the flow of Jack's question. "So, I called Kathy to tell her I was home and she jumped all over me and insisted I go to the emergency room."

"Nothing surprising there," Jack laughed.

Everyone else was busy around the kitchen, the apparatus floor, or the watch room. He wanted to pitch in, but somehow got the feeling that they all wanted to hear what he had to say. Why did he have to fall in love with a woman who had been adopted by his crew? He felt like an eighteenth century suitor preparing to ask a girl's father for her hand in marriage.

"When I got to the emergency room, the doctor had to use a catheter to empty my bladder," he explained

Jack winched when he heard that. Ray just said ouch from the sink, showing he was listening to every word. The Captain made a sympathetic noise from the watch room. Hank had a grimace on his face. Hector walked into all of this from the apparatus floor.

"What happened?" he asked.

"Bob had to have a tube put up his Johnson this morning," Jack told him.

"Oh, God," Hector muttered. "That must have hurt."

"Something to be avoided at all costs," Bob laughed.

"Was Kathy with you?" Hector asked innocently.

"Well, ah, you see, ah, the nurse said only family members could accompany me into the exam area," Bob began. "And I knew she wasn't going to accept that."

"So what did you do?" Jack asked. "Tell them she was your sister?" Everyone laughed at the suggestion. Bob's mind began to ease a little. Apparently the girls had not spoken to the men yet.

"No," he said, then took a deep breath and blurted out. "I told them she was my fiancé."

At first there was complete silence in the kitchen as everyone looked at him. A collective moan was followed by a steady stream of questions.

Jack held up his hand to quiet the room. Bob waited to answer the questions and comments.

"How did she respond to such a presumptuous statement," Jack asked with mocking pomposity. He had never had any doubt about Kathy's answer. His doubts had always been about Bob's nerve.

"She had the biggest smile on her face I have ever seen," Bob described. "And tears in her eyes."

There were shouts and hoots after he said this. Jack and Ray reminded him that they had said this would happen. The Captain, Hector, and Hank congratulated him. After the celebratory outburst had run its course the method of his proposal came into question.

"Let me get this straight," Ray said. "You didn't ask her; you told her she was your fiancé?"

Bob laughed at Ray's interpretation. He had expected a reaction from Stacey's husband knowing the story of his marriage proposal.

"That implies I knew what her answer would be," Bob answered. "She could have slapped me in the face and called me a presumptuous bastard, as Jack pointed out."

"Only you doubted it," Jack reminded him. "It was obvious to the rest of us that she had you in her sights and wasn't going home without her prize."

"No ring, no flowers?" Hank asked. "Did you get down on her knee at least?"

"No," Bob admitted. "It was kind of a spontaneous thing. Just wanted to solve the problem of her not being allowed in."

"Where'd this generation come from?" Hank muttered as he shook his head.

"I'll do all that after the test," Bob reassured him. "Kathy happily took a rain check." He considered himself to be the luckiest man alive, not because of how he proposed, but because of her answer.

"It's just not fair," Ray whined quietly. "After the hell I went through, you just do it as a side thought. Just spontaneously ask a beautiful, talented, warm, loving woman to spend the rest of her life with you and she chirps 'yes'. No deep thought or discussions about the future. No secret planning, no sweating details, just a nonchalant statement. 'I Tarzan. You Jane. You marry me.' Some guys get off so easy."

Laughter filled the room. "What a crew," the Captain commented. "You know, Bob, you really give us something to talk about besides baseball, football, and fires. Now for a change of subjects, what did the doctor say?"

Bob was not surprised the Captain was the one who changed the subject to his health. A captain has to be certain his firefighters are not denying any health issues that would put the company members at risk. "You mean Doctor LaConti?" Bob asked, throwing the doctor's name out to see if it got a reaction.

"Doctor LaConti?" Hank asked as expected. "It wouldn't be old John LaConti, would it?"

"No," Bob replied. "His son, he said he wanted to have a look at my bladder."

"Look at your bladder?" Hector reacted. "How's he going to look at your bladder?"

"With a tiny camera after they put me out," Bob sighed. "I'm not looking forward to this, but a man's got to do what a man's got to do."

This brought moans from around the kitchen. Bob purposely left out the doctor's comment on all his symptoms leading to one diagnosis. He would not be able to answer the questions that information would provoke, so he let it slide.

"What can I do to get dinner on the table?" he asked. "We're not going to eat until midnight unless we hustle."

Jack pointed towards Ray, who was at the sink. Bob walked over to give him a hand peeling shrimp. Hopefully they would be able to finish their meal before another alarm came in.

The last of the dishes were in the sink ready for clean up when the next alarm came in. The Hotel Carlton reported a fire on the fifth floor. Bob had a feeling he was not going to be able to review tonight. A fire of any consequence in a hotel usually went to an additional alarm just for the potential rescue problems. He walked into the watch room and found Hector checking the running cards to see where they were listed for subsequent alarms. Jack poked his head in the door.

"First due on the second," Hector told them. The sound of footsteps on the metal stairs from the second floor could be heard in the background. Before any companies were on the scene, the entire crew was in the watch room listening.

"Truck One to quarters, on the scene. We have a fire on the fifth floor of a seven story brick hotel with a rescue problem."

As soon as they heard the radio report, they all moved as one toward the rig.

"Deputy Two to quarters, transmit a second alarm."

Hank stood by the door as Six rolled out into the warm summer air and turned east. The door began its descent and the chief's driver walked to the watch room to listen. Six rolled down the hill towards the city's business district. They would be the only company on the second alarm coming into the fire from this direction.

Hector pulled the rig into a parking lot beside the hotel. Truck Eleven had its aerial to the front of the building with people climbing down it. They could see Truck One's snorkel operating on the far side of the building. No one was working the side of the hotel facing them. When Bob looked over the windows of the upper floors, he saw a woman leaning out of the fifth floor. Captain Pete saw her at the same time. They all knew this side of the building would be theirs.

"Go to the back of Eleven Truck and take out the fifty footer," the Captain ordered.

All four of them went to Eleven Truck while the Captain tried to keep the woman calm. Bob had not worked with a fifty foot ladder since the Academy and doubted any of the firefighters on his crew had either. At least they had Pete. All those years in a truck company were going to be invaluable in the next five minutes. They quickly pulled out the largest ground ladder carried by a truck company. With each man on a corner of the behemoth, they walked it to the area under the window. Jack and Ray were at the foot of the ladder. Pete barked an order to drop the foot. Then Hector and Bob began to push it to a vertical position while Jack secured the bottom so it would not slide. When it was vertical, Jack and Ray grabbed the bangor poles from the sides of the ladder and moved to where the Captain ordered. This placed them at a ninety degree angle from each other and stabilized the ladder. Bob grabbed the halyard and extended the ladder until Pete told him to stop. After locking it, he put his hands on a rung at shoulder level and placed a foot on the bottom rung. They lowered the ladder into the building, dropping it just short of the fifth floor window. By now a man had joined the woman in the window. Between memories from the Academy and his readings, Bob knew it was not a perfect raise, but it was damn close and was the best they could do. The tip of the ladder should go through the window, but the ladder was too short. He found himself at the foot of the ladder, so Bob began to climb. Kathy had told him more than one funny story she had collected in her oral history about ladder rescues. They were only funny years later. Nerve wracking was a better way to describe such a rescue while it was occurring. Panicky citizens frequently knocked firefighters off ladders. A fall of two or three stories might be survivable. One from five stories up onto a paved parking lot was certain death. This was turning out to be one hell of a night.

"Bob, watch out," Jack shouted. "She's on the ladder."

Bob looked up and saw the woman had crawled out of the window and had begun to cautiously climb down. He wished she had waited. There was no smoke coming from her window. Companies were inside attacking the fire. It might have been possible to get out by the interior stairs. Now they were committed to the most dangerous means of egress. He climbed quickly so he would be able to catch her if she slipped. When he reached her, the first thing he noticed was she had no shoes on and was climbing down on her toes. She was trying to avoid putting the middle of her sole on the rungs' grooves.

"Ma'am, I know it's uncomfortable," Bob coaxed her. "But there's less of a chance slipping if you go down using your feet instead of your toes." She shifted her weight from her toes to her feet and continued down. Bob had his arms on the rungs around her and timed his steps down so his leg was in position to catch her if she slipped. As he monitored her climb down, he saw her companion had joined them on the ladder. The slow, cautious descent took a couple of minutes, but seemed to take an eternity to Bob. He much preferred crawling on his stomach working a hose line inside a building. A fire building was predictable. Human beings were not always.

"Chief," Ray said. "He just climbed that ladder like he did it every day, like he was cleaning a gutter. This woman dove out of that window. I thought she was coming right down on top of him. And when he gets down, he's like, 'What? So I climbed a ladder. No big deal'."

It seemed like it was pile onto Bob night. He did not feel like a hero that was for sure. First he suckers some guy then he coaxes a woman to climb down safely, not exactly fire eating valor. "I think you're getting carried away," Bob insisted, attempting to calm everybody down. "It's not like I crawled past fire to rescue an infant. You do what you have to do on this job, right?"

This brought a cascade of verbal abuse down on him. The Chief had listened to the crew's description of Bob's ladder work. He picked up the phone and called the Second Deputy. After a short conversation during which he recounted the details of what happened on the side of the fire building away from where the Second Deputy had set up, the Chief hung up the phone. He told them the Second Deputy was grateful for the job they did. Bob hoped it would end there, but had a feeling it would not. Having given up on studying, he decided to try and get some sleep. He would not remember what he studied now anyway.

Chapter Twenty-four

"Hello," the accented voice of Kathy's mother answered the phone. Kathy knew her mother had always wanted to shake off her foreign accent and speak like a native born American. It was a dream of hers she could never achieve. The neurons welded in place during childhood do not change easily. Although frustrating to her mother, Kathy had always found the sound of mama's voice to be loving and reassuring, Kathy's friends had always thought mama's accent was cute.

"Mama, I have news," Kathy began. She had thought long and hard about her decision not to tell her parents until Bob had shown his commitment by informing his. In the end, it made no sense to put off sharing the news. If Bob got cold feet it would be a catastrophic heartbreak needing all the support she could muster to get through. Kathy was many things, but a good loser was not one of them. She had not told Bob about her basketball days in high school or the fierce competition for valedictorian of her graduating class. When she competed it was no holds barred; no quarter given; no prisoners taken. She did not dare think of how she would react if he attempted to back out. Whatever her reaction, it would not be a pretty picture.

"What kind of news?" her mother asked in a voice laced with concern.

"Good news, mama, good news," Kathy reassured her.

"Don't frighten me like that," mama admonished her.

"Mama, he asked me to marry him!" she blurted out. There was a moment of silence on the other end of the phone then her mother asked, "And how did you answer?"

"Yes, of course," Kathy laughed.

The down side of informing mama over the phone was she could not see her mother's initial reaction, but she felt in her heart that mama was smiling and probably crying.

"Mama?" Kathy asked.

"Shh, let your mother control herself first," mama replied in a voice laced with emotion. "*Wo mashang daguo lai.*" Then there was a click.

Kathy was nervous now. She gently placed the phone back on its hook. "I'll call you back." Why not talk now? Was mama upset or overcome with joy? She had reverted to Mandarin which happened when she was overwhelmed. When her acceptance letter from Columbia had arrived, mama was overwhelmed with happiness. When she had been told by her brother that their grandmother had died, she was overwhelmed with grief. If mama's reaction was the latter, could Kathy go through with her engagement? Her mother had been nothing but supportive and encouraging as her relationship with Bob had evolved. Why were doubts now crowding in on her feelings? She jumped when the phone rang and picked it up with the trepidation of an errant child about to explain a broken window to her mother.

"Hello, mama?" she asked into the phone. The voice that answered revealed how silly she had become. When you want something this badly, the mind seeks out all the negatives as if to prepare for the worst.

"Hello, Kath," her father's voice answered. "Your mother tells me you have some happy news. She just can't verbalize it right now."

Kathy laughed at herself for being a worry wart. The mind games we play with ourselves. She was not telling her parents news that would have been considered out of the realm of possibilities. It was just coming a little earlier than expected.

"Dad, Bob asked me to marry him!" she bubbled. "And I said yes!"

"You're engaged?" her father laughed. "Congratulations, how did he ask you? Your mother is going to want to know."

She should have been prepared for that question. Mama had all sorts of romantic fantasies because her own engagement and marriage had been so simple. Should she create a story to make her mother happy? In the end, Kathy knew that probably would not work. She was horrible at lying.

"It's a little complicated," she began, "You see, he's been having some troubles."

"Complicated?" her father asked. "Troubles? What kind of troubles?" His tone had changed to one of concern.

"He's been studying so hard, putting a lot of pressure on himself," she explained reluctantly. "And the stress has been getting to him."

"He didn't go out and blow off steam somewhere, did he?" he asked.

She knew "blow off steam" was Fire Department parlance for drinking. "No, dad," she chuckled. "He really doesn't drink, just an occasional beer. He's been having some weird, stress related symptoms." Kathy could not believe what she was telling her father. Bob was the one insisting his symptoms were from stress. She was the one insisting there was something else wrong. She felt like a used car salesman trying to sell a car that might have some defects. It was not a good feeling.

"Weird, stress related symptoms?" was the response from her father. "What kind of stress related symptoms? Has he seen a doctor?"

She felt so false holding back like this and knew the guilt would eat at her happiness if she went through with it.

"I've pushed him to get checked out," she said truthfully. "No one will say what it might be right now. It's still a work in progress."

"So, what are his symptoms?" he persisted.

"He has some loss of sensation in his hands and frequent urination," she answered. There was no way she was going to describe to her father some of his other symptoms!

"You know," her father told her. "We had a guy on the job who had similar symptoms. It turned out to be diabetes. Of course, he was an older fellow, but maybe you should have him checked out for that."

"We will," she assured him. "It's one step at a time right now. I have to make an appointment to see another doctor."

"Kath, can I ask you a hard question?" he said quietly.

She was expecting hard questions from her father. After all he had not met Bob yet. The way the conversation was going, Kathy knew the hard question was not about Bob's character or his prospects. "Yes, of course you can," she replied.

"What if it isn't stress?" he asked. "What if it's something serious? What will you do?"

"I'll love him," she answered. There was a pause before he responded.

"Then I guess I will too," he replied.

"Thank you dad," she said in an emotional whisper.

"So, how did he propose to you?" was his next question.

"It wasn't exactly the romantic interlude mama has dreamed of," Kathy began. She could not remember another time when she started a story with more of an understatement. How to craft the tale so it would sound romantic enough to please her mother? It took only a moment to realize it would be an impossible task. He had not even given her a ring. Mama would consider it a business arrangement more than a love story. If she was going to please her mother, she would have to doctor the story considerably. Careful girl, she told herself, you always give yourself away when you stray from the truth.

"No one experiences a romantic interlude like your mother dreams of," her father chuckled. "How far off the mark was it?"

"Quite a bit," Kathy admitted. "It went like this. We had to go to the emergency room and the nurse said only family could accompany him into the exam room."

"And you weren't going to be left out," he interrupted with a laugh.

"Before I could say anything," Kathy continued, ignoring his comment. "Bob said I'm his fiancé, did that count?"

"Good for him," dad commented. "He's quick on his feet and knows you well."

"Dad, I'm trying to tell you the story," she chided him.

"Opps," was the response with a hint of contrition. "I'll try to be quiet."

"Thank you," Kathy chuckled. "So the nurse turned to me and asked if that was true and I said yes."

"So, you had a facilitator," he observed. "Kind of like an arranged marriage."

"Dad!" Kathy scolded. "Don't say that, mom will freak!" Firemen and their off kilter sense of humor.

He became serious again with his next question, but she had been prepared to answer it months before and had just answered the same type of question from Chingli.

"You know, when you were up here over the holidays, you told us all about him. It was obvious you were smitten, but you never explained why. So, why do you love him?" he asked.

"Because he's a poetic fireman," she answered without thought. Of all the people in her life, he would understand her answer best. When she was growing up, mama could not really help with her homework. That task had fallen on her father. He knew all her literary strengths and weaknesses.

"A poetic fireman?" he muttered. "I'm trying to get my mind around that. From the picture you showed us, he's not your stereotypical poet. I remember that poetic kid from your freshman year. He didn't have what it takes. A poetic fireman, he's really dangerous for you isn't he?"

It was sometimes unnerving how well her parents knew her. There seemed to be no part of her life where she could surprise them. Was that because she was an only child or was she that simple a read? Was that a good trait or something else? Whatever it was; now was not the time to ruminate about it.

"Yes," she confessed. "I knew from the first day we met and I've been very defensive around him, trying to slow myself down. But he got under my skin anyway."

"I'm happy to hear that," he told her. "I was afraid of a Florence Nightingale relationship."

"I loved him before he started having problems," she reassured her father. "I think we make a good team."

"A good team?" he laughed. "So who's the point guard?"

"Dad!" she reacted, then could not resist answering. "I am, of course."

After she spoke with her mother again, Kathy hung up the phone. Now it was on to the girls, although she doubted it would be new to them. Chingli had probably spread the news as far as possible. Before Kathy could pick up the receiver to dial Stacey or Gloria, it rang. Gloria screamed an enthusiastic "You did it" when she answered the phone. It was off to the races after that.

"We want to go out to celebrate," Gloria insisted. "Stacey accepted the scholarship today; you got engaged; and Chingli found out she was pregnant." In spite of her friend's enthusiasm and energy, Kathy suddenly felt bad for Gloria. She would be celebrating for everyone but herself; realizing that put a bit of a damper on Kathy's joy. How should she approach the subject?

"Are you sure you're okay, Glor?" Kathy asked awkwardly. "You seem to be the only one not celebrating for herself."

Gloria laughed and then reassured her, "Kathy, I'm the only one who didn't work for something to celebrate. My turn will come. Right now all of my best friends need my support to celebrate."

Kathy felt the weight that had suddenly dropped on her lift off just as quickly. Tonight was the girls' night to celebrate as long as Chingli could shake Frank. The guys were in the firehouse.

"So, where does your brother fit in all of this?" Kathy inquired lightly.

"He has things to clear up at the office," Gloria told her. "Then he'll go to the gym and pick up a pizza or something. He didn't express a desire to hang out with us."

"I wouldn't expect him to, he got beat up the last time he did." Kathy observed. "So, let's do it. What did you have in mind?"

"Stacey knows a place in Clifton," Gloria said. "It's called Bella Napoli and the food is supposed to be exquisite."

"Sounds good," Kathy agreed. "How do I get there?"

"We'll pick you up," Gloria offered. "Parking is limited, so it'll make everything easier."

"Dress code?" was Kathy's next question.

"Casual," Gloria reassured her. "It wouldn't be fair if we had to work."

"Then I'm ready to go," Kathy bubbled.

Bella Napoli was a tiny restaurant not far from Bob's apartment. It appeared to be in what was once a small diner with a half dozen parking spaces on either side of the rectangular building. Stacey pulled into the only empty space available and appeared very content that she could do so. They all hopped out of the car and headed for the entrance. A wall greeted them as the stepped into the building. A sharp left turn and a few paces brought them to the dining room door made up of small beveled windows set in wooden frames. Dark paneling lined the walls of the short hallway. A waiter opened the door and made an inviting gesture to welcome them into the dining area. Glancing at her surrounding, Kathy estimated there were perhaps twenty small tables lining the walls and scattered about the middle of the room. These were covered with white table clothes and surrounded by cushioned chairs. The coloring of the room was dark and subdued. Large windows ran along two of the walls while a mural depicting Italy, most likely Naples when she remembered the name of the restaurant, occupied another. The four of them followed the waiter to a table by a window. Sunlight still flowed in through the glass, but Kathy doubted there would be anything but moonlight when they left. As they settled in, Chingli excused herself to go to the ladies room. Kathy chose the seat with its back to the window to avoid the distractions outside the restaurant. She wanted to focus on her friends.

There were so many questions she wanted to ask. The first one was practical and directed at Stacey since she had chosen the restaurant.

"What would you recommend?" Kathy asked.

Stacey opened the menu and scanned down through the offerings. "I'd recommend the chicken cordon bleu," she stated confidently. "They do a good job on the chicken, but the sauce will change your life. It's that good."

Kathy had never seen her friend so enthusiastic about a meal. With such an endorsement how could she not try it?

"What kind of sauce is it?" she asked.

"It's a white wine sauce with garlic," Stacey told her.

"I feel like I'd be a fool if I passed up the opportunity," she sighed. "I usually like to try the red gravy first at Italian restaurants, but with such a ringing endorsement I guess I can't this time."

Gloria had been listening to the exchange. She shook her head and laughed. "You would think the two of you were food critics for some gourmet magazine," she chided them. "The chicken comes with a bowl of pasta. Just have them put the gravy on that and you have the best of both worlds. Make sure you write a good review."

Kathy laughed at Gloria's observation while basking in the warmth of the friendships that surrounded her. Chingli returned with the waiter, who quickly took their order. As he walked away, it dawned on Kathy that the four of them spent an inordinate amount of time talking in restaurants or at least enjoying a meal when they got together. It seemed there was always a reason for them to sit down to good food and chat. She wondered if any of her friends had also noticed this. It would be a good starter point for all the questions she had.

"Do you realize," Kathy said after the waiter returned with wine for three of them and water for the expecting mother. "That whenever we get together we eat?"

They all laughed at her observation although Gloria and Stacey denied its validity. "We have sat for hours talking without consuming a morsel of food," Stacey contested. "But tonight we celebrate and celebrations call for good food."

Kathy could not deny that. The two culinary traditions that were her heritage demanded food when celebrating. Did Stacey and Gloria grow up with the same emphasis on food and celebration? "So, do you think all of mankind eats when they celebrate?"

"Of course they do," Gloria laughed. "Birthdays, holidays, weddings, even Irish wakes, people celebrated with food. Of course an Irish wake celebrates the life of the deceased, not their death. At least that's what my mother always told me. But anyway, people eat to celebrate. It's only natural."

"I agree," Chingli chimed in. "You know what the lunar New Year celebration is like and the San Gennaro celebration in Little Italy is so much about food, no?"

"Yes," Kathy conceded. "But if we keep this up, we're going to get fat. After all we have three reasons to celebrate tonight. Does that mean we have to eat three times as much?"

Moans followed that question. "We're only celebrating one thing tonight," Gloria declared. "We celebrate friendship. Raise your glasses to friendship, girls."

All four agreed with Gloria's assertion. Kathy looked around the table and did a quick review of each woman's story. They all had one thing in common, so she offered a second quiet toast. "And here's to feminine conspiracies," she said softly. "May men never catch on."

"Careful," Stacey whispered. "The walls have ears."

The frequent laughter from their table was drawing the attention of everyone around them. Kathy motioned for her friends to calm down. They could not see the reactions around the room.

Chingli added a bit of wisdom to the conversation. "Most older men know," she said. "It's the younger men who have cloudy minds, but that's the way of nature, isn't it?" They all agreed to this just as their meals came.

During dinner Kathy caught up on Stacey's news and learned the details of what Chingli was experiencing. One of the changes was the frequency of her friend's visits to the ladies' room. She gave them her own details of what had transpired that day. When Stacey heard the theory of diabetes Kathy's father had floated, she was skeptical. There were too many other symptoms. They had all agreed when dinner came to save half their meals for their men. That way they could enjoy dessert. When the waiter came with coffee and dessert, Kathy decided it was time to ask the questions that worried her.

"So, I'd like to tap the wisdom that surrounds me," she began facetiously. "When do I reveal all those little secrets I kept hidden while we dated?"

This brought a burst of laughter. If nothing else, they were enjoying each other's company. Gloria put a shocked look on her face and asked, "Kathy, do you have secrets? You have tarnished your image beyond repair, a news reporter who chased down the truth, now confessing to withholding information from Bob. I knew it!"

"And how many secret lovers have you entertained Miss Stanley?" Stacey asked.

Kathy felt her face redden a bit. Lovers were not the secrets unfortunately, she thought. "I wish I could confess to passionate lovers," she sighed. "But I've been too busy pursuing a career for such distractions. I have held back certain parts of myself because I thought they might get in the way." She sipped her coffee after sampling the rum cake in front of her. There was a momentary pause in the conversation as it down shifted to a more serious topic.

"Some secrets you never reveal," Chingli admitted quietly. "That is easier for me because my past is in Taiwan."

"Oh, we have our secrets," Stacey confessed. "Just because we grew up together doesn't mean Ray knows all. It's best to keep a little mystery in a relationship. Of course, if your secret is going to ring the doorbell and say, 'Hi, mom', you should talk about it." Quiet chuckles followed this bit of advice. The tone of the conversation had definitely changed.

"I'm a little young for that," Kathy replied.

Chingli felt obliged to point out, "Two hundred years ago, you would have been married for ten years, would have five children, and would be middle aged."

"We've come a long way," Kathy laughed. "Thank God."

"What's eating at you Kath?" Gloria asked.

Kathy thought about how to present her concerns concisely. "There's this part of me he hasn't seen," she began. "You see, my mother was determined that I wouldn't be overshadowed by the boys in school. She had this thing about making sure the Chinese penchant for . . .in Mandarin the expression is zhong nan, qing nu. It literally means heavy male, light female. That's how she was raised; so my uncles went to college, but she didn't. That wasn't happening to her daughter. To prevent it, she encouraged me to compete and my dad didn't have a son, so all his attention was on me."

Her friends were listening intently. Chingli had smiled knowingly when Kathy quoted the Chinese expression. Gloria and Stacey shook their heads in understanding, so she pushed on. "I developed a keen sense of competitiveness. I'm not a good loser and I tend to be a showboat when I win," she laughed at herself. "I played basketball in high school, never told Bob that. But I had a problem with technical fouls for arguing with the ref. Then there was the competition for valedictorian."

"You were valedictorian of your school?" Gloria interrupted.

Kathy smiled and involuntarily bowed her head for a moment. "It came down to one final exam. I was competing with a kid named John Steinbeck; it's funny, he couldn't write very well. He was a math and science wiz. The last I heard he was in med school, so Stacey might run into him some day. If you do, don't mention my name. I humiliated him in the middle of the school hallway."

"Kathy!" Stacey exclaimed in feinted shock.

"You see the teacher posted the final grades on the wall outside his classroom. They were listed with our social security numbers and I had gone through the trouble of memorizing John's. When the grades were posted and I saw them, I did a victory dance in the hallway pointing at John and telling him he lost. Bob doesn't know I was valedictorian or that my character has this flaw. Competition brings out the worst in me."

The girls sat quietly for a moment; this was followed by a chorus of protests and questions. "I don't think Bob would be put off by your competitive side," Gloria opined. "Guys like feisty women. Just don't spike the ball when you beat him."

Everyone agreed with Gloria. Then Stacey asked, "Why haven't you told him you were valedictorian?"

Kathy thought about it. Why had she held that bit of information back? Her stomach felt uncomfortable just thinking about it. It was a deep seated fear; Bob knowing that would have chased him away. She had told other men and it had changed their attitude towards her, some for the better, some for the worse. Knowing Bob, she was certain holding back had been the right decision. "I didn't tell him right away because he was so attractive and I didn't want to scare him off," she confessed, then cut a piece of cake and waited for the response.

Stacey put down her cup of coffee and asked in disbelief, "You thought it would intimidate him if he found out you were that smart?"

Kathy shook her head yes. Before Stacey could contest this assertion Chingli chimed in. "I think, for Bob, that was a good choice. Frank tells me that Bob is so smart, but doesn't think so because of his high school."

Gloria shook her head in agreement after she finished sipping her coffee. "From what Jack tells me, and believe me he is very closed mouth about it, Bob might have been spooked at the beginning. But if it comes up in conversation now, you can tell him. You set the hook already, Kath. Now you just have to play with him a little more and reel him in."

Stacey did not appear convinced. "I don't know," she said. "It's best to have a relationship based on the truth."

Kathy agreed with that, but after she had read the poem Bob wrote at Gloria's wedding, it was too risky. "It's not like I lied to him," she asserted. "I just held something back. Haven't you held back on Ray, Dr. Stacey?"

They laughed while Stacey put up her hands in surrender. Then Chingli stood up and scooted to the ladies' room one more time.

"She's acting like Bob," Kathy laughed.

"Ladies, if you ever plan to have children," Stacey warned. "That is your future."

They leaned back in their chairs, sipping coffee and quietly enjoying each other's company. Kathy was content. She had confessed her transgression and been absolved by the feminine tribunal. Now she just had to reveal her secrets a little at a time and then reel in her catch. It was fortunate that her dad had taught her how to fish. She knew she would have to explain Gloria's metaphor to Chingli later. Poor girl could not ask the question when she heard it. Her bladder was in control of her life right now. Men could never appreciate what women do for the species.

Chapter Twenty-five

McGovern's was slowly beginning to fill as guys trickled in from test sites around the state. Bob sat at the bar waiting for his crew to show up. They had chosen different sites for one reason or another. His reasoning had been strictly convenience. It had not mattered to him what his surroundings would be like while he wrote. His focus would be on the paper in front of him. Bloomfield Tech had been the closest. Hector had picked Piscataway High which meant he had an hour drive from North Newark to Middlesex County. Bob suspected the reason was there would be fewer Newark guys at that site. Hector was still a little sensitive about taking the test with only a year's experience even if it was just for practice. Jack and Ray had chosen a site midway between their homes so they could meet there. Hank lived down the shore and so had chosen a south Jersey test center. He doubted the chief's driver would come all the way up to Newark to talk about the test over a beer. They would have to wait until their first day back in the firehouse to hear his take on the morning.

Bob took a sip of his beer and reviewed his answers. After all these months of preparation, all the reading and memorizing, it turned out that Kathy's insistence on writing carried him through. Sister Mary Elephant had hammered away at two points, writing responses that mimicked the examples in the study guide and following directions. As far as he could tell, doing well on this test required just those points, following the directions, writing a good size-up as part of an initial radio transmission, and making sure you did not order your firefighters to do something that might get them injured or killed. Spelling, grammar, and punctuation did not count. Any factors left out of the information provided on the test could be inserted by the test taker. In the end, it resembled writing a novel more than a non-fiction essay. Naturally, everything went quite smoothly at the fires he had written about. There were no bad hydrants, no burst hose lines, no holes in the floor, no weakened or non-existent stairs. It had been a simple stretch in; order everyone to throw on a mask after making sure they were wearing the proper turnout gear, ascertaining no rescues were needed, and dragging a hand-line in to the seat of the fire. If only things worked out that way in the real world. The biggest challenge he had was sitting through the last forty-five minutes with a bladder screaming for relief.

Jack and Ray popped in through the door as Bob took another swig of beer. He felt fairly confident that his answers would allow him to move on to the second part of the exam. From what he was overhearing, not everyone around him felt that way. One of the guys from the Bureau of Combustibles moaned after realizing he had fought the fires like a Newark captain instead of an "Alexandra City" captain. That meant his essays had too many companies on the scene, so he had failed this part of the exam. Bob tilted his bottle and drank a silent toast to his girl. He owed her for teaching him the importance of discipline when taking a test. No shortcuts or assumptions were allowed. Just follow the instructions and you can defend what you wrote if you appeal the test grade. Jack reached him as he swallowed the toast.

"How does the student feel he did?" Jack shouted.

"Alexandra isn't such a tough town," Bob answered. "My guys fought those fires flawlessly. How about you?" He figured Jack would have been able to write a respectable answer to the first two scenarios. The third one involved truck work. Since Jack had spent all of his time assigned to an engine company, he had little truck experience. Bob had devoted a lot of his study time to truck work because he was in the same boat. Jack had not cracked a book, so any instructions he had given his truck men were suspect.

"Let me get a beer," Jack laughed. "Then we can talk." Ray walked up as Jack was hailing the bartender, so the two waited for beers while Bob moved to a table. After settling in, Jack began to give his take on the morning.

"I haven't written longhand like that since high school," he complained. "It was a challenge and I think they screwed the truck men." Ray shook his head in agreement while nursing his beer. The room was beginning to really fill up. Guys from central Jersey test sites were wandering in. Bob knew Hector would show up in a few minutes, so he wanted to wait before they analyzed the test. The new arrivals were making a lot of noise about a fire drill, but the details were drowned out by laughter. Hector walked in on the tail end of the commotion. He spotted their table, waved, pointed at the bar, and began to weave through the growing crowd.

"Hector's here," Bob told his buddies. "It's getting crowded. If we want to order something to eat, we better do it quick." With that the three of them made their way to Hector and ordered burgers. The bartender was swamped and asked Jack why so many firefighters were in on a Saturday afternoon. As soon as he heard of the captain's test he made a quick phone call. Bob was sure the bartender had called for help. Hopefully, a couple of waitresses would be in early to shorten the wait for food and drinks. It was twenty minutes before all four of them were settled. Between bites Hector told them about what had happened in Piscataway.

"I couldn't believe it," he complained. "We were like thirty minutes into the test and some wise ass decides to pull a fire alarm in the school." Jack almost choked on his food when he heard this and started to laugh. Everyone thought it was hilarious except for Hector "We had to leave our stuff on the desks and evacuate the building," he continued. "I couldn't help thinking how stupid it was. You have a school filled with city firefighters and they have to leave the building? If there was a fire, who better to be inside? We'd put it out before the local department showed up."

"Not your jurisdiction," Ray pointed out. "You have to respect the guys rolling in. They're responsible for the school and everyone in it."

"Yeah, but I still felt dumb," Hector moaned. "I thought maybe we should just ignore the whole thing and keep writing."

"I feel sorry for the vollies pulling up," Jack pointed out. "They probably knew who was using the building. I imagine it would be a little intimidating. You see more fire some nights than they see in a year. That's not easy."

"You're right," Hector admitted. "My first taste of a suburban school and there's a false alarm. I can't win."

They all laughed with Hector. Bob wondered if someone wanted to check a book in their car and so pulled the alarm. He hoped that was not true, but you could never be sure.

"I can't help but compare this test to the last one," Jack said after looking around the room. He was the only one who had been on the job when the last test was given. "Guys came back to the firehouse and wrote down all the questions they could remember. Then they called around the city to the houses that had guys in the books. By the end of the day they had reconstructed the entire test."

"You can do that with multiple choice tests," Bob pointed out. "But it doesn't help much with essays. This was not my father's promo test."

"I'm not even sure what they were looking for," Ray admitted.

"They wanted something like the examples in the study guide," Bob told him before taking a bite out of his burger. He washed it down with a little beer and glanced around the room. There were not a lot of cocky firefighters in the place. He felt confident about his test although they would not know the results for weeks. The format of the test was so new his confidence could easily be misplaced. If that happened he would be really pissed off. Right now he was just glad the first portion was over.

"So how do you boys feel about your chances?" he asked.

"I just took it for practice," Ray told him. "That being said, looking around the room at all the glum faces, you never know. The only problem I had was the truck scenario. That was a shot in the dark. The engine scenarios I just fought the way we fight fires."

Jack shook his head in agreement while biting into his burger. Hector had been unusually quiet. He was a hard read. It seemed the fire drill really bothered him. Whatever the reason, he was not volunteering his opinion. Instead Hector appeared to be in one of his brooding phases. Bob figured he would begin talking in a few minutes, so he moved the conversation in a different direction.

"I've been wondering if any of you could throw a little advice my way on adjusting to my new situation," Bob began ambiguously.

"New situation?" Jack asked. "Are you referring to your change from single and free to betrothed and confused?"

Bob laughed at the description. "Yeah, very confused, I have to admit I'm still getting used to her being in every corner of my life."

"Listen to Mr. Experience," Ray laughed. "It's been less than a month since he backed into proposing and he's still getting used to it. Want to know a little secret, Bob? You never get used to it. You just accept it."

He was afraid of an answer like that. How do you accept giving up your independence?

"Sounds like you're having issues with her accompanying you to the doctor. Do you remember Frank's take on men, women, and worrying?" Jack asked.

"You mean the possible/probable difference?" Bob replied.

Jack shook his head yes. Of all the bits of advice Bob had been given, that was the most useful in understanding Kathy. He had been living with it for months. It was probably nothing, but possibly everything. "I am reminded of that every time I sneeze, cough, or yawn," Bob said. "Remember, I've been to more doctors over the past month than I've seen in my entire life and next week she has me going to another type of doctor. Then I go for an outpatient thing with the urologist. It doesn't seem to end." Bob had to admit the incessant worrying was getting old.

"That's the way they are," Ray pointed out. "You learn to live with it or you learn to be celibate. Just don't tell her every time you stub your toe. Now that the pressure is off, you can take a break from the books and relax with her. You'll both feel a lot better, believe me."

Bob took a deep breath and then emptied his mug. It seemed his friends were as confused about their wives as he was about Kathy. He remembered the Chief's advice about acceptance. Ray apparently agreed, so striving to accept seemed the most direct path to nirvana. Hector had yet to give his take on the test. Bob knew the longer he held back, the deeper the problem was.

"Hector, how do you think you did?" Bob asked. The question seemed to startle him. He took a second to think before answering. "I had the same problem Jack and Ray had," Hector explained. "The only time I've done truck work is when I was detailed to a truck company. That hasn't happened much, so the truck question was guessing."

"Hector, you've got to do well," Jack teased. "They'll throw the test out if they don't get the consent decree numbers."

Hector bristled at the mention of the decree. "I don't need a consent decree. I can do it on my own, but I don't know if I want to do well on this test. They can give me all the back seniority they want. Without the experience, I might get someone killed."

"We're paying for the sins of the Fire Department's past lives," Bob reminded everyone. "The decree is our reality. Your perfect outcome would be coming out like fifty. Then you won't get made for a couple of years. You'd get your experience and get promoted off this list."

"When does anything work out perfectly?" Hector asked. All of them shook their heads in agreement. They were all quiet for a minute then Jack shot a question at Bob that changed the subject completely.

"So, did you tell your parents yet?" he asked with a sly smile.

Did I tell my parents? How does he come up with these questions? Bob thought. "I've been busy," he explained. "I'm going to call them tonight."

All three of his friends looked at him in disbelief. "That wasn't supposed to be a serious question," Jack said sounding flabbergasted. "You can't be serious. You haven't called your parents to tell them you asked a woman to marry you? Are you nuts?"

He did not know how to respond to Jack. Bob knew he was pushing his luck a little, but his friend's reaction gave him doubts. It was not like he did not want to tell them. They already knew about Kathy and were in love with the girl he described to them. It had all happened so suddenly, so he had not prepared. How do you tell your parents something that hopefully will only happen once in your life?

He just did not have time to work on that question. The delay in his answer produced a barrage of abuse from all of his buddies.

"Okay, okay," Bob surrendered. "I'll call them tonight."

"You better pray Kathy doesn't ask the same question," Ray warned. "Or it could be the shortest engagement on record."

"I still have to buy a ring for her," Bob reminded them. "You two have done this. Where's a good place for a nice ring?"

"Didn't you say Kathy wanted to help pick the ring?" Hector asked, obviously interested in picking up pointers for the future.

Bob shook his head yes. "If she's going to be involved," Jack warned him. "The best place to pick out a ring is where ever she wants to go." Ray agreed without hesitation. Bob was disappointed with the answer, but knew pursuing the question any further was pointless. He figured their little session was over until Jack threw another question at him.

"You're going to another doctor next week, right?" he asked out of the blue.

"Yeah, why?" Bob answered.

"What if this guy finds out there's something wrong and orders you out of the firehouse?"

"Where did you come up with that?" Bob shot back. "It's not like I'm on the floor clutching my chest."

"Just asking about the worst case scenario," Jack reassured him.

"That's not a worst case scenario," Bob laughed dryly. "That's a nightmare."

314

Ray and Hector were listening intently. The question went to the heart of their existence. None of them had any intention of leaving the firehouse, not until their bodies gave out. Just the thought of being ordered out of the firehouse made Bob's stomach flip. Why was Jack asking the question? Did Stacey say something to Gloria? He had spent the morning answering difficult questions, now this?

"Agreed, it's a nightmare," Jack pushed. "But what would you do?"

"Ignore him," Bob stated flatly.

"With Kathy sitting there?" Jack asked skeptically.

"She'll understand," Bob answered unconvincingly.

"Really," Jack doubted. "I hope you're right."

Until Jack had asked that last question, Bob had felt pretty confident about his future. What if this guy tells him there was a problem and he should leave the firehouse? Would he have to listen? The Fire Department could not find out about any condition until Bob allowed it. He resolved right then to stay in the firehouse until he became a threat to the safety of the guys. If he got a little banged up it did not matter. He would be living life as he chose, on the edge and with a purpose.

Chapter Twenty-six

Kathy eased out of the fast lane as she approached the Essex toll plaza. Her mind had been all over the map on the drive up from South Orange, so she put extra effort into paying attention to the traffic around her. The Parkway gradually widened from three to eight lanes, but there were no markings on the road surface indicating lanes as she entered the plaza. A line of green toll booths swept across the north and south bound lanes of the roadway. A few had toll collectors for those drivers who did not have exact change. The other lanes had white baskets reaching out from the wall of the booth. Bob called them white gloved bandits. These were still extracting the proper coins from the driving public, even though it had been promised decades before that the tolls would cease as soon as the cost of building the road had been collected. Since then the Garden State Parkway had become a living entity that grew a little each year and so was never completely paid for. Kathy slid into an exact change booth and tossed in her contribution to maintaining the Parkway bureaucracy, the forward momentum of the car only hesitating a moment before moving to the far right of the road and rolling into the Hoover Avenue exit. She made a conscious effort to change her driving mindset after leaving the insanity that was highway driving in New Jersey. A calmer approach was more appropriate when navigating through suburbia.

The trees across from the exit ramp were a deep healthy green. Patches of puffy clouds floated across the sky and the air was comfortable for the first time in weeks. An unusual cold front was passing through the mid-Atlantic states region. This was denim weather, a time to wear jeans and a jacket of that material. No need for a fashion show, they were only seeing a doctor. There would be no fashion police in attendance. Overall the day did not appear to be the type that would change her outlook on the future, but she had a feeling of dread sitting like a stone in her stomach. Maybe Bob was right and it was just stress. She immediately laughed at herself for even thinking that. In her heart she knew there was something else going on and prayed that something was not a brain tumor or some other life stealing malady. Stacey had called the night before to give support and tell her of an offer from Doctor Dunn, the neurologist who was one of her professors. "Doctor Dunn said if you need to talk with someone, to get a second opinion or some guidance, he's willing to help out, pro-bono." Why would a neurologist on the staff at University Hospital even think they would need to speak with anyone unless he suspected Bob's condition was serious? That was why she had insisted on driving. Of course, she did not tell him that. As far as Bob was concerned she was saving him a round trip to South Orange. If what the doctor said threw him for a loop, she would guarantee he did nothing stupid.

There had never been a busier, more emotional period of her life. So much seemed to reach fruition at the same time, not all of it had turned out as expected. Bob should have been cheerful or excited or at least relieved after completing the first portion of his test. Instead he was preoccupied, almost brooding. When she had asked why, he had responded that it was something Jack had asked him. That was the last honest answer she got. She inquired about what Jack had said and he had dodged the question and then finally said something about buying an engagement ring where ever the woman wanted. That was an obvious blatant lie. Something as silly as that would not put him into the funk he was in. She did not push it, deciding instead to wait him out until the truth slipped from his mouth.

The phone calls to both sets of parents had been nerve wracking. Each wanted to make as good an impression as possible. Mama had been so excited to speak with Bob. The first thing she asked was if he could really speak Mandarin. He had given the truthful answer of yidian-diar, a little, not realizing that was a polite way of saying yes. Mama had taken off leaving Bob behind and very confused. Kathy had to take the phone from him to hear what her mother was saying. After straightening that out, dad had picked up the phone. The two of them were like kindred souls. The whole brother firefighter, fire service subculture came into play. In the end, her parents loved him. After that it was on to his folks. That was when things got dicey. Bob did not want to tell his mother about doctor visits until he had completed all of them. Kathy had to promise she would play along with his subterfuge. They had a pleasant conversation, but something told Kathy that Bob's mom knew he was holding back. That suspicion was confirmed by a surprise call from her the following day.

Without Bob around the two of them had spoken for an hour. His mother knew he had not been completely honest and she was worried. She assured Kathy that Bob had spent his life trying to hide things from her and she had spent his entire life seeing through him. Was their relationship okay? Was his job secure? Kathy could not allow her to continue worrying, so she had opened up after pleading for secrecy. Hearing about Bob's health issues, his mother had understood why he held back. She then thanked Kathy for her honesty because now she could prepare herself. Then she requested Kathy call her with any results in case Bob decided to protect her. Now Kathy had one more secret to keep from Bob and an additional conspirator to talk with. Men just did not appreciate how complex a woman's life was. An idea crossed her mind to write a book about the secret lives of women. The thought reminded her of the dinner conversation with her fellow conspirators and the secrets they admitted keeping. Chingli had said some would never be revealed. That had an ominous sound to it.

Bob was waiting on the sidewalk when Kathy arrived at his place. She pulled the car into the driveway leading to the back of his building. He scooted around to the front of the car, hopped up on the hood, and slid on his rear across it to the passenger side, landing on his feet with a triumphant smile. Any concerns that might be weighing him down were well hidden under his exuberance. At least she had the car washed recently. He would not walk into the doctor's office wearing filthy pants.

"You're full of spunk today," Kathy pointed out when he dropped himself into the car.

"It's going to be my day of release," Bob told her as he slammed the door closed. "This guy's going to say it's just stress, go take the lovely lady out for a romantic lunch and relax. It'll all go away in a little while."

Kathy wanted to slap him and yell "wake up." Was he putting on a brave front or was he in complete denial? She put the car in reverse and backed out onto Prospect Street. While she shifted the transmission into drive she asked, "You have your insurance card?"

Bob chuckled at the question. "Yes, Kath, guys are self-contained. Their lives are held in their wallet. Money, credit cards, insurance cards, pictures of the love of their life, all held in that billfold stuffed down their pants rear pocket."

"Good," she replied. "I hope Mr. Self-contained is right about the effects of stress and has learned how to control it for the second half of the test."

"I'm right, don't worry," he assured her. "You really didn't have to come all the way up here. I could have gone by myself."

Kathy laughed quietly as she stopped at Center Street and waited for traffic to clear. "Not after sitting through your act at the urologist's office," she informed him.

"My act?" Bob bounced back at her. "You were unimpressed with my interview at Dr. LaConti's?"

"Oh, it was impressive," Kathy said. "There's no need to impress this guy. Just give him the facts, all the facts."

"You don't doubt my honest heart?" Bob asked.

"The heart I don't doubt," she told him. "It's the mouth that sometimes sways from complete disclosure. If you don't give the doctor all the info he needs, you'll only make matters worse." By now they were on Franklin Avenue. Clara Maas was ten minutes away. "Are you going to call your folks tonight with the results?"

"I'll call when there are results," he said. "No need to worry them until I have something final." They drove the rest of the way in silence. Kathy did not want to push the subject for fear that he would put two and two together and realize she had spoken with his mom.

After parking the car, they walked silently into the professional building. Dr. Bradinsky was on the second floor. Stacey's professor had assured her he was one of the best in the state. Hopefully, that would turn into a quick diagnosis and resolution of whatever ailed Bob. They stepped into a crowded waiting room filled with patients who appeared to be on the mend. At least they had no obvious signs of illness at first glance. Bob went to the receptionist window to announce his arrival while Kathy found two seats in a corner. She sat and smiled at an elderly couple across from her as she made a quick sweep of the room. It took only a moment to realize her initial impression of the patients waiting to see Dr. Bradinsky was off the mark. Most of the people were elderly. Some appeared to have suffered strokes; others had the tremors of Parkinson's. There was a middle aged woman sitting in a wheelchair close to the receptionist. Kathy could not tell why the wheelchair was necessary since there was no obvious sign of injury.

"Excuse me," the elderly gentleman across form her said. "You look very familiar. Were you a news reporter on television?"

Kathy smiled, delighted that people still recognized her after so many months off the air. "I was," she answered politely. "I took a leave of absence from the station to do some writing."

"You see dear," the gentleman said to his partner. "I knew it was her. My wife didn't believe me when I told her. We watched you every night. Are you going to be back on the news?"

"I haven't decided yet," Kathy answered. She wanted to cultivate the conversation. If they were established patients of Dr. Bradinsky, maybe she could get a feel for the kind of doctor he was from them.

"Have you seen Dr. Bradinsky before?" she asked.

"Yes," the husband replied. "I suffered a stroke two years ago. He's a miracle worker."

"When he came into the hospital room," his wife continued. "He took me aside and said that if we were willing to work hard, rehabilitation could bring back a lot of what was damaged. All that's left is a little bit of a limp. The doctor may not have the gentlest bedside manner, but he knows what he's doing and that sternness was needed at the beginning."

"Thank you," Kathy said. "That's encouraging to hear."

The receptionist called out a name and the couple stood up. "That's us," the woman said. "It was nice talking to you. Good luck." Bob walked up as the couple left. Kathy reached into her purse for a pen and took the papers from her fiancé. By the time Bob's name was called all the forms were completed and handed to the receptionist. They walked into a small office dominated by a desk and shelves filled with books. The wall behind the doctor had a few family photos and one of a younger Dr. Bradinsky in an operating room. The doctor sat behind the desk with a handheld tape recorder next to him and Bob's chart in front of him.

"Hello, doc," Bob began. "Bob Brendler and this is my fiancé, Kathy Stanley."

"Hello, what can I do for you?" the doctor replied.

"Dr. LaConti suggested I see you," Bob began. "I had some trouble voiding about a month ago."

"Any other symptoms?" the doctor asked.

"I've had some stress related issues lately," Bob added. "Nothing major."

"Stress related issues?" the doctor asked. "Tell me about your issues."

Kathy had held back with difficulty when Bob had answered. Thank God the doctor did not let him push his other symptoms off to the side. The elderly couple was right, he was curt and to the point. Hopefully, he was also as competent as they claimed.

"I've had tingling and blunted sensations, first in my legs, then in my hands and forearms then it spread to my chest and back," Bob explained. "There's also a floater in my right eye. I saw an ophthalmologist for that."

"Which ophthalmologist did you see?" the doctor asked.

"Dr. Erhler." Bob told him.

"These sensations, do they come and go or are they always there?" was the next question from the doctor.

Bob appeared a little surprised by the question. "They come and go with the stress in my life," Bob admitted. "I've been studying for a promotional test, so I spend six to eight hours a day studying. I'm a Newark firefighter, so I work days and nights then I work at a part time job occasionally. So there hasn't been a lot of time to relax, but I just finished the first portion of the test. That should give me a little breathing room for a while."

"You study six to eight hours a day while you fight fires in Newark?" the doctor asked in amazement.

"Yes," Bob replied. Kathy was proud of the thoroughness with which Bob had explained his symptoms. About the only thing left out of his report was the effect on his love life. She was not going to push that subject, not after the embarrassment in the urologist's office.

"When the symptoms recede, do they go away completely?" the doctor continued.

"Well at first they went away, but as they came and went it seems there was a little residual bluntness that remained," Bob confessed.

"How long has this been going on?" the doctor probed.

"Less than a year," Bob informed him.

"Now, you said there was trouble voiding your bladder," the doctor asked. "Have you noticed any change in sensitivity during sex?"

Kathy felt her face blush. This guy was good. She could not avoid that subject.

Bob chuckled before answering, "Sometimes I have difficulty climaxing," he admitted.

"Difficulty or inability?" the doctor countered.

"Inability," Bob reluctantly answered.

"Okay, come to the other room so I can examine you." With that the doctor stood up, walked around the desk, and into a room off the office. Bob followed while Kathy remained seated. She was not invited and did not bother asking since she could see into the other room. She had never seen a medical evaluation like the one Bob was receiving. He was asked to read from a card; was poked by a pin; touched his nose and then the doctor's hand; walked on his heels; and stood on his toes. The doctor did not react to anything until he checked Bob's knee reflexes. On the first attempt, he had none. Kathy had a feeling that was significant. How do you not have reflexes? She saw Bob bring his hands together, curl his fingers, join them together, and pull. This time when the doctor struck his knee, the leg jerked up. After that, the two walked back into the office and returned to their seats. Dr. Bradinsky picked up his tape recorder and began speaking into it.

"The following note on Robert Brendler, B-r-e-n-d-l-e-r. Patient came in complaining of loss of sensation in arms, legs, and torso, a floater in his right eye, difficulty voiding . . . ."

Kathy listened to the doctor's monotone drone as he concisely summarized Bob's symptoms. The precision of his description and the routine manner with which he treated the information told her they were finally seeing the right doctor. He was familiar with all of Bob's symptoms and showed every sign that he had a diagnosis in mind. Bob looked a little shell shocked. It was obvious to him as well.

The doctor finished his recording and turned his attention to them.

"You said the young lady was your fiancé?" he asked.

"Yes, doctor," Bob replied. "This is Kathy Stanley."

"Hello, Kathy," the doctor replied. "Have you set a date yet?"

"Not yet," Kathy answered. "We haven't had a chance to work on details. We've been studying."

"Yes, she is the most demanding tutor you can imagine," Bob said while looking at Kathy with a smile.

"Oh, I can imagine," the doctor laughed. "My wife drilled me in medical school. She was relentless. Now, I'm going to send you for a test. It's brand new, called an NMR. There's a center in Union you can go to. What insurance do you have?"

"Crossroads," Bob informed him.

"Crossroads, good," the doctor seemed relieved. "It's an expensive test. Are you claustrophobic?"

"No," Bob chuckled.

"Doctor, can I ask you? What do you think it is?" Kathy asked, praying it was not a brain tumor.

"I think your fiancé may have a form of multiple sclerosis," the doctor answered flatly. "The NMR will tell us. Then we can come up with a treatment plan. Tell the girls at the front desk you need an NMR. They'll set up an appointment for you. Oh, and if you can avoid it, don't go running into any burning buildings." The doctor handed Bob his chart. They picked up some brochures about the disease on the way out.

Kathy felt numb as they walked toward the car. Bob had not said a word since the doctor informed them of his suspicions. Multiple sclerosis, she had heard of it, but knew nothing about it. That was the disease the Foreign Service officer who was released early during the Iranian Embassy crisis had. The only image she had was that of small coin collection boxes at the checkout counter in supermarkets. There was inevitably a picture of a wheelchair on the boxes. Remembering those suddenly became emotional. Silent tears began to course down her cheeks as they reached the car. Bob embraced her while she released all her pent up anxiety from the past few months. She buried her head into his chest, her body shaking with sobs. In the back of her mind was uncertainty about why these emotions had surfaced now. Was it because it could be multiple sclerosis or because it was not cancer? Whatever the cause, her tears were cathartic. After a minute she pulled her head off Bob's chest.

"He said it was a form of MS, not MS," Bob said optimistically. "It sounds like it's not a one size fits all problem."

"We'll get through this," Kathy said with determination. "I have my work cut out for me."

"Why do you say that?" Bob asked.

"You have to start preparing for the oral portion of the test," she said, knowing it was really an excuse. She felt a need to be involved in the fight to beat back the newly named threat to her happiness. "So I'll hit the library and the phones, collect all the info I can about MS, and what the prognosis might be. Then we can plan." She purposely withheld the offer from Stacey's professor. No need to bring that up until they had information to help formulate intelligent questions. They got into the car and drove to Bob's place in silence.

"I have to go to work tonight," Bob said when Kathy parked.

"You're going to work?" she asked incredulously. "He said to avoid burning buildings."

"Of course, I'm going to work," he laughed. "Whatever it is, I'm the same as I was yesterday. Still have to pay the bills. I can drive if necessary and I never run into buildings, I always walk. "

"Couldn't you go on sick leave?" she asked in a pleading tone, knowing it was a futile question and totally ignoring his attempt at humor.

"I'm not sick or at least I'm not contagious," he replied.

"Heart attacks aren't contagious either," she shot back a little too sharply. She did not want this to turn into an argument. She just wanted him to react rationally.

"Got to go, love you," was his cheery response.

"Men!" she spat out as if it were a curse.

Chapter Twenty-seven

Multiple sclerosis, the words reverberated through Bob's head. What did they mean? He had a vague association between those words and wheelchairs. It was not the disease that Jerry Lewis campaigned for every Labor Day weekend. That was muscular dystrophy and affected children. Whatever it was, it was bad. He was sitting in his kitchen, staring at a pile of books on the table, but not really seeing it. Questions shot through his mind at a maddening pace. It was apparently a neurological illness because a neurologist took minutes to diagnose something that had baffled everyone else. Although both the urologist and the ophthalmologist had hinted that one diagnosis could explain all his symptoms, they had left the diagnosis to a neurologist. He felt exhausted and mentally drained. What could be expected? It seemed there was a treatment for the disease because Dr. Bradinsky had mentioned a treatment plan. What would the treatment plan entail?

Bob felt rage building in his gut. He knew it was a good move to have a night away from Kathy. Having the woman you love next to you when feeling enraged at an illness was not advisable. The chance of snapping out of frustration and lashing out at such a convenient target was too great. She deserved much better than that.

After working so hard to find a place in the world, he was now confronted with a problem that could rob him of it. Fighting fires was his life and that could not be done from a wheelchair. Was a wheelchair really a part of his future? Kathy had taken the brochures from the doctor's office with her. He had nothing to grab hold of. An information vacuum had enclosed him. How did Kathy really feel about this? Why would she want to marry a high school graduate, a graduate from a dummy school as his shop teacher had called Irvington Tech, whose future had just turned indescribably bleak? Could he be so selfish, so heartless to condemn someone like her to such a match? He swore under his breath and stood up. There were no answers to be had in his kitchen. Grabbing his uniforms and a few towels, Bob stomped out the door and headed for his car. The only place he wanted to be right now was in the firehouse.

By the time he reached Six Engine, Bob's growing rage at life had turned into a steely determination. Whatever MS was, it was not going to slow him down. When the doctor had said not to go into fire buildings, he should have asked why. The chances that this guy would know anything about the inside of a fire building were slim to none. He would follow the doctor's instructions for tonight possibly. There was no way it would be a permanent decision. If he could fight fires last week, he could fight fires next week. Bob parked in the side lot, took a deep breath to calm down, grabbed his things, and went inside.

The kitchen was busy with everyone pulling together to help prepare dinner when Bob came down from the locker room. While he was changing upstairs, the time blow had hit so Captain Pete was writing up the company journal. Jack was sitting at the table peeling potatoes. Bob grabbed a knife and began cutting then into an appropriate size to boil and mash. Hector and Ray were by the sink and the Chief and Hank were upstairs. He was hoping that no one would remember the doctor's appointment, but realized that was unlikely. Bob had placed his turnout gear on the jump seat behind the driver. If the Captain did not push it, his gear would not be moved.

"So, what did the doctor say?" Jack asked casually.

"He wants me to go for a test," Bob said. "Then go back to see him."

"A test?" Jack asked. "You seem to spend a lot of time taking tests lately. What kind of test is this guy after?"

Bob smiled at Jack's attempt to lighten the subject. Unfortunately, he could not write his way through this one. "It's called an NMR; that stands for nuclear magnetic resonance," Bob answered, happy he had gone through the trouble of asking Dr. Bradinsky's receptionist what the acronym stood for. "Got an appointment in a couple of days at a place in Union."

"Nuclear magnetic resonance?" Jack asked. "Never heard of it. What does it do?"

"It takes pictures of soft tissue in the body," Captain Pete said as he walked in from the watch room. "It's supposed to be the best thing since mother's milk in radiology. My mother-in-law just went to have some tests done at that place. They told her it uses a large magnet to generate images. Also said it was loud as hell. What's he looking for?"

Bob curse silently to himself; everything had been going fine. His answers were ambiguous and Jack did not seem to be expecting any answer to the unvoiced question of what the doctor was looking for. When Captain Pete asked his question, Bob was thrown into a quandary. Should he confess the purpose of the test or play the ambiguity card and say the doctor wanted to see the results before saying anything definitive? The exhaustion he had felt earlier had not improved. It would be irresponsible not to inform his skipper.

He sucked in a lung full of air and explained, "He suspects I might have a form of multiple sclerosis. The NMR will tell him for sure."

There was a moment of shocked silence. Ray and Hector came over from the sink. Captain Pete and Jack were just staring. Bob knew then that his last sentences had altered his world forever.

"This guy thinks you have MS?" the Captain asked.

"Maybe a form of it," Bob minimized.

"A form of it? That's like being a little pregnant," Pete said.

"Why are you even in?" Jack asked. "You should have it taken care of."

How could he explain the need to be here? He wanted to talk it out so he could clear his mind and weigh his options with guys who understood.

"How do you feel?" the Captain asked.

"Same as last day in," Bob lied.

"Okay, why don't you drive until we find out where this is going?" Captain Pete suggested. "This way you'll keep your captain sane."

"Alright, Cap," Bob relented. "Hopefully, I'll know in a few days. The doctor said as soon as he saw the results he would set up a treatment plan. It'll be under control in no time." With that they all went back to prepping dinner. In the back of his mind, Bob was hoping it would be a quiet night. Whatever bounce he had had in his legs was used up impressing Kathy when she picked him up. Now the legs just felt heavy.

They were finally sitting down to dinner when the phone from dispatch rang. An instant later the joker circuit clicked. Ray was sitting under the phone. He picked it up and grabbed a piece of chalk for writing on the blackboard.

"Six, on a full assignment to Sixteenth Avenue and Thirteenth Street."

When they arrived on the scene, a light smoke condition was drifting across the intersection. Bob parked the rig next to a hydrant on the corner and climbed down to hook up. Before he could attach the front suction hose to the hydrant, flames exploded out of the second floor of the building across from the rig. The light smoke condition instantaneously transformed itself into a working fire. Flames were suddenly blowing out the street doorway that Jack and Ray were walking towards. That was not natural, Bob thought. It appeared as if an accelerant had been used. Thank God they had not arrived a minute sooner.

He quickly stepped over to the pump panel on the side of the rig and sent water to Jack's line, then hopped around to the front to hook the front suction up to the hydrant. After slapping a wrench onto the pentagonal post poking out of the hydrant bonnet, he spun the hydrant open and then opened the valve on the front bumper of the rig. Sliding to the pump panel, he adjusted the pressure going to Jack's line. By now Hector and the skipper had stretched a second line into the building. Bob waited for Captain Pete's signal and then wet that line. While busy with all of this, companies had been rolling in. The familiar cacophony of a fire scene filled the air. He had always found it exhilarating, but tonight it just seemed to drain him of what little energy he had. He was running on pure stubbornness. The Captain's insistence he drive had been a good call. Stubbornness would not have carried him through this fire. He realized he was now a liability on the fire ground. All the other problems he explained to the doctor came and went. Will this soul wrenching exhaustion he was experiencing also recede?

"Deputy One to quarters."

Bob paid attention to the radio. It was an unusual time for the Chief to call headquarters. The fire had been declared under control, but it was too soon for the Chief to call back in service. Something was up.

"Deputy One."

"Signal two hundred, have police homicide respond."

"Signal two hundred, requesting police homicide received."

Jack and Ray walked over to the rig as headquarters finished their acknowledgement.

"What's going on?" Bob asked Ray.

"Hector found a guy in a closet on the second floor," Ray told him. "Hands and feet bound with electric extension cords."

* * * * * * * * * * * * * * * ** *

He went to work! Kathy could not believe it. She was beside herself with worry and anger. A doctor told him he might have a debilitating disease and he goes off to fight fires. After reading the brochures they had picked up at the doctor's office, she did not know what to do.

She was sitting on the couch in her living room with the brochures laid out on the floor in front of her. Most of them were published by the National Multiple Sclerosis Society. A glass of burgundy was nestled in her hand. Nini Anna always said a little vino clears the mind and eases the heart. It was not working tonight. Her mind was wrestling with the myriad possibilities presented to her today and her heart was in turmoil. A fire was not the place to discover you cannot do the job. How could he go to work? The answers to these questions were not here, so she decided to reach out for help. Emptying the last sip of wine from the glass, Kathy stood up and marched to the kitchen. She picked up the phone and called Stacey. Maybe she could help get a better handle on it.

"Hello," Stacey answered.

"Stace, it's Kathy, got a minute?" It was at best a misleading question. This would take more than a minute.

"Hi, Kath," Stacey responded. "Of course, I have all the time you need. What did the doctor say?"

"He thinks Bob has a form of MS," Kathy started then found herself beginning to get emotional. She was sure she heard Stacey quietly gasp. "We have an appointment at a radiology place in Union for something called an NMR," she said as she began pacing the floor.

335

"Is Bob there with you now?" Stacey asked.

"No, the stone head insisted on going to work!" Kathy snapped out. "I've been reading the information we picked up at the doctor's office. The more I read, the angrier I get at his stubborn streak." Tears had begun to silently stream down her cheeks. "I'm standing here worrying and he's off playing hero. Can you give me some idea of what we're facing? The doctor wasn't exactly forthcoming with a prognosis."

"It would be best if you spoke with Dr. Dunn," Stacey suggested. "MS is one of his concentrations. I think he's conducting some research on it. Now I understand why he said Bob's case was interesting. I'll warn you, I don't think you're going to get anyone to give you a detailed prognosis. In the lecture he gave us, Dr. Dunn said it's a very complicated, very unpredictable disease. In fact he called it an individualistic disease. Each patient has a unique set of symptoms that fit into broad categories. No one can predict the outcome of any one person's illness. Does the doctor know Bob's a firefighter?"

"Yes, Bob told him."

"And he didn't say anything about Bob going to work?"

"Of course he did!" Kathy snapped. "He said he didn't want Bob in a fire building, but that didn't seem to register." The rate of her pacing and twirling the phone cord had gradually increased as she became more agitated.

"I think Bob is too loyal to the guys at Six to do anything dumb," Stacey reassured her. "He's probably driving. You don't think he'd do anything that could get someone hurt, do you?"

"No," Kathy admitted. "He might be stubborn, but he's not selfish, but a fire's not the place to find out you can't do the job!" She was crying freely now, her anxiety suddenly overwhelming her.

"He has a lot of experience doing this," Stacey reminded her.

Kathy remembered all her interviews and the way the senior firefighters had described the difference between the young bucks and themselves. It was brains versus brawn. "His experience is fighting fires like a bull. Can he still do that?" Stacey did not answer. Kathy stopped her pacing as she built up the nerve to verbalize one last question. "I know this is serious," she began. "How bad can this go and how quickly?

Stacey hesitated for a moment. The silence spoke volumes to Kathy. "I've worked with a few people who have MS," she said. "One woman told me she has had the disease for thirty years and she's still walking. A man is confined to a wheelchair and he's had it only ten years. I wish I could tell you more, but I haven't learned that much yet. Call Dr. Dunn. He's the expert."

Kathy thanked Stacey and hung up the phone. Then she dropped to the floor and quietly sobbed while scolding herself for being so weak. She vowed Bob would never see her collapse like this. Now she had to call his mom.

Chapter Twenty-eight

Bob flipped through a magazine mindlessly as he and Kathy waited in Dr. Bradinsky's office. The room was as crowded as their last visit, but there was little conversation between those scattered among the seats, tables, and magazines. What a week it had been. Things had been quiet at work after the arson job set to cover a murder. Rain and a cold front had kept people off the streets. The NMR had been a trip. He understood the doctor's concern about claustrophobia when they had inserted him into the machine. Bob could not help but laugh to himself as he slid into the tube of the NMR. The first thought that crossed his mind was the picture of a World War II submarine movie. It was Run Silent, Run Deep all over again and he was the torpedo. The almost irresistible urge to shout, "one's away" came to him. Instead he was required to wear ear plugs and lie as still as possible. Before slipping into the bowels of the beast, a small cage had been place around his head. This brought to mind the white helmets of the storm troopers in Star Wars. It was a bit of a stretch, but he seemed to be in a movie reviewing mood that day. After fifteen minutes of loud thumping, they backed him out, shot him up with radioactive isotopes, and sent him back for more of the same. Contrary to the doctor's expectations that he might be fearful, Bob spent much of the time inside this machine dozing off even with the contraption steadily clunking away.

Putting the magazine aside, his mind was wrestling with a quandary. How can he ask questions or give a straight answer with

Kathy sitting next to him? She had tried to hide her annoyance at his going to the firehouse, but he knew her too well for that to work. Thankfully, she was chatting with a couple, leaving Bob to his thoughts. The memory of exhaustion at the last fire haunted him. During their last visit, Dr. Bradinsky had asked about sensations coming and going. He had to know, would this feeling of being completely tapped recede? If this was going to be a good day- bad day thing then he could work around it. Good days hang on the side of the rig. Bad days drive. Bob was sure everyone would work with him, especially because they all hated driving.

How about the effects of stress? It was not his imagination that he felt worse when under stress. Over the past week, they had put the firefighting books away and set up his study space for the oral. Management books replaced ventilation and hydraulics. Kathy was now in her zone teaching him how to give an accurate, concise presentation. Whether he had to counsel a problem firefighter or instruct a new recruit, the way he presented the information was critical. That was what Kathy did best. She knew it and now controlled what he did and critiqued everything he said. Would this phase of test preparation extract as large or even a larger price than the last?

Then there was the question of the blunted sensation worsening. How bad could that get? Could it make him so insensitive that he would be unable to father a child? Kathy would die of embarrassment if he voiced that question in front of her. With that thought, a solution to his dilemma sprang into Bob's mind. As long as the doctor continued to take him into the exam room off his office and Kathy did not follow, he would have an opportunity to ask unguarded questions. If she became suspicious he could always play the trump card of embarrassing questions.

"You gave up reading?" Kathy asked snapping him back to reality.

"Oh, sorry, yes I did," Bob blurted out. "I was just thinking of the oral."

"We should go over everything we found out so we can ask intelligent questions," Kathy reminded him.

He could not argue with that. Even if he wanted to, he knew better than to resist the runaway train she was about to become.

"Now, the brochures from the MS society said it's a disease that is not genetic and occurs in countries with good sanitation. There are two forms of the disease. One is relapsing remitting and the other is progressive. It's an auto immune disorder that attacks the nerves and strips them of their insulation, so your nerves get short circuited," she reviewed the information they had collected. Bob was impressed with how thorough she had been, but what did it all mean?

"If he confirms it's MS," Bob interrupted when she took a breath, "The first question should be what form do I have. Then we need to know about treatments."

Kathy shook her head in agreement while never taking her eyes off the notes she had written. "Then I want to ask him about his experience treating the disease and your prognosis. Stacey said she's worked with a woman who was diagnosed thirty years ago and is still walking, but she's also worked with a man who was diagnosed ten years ago and is confined to a wheelchair. So does that mean women do better than men as a rule?"

"So, if I spend more time around you with your estrogen I should do better, right?" Bob quipped.

She slapped his knee. "This is serious," she reminded him. The receptionist called Bob's name before their review could continue. They walked over to the receptionist's window, picked up Bob's folder, and headed to the back where Dr. Bradinsky waited.

"Hello," the doctor said as he accepted the folder from Bob. "Let's see what we have here." He began reading a report from the radiologist, muttering "interesting and "really" to himself. When his perusal was completed, the doctor looked up at them as he reached for his tape recorder.

"The following note on Robert Brendler B-r-e-n-d-l-e-r. Patient had an NMR of the brain, cervical, and thoracic spine with and without contrast performed at Union Radiology. Abnormalities appeared in the cervico-medullary junction, right frontal lobe, and periventriclar matter bilaterally. Abnormal signals were also demonstrated at the C2 and C5 levels all of which is strongly indicative of multiple sclerosis." He switched off the machine and looked at Bob. "I'm sorry, but the images show you have MS. From the way your symptoms come and go, I would say you have a relapsing remitting form of the disease. So, here's what we're going to do. First, I'm going to evaluate you to see if I can detect any changes. Then we can discuss what all this means and how we can deal with it. Okay?"

"Okay, doc," Bob replied. His stomach had dropped when the doctor pronounced his diagnosis even though he did not understand the medical terminology that preceded it. Bob had not realized how stubbornly he was clinging to the hope that it was not MS. Kathy had been deathly still the entire time which meant she was struggling to maintain control. Dr. Bradinsky stood up and strolled toward the exam room. Bob snapped out of his stunned state, rose, and followed the doctor, reminding himself this was the only opportunity to ask a few quiet questions without upsetting Kathy. He sat on the exam bench and allowed the doctor to prick him with a pin and hit his knees with a hammer. After walking and reading, Bob glanced through the doorway to check on Kathy then quietly asked the doctor, "Doc, will the tired feeling I get come and go like the rest of my symptoms?"

"I can't assure you of that and even if it does, you may have a gradual or even sudden worsening of any symptom," he answered quietly, apparently picking up on Bob's desire for personal privacy.

"Will stress worsen the disease?" was Bob's next query.

"It can," the doctor informed him. "I would caution against taking on anything that would give you undue stress."

"Will my sensation during sex get worse?" Bob asked the hardest question last. "We would like to have children if we get married."

"There is no way for me to answer with any certainty, but it's been my experience that the symptoms you present to me on your initial visit usually worsen," was his guarded response. "Bob, it's difficult to say what will happen with this disease."

"I understand," Bob accepted. "Thank you for your candor. Kathy's going to have questions for you also."

"Then let's go back so we can discuss it with her," he suggested.

The doctor recorded a quick synopsis of the results from Bob's evaluation before he asked, "Do you have any questions?"

"What is his prognosis?" Kathy asked seeming determined to follow the questions discussed in the waiting room.

"That's very difficult to say with MS," Dr. Bradinsky answered.

"In your experience treating this disease," Kathy plowed on. "What therapies work best?"

"In the case of your fiancé," the doctor answered. "I'm going to start him on Predinose, which is an adrenal cortisone medication. The disease usually responds well to this. We'll see how Bob reacts. I think we can get this exacerbation under control fairly quickly."

"How will this affect his job?" she asked next. This caught Bob by surprise. They had not talked about MS and the Fire Department.

"I don't want you in a fire building," the doctor told Bob.

"I've been driving, doc," Bob informed him. "The Fire Department takes care of its own. Besides I know what it takes to fight a fire. Right now I don't have it. We'll see with the medication."

Kathy became agitated when she heard what Bob said. "If there's an emergency . . . a building collapse or something, he would run right into the building!" she pleaded. "Can't you write a prescription to limit his duty? There are positions on the department that don't require his doing fire duty."

Bob was stunned at the direction Kathy was taking this conversation. Before he could counter her plea, the doctor jumped in to reassure her.

"I don't want you to just give up," he counseled them. "A man has to do his job. If they can give you a position that would allow you to do lighter work when you have a flare up, then there is no need to seek preferential treatment."

This seemed to calm Kathy a bit, but Bob could tell she was primed to explode if he said the wrong thing.

"Would you recommend he rest for a few days to build up his strength after he starts the medication?" she asked next.

"The medication should make him feel stronger," the doctor assured her. "But in the end, he knows how he feels. I'll leave it up to him."

Kathy finally collapsed, relinquishing control of the conversation back to Bob. The doctor picked up his recorder and said his final words for this visit, "Patient started on Predinose, 80 milligrams, daily on a tapered schedule and will be re-evaluated. Return in two weeks." He put down the recorder and handed Bob his folder. "Try to avoid excess heat, exhaustion, and infections. Any of them can worsen your symptoms," the doctor advised. "Oh, one other thing, do you have a belief system?"

Bob was taken aback by the question. A belief system, why would a medical doctor ask such a question? It had an ominous ring to it.

"Well, I was raised Catholic," he informed the doctor.

"Catholic, good, good," Dr. Bradinsky smiled. "I'll see you again in two weeks."

Bob saw the doctor write a number on his chart before handing it to him. "Doctor, could I ask you one more question?"

"Sure."

"What does the number you just wrote mean?"

"The number?" the doctor questioned. "Oh, that's the diagnostic code for MS. Why?"

"That's my badge number."

The tension was palpable as they walked to the car. Bob had the feeling things were going to go from bad to worse. Kathy was mum until they were in the car. He started the engine and started the drive back to South Orange, waiting for the storm to strike.

"He seems to be confident this medication will improve things," Kathy began awkwardly.

"That's the impression I got," Bob answered cautiously.

"What did you ask him in the exam room?" Kathy asked circling her prey.

"I asked if my sensation will come back so I'll have a normal sex life," he answered leaving out any mention of his other queries.

"You didn't, did you?" she laughed, turning a delicious color of pink.

"Yes," Bob assured her. "It's a legitimate question, but not one to be asked in mixed company."

"Why are you guys so obsessed with the subject?" Kathy asked attempting to keep the conversation light. She seemed to be trying as hard as he was to avoid the mines scattered around the conversation.

"I'm concerned about my ability to father children," Bob said, deciding it was too important a topic to sweep under the rug. "All of our parents have indicated they would like to have grandchildren, right?"

Kathy reverted to her silence for a moment. Bob feared she was at a breaking point, but she rebounded quickly and replied, "Then we should move things along, so we can produce what they want before you turn into a permanent, life size sex toy."

Bob burst out in laughter upon hearing her description of his possible future self. Kathy laughed along, giving him hope they had successfully navigated the afternoon's minefield. The subject Kathy raised next showed him his assessment was premature.

"Are you intending to go to work tonight?" she asked hesitantly.

"Of course," Bob answered. He was not going to lie, even if he could get away with it and he knew he could not. "He said no inside work until the meds work. I'm driving so you don't need to worry."

The change in her attitude was instantaneous. "Don't worry!" she bristled. "Are you crazy? If something happens you'll be inside in a heartbeat! You're no good on the fire ground! You're going to get someone hurt!"

"Kathy," Bob pleaded. "Be reasonable. I can't just abandon the rig. There are plenty of guys on the scene to play hero. My job is to keep the water flowing."

What he said had no impact on her. When she spoke again, her voice was laced with venom. "You just don't get it do you? You think it's your life and you'll do what you want."

"Kathy," Bob started to try to reassure her.

"No!" she snapped back to silence him. "It's not just you anymore, I love you."

The last sentence was whispered, but her temper quickly regained control. "Just, just stop the car, let me out," she demanded. "I can't be with you right now."

"What do you mean?" Bob asked astonished. "How will you get home?"

"I'll get home," she insisted. "They have pay phones and I have friends. Just let me out!" She emphasized the last four words in staccato fashion. Bob relented and pulled into a gas station. Kathy stepped out of the car crying quietly and walked toward the phones, leaving the door open. She stopped after a few steps, turned to face him and shouted, "Go, you have to get to work remember!"

He could think of nothing to say or do that would comfort her, so he reached over to close the door. Pulling onto the street, he parked a discreet distance away, and watched her until Gloria pulled up to pick her up. Then he headed for the firehouse.

* * * * * * * * * * * * * * * * * * *

347

Kathy watched Bob pull away as she opened the door to Gloria's car. He could not think she would miss his little protective ploy. So busy protecting his woman, yet he could not protect himself. How was it that men did not understand that protecting themselves was the ultimate way to protect their ladies? She slid in next to Gloria, slammed the door, and began to rant. "Damn him! Damn him and his pride!"

"Things didn't go well at the doctor's office?" Gloria asked sarcastically.

"That's an understatement," Kathy laughed bitterly.

"He didn't just leave you, did he?" Gloria asked with doubt.

"No," Kathy answered. "Mr. Chivalry parked down the block and waited for you to rescue me. I demanded he let me out of the car. I just couldn't be with him right now. He's going to have to hustle or he'll be late. Serves him right!"

Gloria pulled out of the station and headed for the Parkway. Kathy sat quietly, reviewing what had transpired. What could she have done differently? In the end, she knew it was beyond her. She should have prepared for this. When he had insisted on picking her up because if ordered out of the firehouse he could drop her without worrying about the time and if not he had to go to work. The "could drop her without thinking of the time" part of his explanation was bull from the moment he said it. The man had no intention of staying out of work. She had all but pleaded with him and the doctor. Just give him a few days to build his strength.

"What did the doctor say?" Gloria asked.

"The NMR confirmed it," Kathy told her. She felt the emotions welling up inside and so took a moment to regain composure before continuing. "Bob has MS. There is no way to give a prognosis. He suggested Bob avoid excess heat, exhaustion, and infections because any of these could worsen his symptoms."

"So, he shouldn't be in the firehouse," Gloria pointed out.

Kathy swore in Taiwanese under her breath. "I'll leave that up to him," she spat out imitating a male voice. "I felt so helpless. It was obvious he was making a mistake, but I couldn't persuade him."

Gloria pulled onto the Parkway after flipping a coin into a toll booth basket. She accelerated smoothly and eased into the traffic flow before responding. "You shouldn't feel helpless. You have more control than you think. Remember, if he gets promoted, his job will be less physically demanding," she pointed out. "But, right now he's going to the firehouse and you're miserable."

"Miserable?" Kathy questioned. "No, right now I'm furious. Miserable will probably come later when the worry takes over."

"You said the doctor couldn't give you a prognosis," Gloria said. "What did he say?"

"He spent a lot of time speaking into a tape recorder laying out his diagnosis for transcription. He said he didn't want Bob in fire buildings and Bob said he doesn't have the strength right now. He'll see after the medication kicks in! He's going to try to stay in the firehouse on full duty! When I told the doctor there are light duty positions, he comes back with 'I don't want you to give up.'"

Gloria had a surprised look on her face even as she negotiated through traffic.

"Then - - - then he said," Kathy found herself stuttering with fury. "If there's a position he can do when he has a flare up, great, but don't look for preferential treatment when you don't need it!"

"We have to call Stacey," Gloria insisted. "I don't know anything about this disease, but you need to talk with someone who does."

"I need to speak with someone who can make a man think rationally is what I need," Kathy countered.

"Does Bob have this medication with him?" Gloria asked.

"No," Kathy answered in a quieter voice. "I have the prescription and his card. If we could swing past a pharmacy, I'll try to have it filled." With that the two women fell silent. Kathy had a feeling it was going to be a long, sleepless night. One thing was certain; he was getting promoted if she had anything to do with it.

Chapter Twenty-nine

If he was going to ask the guys for help to in the firehouse, Bob knew he would have to be completely honest. He had wrestled with how to present his prognosis or lack of prognosis to the Captain. A minor slip of the tongue could make the situation sound dire, when it was only bad. Bad meant riding out the storm driving until the prednisone did what Dr. Bradinsky thought it would do. Dire meant ordered out of the firehouse and an end to life as he knew it. Was there no middle ground?

He pulled into the side lot at Six Engine and shut down the car. How did he end up in this situation? A year ago he was trying to score a dance with the most fascinating, most exotic woman he had ever met. Now he was engaged to her, but felt his world was imploding. Is this how passengers felt on the Titanic? The plunge from the heights of happiness and fulfillment to the depths of misery and fear was harrowing. Give me a fully involved three story frame any day, he thought. It would be so straight forward, so simple a problem to solve. The complex tale his life had become was disheartening. There was no time to contemplate the situation. If he did, he would be late. He grabbed his clean uniforms and dragged himself into the firehouse to face the inevitable inquisition. Suppressed in the back of his mind was Kathy's fury. That would have to be dealt with tomorrow when he was off duty. His focus had to be on the job tonight. There was no reserve for error.

When he stepped in, the kitchen became unnaturally quiet. Bob felt like a rabbit that had wandered into a wolves' den. The time blow hit as he put his uniforms on the table.

"Everything okay?" Jack asked.

"You'll hear about it when you get home tomorrow," Bob assured him.

"That doesn't sound good," Jack replied.

The Captain stepped in from the watch room as Jack muttered this. "You made it," he said. "I was worried things wouldn't go well. What did the doctor say?"

Bob refrained for the moment from saying how things had gone, deciding instead to share some of what the doctor said. "He said the test confirmed I have a form of MS, but he can't tell me where it will go. Just that he trusted my judgment on how I felt and what I could do on the job. Then he prescribed some medication and said to come back in two weeks to see how well it works. That's where it stands right now." It was about as short a synopsis as he could think up. If it left out some of the gory details, well he could fill in the blanks later. Right now he had to get his turnout gear on the rig and change.

"He trusts you to police yourself?" the Captain asked. "I trust you're not going to do anything stupid. Am I right?"

Bob laughed. "Don't worry Cap," he reassured him. "I'll drive until the meds work. Not going to give you undue cause to worry."

"Thanks Bob," Captain Pete said then he went to complete writing up the book. Bob headed to the back for his gear and then upstairs to get changed. As he climbed the stairs his head began to

352

spin a little. It was nothing like the vertigo from his supposed middle ear infection, so he brushed it off and went about the business of getting ready for the night.

"What did you mean by I'll hear about it when I get home?" Jack asked Bob as they dragged the house garbage cans out to the curb behind the firehouse. It was a moonless night and the stars not drowned out by the city lights danced in and out of the clouds. The air had a bit of a mid-autumn nip to it. This was the kind of night that reminded firefighters the cold winter was fast approaching. Bob remembered more than one night of shivering in ice coated turnout gear outside a building that had been fully engulfed in flames. Those were the type of jobs where the machinery did the work of throwing water and firefighters struggled to contain the fire to the building of origin and the buildings on either side of it. But the ice in those memories was still a few months away. The thought crossed his mind that he might never experience a night like that again. This was quickly put to the side. He just had to get through tonight and the weather would not be a significant factor.

"What did I mean?" Bob chuckled realizing his mind had wandered off a bit. "Well, Kathy had a really bad reaction to my coming to work and she decided that she didn't want me to drop her home. So she suggested I pull into a gas station. Then she called Gloria to come pick her up."

"What did the doctor really say?" Jack asked knowingly.

"He said he doesn't want me inside a fire building right now," Bob revealed to his best friend. "There is no way he can give me a prognosis, but did put a more precise name to the illness. I apparently have what is called relapsing remitting MS which means the symptoms come and go. He thinks the medication will get it under control quickly. Right now the worst part of it is the exhaustion, but he thought that would recede with the medication."

"So why are you in tonight?" Jack challenged.

"We work tonight, remember?" Bob countered.

"Let me get this straight. This disease has affected your stamina, your equilibrium, and your sense of touch. So you get tired fast, lose your balance, and if your ass lands on some embers you won't know it," Jack said. "You are one crazy bastard."

"Slow down, I'm driving tonight," Bob defended himself.

"Like the Captain said," Jack reminded him. "No heroics. Now tell me, what can I expect when I get home?"

Jack's question pulled the memory of Kathy's anger out of the deep cellar in his mind into which it had been sealed. He knew if these thoughts were allowed free reign, he would not get much sleep tonight even if they did not turn a wheel. Deal with it quickly, Bob told himself. Since he did not think Jack would want to discuss it in front of the entire crew, he turned around and started walking toward the firehouse door. "What can you expect when you get home?" He laughed as Jack followed his lead. "An earful, my boy, an earful."

Bob made his bed after talking with Jack and lied down to rest. It would be best to get a little sleep now so when the bar crowd let out later he would at least have some rest. After lying for a few minutes, he drifted off into a light sleep. His last thoughts were about persuading Kathy to accept his desire to remain in the firehouse. Dr. Bradinsky had said to not just give up, right? Something told him even bringing that up would cause an explosion.

Bells sounding pulled Bob out of a fitful sleep. The bunkroom lights came on automatically when the first bell sounded. He glanced at the clock on the Hunterdon Street wall and saw it was one o'clock. Jack and Ray were in their bunks. Hector had the book watch. Before the first round of bells was complete, Hector was shouting, "Everyone goes, Fourteenth Avenue and Sixth Street."

The three firefighters jumped out of their bunks, slipped into their pants and shoes, threw on sweatshirts, and slid down the front pole. Bob heard the Chief and Captain open their doors. Hank could be heard climbing down the stairs on the far side of the rig as Bob hit the floor. After slipping out of his shoes and into his boots, Bob reached into the rig and turned on the power. The radio came to life as he climbed into the cab. Captain Pete pulled himself up into the seat beside him while the overhead door started its climb. A turn of the key produced the low rumble of a large diesel engine. Bob looked at the seats behind him to make sure everyone was aboard then pulled out onto Springfield Avenue. By the time he turned from Bergen onto Fourteenth Avenue, they could see a glow in the sky. He felt bone tired, but knew he had to perform.

"Take the hydrant on the corner," Captain Pete ordered.

Bob stopped the rig just beyond the corner hydrant. Ray jumped down and quickly walked to Bob who handed him the hydrant wrench from under the driver's seat. Jack and Hector moved to the back step,

355

pulled down their newly acquired four inch hose, and wrapped it around the hydrant barrel. They jumped onto the back step and pressed the signal button twice. Bob rolled the rig to just before the fire building while Ray walked to the hydrant to begin hooking up.

"Put the deck gun between the buildings," the Captain ordered.

Bob inched the rig forward until its midsection was aligned with the alleyway separating the fire building from the exposure. After setting the parking brake, he climbed down from the seat and made his way to the rear compartment. The rear of the building was ablaze, with fire spreading to the exposure. He pulled a wooden chock from the compartment and threw it under the rear wheel. Then he made his way to the back step. Jack and Hector were throwing on their masks while Bob broke down the hose and dragged it to the side suction on the pump panel. When he had connected the hose to the suction inlet, he waved for Ray to wet the line. Water quickly filled the line snaking up the block. By now Jack and Hector were in the building. The Captain stood in the doorway. "When Ray gets here, have him put the deck gun between the buildings, then stretch in another line. I'll meet him inside!" the Captain shouted. "Now wet this line."

Bob tried to pull the handle that controlled the outlet for that line, but could not move it. After several tries standing on the rig's side diamond plate and leaning out with all he had, it was obvious that there was something jamming it. He quickly hopped up into the side bucket seat to try and loosen the hose from the outlet connection and move it to a working outlet. That was when he discovered that the short length of hose that allowed you to easily disconnect the line was no longer there. The guys were already in the building, so he had to solve this problem quickly. It was obvious he would not be able to quickly loosen the hose from the outlet. It was buried too deeply below the Mattydale floor for that. He would have to abandon the last length of hose, attach another length from the rear compartment to a side outlet, and then hook that length into the line running in. It took seconds for this calculation.

Bob jumped down from the rig and started running to the rear compartment. Half way there he lost his balance and crashed to the ground. His right knee hit first, the full weight of his body coming down on it. With hands instinctively extended to break his fall, Bob slid along the pavement. His left wrist folded under him while both hands scraped along the tarmac. Stunned for a split second, the firefighter recovered, pulled himself up, and completed his task. He had water flowing to Ray on the deck gun before taking the time to inspect the damage.

His hands were a mess, having suffered deep abrasions on the knuckles and palms. The right knee was screaming and the left wrist was getting very stiff.

"You okay?" Ray asked as he climbed down from the top of the rig.

"Scrapes and bruises," Bob brushed it off.

"That was one hell of a fall," Ray said as he threw on his mask. Other companies were arriving on the scene from either side of the fire building.

"I'll live," Bob said. "Pete said stretch another line in. He'll meet you inside. Just signal when you want me to wet it. I'll take care of the excess line out here."

Ray climbed up on the side of the rig, pulled the four lengths out of the Mattydale, twisted the folds, and headed for the building. Bob grabbed the remaining hose, pulled it out, and flaked it along the sidewalk. Doing this pushed his left wrist to its limit. His hands felt like they were on fire while his knee was howling. The sound of the revving engine filled his ears as he limped back to the pump panel. The Chief called for a second alarm as he reached the pump panel. Bob's head was spinning and all he wanted to do was lay down and die.

* * * * * * * * * * * * * * * * * * *

The amount of bandages wrapped around his hands was ridiculous. X-rays had showed no broken bones, but his knee was swollen and his left wrist was immobile. Bob stood outside the emergency room entrance waiting for Hank to pick him up. The sun was cracking the eastern horizon, bringing a new day with new problems. How could he have fallen so hard? There was nothing to trip over. His center of gravity had just pushed out ahead of the rest of him. Not running and always wearing gloves at fires were basic rules to live by that he had broken. Now he would have to explain to Kathy. This whole relationship thing had complicated life. Before if he had gotten banged up, there was no one to explain it to but himself. Now she was going to be pissed.

By the time he stepped out of the gig in quarters, Bob was resigned to a bad day. Everyone was waiting in the kitchen, nursing cups of coffee and waiting to pounce on their prey. The Chief was the first one to strike.

"Bob, I think you should take a few days off," he started. "Give your hands time to heal and the medication time to work."

Bob knew that was a nice way of ordering him off duty. He had been expecting it. At least he had not been ordered out of the firehouse.

"How's he getting home?" Jack asked.

"I'll drive," Bob replied wondering where that question came from. Did he look that bad?

"Maybe you should let someone take you home," Captain Pete suggested. "The way Ray describe your fall, it might be better."

"Who gets my car home?" Bob countered.

"I'll have Gloria drive it back," Jack offered.

Bob swore under his breathe. "That means Kathy will know."

Everyone laughed. "You think you can hide this from her?" Ray asked.

"No," Bob admitted. "Just a wishful thought."

"Then I'll have Gloria drive down with Kathy now," Jack suggested. "Kathy can drive you back."

"Me in the car alone with her?" Bob laughed, shaking his head no. "Besides, she's not talking to me."

"No woman would pass up a chance to say I told you so." Jack reminded him.

"I think it's more serious than that," Bob muttered, exhaustion now hitting him like a rogue wave.

"Just get home," Jack told him. "We can talk about it there."

"Hank can take you home in the gig," the Chief offered. "We'll worry about details later."

"I'll get his car home one way or another," Jack promised.

"And Bob, a little advice from experience," the Chief suggested. "Call her when you get home. It'll go better that way."

* * * * * * * * * * * * * * * * * * *

"What did Jack say?" Kathy asked as she turned onto Springfield Avenue.

"He just said Bob got a little banged up and Hank took him home," Gloria told her. "Then he asked me to come down and pick up his car because he was driving Bob's up to Nutley."

The rush hour traffic going into the city was bearable. Stop and go with the lights, but flowing. Kathy had received one anticipated call and had made one unusual call that morning. Bob had called, just earlier than normal. The timing had made her nervous. Her heart was in her throat when she picked up the receiver, only to relax as soon as she heard Bob's voice. The respite from worry lasted a moment, shattered by Bob's lame excuse for calling so early.

"I got a little scraped up when I tripped while hooking a line into the rig," he had explained. "So I'm home early."

Everything about that story cried foul. A little scraped up so I am home early? She knew too much about firemen and their macho attempts to minimize so they did not upset their loved ones.

"Describe 'a little scraped up' for me," she insisted. Little scrapes do not get you sent home early. She knew he was hurt, but how bad were his injuries?

"Well, the bandages they wrapped around my hands are impressive," Bob confessed. "But it's only scrapes on my knuckles and palms."

She tried to picture how he could scrape both his knuckles and his palms in one fall, but was having a hard time with it. A quick mental assessment produced a fall that was broken by his palms, but then had so much momentum that his hands twisted under and dragged his knuckles along the street. At least he was able to drive home.

"Any other aches," she asked nervously.

"Well, my right knee's a little messed up and my left wrist is stiff, that's about it, no broken bones," he finished trying to sound cheerful.

No broken bones! What kind of fall was this? She wanted to rush over to his place, but was not sure she could handle it without getting emotional. Why could he not have just taken the night off? That was what sick leave was for and no one could deny he was sick. As far as she was concerned, his illness was both mental and physical!

"How about I come over and help you get settled," she suggested. "It sounds like you're tired and in pain."

"I am a little achy," he admitted. "But I think Gloria is going to call you."

"Why would she call me?" Kathy asked. "Is Jack alright?"

"Yeah, yeah, Jack's fine," Bob reassured her. "But Hank dropped me off with the gig, so my car's at the firehouse. Jack's going to need a hand getting it here."

"You couldn't drive home?" she asked incredulously.

"I could have, but the Chief saw the knee and thought it best I didn't push it," he explained.

The more he talked, the worse his condition became. She wanted to hang up before he fessed up to something really serious.

"Look, I have to hang up right now," she stammered, oscillating between wanting to cry and wanting to scream at him and his pigheadedness. "Gloria's probably trying to call," she fibbed about her reasoning. Before he could reply she gently replaced the receiver on its hook. Struggling to control the emotional conflict being waged inside her, Kathy waited for the phone to ring. After half a minute, she could not wait any longer and called. Then she threw on a pair of jeans and a top before driving to Gloria's. Now they were in rush hour traffic and her emotions had come down on the side of anger.

"I begged him not to go in last night," Kathy hissed as she negotiated through traffic. "Why couldn't he listen to me?"

"Do you think his fall had anything to do with MS?" Gloria asked. The way she voiced the question put doubts into Kathy's mind.

"I don't know," she admitted.

"Guys do get hurt at fires all the time," Gloria reminded her. "Cuts, burns, bruises, falls, sprains, strains, I thought you were the one who knew all about it."

Kathy laughed at herself. She had claimed that she could handle it because she was a fireman's daughter and had done all those interviews. She knew the job well. Now look at her.

"Sorry Glor," she apologized. "It's different when it's your man getting hurt."

"You don't have to be sorry," Gloria said. "Oh, Jack arranged for Ray, Stacey, Frank, and Chingli to meet at Bob's around two so they can discuss his options and how everyone can help. Interested in taking part?"

The last question was spoken facetiously. Kathy felt surprised and then deeply grateful for their friends' concern. "Of course, I am," she whispered,

"Just be nice to him," Gloria advised. "He's had a bad night and needs a little TLC."

As they passed through the light on Springfield and Bergen, Kathy hit her left directional. She wanted to give the traffic around her plenty of warning. Turning onto the firehouse apron was not a predictable move. A break in west bound traffic allowed her to move out of the traffic flow easily. Jack's car was parked on the apron in front of the firehouse parking lot. Gloria had a spare set of keys, which was fortunate because the firehouse appeared to be empty.

"Right now, I'm driving up to Bob's then Jack and I are going out to breakfast," Gloria said. "Do you want to tag along?"

"No," Kathy answered not feeling up to socializing, especially without Bob. "Thanks, I still have to pick up Bob's prescriptions. Then I plan to go up and nurse the lug."

"Okay, be nice," Gloria advised. "Maybe we'll see you later."

With that she closed the door and walked to Jack's car. Kathy backed up enough to make a u-turn on the apron and headed back to South Orange. How did she get herself into this situation? A year ago, she had just wanted to have a casual conversation with the cute firefighter she had met on a visit to Six Engine. Now she had committed her soul to him and his obstinate pride.

Chapter Thirty

Bob poked his head out of the bedroom window and dropped his front door key to Jack. There was no way in the world he was going to subject his knee to the down and back up required to open the door. After closing the window, he hoppled over to his apartment door, opened it, and then dropped himself into a seat in his living room. Past experience told him he would feel worse before he felt better, something to look forward to, he thought wryly. Exhaustion clouded his mind. When Jack left he intended to get some sleep. The afternoon would be reserved for studying. Maybe Kathy would have forgiven him by the evening and they could enjoy some Chinese take-out and watch a movie on his VCR. That would be the most he could hope to pull out of the rubble of this day and he would be very thankful if it happened.

"How's the knee?" Jack asked when he stepped in.

"Sore, swollen, a little bloody," Bob laughed. "All in all, it was a good night's work." He saw the look of doubt in Jack's eyes. "Look I lost my balance, tripped, and fell. These things can happen to anyone. That's why you're not supposed to run at fires, remember?"

Jack smiled as he closed the door and dropped himself into the only other chair in the living room. "You were running?" he asked. "You didn't tell me that. I thought there would be no heroics last night?"

Heroics, Bob thought. Running was heroic? "You boys were in the building without water, just trying to do my part," he answered defensively.

"We could have backed out," Jack reminded him. "No reports of people trapped. We were enjoying the multi-colored display of plastics burning. The milliseconds you might have saved wouldn't have made a difference. With your fall, you ate up a lot more time than you would have eaten up walking, no?"

Was he trying to make me feel better or was he trying to drive home the lesson? No need to run. It made no difference. Don't you feel foolish? Or why did you rush, we were enjoying the view.

Bob knew what he had done was inexcusable. Certain rules were never broken unless under extreme duress and last night was not even close. He realized he had been compensating because of his new found friend MS. Did that play a role in his fall? There was no way to know for certain and he was too tired to think about it anyway.

"Can I ask you a question?" Jack inquired.

"Who wants the answer?" Bob asked.

"Just me, Bob," Jack assured him. "How do you really feel?"

Bob inhaled deeply before beginning his description. "I feel wiped out, like I just spent the night at a three bagger being ordered in and out of the building. You know, one of those nights where you watch the sun rise."

"You mean something like last night?" Jack pointed out.

Bob laughed at himself. "No, like Sixteenth and Littleton, the job where Pete went down."

"That was a long day," Jack agreed.

After thinking about it, Bob felt obliged to add, "And I feel pissed off. Everything was going my way. Kathy seems to really have something for me. The test went well. I was feeling good about life. Now this." He followed that with a quiet curse.

"Kathy seems to?" Jack laughed at him. "Gloria tells me Kathy says she's found her dream, a poetic fireman."

Bob gave an ironic chuckle in response. "I haven't written a thing in months."

"You've been studying," Jack reminded him. "It'll come back. So, why don't you lie down when I go to breakfast with Gloria? You'll want to be rested when everyone gets here."

"Everyone gets here?" Bob asked in surprise. Now what was going on? He got the feeling from Jack's last comment that he was hosting an unexpected party. A sensation similar to what Bilbo must have felt in The Hobbit began creeping into his consciousness.

"Yeah, didn't I mention it? Ray and Stacey, Frank and Chingli, Kathy, and Gloria and I are going to have a conference about you. It starts around two. You might want to sit in on it."

Bob could not help but smile. He shook his head and said, "Jeez, can't a guy have a little peace?"

Jack looked at him seriously and answered, "Only guys with no friends have peace when they're wiped out. Now get some rest and don't worry about playing host. We've got all that covered." With that he stood up and headed for the door. Gloria was probably waiting downstairs already. Bob set his alarm for twelve and crashed onto his bed where he fell into a light, restless sleep. It was so difficult to drop off with his knee throbbing and so many questions humming around his mind. The thought of a poem drove him out of bed. It must have been the power of suggestion after Jack's comment. He picked up pen and paper and began writing.

Dream Stealer

I had found happiness
After searching so long
A new meaning for life
And a new harmony for its song

Based on love
With dreams beginning to bloom
A new partner to share with
But all was ended too soon

By the Dream Stealer

The thief does not come from without
But dwells within
Waiting expectantly
For the dreams of the young to begin

Shielded only by a new found bitterness
No other defense to deter the attacks
You are robbed of your strength to resist
While the world shows you all that your life lacks

Because of the Dream Thief

Others look at you
With questions in their eyes
Knowing not how to deal
With one whose dreams have died

The world has little pity
Needing only productive work
No others can understand the frustrations
The questions of self-worth

Only its victims know the Dream Stealer

You are filled with a frustrated feeling
As if trying to clutch the air
Like grabbing a fist of water
And no one seems to care

You can only shield yourself in bitterness
Against the enemy from within
Betrayed by your body
Fighting a battle you can never win

Against the Dream Stealer

Satisfied with the results of his work, he slipped the paper under some others in his desk drawer thinking it better to not share these thoughts with anyone right now.

He did not need the alarm to wake up. Kathy arrived ahead of everyone else, sneaking in as quiet as a mouse. Bob let her putts around the kitchen for a few minutes hoping to gauge her temperament. By the sound of it, she was putting things in the refrigerator. Then he heard her slip off her shoes. Why would she do that in his apartment? She had that habit in her place, but Bob never said anything about shoes on his carpet. He thought she must be getting comfortable for the long conference. It was supposed to begin in a couple of hours. That did not make sense either. She was the only one who had a key. With the condition of his knee, Kathy would have to play doorman. That probably was the reason she showed up so early. He closed his eyes and tried to relax for a few more minutes. A quiet noise pried them open.

There she stood in the doorway in all her natural glory, her breast firm and high, her skin supple and milky white. How could a woman who was half Chinese and half Italian have such beautiful, translucent skin? That skin wrapped a slender, athletic body. The seductress had returned. His grin was matched by her suggestive smile.

"I wanted to provide a little comfort before everyone arrives," she said quietly. "To find out how damaged you really are. Gloria said I should give you a little TLC."

God, she is gorgeous, he thought. His body had an instant reaction which his lover picked up on immediately. She stepped into the room, closed the door quietly, and walked to his bed. He started to get up, but she touched his shoulders gently and said, "I'll do the work today. We don't want to tax you knee, right?"

Bob winched a little as Kathy finished drying him off after their shower. The day had gone well beyond what he had hoped for. She had forgiven him and taken the day so far beyond Chinese take-out and a movie that it was bordering on the surreal. His body ached, but his soul was floating. Their only problem now was getting ready for the "conference on Bob." Kathy slipped clothes onto him and then quickly dressed herself. They had ten minutes before the crew was scheduled to arrive.

"I think we should close the bedroom door," Kathy suggested.

"We can just throw the comforter over everything," Bob countered. "No one will pay attention."

"It's not the sight, silly," Kathy laughed. "It's the scent."

"The scent?" Bob asked. "What scent?"

"You can't smell it?" Kathy quipped. "There's a certain scent that goes with love and this room has it."

A scent that goes with love? What was she referring to? Then it dawned on him. She was afraid their friends would pick up on Kathy's method of comfort.

"Do you really think they'll be able to smell that?" Bob asked skeptically.

"Maybe not the guys," Kathy told him. "Between being male and all that smoke you're exposed to they might miss it. But the ladies are programmed to pick up on all the subtle hints. They'll know and I'll be embarrassed, so we just close the door. Where do you keep that potpourri I gave you? We can use that."

Bob dug out Kathy's forgotten gift which she opened and placed in two bowls, one in the living room and one in the bedroom. The bedroom door was closed and they had time for one last embrace before the crew arrived. The gang descended on him bringing pizza and a little laughter before getting down to a serious discussion about how to deal with Bob's good days and bad days.

"So, let's get this straight," Ray began, setting the tone of the conversation. "From what this doctor said, you have a form of the disease that comes and goes. When it comes, you feel exhausted and he'll put you on this medication that winds you up."

Bob and Kathy shook their heads in the affirmative. He was not surprised that the former detective was taking the lead with the questioning. The disease was a mystery and that was what detectives, current or former, were good at solving. They were spread on the floor around the living room. Chingli occupied one chair in deference to her condition and Bob sat in the other because of his knee. Frank and Kathy sat next to their significant others while the other couples took up the floor space in the middle of the room. Paper plates with the remnants of pizza lay in front of each of them. Plastic cups with soda rested on small plates for stability. No beer was allowed today because the boys were working in a few hours and their wives would not hear of it.

"On your good days, do you think you have the stamina to ride on the side of the rig?" Jack asked.

"So far I've been able to," Bob answered truthfully after attempting to stifle a yawn.

"What that means," Kathy interjected. "Is he'll have to take it one day at a time." Bob looked up at the ceiling which earned him a slap on the leg. He exaggerated his reaction to this spat of violence, but she ignored him. It was obvious he would get no sympathy from the woman she had become when the conversation became serious. The party atmosphere suggested by the smell of pizza and soda was belied by the looks of concentration and concern on everyone's faces.

"We ran a plan past Pete before we were relieved this morning," Jack told Bob. "We figured, on your bad days you drive. On your good days you hang on the side. You know Pete doesn't want a steady driver, but if you have days where you can hang, then we'll all keep up our pumping chops and you'll get to have some fun inside."

It sounded like a workable plan to Bob. If the Captain and the Chief were both willing to trust him, then this was doable. He could see Kathy was not thrilled with the idea, but she was holding herself in check for now. "That sounds great to me," Bob told them. "After I start this medication and adjust to it, I think I'll be ready to switch to hanging. Just don't know how long it'll take."

Stacey had been sitting quietly listening to the exchange. This comment brought her into the fray. "I think you're all getting ahead of things," she pointed out. "Prednisone is not a cure for MS. There's no guarantee it will do anything. This isn't a headache, guys, and prednisone is not aspirin."

Kathy showed her agreement and felt obligated to add her own dose of reality. "This medication is only half of what the doctor prescribed," she reminded Bob and informed everyone else. "The second half is something called Zantac which protects the stomach from prednisone."

"Okay, but in the end it's still one day at a time, like you said," Ray insisted. The guys all shook their heads in agreement, so Bob felt at ease with his desire to stay in the firehouse.

"Are you still studying?" Gloria asked. "If you make captain, your duties will be less physical, no?" Kathy reacted very strongly to this.

"Yes, as you can see from the books piled in my kitchen," Bob said, "I'm still studying. The nun who was tutoring me is expected to return any day now." This last comment produced laughter from everyone but Kathy. Her response was another slap on the leg.

"Has she always been so violent?" Jack asked.

"That's the secret to our relationship," Bob quipped.

Kathy did her best to put on an evil grimace, but failed. Bob chuckled at her attempt. Some things have to be learned and continually practiced. Her grimace was not there, but her words made the point. "He hasn't seen violent yet."

"Tread lightly, Bob," Jack advised. Then he looked at his watch and stood up. "Time we headed in, Ray, we're short one body tonight. Getting dinner together is gonna be tough."

"Will you listen to the macho fireman," Gloria laughed. "It's not the fires he's worried about, it's dinner."

"Fires are easy," Ray told her. "Getting dinner in between everything is the challenge."

This produced groans from the women. As Jack and Ray stood up, said their good-byes, and walked to the door, Bob was hit with a wave of melancholy emotions. He should be leaving with them. The attempt to hide his feelings fell flat. Kathy reached up to grab his hand and gave a little comfort. Frank picked up on it and commented, "Bob, you're on injury leave, not going to be much use tonight with that knee."

"That's what sick leave is for," Kathy insisted.

"He's not on sick leave," Jack reminded her from the door. "He's on injury leave. There's a difference."

The women gave a collective sigh of tolerance which brought Ray in on the conversation. "Bob was injured performing his sworn duties to protect lives and property. But alas, you girls just don't seem to understand the concept of a man's word and honor. After all, a man is only as good as his word, but it is a lady's prerogative to change her mind." With that he ducked out of the apartment, leaving Bob and Frank in the hornets' nest.

"Oh, I hate when he does that," Stacey scowled. "When he gets home tomorrow, he'll say I took it the wrong way. If he's not careful, this lady might exercise her prerogative and change her mind about him!" The ladies laughed with her while Frank and Bob knew to be quiet. When the girls calmed down, Frank brought up the subject of part time work.

"Bob, got a question for you," he began. "Chingli is going to be spending less time in the office, for obvious reasons. I was wondering, would you be willing to pick up some Chinese business terms and help fill in the gap?"

Bob was surprised by the offer and flattered at Frank's confidence in his language ability. He also knew that confidence was misplaced. He would not be able to hold even the most rudimentary conversation by simply picking up a few business phrases. "It sounds interesting Frank," Bob commented. "But my speaking ability isn't up to it."

Frank chuckled and then assured him, "I won't expect you to get on the phone with Taipei. If you can learn to read a couple of dozen characters, you can organize and file paper work. That would free me up to do the talking. It would just be for a few days a month really. But you wouldn't have to run all over the state or through the Holland Tunnel."

Kathy reacted before Bob could. "Frank, that's a wonderful offer. We're going to have to concentrate on test prep, but I think we can get a few characters in."

"I have one character here that is hard to read and she's only half Chinese. Suddenly, I'm beginning to doubt my ability to read anything Asian."

This earned him a third slap on the leg. "Even Confucius admitted the difficulty of dealing with that type of character," Frank laughed.

"He did not," Chingli interjected.

"The beginning of Chapter twenty-five of the Analects," Frank sited. "The Master said, 'Of all the people, women are the most difficult. . .' That's a paraphrase, but you get the idea."

"You read too much," his wife told him.

"This is getting too deep for me," Gloria admitted. "You look exhausted Bob, should we leave so you can get some sleep?"

Bob had to admit to himself that he was exhausted, but needed the support surrounding him right now. "No, no," he claimed. "The party's just begun. Frank and I have the opportunity to be flies on the wall. You girls should feel free to chat. Maybe I can pick up some pointers."

Kathy jumped in with a suggestion that seemed to be the perfect compromise, "Why don't you lie down for a bit. Frank's here to protect your masculinity and we girls can clean up and plan for the evening."

Bob considered this a great idea. In the state he was in, chances were he would forget anything that was said anyway. There were questions he wanted to ask Stacey about prednisone and how long it would take to get him back to something resembling normal. He also wanted to speak with Frank about his offer.

"Come on, babe," Kathy said. "I'll tuck you in." She stood up and helped Bob ease out of the chair. His knee was throbbing and his hands felt like they were on fire. Now that the conference on him had concluded, his body was crashing and complaining. He hobbled into the bedroom and crawled into bed. Kathy covered him with the comforter and gave him a peck on the forehead. As she closed the door, Bob resolved to fight to be the guy who was still walking after thirty years of MS. He had been fighting successfully all these months without the help of any medication. Think how much better he would do with that help. As he dozed off, his left cheek developed an itch. Brushing it with his hand, he fell into a deep sleep.

The sound of Kathy's voice woke him up. She was sitting on the bed running her fingers through his hair. "Hey, you don't want to sleep too much," she said. "You won't be able to sleep tonight. Everyone decided you needed to rest, so they left. It's just you and me. What do you want to do for dinner?" She bent down and kissed him on the cheek. This snapped him out of his lethargy. He had not felt her lips touch him. It took only an instant to realize the left side of his face was completely numb. It was as if some crazy dentist had gone wild with Novocain. Sitting up quickly, Bob began to feel his face. There was no sensation. He cursed softly. "We've got a problem," he said flatly.

Chapter Thirty-one

Kathy had been too busy reaching Dr. Bradinsky to really think of what had happened. The first call to the doctor's office had produced an answering service. She had explained the situation and requested the doctor call back. Her mind knew this was not a life-threatening situation, but her heart would not allow a casual response. Bob was resigned to seeing the doctor in a day or two. Kathy considered this ludicrous. Dr. Bradinsky agreed with her. His office returned her call in a matter of minutes and said to come in immediately. Her beau was unenthusiastic, so she took the lead and all but dragged him.

They stepped into an empty waiting room. When Bob walked up to the receptionist, he was immediately handed his chart and told to go right in to see the doctor. Kathy followed him, determined that the patient would be completely honest. Stepping into the doctor's office, each of them naturally sat in what now seemed to be their assigned seats.

"Bob, tell me what's going on," Dr. Bradinsky requested.

"Well, doc, I took a nap and when I woke up I couldn't feel the left side of my face," Bob told him.

"Couldn't feel the left side of your face, you mean completely numb?" the doctor asked.

"Like I was shot full of Novocain," Bob said.

"Okay, let's go to the exam room," Dr. Bradinsky suggested. As Bob stood up, the doctor noticed his hands. "What happened to your hands?"

Kathy perked up when she heard this question. How was Bob going to explain his injuries? What if the doctor said he should leave the firehouse? She knew the question had been lurking unacknowledged in the back of her mind, unacknowledged because of fear. Chingli's comparison of Bob and Frank all those months ago filled Kathy with trepidation. Bob was more of a physical type of man. If he were told to leave the firehouse, it would devastate him. Now that she had a chance to think about it, she was not so sure being ordered out of the firehouse so suddenly was a good thing. He would need time to reinvent himself, to tap into all his potential, and come up with another way to help others. She had to find a way to help him or the man she loved might simply die. It was ironic, but Kathy now found herself praying the doctor would leave it up to Bob, if only for a few weeks more.

Bob sighed and explained, "I fell at a fire running to get a length of hose from the back of the rig."

"You fell running?" the doctor asked. "Did your leg give out or your foot drag?"

"No, no," Bob chuckled. "No, doc, simply tripped. I broke a cardinal rule at fires. Never run, it only increases your chances of getting hurt. A firefighter falling is not unheard of."

"If you say so," the doctor said. "Let's have a look at you." He stood up and walked toward the examination room with Bob trailing behind him. Kathy felt they had dodged a bullet, at least for now.

She remained in her chair, relenting to the evolving routine because she could watch from that vantage point. Bob sat on the exam table while the doctor took out what must have been a pin. He began poking the top of Bob's head, moving from the front to the back. Bob had no reaction. Kathy began to doubt it was an actual pin being used until the doctor reached the back of Bob's head. As the poking started down the back curve of his skull, he made a sudden violent movement to avoid the pin. The doctor immediately placed the pin down and motioned for Bob to follow him. The two returned to the office and sat in their respective seats. Then the doctor picked up his micro-recorder,

"The following notes on Bob Brendler, patient came in complaining of complete numbness on the left side of his face. Evaluation with pin confirmed he has no sensation on the left of his face and along the left side of his scalp. Apparent exacerbation of MS involving the aphthalnic and maxillary branches of the trigeminal nerve. Will require hospitalization with Solu-Medrol therapy."

Dr. Bradinsky placed his recorder on the desk and looked at them. "I'm going to have you admitted to the hospital because of the high doses of steroids you'll be receiving. The nerve involved is a cranial nerve, so I want to hit this hard. This therapy works well with muscular weakness. I think it should bring this under control quickly. Any questions?"

381

Kathy had countless questions, but none that could be answered by this doctor. Bob shook his head no, appearing a little shell shocked.

"All right," the doctor continued. "When can you check into the hospital? The sooner we begin this therapy the better."

Bob hesitated for a moment which gave Kathy the time to insert herself. "He can go there right now," she insisted.

"I'd like to get some things together," Bob retorted. "It sounds like I'm going to be sitting in bed popping a lot of pills."

"Solu-Medrol is the liquid form of prednisone. I'll begin with an I.V. then after four days we'll go to pills," the doctor informed him. "I usually do two more days to make sure you're okay."

"I can pick up whatever he needs," Kathy assured them. "We can drive over there now and get him settled."

The doctor looked at Bob who raised his hands and shrugged his shoulders in resignation. "I'll call admitting and arrange it," he said as he offered Bob his folder.

"Okay, doc," Bob said as he stood up, took the folder, and headed to the receptionist. Kathy followed behind confident she had made the right decision for her man.

The two walked quietly to the parking lot with Kathy trying desperately to read Bob. He seemed subdued; as if he were too busy thinking to speak. She knew to let him consider all his options. When he needed to, he would talk. Before they reached the bottom, of the stairs and stepped into the parking lot, Bob turned to her and suggested, "Let's walk instead of driving."

Kathy put her arm into his and shook her head in agreement, resisting the urge to protect his knee. They reached the bottom of the stairs and began a slow stroll toward the hospital. She knew he wanted to walk so they could discuss things. Her patience would soon be rewarded.

The evening air was beginning to cool with a light breeze helping to ease the temperature. It was a cool late summer day. The pop up thunder showers of mid-summer had been replaced with chilly evenings meant for strolling through a park with your love. The sun was still strong as it danced in and out of puffy clouds floating past. Kathy breathed in the tainted air as she looked at the clouds and waited.

"I'm sorry," Bob started. "This wasn't part of the plan."

"We really haven't begun to plan," she reminded him. "We've been too busy with the test and seeing doctors. But even if we had planned, I always keep in mind one of my father's favorite sayings, 'Life is what happens when your plans go astray.'" Bob chuckled at this little bit of wisdom which encouraged her to continue. "What's happening to us right now has been part of the landscape since that softball game. The difference is we know what it is, so we can deal with it. My mother always used a Chinese saying for situations like this, 'Jing ren shi, ting tian ming.' It means do everything humanly possible then listen to God. We'll get through this." She realized how chatty she had become. Throwing two sayings at him in a minute was over the top and indicative of how nervous she was. Bob had listened patiently. When she stopped to catch her breath, he jumped in to fill the void.

"It hasn't been a year since we shared that first dance," he pointed out.

"True, but you bared your soul to me," she countered "And I gave you a peek at mine." The way she put it brought the desired response.

"That didn't sound like an equal exchange," he laughed.

"A lady always holds something in reserve," she informed him. "That's how she keeps her man interested."

"So, if you saw my soul," he supposed. "Then you know it might not be worth your trouble."

Kathy laughed at him. "I think you're grossly undervaluing yourself, but that's okay. Getting a bargain is half the fun. I've been looking for a knight in shining armor who is also a poetic troubadour. Didn't think I would find one until you wrote that poem inside that card."

"A knight in shining armor?" Bob chuckled. "We were sitting at a round table, but still you got a fireman in a sooty turnout coat. That doesn't sound like your dream come true to me."

"Oh, but it is," she assured him as they climbed the last of the hill to the hospital entrance. "You'll understand some day just how fit for the part you are, Mr. Brendler."

They reached the entrance and Bob pulled the door open. A scan of the signage revealed the direction to admitting. They walked quietly for a minute until they bumped into the nurse from the ER.

"Are the two of you back again?" she asked.

"Unfortunately, yes," Bob smiled. "They finally put a name on my problem. I have MS."

The nurse held back for a moment, seemingly unsure how to react. Kathy jumped in quickly. "At least we now know what we're up against," she said. "We'll get through it."

"That's the proper attitude," the nurse responded. "Never give up. How's the engagement?"

They both smiled. "We're still working on that," Bob told her. "It's only been a month or so and we've been seeing doctors, so no ring yet."

"It's not the ring," the nurse told them. "It's the commitment. I have to confess to you, the entire staff has heard your story. It's not that often we see romance around here. Thanks for letting us share the moment."

Bob and Kathy both laughed. "It wasn't intentional," Bob declared. "I mean the thought had been there, but I never pictured it happening in an emergency room."

"Oh, I realize that," the nurse admitted. "That's what makes it so romantic. Where are you going now?"

"Admitting," Kathy sighed. "He has to have a little hiatus from life and get an I.V. cocktail."

"Admitting? Just go down this hallway, you'll see a counter on your right," the nurse directed.

"Thank you," Kathy said.

"You're welcome and good luck," the nurse smiled.

"Hiatus?" Bob asked as they strolled through the hall. "You make it sound like a vacation."

"Sorry, Bob," Kathy apologized. "Poor choice of words. Now, you're going to have to give me a list of what you need and I'll run to get it after you check in."

Thank God she still had the habit of carrying a note pad in her purse. Kathy had the list of what her beau would need for the next few days. She quick stepped across the parking lot, hopped in her car, and headed for Bob's. After parking across the street, Kathy made her way into the building. When she opened the door, the sounds emanating from the second floor caused her to switch to stealth mode. Bob's eighty year old landlord was having words with his wife. She crept up the stairs quietly, not wanting to embarrass the elderly couple who were arguing at a high volume. As she slipped past the second floor door, the disagreement reached a crescendo. Angry words passed through the apartment door easily. "If you leave me I'll die!" the wife shouted. There was a pause before her husband responded loudly. "Die! Die!" each word building. "You're an evil spirit! You'll never die!"

Kathy could not believe what she had just heard. She stifled a laugh and quickly eased up the stairs to Bob's place. After closing the door, she shook her head and quietly released her laughter. That had to be the wittiest come back she had heard in a long while. To be that quick and that passionate at their ages was admirable. Bob was going to enjoy the story. She wondered; did he know his landlords were so

386

feisty? Taking out her notepad and reviewing it, she scooted to his bedroom.

The smell of pizza still permeated the living room. It had not been that long since they had sat here discussing Bob's options. Was she really ready for a life that included such sudden, dramatic swings? Her mind screamed caution, but her heart had decided. Where in this crazy world would she ever find someone who matched her intellectual and emotional needs so well? The smell of pizza reminded her of something much more mundane. Bob's garbage went out tonight. Did her knowing that say something about their relationship? Pushing the garbage question to the side, she went to his underwear drawer. As she opened the drawer, the question she had just push to the side reasserted itself. Did knowing in which drawer he kept his underwear say something about their relationship? There was no denying it this time around. She was in deep. Their lives were already intertwined. Reaching into the drawer told her laundry had to be done. He was going to be in the hospital for six days and only had three days' worth of underpants. Was she now going to do his laundry? How domesticated, she thought, knowing it was not the first time that had crossed her mind. Scooping up what was there, she dashed to the kitchen for a management book and a legal pad. When she grabbed the pen on the kitchen table, something made her stop. He had been writing with this pen forever. Where does he keep spare pens? Most likely in the spare bedroom that he used as an office.

Walking into Bob's office brought Kathy up short. This was a man's cave, the equivalent of her father's space around his workbench in the basement. Bob called the room his office, but since he studied in the kitchen it was more a storage area now. There was a desk against one wall and a bookshelf against another. Bob's guitars stood next to the bookshelf. The two each occupied a guitar stand, an electric in one and an acoustic in the other. On top of the bookshelf sat two motorcycle helmets. All of these had one thing in common; they were covered in a thin layer of dust. It was a sad sight. She remembered their conversation at Jack and Gloria's wedding. His main interests were his guitar and his motorcycle. The dust on the helmets and guitars said it had been quite a while since he had touched either. They had never gone on another motorcycle jaunt to west Jersey and she had not heard him play guitar even once over the past eleven months. Preparing for the test had consumed him and she had been his distraction when they were not studying. There were parts of him she did not know. Thank God it was the musical part which could only enrich their relationship.

Kathy pulled herself out of the trance she had fallen into upon stepping into the room. She wanted to get these things to Bob before his dinner. Where would he store pens? The desk was the logical place, especially since Bob was so organized. Stepping over to it, she opened the main drawer and was rewarded with the sight of several pens. As she reached for one, a piece of paper caught her eye. Several more pages were uncovered when she picked it up. "The Dream Stealer", she read the poem and stood quietly thinking of the pain that produced it. Determination to ease that pain and fill the void with love rose inside her. The author then reached for the other papers, feeling a tad guilty at perusing through Bob's poetry without his knowledge. The first page had simple thoughts jotted on it, "The hand life dealt you – Mrs. Banks." Who was Mrs. Banks? Putting that aside in favor of the next page, she read:

Buster, the House Guardian

Boom, the thunder adds its roar
To the splash of the rain outside the door

Up pops Buster's head from under his cover
He whines, he barks, he moves out and shudders

Drip goes the water after it splatters against the window glass
Whimpers from the dog continue to grow with each thunderous crash

Pitter-patter up the forbidden stairs when he can take it no more
"Boink" his head hits the closed bedroom door

Squeak, the door opens to a bleary eyed dad
Who growls out the words to tell him he was bad

Tail between his legs, his nail clicking on the floor
Whimpering, he descends knowing he won't get beyond the door

Crash, boom, bang the thunder continues its cacophony
It's times like this when being the house guardian is so lonely

Did Bob have a dog when he was growing up? He had never mentioned it. Writing an onomatopoetic poem was clever. She would never have thought of it, but then she was not very poetic. The last page contained:

Insomnia

Sleep, sleep precious sleep
At times you are such an elusive state
Wanted, needed so desperately
Yet the pressures of life can prove too great

The body may be exhausted
Wanting only to nestle in your soft caress
But the mind will not surrender to you
Too busy for even a short rest

To close my eyes and find peace
Seems such a natural thing
To seek that pleasant twilight
When the body seems to float as a feather fallen from a wing

But the mind resists
With a strength hard to overcome
After hours of turning the sky lightens
To proclaim the mind has won

Problems have not been solved
The day's tasks must be faced
And one more night of tossing
Has proven a frustrating waste

After finishing her little surreptitious poetry reading, Kathy carefully returned the papers to their original positions and closed the drawer. This quick stop in Bob's man cave had been eye opening and reassuring. What she saw and read reaffirmed her judgment and revealed tantalizing hints to parts of his soul she had only begun to plumb. It seemed he had held a little back also. It was going to be interesting for both of them. Before she dashed out of the room, she took one more glance around. Something on the bookshelf caught her eye. James Clavell's works rested in the corner of the middle shelf. Among them was an obviously unread King Rat. She remembered that he had claimed not to have read this particular novel when they had discussed Clavell's works that first date. Impulsively she swooped over and scooped up the book. Management books were so dry. The boy needed something to spice up his day and she could not be it while he was in the hospital.

Gathering up the materials that would make Bob's stay bearable, Kathy grabbed the garbage and ran out the door. She eased down the stairs past the second floor. All seemed quiet on that front. Descending the final flight of stairs as quietly as she had the first, she opened and closed the outside door gently and made for her car, leaving the garbage by the curb. While placing her findings in the truck she remembered her promise to Bob's mom. It had been so hectic and so emotional since his diagnosis. The call would have to be made tonight.

When she stepped into Bob's hospital room, he was lying in bed dressed in a hospital gown with an I.V. in his arm looking none too happy about his situation. Kathy was surprised to see bandages back on his hands. She put on her best happy face and tried to be a breath of fresh air.

"I'm back," she bubbled. "How did you get your hands wrapped up again?"

Bob lifted up his bandaged hands with chagrin and said, "The nurses saw my hands and couldn't leave them alone. I don't know how my medical insurance is going to take this when they see the bill.

The hands are workmen's compensation; the hospital stay is on Crossroads." He was sitting in his bed with the mattress behind him elevated. It could not reach a ninety degree angle, but he could easily lean back and rest if he tired of his position.

"Well, I guess they'll have to fight it out," Kathy speculated. Seeing the bandages reawakened her doubts about his insistence that his fall had nothing to do with MS. She suppressed her doubts, knowing it would be futile to speculate about it. She decided to move on to her main purpose. "I have everything you ordered and then some."

"Was it hard to find?" Bob smiled as she unpacked.

"You know, that's the worrisome part," Kathy admitted. "It wasn't, for the most part. I wouldn't say I had to look for anything except a pen." She waited for his reaction, hoping he did not put two and two together and ask about his poems, still unsure how to react to the Dream Stealer.

"Welcome to the country club," Bob chuckled.

"The country club?" Kathy asked, confused. Her idea of a country club did not include an antiseptically clean room with an I.V. going into its member's arm.

"That's what the orderly who wheeled me here called this unit of the hospital," Bob explained. "It's the CC unit, that's continuing care, which is the opposite of the IC unit."

"Cute," Kathy muttered while placing her gatherings on the bed. He picked up King Rat before she completed unpacking. Flipping through the pages nonchalantly, he commented, "I forgot I had this."

392

She became a little flustered, but quickly rallied. "I remembered you said you hadn't read it. It looks like you still haven't, so I grabbed it for some variety. Management books can be so dry. It'll give your mind a break."

Bob shook his head in agreement. "I've been studying for so long, haven't had a chance. I picked it up on your recommendation," he told her. "You know I haven't been in that room in God knows how long, used to spend a lot of time there."

The poignancy of that statement pulled at Kathy, but she resolved to be little Miss Sunshine and so tried to make light of it. "Yes. I noticed," she said. "Your guitars are gently weeping, pining for your touch." Her words had the desired effect.

"George Harrison I'm not," Bob laughed. "What drew you to that room?"

"That's the thing," she began. "I knew where your underwear was. I'll have to do some laundry tonight. The books and pads were in the kitchen. I even remembered the garbage had to go out. But you really needed a new pen and I had to guess. I guessed right. I'm just not sure if that's comforting or worrisome."

From the look on Bob's face, he was clearly enjoying Kathy's take on how well she knew him. She began to gather up all his things from the bed and shift them to the dresser on his right. Shaving kit on top, underwear inside, and the books beside the razor then she sat in the chair beside the bed.

"I don't think you have to worry about all you know," Bob said. "I'm not that hard a read. What else did those beautiful orbs see?"

Kathy found herself feeling a little disconcerted. She instinctively became coy as she explained. "I couldn't help noticing some papers," she confessed. "It was so hard to resist picking them up and kind of glancing over them." Even to her that sounded ridiculous. How does that explanation justify invading his privacy? It was about as lame an excuse as she could imagine, but it was also true. His reaction showed he realized that.

"Glanced over?" he laughed. "So now you have read over some of my inner most thoughts. What did you think?"

Kathy considered how to approach the subject of his Dream Stealer poem and decided it was useless to pretend she had not read it. "Should I be worried?" she shot back.

"Worried?" Bob asked then paused for a moment as if remembering what was in the drawer. "You're thinking about the last poem, The Dream Stealer?" She shook her head.

"They were just thoughts," he answered. "I'm fighting to be the 'thirty years still walking' guy, remember?" His answer sounded very hollow to Kathy, as if he were hiding behind a shield of false bravado. Something had happened while she was gone. Reminding herself that she was there to give support and encouragement, she pushed on. "Who is Mrs. Banks?"

Bob laughed at the question and told her the story of Janet Banks. "That idea has been sitting in the drawer for months. We've been so busy studying I haven't had a chance to develop it."

His story of Mrs. Banks reminded Kathy of what she had overheard when she was climbing the stairs at his place. The tale gave him a laugh and allowed her to organize questions in her mind, some having to do with poetry and others about his mood. The latter would be put to him another time. "I've never seen you have a hard time sleeping," she pointed out. "Do you really suffer from insomnia?"

Bob smiled remembering the poem, "When you're with me, all is right with the world," he chuckled.

She smiled and tapped his leg, "You surely exaggerate, but I'll take the compliment."

"Any other questions?" he asked.

"Yes, there is one," she replied. "You never talked about having a dog. Is this a secret guy thing? Did you have a dog?"

Bob looked puzzled, "Why would you ask that?"

"Who is Buster the House Guardian?" she shot back.

Bob laughed, "I forget about that one," he told her. "God, when did I write that? Buster is my cousin Dennis' dog. His daughter had to read a poem before her class and the teacher said something about booms and crashes, meaning something onomatopoetic. Den knew I wrote poems and he had no idea where to find something like that, so he called me. I knew Buster was afraid of thunder, so the poem grew out of that. That had to be a year ago. I honestly forgot about it."

"It's cute," Kathy said. "I'm sure it got the expected laughs in class." As she said this, Bob's dinner arrived.

"You should go," Bob told her. "I'll be fine. You brought lots to distract me."

Kathy's heart felt heavy as she stood up. There was no arguing with what he said. She had to eat dinner and the hospital was not going to feed her. A load of laundry awaited her and she owed a phone call to Bob's mother. "I'll see you tomorrow, babe," Kathy said. "You know, I'm glad I couldn't find a pen easily. It let me look into a little bit of your pre-study, pre-Kathy past. I think I know you better now. Every little bit helps, don't you think?" She knew she sounded awkward, but there was nothing she could do about it. The feeling was genuine. With that she bent over and kissed his forehead. "Now just rest and let the meds do their magic." Then she gathered her purse and walked into the corridor.

Kathy gave herself a little time to organize her thoughts and get a handle on her emotions. Dinner and the cleanup were complete before she called Bob's mom.

"Mrs. Brendler, this is Kathy," she began.

"Kathy, please call me mom," she insisted. Kathy had anticipated this and had no problem with it. She always called her mother mama, so there would be no mix ups in conversations with Bob. As she explained Bob's condition, Kathy began to regret volunteering for the task. Would she always be associated with the misfortune of MS? How does a mother feel when she is told her son has this disease? Her future mother-in-law picked up on Kathy's misgivings.

"My dear," she said. "I don't want you feeling guilty about telling me and I certainly don't believe in killing the messenger. How do you feel?"

"Scared," Kathy confessed, although she did not say what her worst fears were because she did not know them herself. There was a gnawing feeling deep within her that she was facing a challenge greater than MS.

"I understand," Bob's mom sympathized. "My mother's cousin had MS. She was her oldest cousin, Sister Clarisa, a Sisters of Charity nun. She was able to walk until she passed away at seventy-eight, so don't despair."

When she got off the phone, Kathy felt a little better. She gathered up laundry and headed for the laundry-mat, the feeling that another shoe would drop still eating away at her.

Chapter Thirty-two

Bob sat up in bed picking at his dinner and thinking. The vegetables were not Frank's broccoli, let alone Kathy's stir-fry. The bandages on his hands were making it difficult to eat, but he hardly noticed. His mind was in a loop with thoughts of Kathy and the realization that his health was only going to decline swirling around in an angry dance. She was young, exotic, intelligent, talented, and her fiancé had MS. There was only one blemish in that description. He put that thought off and focused on the chance encounter he had while Kathy was at his apartment.

A couple had been standing outside the room next to his as the orderly delivered him to the CC unit. There was something familiar about them. It took a moment for Bob to put it together, but after a little pondering he recognized them from Dr. Bradinsky's office. Before he changed into his hospital gown, he walked out into the hallway and approached the couple.

"Dr. Bradinsky's office?" Bob asked.

"Yes," the woman replied. She was dressed in an elegant yet understated outfit; striking Bob as the wife of a professional or stock broker. "Oh, you're the young man we saw the other day in the doctor's office. Was that lovely girl your wife?"

"My fiancé," Bob corrected her. He wondered if this was how he would be identified for the rest of his life, the companion of Kathy. There was a downside to being attached to an attractive woman.

"I don't mean to pry," the husband interjected. "But maybe you could settle a little debate we had. Is your fiancé a television reporter?"

Bob chuckled to himself. Not only was she attractive, but Kathy was recognizable to many people in the area. His identity problem had more than one element. "Well, she's on a leave of absence from the station, but she was a reporter."

"You see," the husband said with a satisfied grin, "I knew it was her."

"Okay, okay," the wife sighed. "No need to gloat. You never forget a pretty face."

"That's why I married you," the husband answered diplomatically.

"Don't try to butter me up," she warned with a smile then turned her attention back to Bob. "What brings you to the country club; does it have something to do with your hands?"

"My hands?" Bob asked. Then he remembered his bandages. That would be the first assumption anyone would make. Before diving into a long explanation, he paused to consider why he had impulsively jumped at the chance to speak with this couple. One obvious reason was to get their opinion on Dr. Bradinsky. Bob's initial impression was one of high competence, but that view was based on three visits for MS. How long have they known the doctor? They both appeared healthy. What was the reason for their visit to his office? How do you start a conversation like this anyway? Kathy had a way of casually chatting that drew the information she wanted out of whomever she was speaking with. That was why she was a reporter. He did not have that skill. That was why he was a firefighter. Standing ruminating about it solved nothing, so he decided to approach it like a fire, dive in and hope for the best.

"No, the hands are from a fall at work. The doctor just diagnosed me with MS," Bob began. "And I developed a problem he thinks can be helped here." The demeanor of the couple changed instantaneously when he mentioned MS. It was as if he had thrown a bucket of ice water on them. The smile receded from the wife's face while the husband instinctively gave her a supportive glance and took control of the conversation.

"He gave you a definite diagnosis?" was his first question.

"Yes," Bob answered suddenly feeling defensive. "I went through an NMR which confirmed the disease."

"An NMR?" the husband asked. "That's the new magnetic imager, isn't it?"

Bob stepped toward the wall to make room for a nurse making her rounds before answering. "Yes, it's supposed to be the latest and greatest for detecting MS." The hospital flowed past them as they spoke, but he paid no attention. From the tone of this conversation, MS was not foreign to this couple. Could he get information from them and learn from their experiences? His mind was now completely focused on the conversation.

"They didn't have those eight years ago. Back then it was a clinical diagnosis backed up with a spinal tap," he told Bob sounding very frustrated.

"Our daughter Susan has MS," the wife said sadly. Bob felt he heard a hint of bitterness mixed in, telling him to proceed cautiously. "It took so long to diagnosis, but that made no difference. There's little that can be done. At first her disease slowly ate away at her independence then it became very aggressive and . . . . I'm sorry. I shouldn't be saying this to you."

"No, please," Bob reassured her. "I really appreciate you sharing your daughter's experiences." He suddenly felt it was important for him to keep the conversation alive. It was one thing to hear coached, cautious information given by a doctor. To hear of someone's actual experiences was quite another.

"Dr. Bradinsky discourages comparing patients," the husband reminded his wife. "No two patients are alike is what he tells us." His wife shot a disapproving look at her mate before continuing.

"The doctor has his reasons, but what harm can there be in telling the truth?" she asked. The question produced a look of acquiescence from her husband, allowing her to continue. "How long have you felt symptoms?" she asked Bob.

"Less than a year," he told her. "I lost some sensation in my leg, but it came back after a week or so. Then it happened again and worsened. That's the way it's been; kind of back and forth, but each time it comes back I seem to lose a little bit more." The details he was sharing surprised him. He had not even given Kathy such a complete description.

"You have a relapsing remitting form of the disease," she informed him. "That's how our daughter's disease started. She was

401

able to work and live independently until about three years ago. Then it took a turn for the worse. The symptoms began about twelve years ago. It took almost five years to find Dr. Bradinsky and get a diagnosis."

"But that's not how it goes for everyone," the husband interjected. "From what I've seen over the years, guys seem to do a little better than women. Can't say whether it's because of a difference in chemistry or because guys just don't complain as much."

"You do your fair share of complaining," his wife reminded him. She then sighed, "Oh, what we could have done if this hadn't happened. But I'm painting a bleak picture aren't I? Dr. Bradinsky is one of the best. He doesn't sugar coat anything and gives you the best medicine can offer."

The best medicine can offer. That statement resonated through Bob's mind as he picked at his meal. From what he saw today, there was not much that medicine had to offer. After Susan's parents left, Bob had glanced in on their daughter. She had been sleeping, but it was obvious by the set-up of the room she could not care for herself. This was not a country club for her. It was simply a different location in a personal hell. How could he subject Kathy to such a life? She had tried so hard to be bubbly, but had only partly succeeded. Did he love her enough to break her heart now and save her a lifetime of pain? The question assaulted the very fabric of his being. She had seemed so content with her ability to figure out where he kept something as small as a pen. Over the months she had woven herself into his life. To pull those threads out would cause agony. To continue on as they were going could expose her to daily hardship and disappointment. He remembered the wife's comment about what they could have done if not for MS. The statement had contained an element of bitterness. Kathy deserved better.

Did he have the strength to set her free? This would be his last chance for happiness and a loving relationship. He was now damaged goods. Who would want a man with MS in her life? Could desperation make him so selfish that he would cling to this last hope and condemn her to a life of sorrow? In the end he knew he could not and so he resolved to find the strength to save Kathy from such an existence. If he had the nerve to fight fires, then he should have the courage to save her from that life. He loved her too much to do otherwise.

"You look like you have a lot on your mind," Dr. Bradinsky's voice commented, pulling Bob's mind back into the hospital room.

"Hello, doc," Bob answered. "Thinking about my future and the choices I'll have to make. They got me hooked up. How long before I feel the effects?" He was trying to stay upbeat and had not meant to say anything about thinking of the future. That slipped out as filler while he transitioned from his ruminations back to the world. The doctor appeared to take it into stride.

"Hopefully, we'll see some results by tomorrow," the doctor informed him. "I'm starting you off with one thousand milligrams. Tomorrow it drops to seven fifty and the next day to five hundred, then to two fifty. After that you'll be taking the medication orally and can leave your friendly I.V. tree behind. A couple of days on oral meds and we'll send you home."

Bob listened attentively, trying to read how the doctor felt about his case. From the casual tone of the conversation, it appeared that this was standard treatment for a routine flare up of the disease. It was just a walk in the park for the good doctor. Probably would not mention it in a conversation with his wife about how his day went. Bob realized that the doctor's perspective toward MS was about the same as he had at a fire. This exacerbation was a Signal Five, a single company response. If they got a quick knock down with this therapy, then it would be recorded in his medical file as a forgettable episode, forgettable to everyone but the victim.

"From your experience, how effective is this treatment in cases like mine?" Bob asked, his mind still struggling to recover from the sudden switch back to reality.

"It should calm the exacerbation, but it's not a cure," the doctor stated. "We'll have to wait and see."

By now Bob had pulled himself fully into the present situation. Questions began flooding his mind. He knew there was a limited amount of time to ask them. Which were the most pressing? "Doc, can I ask you a few questions?" he began lamely.

"Of course, shoot," was the answer.

"I've heard stories of people with MS who are in a wheelchair after ten years and stories of people who are still walking after thirty years. What are my chances?" Bob asked.

"That's hard to say," Dr. Bradinsky replied, looking a little frustrated with this answer. "The symptoms you are presenting and the way you described them, indicate you have a form of relapsing/remitting MS. Many patients with this form of the disease progress very slowly, for others the disease turns progressive and their decline becomes more rapid. There is no way to determine which route your case will take. We'll have to deal with it one day at a time."

Bob had guessed that would be the doctor's answer, but continued along the same track. "This is the first time I've had such a sudden attack with such obvious symptoms," Bob push on. "Does that mean anything?"

"From your description of the symptoms you experienced, your previous attacks have also been sudden," the doctor pointed out. "The symptoms have just been more subtle. That's not unusual. Bob, you have to remember, MS is one of medical science's most puzzling diseases. It is very individualistic and very unpredictable. You're going to hear all sorts of stories from other patients. They have little to do with your case and can't be used to predict where you are going to be next year let alone thirty years from now."

As Bob listened, it became increasingly apparent that it would be very difficult to make any long term plans for his life. He had always known there were no guarantees. His experience on the fire ground had taught him that. But there had always been a semblance of stability on which to build his life. Now there was nothing but quick sand. The doctor took his momentary silence as a sign that the questions were finished.

"The best advice I can give you right now is to avoid heat, infections, stress, and exhaustion," he finished. "That and a good partner should improve your chances. Kathy seems like a wonderful girl."

The last statement cut through Bob like a knife. He was not going to mention his inner quandary to the doctor. No doctor could tell him how to prevent this disease from taking over every aspect of his life. Was there any way to avoid that? The hardest part was going to be giving up the dreams he and Kathy had just begun to formulate. He wanted to shout his frustrations at the top of his lungs. Life had finally been going his way. Why did he get cursed like this? The turmoil inside him drove what little appetite he had away. A glance at his unfinished meal nauseated him. He just wanted to be left alone.

"She's more than I could have hoped for," Bob responded to the doctor's last statement a little too coolly. "Thank you for your honesty doc. One other question, would you be offended if I sought the opinion of another doctor?"

Dr. Bradinshy smiled confidently. "No, not at all. Do you have anyone in mind?"

"Dr. Dunn at College Hospital," Bob told him.

"Tom Dunn?" the doctor reacted enthusiastically. "Good choice. He's on the research side of things. If there are any new developments, Tom will hear of them first. But you have to hustle. I'm having dinner with him next week, so we can discuss your case then." With that the doctor stood up, shook Bob's hand, and walked to the next room to see Susan. The void he left was foreboding.

After considering all that Dr. Bradinsky had said, Bob doubted seeing Dr. Dunn would make any difference. He could feel the medication was beginning to kick in. The first sign was a receding of his exhaustion. The nurse had explained that prednisone might interfere with his sleep. A restless sensation was creeping into his body. Was it the medication or the unanswered questions? Whichever, there was no sleep in him right now. The hard reality of his situation kept pounding him like a huge wave crashing ashore, eroding the beach of his dreams. Bob reached for a paper and pen. First he wrote the metaphor of a beach of dreams. Then he began a poem that would break Kathy's heart, but would also release her from unthinkable sorrow.

Should You Stay

Should you stay with me?
When my body is burned and battered
After you have rejected my world
And so many of our dreams are shattered

Should I expect so much of you
Be that selfish, that cruel
To cling to a broken body
And watch it decline into a useless tool

I have been lost in your love
And yet found in your embrace
But can I demand you cling to me
While all your hopes and talents fall to waste?

Must you surrender yourself to this hardship?
Should I release you from the pledge you made to me?
Your investment is still not too great
It is time I set you free

You must be strong for both of us
There is no need to suffer daily heartache
I hope you will remember me with kindness and treasure our love
Keeping it in a special place

He had a feeling that she would not go down without a fight. Did he have the strength to carry this through? Something in the back of his mind told him he was not really in control of the situation.

Chapter Thirty-three

Kathy had made the trip from South Orange to Belleville so many times over the past six days she was sure the car could get to Clara Maas Hospital on its own. Between trips to visit Bob, jaunts to his apartment to pick up or drop off assorted articles, and dealing with her publisher and the station she was exhausted. It took an enormous amount of energy to pull off the little Miss Sunshine act. She knew Bob saw through her, but they had settled on a quiet acceptance of the roles each played in their situation. She remembered Bob had once said something about acceptance and wisdom. Hopefully they were approaching that as a couple. It would be so much easier to deal with MS if they could accept it and move on to constructive strategies for living with it.

She found the lack of private time with him to be frustrating. In the whirlwind that this hospital stay had become, so many issues had to be put to the side for later because people were around. Her old camera man from the station had called to see if she might be interested in returning. It seemed the New Jersey bureau reporter had made contract demands that Max felt would result in her being asked to leave. Would Kathy be interested in coming back? When she said she wanted to discuss it with her fiancé Max had howled with laughter. After a short conversation, they agreed she would call by the beginning of the following week. Time was slipping away and Bob was unaware of the upcoming offer. She had responded positively to Max's inquiry because the oral history book was coming together.

After all the interviewing, transcribing, indexing, and organizing, chapters were falling into place. Over the past week, she had finally interviewed Jack, Hector, and Ray to get the perspective of young firefighters. A little more effort at editing was needed to make sure her conversion from spoken English to written English was true. Then the publisher would have something to wrestle with and turn into a published work.

What was most maddening about the lack of privacy was that Bob obviously had something on his mind, but there was no opportunity to voice it. She was unsure what it could be. He had avoided any conversation about their future. All of her energy had been focused on him and his needs. It could not be made any plainer that she was not going anywhere. They would see this through together. She would be the point guard and run the game. He could be the center and take all the glory. What a team they were going to make.

The car pulled into the visitors' parking lot almost by itself. Kathy stepped out, waved hello to the security guard, and walked toward the entrance. Frank and Stacey were going to meet her. Chingli had declined to join them, not wanting to be in a hospital in her condition. Kathy was not sure if it was because of the inconvenience or from a feeling that it would be bad luck, but both she and Bob understood. Bob had improved quickly with the steroid therapy. The doctor was very happy with the results which made her upbeat. Her beau had not reacted the same way. The sunshine charade had been matched by a similar effort on his part, but he was no more successful. Instead he seemed to spend his time thinking. The sense of anticipation that hung in the air was heightened with each passing day. Stacey had commented that Bob resembled Frodo in Tolkien's The Lord of the Rings when he planned to set off on his quest alone. Why would he think of fighting this battle alone when he was surrounded by friends? This brooding made it hard for him to study, although he never admitted that. He seemed to oscillate between optimism and pessimism which inspired him to write, but was making it harder to catch up on his study plan.

When she stepped through the entrance, Kathy was greeted by the usual antiseptic laced ambiance of a hospital. She stopped for a moment at the front desk to speak with the receptionist. Delores was on duty and greeted her with a smile. After exchanging a few friendly words, she jogged to catch the elevator, slipping through the doors just before they began to close. The button for the third floor was already pressed. She stood expectantly as the elevator began its ascent; sharing the ride quietly with a young couple who appeared none too eager for conversation. It struck her that a hospital was a unique place filled with a myriad of emotions. Some came with joy, holding congratulatory balloons with the proud smiles of new fathers or grandparents spread across their faces. Others wore a mask of anxiety as they thought how to react to illness or tragedy. The expressions on the faces of those going to the continuing care unit tended to be worried but not anxious. Kathy felt confident the doctor had Bob's condition under control and so wore a neutral expression. This easily slipped into a warm smile when she saw him. The elevator door opened to a busy hallway. Visitors, nurses, and even some of the patients were moving around the "country club". Her fellow passengers turned to the right which left Kathy alone going to the left and strolling the last few steps to Bob's room. She tried to clear her head of the worries that had been assaulting her. In the back of her mind she knew it was the last day of the sunshine act, time to try for an Oscar winning performance.

Frank and Stacey were in the room when Kathy stepped in. The remains of a large pizza rested on the dresser, apparently an advantage that came with a stay in the continuing care unit.

"Is that considered contraband or did the nurses approve?" she asked Frank.

"They said it was good therapy," Frank replied with a mischievous smile. "A bit of normalcy to lift the spirits."

"Really?" Kathy asked as she leaned over and gave Bob a peck. He was resting upright in bed holding a small book entitled "Business Chinese." The bandages on his hands had finally been replaced by Band-aids.

"Is that going to be part of the oral?" Kathy teased.

"That's for after the test," Bob assured her. "Don't tell Sister Mary Elephant. It'll upset her."

Kathy noted the other bed in the room was empty. Although not complete privacy, the small circle of close friends allowed for a freer conversation.

"I have some news for you," she said. "Max from the station called me. He said there was a strong possibility I would get a call inviting me back."

Everyone started talking at once; words of encouragement and congratulations filling the room. She paid close attention to Bob's response, trying to pick up any nuance that might indicate he was less enthusiastic than his words revealed. There seemed to be nothing but genuine encouragement in his reaction.

"Nothing official yet," she said trying to dampen down the tone of the conversation. "Max just put out a feeler, but he was upbeat. The book should be going to the publisher shortly and my evil twin's tutoring gig will end soon, so I think it should be given serious consideration."

"Serious consideration?" Stacey laughed. "How about jump at the opportunity?"

Kathy appreciated her friend's encouragement, but the main actor was still holding back. She stood beside the bed expectantly.

"Your evil twin should be out of a job in about a month," Bob pointed out. "She's going to need something to keep her occupied, don't you think?"

She smiled at him as one nagging question was put to rest. Everything seemed to be falling into place. Why was she insecure? The answer was sitting on the bed. He was still holding something back. How to pry it loose? Frank jumped in while she considered her options.

"You said the oral should be in about a month?" he asked Bob. "So, you have a lot of studying to do in a short period of time."

The movement of the conversation back to Bob's reality seemed to deflate him a little, but he quickly rallied and regained his equilibrium. "Yes, I lost a lot of time with this distraction," he answered. "There's only so much you can do with books for an oral. I have to practice my presentation." Kathy took this as her cue to jump back in.

"Don't worry, Sister Mary Elephant is waiting in the wings," she interjected. "She is cold hearted and cuts no slack for laggards with lame excuses." Frank and Stacy laughed.

"What a couple," Stacy observed then turned serious. "Have you been in touch with Dr. Dunn?"

Kathy sharpened her focus on Bob to see if she could pick out any clues about what was eating at him. His immediate reaction to the question indicated the conversation had drifted closer to the problem. A look of doubt swept across his face before it settled on a neutral posture. The response which followed revealed a little more.

"Not yet," he said flatly. "I don't know if it's worth the trouble. He's not going to be able to change anything."

Stacy seemed to be taken aback by his words. "He can give you information so you know more about what you're facing."

"Well, maybe," Bob said sounding skeptical. "We'll see."

Kathy placed her hand on Bob's forearm to quiet him then turned to Stacy and said, "We're going to reach out for him soon. If I have to whip him or love him, my sweetheart is going to speak with your professor." Frank and Stacy laughed; Bob did not. This was followed by a momentary lull in the conversation. Bob took the opportunity to redirect the topic to one he had more control over.

"I called my folks and broke the news," he informed them. "They took it well enough. My mother was optimistic. It seems my grandmother had a cousin who had MS. She was able to walk until the day she died at seventy-eight. Of course, she was a nun, so she had an in, but mom felt Sister Clarisa's experience was somehow indicative of what I could expect."

"It sounds encouraging," Stacy commented. Bob's demeanor implied he did not agree. It appeared to Kathy that he was intent on rejecting anything that had even a hint of optimism. What was eating at him?

"Ray said the guys worked out a plan to help you stay in the firehouse," Stacy continued. "The Chief and the Captain are on board."

"Yeah, but I don't want to be a drag on the company," Bob muttered continuing to resist anything positive.

Frank jumped in when he heard this. "Whoa, my boy, you were a kick ass fireman last week and now you're going to be a drag on the company?" he snapped with more than a hint of sarcasm. "Nothing has changed physically in the past week. It's all in your mind. On your good days you drag hose. On your bad days you pump water. Nothing you haven't done before. Just don't run at fires."

Bob laughed at the last remark and raised his scraped hands in surrender. His mood seemed to lighten after that. What was it about men? Their friends slap them down, denying their concerns and ignoring their feelings. How do they react? With laughter, it just did not make sense.

Frank and Stacy had to leave shortly after this which gave Kathy a few minutes alone with Bob for the first time in five days. Before Frank left, he told Bob to call him if he needed to talk. Her gut reaction was "Why call him? Bob can talk to me." She had spoken with enough firefighters to know not to go there. It was a guy thing. They had to bounce ideas off other men. A woman just would not do. Kathy put that to the side and focused on trying to find out what Bob was holding back. She did not want to jump right in with direct questions, deciding to probe around the perimeter instead.

"You should be released tomorrow right?" she asked tentatively. He appeared to be distant, as if he was wrestling with something in the deep recesses of his mind.

"That's what the doctor said," he answered. "It'll be good to get back home so I can begin prepping for the oral."

"You weren't able to work on it much here were you?" she asked dancing with him around the important issues.

"No," he chuckled. "I'd have to practice a long time before I could give a coherent presentation in a place like this."

"So, how have you been occupying yourself when I'm not bothering you?"

"You're never a bother Kathy," he replied. It struck her that they sounded like two people who had just met.

"That's encouraging," she chortled. "But you seem to be avoiding my question. Were you chasing the nurses around and don't want to confess?"

Bob laughed. "No, they were all sterner than Sister Mary. I just thought and read and wrote."

Kathy knew he had spent a lot of time thinking about the sudden changes in his life. If she could read some of what he had written, maybe it would tell her what was eating at him. "What did you write?" she probed. "Notes for the oral or something more profound?" He appeared very reluctant to show her. The last time he was this hesitant, they were at Jack and Gloria's wedding. "I won't be critical," she promised. "The agreement we came to at Jack and Gloria's reception is still in effect." He did not react with the anticipated smile, but he did stand up and reach into a drawer in the dresser, retrieving several pieces of paper. After glancing at them, Bob handed her one. She began reading nervously.

When Love Is Not Enough

What do we do when love is not enough?
When the cold reality of life breaks through stalwart walls of
    tenderness
Wreaking havoc on our commitment to each other
Disrupting a dance we had so carefully choreographed

How do we endure when the hardships of life become too great
When pent-up frustrations burst forth like the torrent of a
    swollen river
Immersing us in a whirlpool of seemingly endless sorrow
Drowning our every hope for a happy existence

Where do we find strength when the foundations of our life
*   together begin to fail*
When the tide of change pounds our once tranquil shores
Eroding the warm, comfortable beach we shared
Robbing us of all the world takes for granted

Who possesses the stamina to persevere when a thief comes to
take
*   our dreams*
When our vision of what life should be becomes shrouded with a
*   haze*
Distorting our view of both what is and what is to come
Covering our eyes with a veil of doubt

"Why" is the question often crossing our minds when life's
*   sweetness becomes unpalatably bitter*
When fermentation changes the wine we shared
Turning it sour and indigestible
Converting it to useless vinegar

When can we expect improvement, when will our dreams be
replaced
When do we begin to blot out our past troubles
Erasing forever the bitterness we have felt toward life's changes
Replacing it with silent determination to endure what we once
*   thought we could not*

And endure we must because love itself is not always enough

The sadness of the poem brought tears to her eyes, but these were held back. She was supposed to be Miss Sunshine. When she looked back at him, he slowly handed her another poem. His eyes told her it was one of the most difficult things he had done in a long time. The poem did not begin well. "Should you stay with me?"

At first she was at a loss for words. Instinctively, what came out when she found her voice was defensive. "I haven't rejected your world," she began. "It's the only world I know." She was looking directly at him when making her plea. Bob avoided her eyes as he responded.

"It's not referring to the Fire Department," he told her. "My world is now MS."

Kathy could not believe what she was hearing. Did he feel some sort of misguided need to suddenly apply a distorted code of chivalry to their life? Was he trying to be a strong alpha male who dealt with his troubles by himself? This was bullshit! He was too far into her soul. If he went through with what the poem suggested, she would never recover. It was the base of his brooding. Her initial defensiveness quickly gave way to anger. The battle had begun. It was her against MS. She would have to fight for both of them until Bob regained his strength and balance.

"MS is your world only if you allow it," she spat back. The words hit him like a slap across the face. After a moment he came back, bitterness lacing his response.

"Allow it?" he asked incredulously. "What? Are you crazy? Haven't you read? Don't you see what this disease does?"

It was obvious this conversation could degenerate into a heated argument. She had to tread carefully because he needed her to carry him over the mountain.

"That's not going to happen to you," she said with supreme confidence, wanting to add "because I won't let it", but knowing that would just be false bravado.

"Oh, you know."

"I know."

"I wish I shared your confidence," he countered.

"The medicine worked, didn't it?" she asked confidently.

"For now," was the resigned response.

With that she changed tactics, hoping a more reasoned, less emotional approach would sway him. "The guys have you covered in the firehouse. You'll get promoted which will make it a little easier. When you make chief, you won't be dragging hose or pulling ceilings. You have a future on the Fire Department."

Instead of relenting to the logic of her argument, he snapped back, "Are you writing a novel? How do you know? I could be a quadriplegic next month."

Kathy had no idea what wall that came off of. Something had spooked him and he was not about to tell her what it was. She had to calm down and get him back to reality. "Where did you come up with that?" she shot back. "You have relapsing/remitting MS not the progressive form."

"Right now maybe," was his response. "But I can't plan on that. They don't know. From what I see, it's all a numbers game. Statistically I can expect one thing, but realistically they can't say."

Was that the problem? That he could not plan out his life? Who could? No one knew that better than a firefighter. He had lived life on the edge for years now. Why was he suddenly looking for guarantees? What happened to his fight? She knew it was still in him. Her job was to drag it out. Deep down she knew to attack his pride. He had told her once that the only fire he could not put out was the one inside him. She was going to stoke those flames.

"You won't back down from a fire, but now you're going to surrender without a fight?" The question had the desired effect. It struck him like a physical blow.

His response was still subdued. "No, but it's my fight, not anyone else's."

"You're wrong," she calmly reassured him. "It's my fight also and I don't give up. We'll get through this together." She felt calmer now that the tone of the conversation had veered away from confrontation.

"But this is forever," he reminded her. "It's not going away. I can deny it all I want. It will extract its toll."

"And I will pay my share," she assured him.

Bob seemed deflated. He pointed to the poem and admitted, "They were just thoughts. We can talk more when I get home."

Kathy did not believe him, but knew better than to voice her opinion. Instead she chose a conciliatory stance. "Just thoughts, I understand," she told him. "We'll put them aside for now. There's an oral to prepare for and your tutor is heartless, remember?"

He chuckled at that, but his acquiescence was obvious. She had fought him to a draw today. The battle was sure to be rejoined another time. Vigilance and tenacity would be required before a complete victory could be declared.

Chapter Thirty-four

Bob laughed quietly as he stepped into Dr. Dunn's office in College Hospital. The last time he had been in this particular medical facility involved a trip to the emergency room to repair the damage done during his argument with the street pavement. He glanced at the scabs on his hands and flexed the left hand without thought. Even after a week, it was still sore, but not as sore as his knee. All of this was a minor distraction now. The issue that dominated his consciousness at the moment was how Kathy had manipulated him into this visit. Bottom line was he had wimped out after she had read that poem. Going into burning buildings was so much easier than telling her it would be best that they stop seeing each other, at least in a romantic way. He would always love her and value her friendship, but to ask her to become his partner would be cruel. His cowardice would cause her unspeakable pain. Was he selfish in putting off the inevitable? Maybe it would be better if she had the opportunity to truly understand the ramifications of his disease. Then she would break it off and he would be the only one suffering. It was an approach that he really needed to consider.

They stepped into a small, sparsely decorated waiting room. He would be the doctor's last patient before lunch. Kathy went to the receptionist while he sat in one of ten seats. This was obviously not Dr. Dunn's primary office. Dr. Bradinsky had mentioned something about his colleague being into the research end of MS. Dr. Dunn was also a professor at the medical school. Bob was hoping he was as sharp as Stacy and Dr. Bradinsky said, then he might answer some questions a little more forthrightly than Dr. B. He had picked the seat furthest from the receptionist. Kathy would probably not approve, especially since the only other people in the room were a middle aged couple sitting by the receptionist. As she began walking back toward him, Kathy started a conversation with the woman. After a minute, the man stood up and strolled over to Bob.

"Hi, I'm Tony Scotto," he began. "The ladies or at least my wife chased me away. Mind if I have a seat?"

"Please," Bob replied even though he really did not feel like socializing. Something told him that he could gain a lot from a conversation with Mr. Scotto. Kathy and Mrs. Scotto were deep in conversation which probably meant they were talking about this doctor and MS. The first question that crossed Bob's mind was did either of them have the disease and if so which one.

"Is that your wife?" Tony asked.

"Fiancé," Bob sighed.

"Lovely girl," Tony complimented. "She did the news not too long ago, didn't she?"

Bob realized he had not even introduced himself and was already identified as the fiancé of a news reporter. "Yes, she did," he replied. "Oh, I'm sorry. I didn't introduce myself, Bob Brendler."

Tony chuckled. "No need to apologize. I didn't give you a chance. From what your fiancé says, you were recently diagnosed with MS."

"Yes, I just got out of the hospital two days ago," Bob explained. "We're here for a second opinion."

"Did you neurologist doubt the diagnosis?" Tony asked. "They have a new test now; it's called an NMR, that's supposed to give an accurate diagnosis."

When he heard this, Bob knew Tony had some knowledge of MS. This reinforced his conviction that he could gain from a conversation with this man. He just had to ask the right questions. Kathy was still talking quietly with Tony's wife. Whatever the older woman was saying seemed to be upsetting Kathy. There was a subtle change in how she was sitting; an unnatural stiffness that told Bob trouble lay ahead. Tony noticed his glance.

"I think I'm going to owe you an apology for my wife," he sighed. "She is probably not saying anything that will make your life easier."

Bob snapped his focus back. "How so?" he asked, hoping a simple question would illicit a detailed answer.

"Let me give you a little background info," Tony began. "I also have MS; have had it for twenty-eight years. First ten years were rough; then my disease became quiescent. Eighteen years since I've had a flare up. In those eighteen years the wife has grown more and more anxious. I don't know if it's the whole change of life thing or a disbelief in how fortunate we've been and it can't last forever. But whatever it is, she's scared."

Bob could not believe his luck. Here was a guy with MS who had not had an exacerbation in eighteen years, living proof that life goes on after MS. At first he wanted to throw dozens of questions at Tony, but then the meaning of the last sentence sank in. His wife was scared. Anxiety was eating away at her.

"She's scared?" Bob asked. "She's expecting things will suddenly go bad?"

"According to her, I've probably been having quiet flare ups," Tong shared. "She claims these have affected my brain and that I'm suffering from cognitive dysfunction. When she forgets something it's because she's over fifty. If I forget something it's because MS is eating away at my brain. We're here because she wants me to see another neurologist and get a complete evaluation of my mental capacities."

Evaluate his mental capacities? Bob was shocked by this. No one had told him that this disease could affect his intelligence. Tony appeared to be normal, but he did not live with the man. The funny thing with questions about the brain was without spending years around someone, you could never tell if there had been a change. He assumed there were tests that could measure mental capacity, but how could they determine if change had occurred without a baseline? How prevalent were cognitive problems? Could he even ask a question like that? The receptionist called Tony's name before Bob had a chance to say anything. The older man wished him good luck and went into the doctor's office, leaving Bob with more questions than ever. Kathy walked over to him, sat down, and held his hand. She said nothing until the receptionist called them.

The doctor's inner office was as Spartan as the waiting room. Bookshelves lined the back wall. Copies of diplomas hung on the wall beside his desk. It was a white washed room dominated by that desk. Two chairs sat across from this, facing a man who appeared to be north of fifty, but had dark hair and a broad smile. Bob and Kathy sat in their self-assigned chairs, he on the left, she on the right.

"You're Stacy's friends, right?" the doctor asked pleasantly as he stood up and offered his hand.

"Yes, Bob Brendler, doc," Bob responded shaking hands as he spoke. "And this is my fiancé, Kathy Stanley" Dr. Dunn reached for Kathy's hand. Bob was struck by the lack of warmth she displayed. She appeared to be turned inward, preoccupied with her thoughts.

"Stacy tells me you're a firefighter here in Newark," the doctor chatted. "Are you on one of the companies that respond here so often?"

Bob smiled at the question. The automatic alarm in the hospital malfunctioned on an almost daily basis. Seven Engine was first due for most of the hospital complex, but Six was due on the southern most buildings.

"Yes, doc," Bob informed him. "We're first due on the south side of the hospital."

"They really have to fix that system," Dr. Dunn said. "It's too sensitive. It seems when the heat or air conditioning kicks off in the morning, the alarm gets tripped. People are starting to get complacent."

"Complacency is a bad thing if there really is a fire," Bob observed. Why they were talking about fire safety was beyond him. He put it down as small talk to break the ice and waited for the doctor to get down to business.

427

"As I understand it, you were just diagnosed with MS and are looking for confirmation," the doctor began. Before Bob could respond, Kathy pulled an envelope out of her purse.

"I think you'll want to read this, doctor," she said as she handed him the envelope. Dr. Dunn opened it, removed a piece of paper, slid a pair of glasses over his eyes, and leaned back in his chair. After pursuing the paper he removed his glasses, placed the paper on his desk, and looked at Bob. "The NMR was positive for MS," he started. "How long have you had symptoms?"

Bob thought for a moment. It would have been an easy question until his conversation with Tony. Quiet exacerbations, was that possible? How could he give an answer that took silent flare ups into account? Quickly rejecting that thought, the firefighter settled on the obvious. "The first sign appeared about a year ago after a three alarm fire," he informed the doctor.

"Only a year?" The doctor asked skeptically as he glanced at the NMR report again. "I think you were having clinically silent attacks before then, but that's just an opinion. What have your symptoms been?"

"I've had sensory problems and bladder problems," Bob informed him.

"Sensory and bladder, that's encouraging. The only reason I brought that up is because statistically the first five years of experience with this disease are a good indication of how well you will do."

When Bob heard that he perked up. Here was a doctor who was willing to express an opinion and give information useful for planning a future. Kathy seemed to share his reaction. Questions that had been resting quietly in the back of his mind waiting for an informed answer sprang out of that darkness. "Doc, you just gave me more information in a few sentences than anyone else was willing to give since I was diagnosed," Bob declared. "Can I put a few questions to you?"

"Sure, what's on your mind?" the doctor replied.

"From what little I've been told," Bob began. "It seems everything about a prognosis for MS is based on statistics. Is there anything definite you can say about my case that will help me plan my life?"

The doctor sighed when he heard this. Kathy sat up expectantly. "The VA conducted a thirty year study of veterans with MS. It showed that your past experience with MS was indicative of your future disease. Unfortunately, we can't say with any certainty what will be the outcome of any individual's disease and even if we could, it's really too soon to make a prediction in your case. But things are improving. Pharmaceutical companies are working on medications that look promising. My advice would be to plan your life as you would if you didn't have MS. There's no need to roll over and play dead. Your experience so far has been sensory loss and bladder problems. You haven't had problems with movement. That's a good sign. It is possible that we can expect a relatively mild form of the disease. But I don't want to mislead you. Men tend to do worse than women."

As far as Bob was concerned, what the doctor had just said was a non-answer. "It is possible" did not suffice and the last sentence had an ominous sound to it. It also went directly against what Susan's father had said and reinforced the doubts in his mind. How could he ask Kathy to throw her lot in with him when his health made it such a roll of the dice? Before he could formulate another question, Kathy interjected herself. "Doctor, can you tell me about cognitive dysfunction?" she inquired. "How prevalent is it in MS and how severe?"

Dr. Dunn had a knowing smile on his face when he responded. "You spoke with the Scottos, did you? It's very dangerous to compare MS patients. Impairment of intellect is not common, but it can occur in four or five percent of cases. Mostly, the impairment is mild, but in severe cases it can be dramatic. "

"Mrs. Scotto seemed so sure her husband had deteriorated intellectually," Kathy stated, sounding very apprehensive.

The doctor's expression became more serious. "I can't say anything about another patient, but suffice to say relationships are very complex and not all the problems are caused by MS. Now about your fiancé's prospects, there are no guarantees. Time will tell over the next few years. As I said, the first five years are the best predictor of the future. If he has no major disabilities after five years, then he may not develop major disabilities."

Bob heard the apprehension in Kathy's voice. What had this woman said to her? Would the information Kathy obtained from Mrs. Scotto make his task of at least slowing down their relationship easier?

He suddenly found himself doubting his resolve. Forcing his thoughts back to a realistic assessment of his future, he steeled himself for the conversation that would inevitably follow this visit. No matter what his heart felt about Kathy, his mind knew she did not deserve the torturous life living with MS could become. Kathy had fallen silent after the doctor's last reply. Bob saw no need to bother Dr. Dunn any further. There were no answers to the most important questions on his mind. No one had the answers. As far as MS was concerned, medical science was still in the dark ages.

"Okay, doc," Bob said unenthusiastically. "I think we've taken up more than enough of your time. Thank you for your honesty and the information." With that he rose to leave. Kathy followed, smiling at the doctor stiffly and whispering her thanks.

"I don't think you should be too concerned with cognitive problems," the doctor said as they moved toward the door. "I have only seen them in severe cases."

"Only in severe cases," Bob repeated. "Okay doc, thanks." He made his way out of the office feeling disappointed. He had a knot in his stomach and it was tightening. Kathy walked silently beside him as they left the building. How do you start a conversation about facing the harsh reality that life with MS could become unbearable? He caught himself in mid-thought, realizing how quickly he was falling into the habit of saying could, might, and maybe. You do not build a life on qualified answers to important questions. They walked across the parking lot in silence. Kathy began to cry quietly before they reached the car.

"We'll get through this," she said almost to herself. Whatever that woman had said to her really threw Kathy for a loop. Bob did not know what to say. How do you comfort a woman when you do not have the exact reason she is upset? Paint with too broad a brush and you just make things worse. The only thing he could think of doing was stopping and giving her a hug. She sobbed into his shoulder, which ripped his heart apart. This was just the beginning. He had no disability now. How could she make it through life when his body fell apart?

"We will get through this," she said again with conviction. Bob hardened himself, using the anger and frustration he felt toward his disease to ask the hardest question he had ever asked, "How can you say that? Can't you see it's all a numbers game?"

Kathy pushed herself off his shoulder looking shocked before becoming animated with anger. "No!" she insisted. "It is not a numbers game; it's a diagnosis. You have no major disability so far, which is a sign your case might be a mild one."

"Mild MS is an oxymoron," he replied feeling his courage begin to build. "What we really have to discuss is your options. You are not condemned to a life with MS."

"What's that supposed to mean?" she snapped back at him, her tears drying up.

"Just a statement of fact," he answered. "I'm the one stuck with it."

She pushed him away and took a step back. The look in her eyes made it obvious she was ready for a fight even if they were in the

432

middle of the College Hospital parking lot. A breeze lifted her hair, making her even more attractive and giving him doubts about going through with this confrontation. The sun brought out the red highlights in those floating locks, but the determined look on her face made him nervous. If she had a violent streak, this would be where it showed itself.

"I can't believe you just said that," she hissed. "After all I've done over this past week, how can you even think that I have some sort of option to just walk away from you?"

The last question dripped with sarcasm. He realized his response to it was stupid as soon as the words left his mouth. "I didn't ask you to do any of it."

"That's the point, isn't it," she snapped back. "I did it for love, not to please you."

"Kathy, you deserve better than living a life filled with MS," he pointed out. "We could still be friends. I just don't want to see you suffer because of me."

"You don't want to see me suffer?" she shot back. "We can still be friends? What are you trying to say? That I should breakup with you because you're ill?"

"I have MS," he reminded her. "That goes way beyond ill. This won't go away."

"But that would subject me to a life without you," she said in exasperation. "I'm a big girl. I can make my own choices."

"You don't know what you're saying."

"I know more about it than you do."

"Please don't make this more difficult," Bob pleaded, his voice steadily increasing in volume. "You are young, beautiful, intelligent, and have a promising career. Why would you insist on hanging an albatross around your neck? My body is going to shrink into uselessness."

"Don't you understand?" she asked. "I don't love your body, I love your soul. Bodies are easy to come by. I can go to a club in the city and throw myself at some cute guy for a body. Your soul, I can't find another soul like you."

"You can say that now," he said bitterly. "What happens when my legs shrivel up and I am permanently seated in a wheelchair? No one has use of a sick firefighter."

"You're not just a firefighter; you're a writer, a poet."

"The poet is dead!"

"You don't mean that. If it was that easy I wouldn't love you."

"And when this disease eats up my brain? Why can't you accept that your dream of a poetic firefighter is just a dream, it will be consumed by MS before it can come to fruition."

"Am I talking to the same guy?"

"No, now I'm sick remember?"

"*Gan lin niang ji bai!*" she shouted and began to cry. "You just don't understand how I feel, what I have at stake. I've - - -I've got to go."

"Go, go where?" Bob asked, not understanding what she said, but suddenly remembering; they were in the middle of the Central Ward. "Come, get in the car and I'll drive you home."

"That's okay," she snapped back at him. "I don't want to stress your fragile body."

"Kathy, please," Bob pleaded. "You can't walk through this neighborhood."

She laughed at that. "I was reporting from this neighborhood when a madman was shooting people," she bragged. "I'm not worried. Why should you be?"

"Because I love you and these streets aren't safe for someone like you," he reminded her.

"*Ni ma de!*" Kathy shouted as she started to cry again. "You don't have the right to say that anymore!" She took a deep breath to get control of herself and then said in a loud, cool voice, "You're saying things now that you'll regret. I know you Bob Brendler, you can't bullshit me." After that pronouncement, she lowered her voice and hissed. "Call me when this stranger leaves and Bob comes back." With that she stormed off heading toward South Orange Avenue.

"Kathy!" Bob shouted after her. She did not even turn to face him, but simply extended her arm backward and flipped him a bird. Where was she going? He could not in good conscience just let her walk off through these streets. She stood out as an easy mark, an attractive young woman stylishly dressed with a purse hanging over her shoulder. What to do? She was not going to listen to reason, so he had to follow her with the car. Follow her where? The firefighter decided to wait for a minute to see where she was headed.

Watching her determined strut only made him more nervous about her walking through the streets of his first due district. At first she seemed to be headed for a phone on the corner of South Orange and Bergen Street, but it was obvious the phone had been vandalized and rendered useless. She then veered left and appeared to be walking toward Hunterdon Street. Was she going to walk to Six Engine? That would be the only safe haven in that direction. The first tour was working today and she would know it. He quickly jumped into his car and headed for the lot exit. After a right turn onto South Orange Avenue and a left onto Hunterdon, he slowly cruised behind her as she marched down the street drawing admiring looks from the residents along the way. It took fifteen minutes to transverse the four blocks to Springfield Avenue. Bob found himself praying Six would be in quarters. Kathy reached the side door, hesitated for a moment, then stepped around to the Springfield Avenue side of the building and simply walked in through the open overhead door. He turned onto Sixteenth Avenue and parked across from the entrance to Six's side lot. Jack came out the back door a few minutes later.

"What did you say to her?" Jack asked when he reached Bob's car. "I don't know if I've ever seen a woman that angry and I've pissed off a lot of them over the years."

"I told her I thought we should break up," Bob sighed. "I don't want to see her suffer living with MS. She doesn't have to go through that."

"You really said that?" Jack said with a quiet chuckle. "We have to sit down and discuss the emotional lives of women someday. You're lucky she didn't scratch your eyes out. Why you would say that is beyond me. Anyway, she's going to take my car home. Hector said he'd drop me at the Rendezvous and Gloria will take me to Kathy's to get the car. Oh, and one other thing, just an opinion, but I think you're being a horse's ass. Bit of an overreaction, don't you think? Maybe you should go talk to Frank, ask his opinion." With that Jack tapped the top of the car, turned, and walked back into the firehouse. Kathy came out a moment later, glanced in his direction without acknowledging him, and drove Jack's car up Sixteenth Avenue. Bob was left with a pit in his stomach and countless doubts gnawing at his brain.

Chapter Thirty-five

Kathy drove up Sixteenth Avenue mindlessly. This was a man's car if ever there was one; not pretty but lots of power. Gloria had her work cut out for her. The interior was cluttered with newspapers, assorted other papers, disposable coffee cups, and even clothes in the back seat. She wondered if she was driving away with Jack's clean uniforms. Well, he could borrow from Ray if needed. She did not care, wanting only to get home so she could think. Why had anger so consumed her? Was it because when Bob mentioned cognitive problems he had articulated her doubts?

She turned onto Thirteenth Street and scanned ahead. West Side Park was on her right so she had to focus on her surroundings in case a child in the park decided to run across the street. Her thoughts were put on hold until she turned right onto Eighteenth Avenue and drove past the park. When they flooded back, she grew angry with herself. How could she allow herself to be so upset by a conversation with a stranger, especially one who had obvious issues? From the moment their conversation began, Kathy had a feeling Mrs. Scotto was a little off.

"Hi, can I ask you," Mrs. Scotto had inquired. "Did you report on Eyewitness News?"

"Yes I did," Kathy had replied. "I took a break to write, but might be going back shortly."

"Really! I thought it was you," Mrs. Scotto gushed. "Have you seen Dr. Dunn before? This is our first visit."

"No," Kathy answered. "Our first also, I was hoping you might tell me something about him."

"I've heard he's an expert with multiple sclerosis, that's why we're here," she explained. "I'm afraid we don't know anything else about him."

That explanation immediately drew Kathy's attention. Before she could react; the woman's husband squeezed into the budding conversation. "I'm Tony Scotto and this is my wife Janet," he said.

"Hello Tony, Janet," Kathy said. "I'm Kathy Stanley. Could I ask why you have an interest in seeing an expert on MS?"

"My husband's been dealing with the disease for almost thirty years," Janet told her. "We've come to see Dr. Dunn about tests to determine how it has affected him."

"Really?" Kathy exclaimed then realized her enthusiastic response might seem a bit odd without an explanation. "I'm sorry, it's just that my fiancé was recently diagnosed with MS and we're here for a second opinion."

Janet's demeanor immediately shifted. It was as if a second person had stepped in to take her place. She immediately suggested Tony go speak with Bob. When he walked away, his wife began a minutes long diatribe which still resounded in Kathy's mind. The man she described did not appear to match the man sitting with Bob. The more she complained the more apprehensive Kathy became. Claims of living with a husband whose mind was deteriorating flowed from her mouth. She informed Kathy that cognitive dysfunction was a symptom of MS that few people took seriously, but it was the worst symptom. By the time the receptionist called her husband's name, Janet had warned Kathy that MS would snatch away Bob's intellect and that it would be best that she break off her engagement to him. With that the older woman stood up and stormed into the doctor's office, leaving Kathy shaken and suddenly filled with doubts.

She stopped for the light just before crossing over the Parkway. Why had she not spoken to Bob about his impression of Tony before she panicked? Janet's words were filled with worry, but her tone and movements were those of a deep seated anger. Kathy's initial feeling that Janet had issues should have given her warning to take whatever was said with a grain of salt. The light changed and she accelerated, propelling the car into Vailsburg. Her mind latched onto Dr. Dunn's words. He had tried to reassure her, but Kathy had paid scant attention. Instead she had let her fears and emotions control the situation. Now the situation was out of control. How was she going to get it back to a manageable state? Thinking of what Dr. Dunn had said gave her something concrete to grab onto. She had to get hold of that VA study. The car rolled past Fire Headquarters as she approached the bottom of the Eighteenth Avenue hill. She pressed the accelerator and felt some release of tension as Jack's little baby climbed the hill effortlessly. One advantage to driving a guy's car was how well it responded to an angry foot. She knew in her heart that the anger came from fear. Fear she could not rationalize away. If only she could wipe the words of an anxious postmenopausal woman from her memory.

When Kathy arrived home, she dropped her purse on the couch and immediately headed for her answering machine. A phone conversation with Gloria had produced Jack's car and set the ball rolling for a war council. She pulled up short when she reached the machine. A pile of Bob's clean clothes was neatly folded and stacked on the desk chair. The clothes were supposed to go with her to Dr. Dunn's office, but had been left behind in the rush to get out. At the time it did not seem to matter, he would drop her home after the visit. Quickly shaking off the momentary shock, Kathy looked at the phone to see if there were any messages. Instead she saw the napkin with Bob's poem from their first date. How many times had seeing it produced a smile? If it had not been under a clear desk protector she might have scrambled it up and thrown it out. Confirming there were no messages, she turned to retreat from the memories in this room. Her eyes passed over the bookshelf and locked onto King Rat. Why was she tormenting herself? Enraged, she stepped toward the shelf with every intention of grabbing the book and tossing it into the trash. The phone rang before she could.

Her attention instantly shifted to the phone. She quickly changed her direction and made for the kitchen. This room was too filled with reminders of hope and too restricted in space. She needed to pace while she talked. Stacy's voice greeted her when she picked up the phone.

"What happened?" was the question emanating from the receiver. "I called Dr. Dunn to see how it went and he tells me about some woman who thinks her husband is losing it because of MS. Then he says you only asked like one question and Bob didn't want to hear anything that would give him hope or encouragement."

Kathy could not think of anything to say that would refute that assessment. She had dropped the ball and squandered an opportunity. All she could do now was admit it and try to pick up the pieces.

"I blew it," she confessed, speaking quickly and trying to keep the sense of growing desperation out of her voice. Voicing what happened would pull all the suppressed emotions out. "We ran into a couple in the waiting room and the wife chases the husband away and then begins to tell me how MS has eaten away at his brain and how cognitive problems are the worst and how I should break off my engagement because there is no hope and . . . and . . ." She started to cry, giving up any further attempt at explaining.

"Okay, okay," Stacy consoled. "Look, Ray is going to drop Jack at the Rendezvous to get Gloria's car. I'm going to pick up Chingli and then Gloria. We'll come to you and she can get Jack's car home, so you don't have to worry about that. We can sort through this and come up with a realistic assessment instead of an anxiety laced rant by a crazy woman."

"Thanks, Stace," Kathy whispered.

"Don't do anything rash," Stacy advised. "We'll be there in a little bit."

"Okay," was the muttered response. Then Kathy hung up the phone quietly and walked toward the living room. "Don't do anything rash, I guess I shouldn't throw out King Rat," she thought as she entered the living room. She regretted coming here immediately. He was everywhere. This was where she had committed her heart, where she had conquered his. No matter where she looked, it brought back a memory to slap her. Cursing Bob and his idiotic streak of chivalry, the author collapsed to the floor sobbing.

Stacy walked in with the air of a cool determined player at a poker game. Gloria had arrived with a hug and words of encouragement a few minutes before, but Chingli was not with Stacy. Before Kathy could ask, Stacy told her Chingli was coming in her own car, She arrived before Kathy could offer tea to her friends. She had brewed a pot of *wulong* with Chingli in mind. This was placed on the coffee table with some cups and a few almond cookies on a plate. The three women settled into the couch while Kathy dropped herself to the floor and placed a box of tissues on the coffee table beside the tea cups. Gratitude overwhelmed her along with a touch of guilt when she looked at Chingli. A pregnant woman did not need any additional stress in her life.

"*Miemie*," Chingli began. "Tell us what is happening."

Kathy started to cry as she attempted to explain her day. "I did everything wrong and now I'm bothering everyone. You're expecting. You have better things to do." She was whining, but it was her truth. Verbalizing it to these three friends was a release.

443

"You did so much to help me," Chingli reminded her while she poured four cups of tea. "That's what sisters are for, to be there for each other. Tell us what happened."

She had berated herself so much since leaving the doctor's office that the story tumbled out of her with little effort or thought. When she finished her tale of woe, Stacy tenderly inquired, "What led up to this? How has Bob been?"

How has Bob been? Stacy always asked the pertinent questions. When? Before the hospital, while in the hospital, after the hospital; she had noticed a gradual change over the past weeks. How to describe that in an intelligible manner? "He's been a moving target," Kathy sighed. "It's like he's been wrestling with himself, He appears to be winding himself up, as if he's trying to make a decision, but doesn't have the nerve to do it."

"What decision do you think he's trying to make?" Gloria asked while she reached for tea.

Kathy did not want to vocalize her suspicions. After his act today, it was obvious to everyone in the room what he had been building up to. She drew a deep breath and then blurted out, "Whether or not to break up with me."

It was disheartening that this statement was not followed by protests. Instead all three women shook their heads in agreement.

"What did he say that made you walk away?" Chingli asked.

"That the poet is dead," Kathy told them. "That I should leave him now before his body and mind were eaten up by MS. That he wanted to stop seeing me because he loved me and didn't think I

444

should be subjected to a life with MS, but we could still be friends! He's turned into Mr. Chivalry, trying to protect me. I don't need protection! I need him!" She broke down for a moment, but quickly rallied realizing if she wanted her man she would have to pull herself together and fight for him.

"He said he wanted to break up with you because he loved you?" Stacy asked in disbelief.

"Yes," Kathy began, not trying to keep the bitterness out of her voice. "I've had guys tell me they need more space, that they think we should see other people, that I just wasn't their type. I've never been told, 'I love you, so I think we should break up.'"

"He said you could still be friends?" Gloria asked. Kathy shook her head yes.

"I was supposed to be the Rock of Gibraltar," Kathy pointed out in a voice laced with irony. "Instead I'm Frosty the Snowman. As soon as it gets a little warm, I melt away."

"Frosty," Gloria laughed. "I think he sees you more as a hot temptress."

They all laughed at Gloria's observation. Kathy felt herself blush a little, then she realized where her three friends were sitting. Memories of the first night she had become a temptress flooded back. Did Bob tell his friends about that night? Did Jack tell his wife? She felt her face go from a light blush to crimson. "I didn't mean it that way," she protested. Her life was falling apart and she was blushing like a schoolgirl. The lessons of modesty instilled by her mother just would not go away. She really wanted to change the subject, but Gloria kept pounding away.

"Don't you see," she insisted. "That passion he has for you is your greatest weapon. Use it. Seduce him again. Show him he can't live without you."

That was easy to say, Kathy thought. The last gesture she had made to him was flipping a bird without even looking in his direction. How do you seduce a man after that? "That's the only thing I can do? Seduce him?"

"Not the only thing," Chingli interjected. "But it is the quickest way to remind him there is so much more to your relationship than MS."

"And it is what our relationships with men are all about," Gloria reminded her. "If not for that, then we would all live with women and men would live with men and the world would have far fewer misunderstandings." All of them murmured their agreement.

"You said Bob has been a moving target," Stacy said bringing the conversation back full circle. "Has he been sad, depressed, angry?"

Kathy thought for a moment before giving her opinion. "He's been sad, yes," she answered. "Angry? Definitely. I can't say he's had enough time to become depressed. I've read some of the poems he's been writing. They're really dark. He calls one The Dream Stealer. Another is Should You Stay."

"Let's get back to what he said," Gloria chimed in. "He said you could still be friends. And he still has to prepare for the oral. So why don't you combine the two. You know, go to his place as a friend to help him prepare and then spring the trap. Use his weakness to your advantage."

"You always were the better schemer," Stacy laughed then she turned to Kathy. "If you could somehow get into his place alone with him, I'm sure he'll forget everything that can go wrong and see what he has right there in front of him."

Gloria and Chingli shook their heads in agreement leaving Kathy to ponder how to do what Stacy suggested. She had the keys to Bob's apartment, so getting in was not an issue. What if she showed up and he rejected her? Would she be able to handle that? If he became angry with her, how would she react? From this afternoon's experience the answer would have to be not well. He did need her couching if he wanted to top the test. That would be her ace in the hole. She intended to use every womanly weapon at her disposal to remind him what love was. There would be no settling for friendship alone.

"It's funny," Gloria commented, drawing Kathy back from her thoughts. "Jack told me that Bob was convinced you were eventually going to kick his teeth in and leave him."

"If I kick him, it won't be in the teeth," Kathy snapped back.

"Ouch," Stacy moaned. "Spoken like a true Jersey girl and you're not even from Jersey."

"I'm a quick study," Kathy replied snidely beginning to sense a plan of re-conquest forming in the back of her mind. She reached for a cookie and offered some to her friends.

447

Bob was a jumble of conflicting thoughts and emotions by the time he reached his apartment. Anger, frustration, grief, hope, acceptance, determination, each held his mind's eye for a moment, only to yield to another thought or feeling an instant later. He pulled his car into the back and parked. Frustration filled him once again. Life had been laid out neatly before him. Promotion, a beautiful loving partner, a bright future, all crushed by a short sentence spoken by a stranger in a doctor's office. MS, the big mystery disease for which no one could give a prognosis. Guesses, he had received nothing but guesses.

Who to believe? What did all those statistics mean for him? Was he really a horse's ass or was his effort to shield Kathy the right choice? He remembered his thought of riding it out until she realized it would be too much and broke it off. Was that a viable alternative or just an excuse to assuage his guilt and enjoy her love? The more Bob thought about it, the angrier he became. Stepping out of the car and slamming the door did nothing to release his rage. He marched to the front of the building and stormed up the stairs to his apartment. When he opened the door, Kathy's efforts to straighten up the place and prep it for studying slapped him. She seemed to be omnipresent in his life. The thought only served to stir his confusion and enrage him all the more. Without thinking he found himself grabbing his helmet and walking to the garage he rented down the street where he stored his bike. Jack was right; he should throw his options at Frank to see which stuck.

Frank was sitting at the computer when Bob walked in. He did not seem surprised, so Bob assumed Jack had been in touch.

"I've been expecting you," Frank laughed. "Come on in. Take a load off. Want some tea?"

The Fire Department grapevine was alive and well, Bob thought. He wondered, did Frank also think he was a horse's ass? "No thanks," he replied. "I'm on my bike. If I drink tea, I won't make it more than a block before the vibration shakes my bladder loose."

"Well, sit down anyway," Frank insisted. "I get the feeling you want to talk. What's up?"

Bob dropped himself into a chair and placed his helmet on the floor. He did not want to talk, he had to talk. "You spoke with Jack?" he asked so he would know where to start.

"Briefly," Frank informed him. "He said something about a second opinion from Stacy's professor and a horse's ass. You're going to have to get me up to speed."

Bob smiled. "So you think I'm a horse's ass too."

Frank laughed and shook his head no. "I learned a long time ago not to judge other guys' choices. Would have called Jack a horse's ass countless times. Never knew he'd end up my brother-in-law," Frank said thoughtfully. "But that doesn't matter now. Tell me, why does Jack think you're a horse's ass?"

Bob took a deep breath and tried to clear his mind of any superfluous thoughts. He wanted to get the story out accurately and

449

concisely. No need to take up more of Frank's time than necessary. "We went to Stacy's professor for a second opinion," Bob began. "Not so much a second opinion of the diagnosis, more like a detailed opinion of the prognosis. So, Kathy does what she always does and strikes up a conversation with a woman in the waiting room. To make a long story short, the woman apparently tells Kathy about MS and cognitive problems. The doctor can't give a more definitive prognosis and now I find out this disease could chew up my brain. Bottom line, I told Kathy it would be better if we stopped seeing each other. No need for her to suffer with me."

Frank sat quietly for a moment. Bob was beginning to regret bothering him. His friend had enough on his plate without dumping this on him. "How did Kathy react to that?" Frank asked with a skeptical tone.

"Not very well," Bob sighed. "She exploded, said something in I guess it was Taiwanese because it sure didn't sound like Mandarin. Then she said she knew me and I couldn't bullshit her before she marched off while flipping me a bird."

"What did she say in Taiwanese?" Frank inquired.

"I don't know," Bob said in frustration. "Something like '*gang li* . . . "

"*Gan lin niang jibai*?" Frank guessed.

"Yeah, that sounds right."

"You got Kathy Stanley to say that to you?" Frank laughed. "She must have really been pissed."

"What?" Bob asked. "What's it mean?"

450

"Fuck your mother's cunt," Frank told him with a smile.

He sat for an instant as the meaning sank in then burst out laughing. After this momentary release of tension, Bob came back to his reality and sobered up.

"Spoken like a true Jersey girl," he commented wryly.

It was now lunch time and he was sure Frank would want to eat before his afternoon became too busy. Determined to take up as little of his friend's time as possible, Bob tried to dive into the heart of the problem. "Look, the bottom line is; how can I ask her to commit to a life consumed by MS? I mean, she's got a promising career that will expose her to countless guys with college degrees who make two or three times my salary and are perfectly healthy. It wouldn't be fair to her. I'd be an albatross around her neck. She should cut her losses and move on, don't you think?"

That was the crux of the situation as far as he could see, so he wanted Frank to agree or at least acknowledge the logic of his assessment.

"I'm not in a position to say what challenges she would face, although I may know someone who is," Frank answered. "As for cutting her losses, she says she loves you and is willing to take on MS. I believe her. Maybe in five or ten years she'll change her mind, but right now? You're trying to rip her heart out."

Bob listened intently, having always respected Frank's opinion. He knew from the beginning that it would hurt her, but in his mind that would be temporary. She would move on. Frank's description made it sound like she would be scarred for life. It took him a moment for the first part of Frank's statement to register. He may know someone who is in a position to tell her the challenges she would face. What did he mean by that?

"Wait, wait," Bob interrupted. "You may know someone?"

Frank smiled, appearing pleased that Bob cut through all he had just said and honed in on the most important point. "Do you remember Captain Andrews from One Truck?" he asked.

Bob had to think for a second. Captain Andrews? One Truck? It had been a couple of years since he had seen Captain Andrews. In the back of his mind, Bob remembered something about a stroke and a transfer down to the Academy. "Captain Andrews?" Bob asked. "Didn't he suffer a stroke at a fire down neck? I heard they sent him to the Academy, although I didn't see him when we went down for the intro to four inch hose."

"Well, he's truck man," Frank pointed out. "Why would he give a lecture on hose?" He stopped for a second as what Bob said sunk in. Then the firefighter in him came out. "Did you say four inch hose?"

Bob chuckled, once a fireman, always a fireman. "Yeah, we're getting it to replace the three inch. It was developed in West Germany, supposed to be the best thing since bread; brings water to the front of the fire building with virtually no friction loss, like bringing the hydrant to the fire."

"Oh, I can hear the complaints about the loss of pump time now," Frank moaned.

"Why would anyone complain about pump time?"

"No more need to pump the hydrant. It'll save the city wear and tear on rigs, but pump time is one of the measures in the department annual report to show how much work we've done," Frank reminded him.

"Why do we always have to justify our existence?" Bob muttered.

Frank stood up to get a cup of tea while he answered. "It's the only way the bean counters have of dividing up the scarce resources of the city," Frank stated before getting the conversation back on track. "But getting back to Captain Andrews, at first they thought it was a stroke, but when he got to the ER they found out it wasn't. It took a few days of testing, but they finally diagnosed him. It's a closely held secret or as closely held as it can be on the Fire Department. They diagnosed him with MS."

"MS?" Bob asked mindlessly. Captain Andrews had MS? How could that be? An avalanche of questions rushed through his mind. Did City Hall know of his condition? When did the first signs of the disease show? How could he talk with him? Did Frank know him well? Bob had only worked with Andrews for about a year, but Frank had spent considerably more time working the same fires. Even though Andrews was on a truck and Frank was on an engine, their paths would still have crossed often.

"Yes," Frank answered. "You might want to talk with him. Just so happens he's meeting me for lunch. Hungry?"

"Hungry?" Bob thought, knowing it was a set up. What was it with his friends? Why not ask before arranging something like this?

453

He was beginning to wonder what they thought of him. Was he really that unreasonable? Not having the nerve to ask that question, Bob simply laughed and shook his head yes.

They arrived at the Spain restaurant in Frank's car a little after one. The restaurant was just east of Penn Station in a three story brick building wedged between Raymond Boulevard and Market Street. Captain Andrews was waiting outside under a black canopy with gold gothic lettering identifying the establishment and protecting the entrance. On the drive over, Frank had explained to Bob that he had received a phone call from Pete Andrews at the Rescue Squad on the third tour. Word had circulated around the firehouse about Bob's situation. Pete was aware that Frank and Bob were close, so he suggested they speak with his father. After Jack called, Frank reached out to the Captain who immediately volunteered to help. What bothered Bob the most at the moment was Frank would insist on picking up the tab for all three of them. The Spain had some of the best Portuguese food around. Their prices were not exactly in the Burger King range.

"Frank," Captain Andrews greeted while he grabbed his hand after they crossed the street. "How have you been? I heard business is good and your wife's expecting. Congratulations!"

"Hey, Cap," Frank responded loudly and with enthusiasm. "Pete's keeping you abreast of things?"

"Oh, I don't need him," Andrews laughed. "This is rumor control down here. Every guy on the job comes through here for one program or another. Makes it easy to keep up with what's happening."

Bob had held back, not wanting to dampen the enthusiasm. Frank turned to him and asked, "You remember Bob Brendler, don't you Cap?"

"Yes, I do," the Captain smiled. "My son told me we have something in common."

Bob extended his hand and forced a laugh. "From what Frank just told me, we have a common enemy."

"Common enemy?" the Captain chortled. "I like that. It's appropriate when you think of that saying, 'We have found the enemy and he is us.'" All three laughed as they stepped into the restaurant. There was an instantaneous transition from bright sunlight and warmth to subdued lighting and air conditioning. This was Bob's first visit to the Spain, but Frank appeared to be right at home. A bar on their left with the usual assortment of glasses hanging above the bartender's head and bottles of liquor lining the rear wall ran the length of a narrow room. The host greeted Frank at the doorway to the restaurant and led them to a table along the Raymond Boulevard side of the building. Frank waved hello to a waiter who came over quickly and took an order for a shrimp and garlic appetizer. After scanning the menu, lunch was ordered and Frank started the conversation.

"Cap, we were looking to tap into your experiences so Bob could better weigh his options," he began.

"How did they diagnose you?" the Captain asked.

"I had an NMR," Bob informed him.

"My doctor didn't go for that," Andrews chuckled. "Don't know if it was because they didn't have it or he just didn't trust it, but I had to do the whole spinal tab routine and past history. Then he gave me a clinical diagnosis, not that you could argue with the results."

Bob was not sure what the whole spinal tab routine was, but it did not matter. Captain Andrews had been dealing with MS for at least a couple of years. He must have had symptoms before he collapsed at that fire. How many years had he dealt with MS in the firehouse without knowing it?

"Cap could I ask you, when did your first symptoms show?" Bob asked, hoping the Captain would remember something before he collapsed.

The older man chuckled. "My guess would be when I was about your age," he answered with a grin as the appetizer arrived at their table.

This brought Frank into the conversation. "How many years did you walk around without knowing you had MS?" he asked incredulously.

"Frank, I'm a fireman," the Captain laughed. "There was always a reason that I didn't feel right. I figured I pulled a muscle at a fire or took in a little too much smoke. You're familiar with the excuses guys make to avoid admitting there's something wrong."

All three chuckled at his comments. Bob was beginning to hope that he would finally be able to get a realistic picture of what he faced instead of some pie in the sky scientific, cover my ass excuse for an explanation. Here was a brother firefighter who knew what the firehouse was like and what it took to fight a fire.

"I've used a lot of them myself," Frank agreed. "So how long did it take you to admit there was something wrong?"

"Oh, about twenty years," Andrews laughed.

"Twenty years!" Bob groaned. How could anyone deny they had MS for twenty years? He had to hear this story. "How did you get away with that?"

"Well," Andrews sighed. "The symptoms would come and go. Since I also made captain twenty years ago, I could get away with a little more. Didn't climb ladders as much. No opening the roof. Even with that, at those hot jobs in the dog days of summer I'd end up limping around. Always thought I had strained a muscle. It would go away on its own and I'd forget about it. That worked until we had a two bagger on Niagara and Rome. My left leg collapsed when I came out of the building."

Frank and Bob listened intently. When the Captain finished, Bob jumped right in. "What would you do in my position, Cap? So far I've only had sensory problems, but I don't want to be a liability on the fire ground."

The smile dropped form Andrews' face. He turned to look directly in Bob's eyes and said, "Stay in the firehouse as long as you can. You haven't had any motor problems. There's no need to give up. If you ever develop problems moving, then you'd have to reconsider your options. Are you studying?"

Bob nodded his head, fixated on the Captain and what he was saying.

"Good, get promoted," Andrews advised. "That way if things get bad, you'll have proven that you have the brains to do other duties. They have a hell of a time getting anyone out of the firehouse to do staff work. I guarantee you, you do well on the test the Director will offer you a deal to get you into headquarters or Special Service or the Academy. You'd just have to work straight days and you won't get overtime, but you'll still be on the job."

Their meals came as the Captain finished. His words reverberated through Bob's mind as he ate quietly, listening to Frank and the Captain catch up and reminisce about the fires they fought together. Bob was enjoying the stories and the banter, but he was also formulating a few more questions to ask over dessert. As the waiter cleared the table, Bob asked, "Cap, how do I know when to leave the firehouse?"

Andrews sat silently for a few seconds before venturing an answer. Bob and Frank both moaned when he started. "You go to the projects a lot," he began, becoming reassuring when the moaning greeted his first sentence. "No, no I'm not saying that to bust chops. When you respond to the projects you climb all those stairs in full turnout gear with a tank on your back and a roll of hose under your arm, right? Do you realize how much weight you're carrying? Think how hot it gets in the summer. When you can't handle the projects anymore, it's time to go."

Bob considered the Captain's analysis. It made sense in an odd sort of way. Jack always said the projects were the perfect proving ground for the Fire Department. There were no worries about building collapses or holes in the floor to fall through, no fire in the walls eating away at the structure or sudden flashovers from hidden fire. Fighting a fire in them was like fighting one in an oven. It got hot as hell, but no real damage was done to the structure. Obviously, if he could walk up twelve flights of stairs with seventy or eighty pounds of equipment, he could handle most fires. Dessert, coffee, and his tea were placed on the table while he was considering this.

"What did you tell headquarters?" was the next question.

"As little as possible," Andrews replied. "The city doesn't have the right to ask specific health questions. They just want to know if you can do fire duty. The Director won't push you on it, even though he probably already knows your condition. He'll leave you alone if you show you can do it."

Bob picked at his chocolate mousse cake as he mulled this over in his head. "So, I'm left to self-regulate."

The Captain shook his head yes as he finished a bite of his chocolate cake. "As long as you don't put yourself or others at risk," he told him after swallowing. "I mean at more than usual risk." Andrews added with a chuckle.

"And you agree that I can extend my life in the firehouse if I get promoted?" was Bob's next question.

The Captain took a second to ponder this while he sipped his coffee. "If you're not one of those captains who tries to be a fireman," he warned. "I don't know how you'd approach the job. If you do it properly and watch out for your guys first and then do the other work, yes getting promoted can extend your time in the firehouse. You just have to make the switch from aggressive firefighter to thoughtful, safety conscious captain."

Frank and Bob both laughed. They had each seen men who struggled to make the transition. It was one of Bob's biggest worries. The irony of the situation was MS might make him a better captain. Bob had one last question that had nothing to do with the job. He was reluctant to ask it, but felt there was no better man to put it to. "Cap, can I ask you a personal question?" Andrews raised his hand in assent. "If you knew you had MS before you got married would you have married your wife?" Frank tried to suppress his reaction, but Bob knew him too well for it to work. It was a hard question, he knew, possibly an unfair one, but Captain Andrews was the only one he knew who could possibly answer it.

"That's a difficult question," Andrews sighed. "If I knew my life would turn out like this, of course I would have, but no one can tell you where you're going with this disease. There's no guarantee you won't just fall off a cliff, just wake up one morning and find you can't move your leg."

"That's my problem," Bob confessed. "How can I ask someone to commit themselves to me when there's a possibility that could happen?"

"Bob," Frank interjected. "That's a possibility for all of us. Life doesn't come with guarantees. So, you've got to have the nerve to take some risks. As long as Kathy is aware of the risk, isn't it her decision?"

"As long as it was an informed decision," Bob conceded halfheartedly, still not entirely convinced.

"My personal philosophy is to get up each day and live life without thinking about my disease at all," Captain Andrews told him. "If I have to make a concession to it at some point in my day, I do it and then go back to ignoring it. Bob, you can't let it control your life because then you stop living. If a woman knows you have MS and still is willing to marry you, do it. Squeeze as much out of life as you can. You know, since I've been diagnosed I've thought about my life. All those years I had this disease and didn't know it. I explained away my symptoms by saying it was just getting older. That's how I look at it. MS is just like premature aging. Push through the symptoms until you find you can't ignore them anymore. Then you adjust, you accept that you're getting older. We all have to do it. You may just have to do it sooner than you anticipated."

Bob pulled his bike into the garage still thinking about what had been discussed at lunch. It was three o'clock and he had to study. How to get his head back on straight after a day like today and focus on studying? Getting promoted was the only constant throughout the emotional rollercoaster ride he had been through. It was only three o'clock. There was still plenty of time to get six or seven hours of quality studying in. He took off his helmet, locked the bike and the garage, and walked up the shallow hill to his apartment. The sun was shining and there was a slight breeze to move the humid air around. It would be a perfect day to ride out to west Jersey again with Kathy holding onto his waist; maybe in his next life, but not today. She was not talking to him. He was not sure it would be good to get that intimate until he had sorted through his issues; and he had to study no matter what. It was a thought, now to work.

As he climbed the stairs to his place, Bob realized that his ace in the hole for the oral was supposed to be Kathy. She was livid which meant he was on his own. Could he live with himself if he used her for promotion and then cut her loose? Did he even have the strength to cut her loose? Knowing he could spend a lifetime debating these questions in his head, Bob pushed them aside. Concentrate on prepping for the test. Even as he did this the last words she said to him came back.

"I know you. You can't bullshit me. Call me when this stranger leaves and Bob comes back."

"She knows me? Who did she know, me or who I was before I was diagnosed?" he thought as he unlocked his door. Who was he now? A thought hovered on the edge of his mind while he put his helmet away. How could she know him when he did not think he really knew himself? This question inspired him to write. Other words she threw at him earlier came back to bite as he wrote.

"The poet is dead!"

"You don't mean that, if it was that easy I wouldn't love you."

Shaking off the memory, he wrote a haiku. He had never written one before. The conversation at the diner on their first date haunted him while he composed his questioning verse.

The Illusive Self

Searching, finding, but
What is found, not what I seek
Moving on, searching

It was obvious to him that Kathy had not given up. Deep down he knew he did not want her to, which left him with the same conundrum of the morning. Should he drag her down with him or inflict the inevitable pain she would suffer now? Today was his second attempt at having the nerve to face reality and move their relationship to the calmer plain of the platonic. Was a simple friendship between them even possible considering what they had shared? Did he love her enough to put both of them through hell's fire? Was it even necessary? Maybe he should just let her enjoy their love until MS became too much then she could bow out gracefully and he would at least have those memories. Was he being melodramatic? Captain Andrews seemed to have weathered the storm well. Bob's head was spinning with contradictory emotions and unanswerable questions. It was a struggle to do so, but he pulled himself back to his one constant, get promoted. He dragged himself to the kitchen, opened the windows for some air, and dropped down in front of his books. In his heart he knew if she walked through the door he was chopped meat.

Chapter Thirty-seven

Kathy parked across the street from Bob's. After stepping out of the car, she put the car keys into her purse and retrieved Bob's apartment keys. A car of teenage boys slowed down to eye her before she crossed the street. The reaction of the boys gave her a boost of confidence. Skin tight designer blue jeans and Bob's favorite tight silk blouse clung to her body. This was all out war and she was holding nothing back. She had the figure to make full use of the tight jean fad and felt it necessary to use all her weapons of attraction to their fullest tonight. There was no easier way to manipulate a man. Add a touch of perfume and she hoped he would turn to putty in her hands. A smile crossed her face when she thought of Nini Anna. What would she think of the temptress her granddaughter had become? She knew the answer to that question if it were referring to A-ma. Hers was an arranged marriage. Romance began after the wedding in the Taiwan of A-ma's youth. Kathy was not so sure of the answer when it came it her mother, after all she did capture her dad and it was not through quiet literary discussions.

The writer steeled herself for what might happen. Bob had told her it was over between them because he loved her. The absurdity of that statement still rankled. It was an attack on her womanhood. Was she so lame she could not hold onto the man who loved her? What kind of woman was she? Bob did not know what he was saying and she was not giving up that easily. He was going to have to tell her to her face that it had nothing to do with MS. This could get ugly, but not if she played her cards right. The day would end in total disaster or she would have complete victory. There was no middle ground. Confident she knew her man well enough; Kathy opened the building door and began her ascent.

Not wanting his first realization that she had arrived to be the unlocking of his door, Kathy tried to make as much noise as politely possible while she ambled up the stairs. She came unannounced because that would make the feminine ambush she was about to spring more likely to succeed. Taking a deep breath like a platform diver about to jump, she pushed open the door and stepped into the kitchen. Bob was sitting at the kitchen table. Books were stacked on the table along with note pads and his tape machine. Was he trying to lose himself in studying or had he hopped behind the books when he heard the sound of someone coming up the stairs? Maybe he was trying to build a scholarly wall to hide behind. She would soon find out.

"You look like a preoccupied graduate student doing research in the library," she said with a smile as she closed the door.

"Got to make up for time," he said avoiding her eyes, but not the rest of her.

Kathy could see he was drinking in her outfit and inhaling her perfume. Now to persuade him that she was here to help with his studies and should sit next to him instead of across from him. She casually walked behind him. If he asked why she would just tell him she wanted to see which book he had chosen to concentrate on today.

"Management?" she said quietly. "Why management? I thought they wanted you to counsel a troubled firefighter."

She leaned over him to flip through the chapter he was reviewing. If her breasts pushed against his shoulder, well it could not be helped. The effect of this intimacy could be seen instantly. This was going much easier than she had expected. No protests about having to study or that she should keep a distance. Was he simply surrendering?

How to start a conversation about the day's events without putting him off? After all the advice and the preparation, Kathy found herself at a loss for words. She began to massage his shoulders, but quickly realized that put her at a disadvantage. She had to be the one in control. Getting that intimate too soon would not allow for time to talk through his misguided desire to protect her. "Can I assume you weren't happy with how things went today?" she asked coyly.

Bob chuckled. "That would be an understatement. There are so many unanswered questions."

"Life is made up of unanswerable questions, don't you think?" she countered. He did not appear to be angry. Frustration seemed to be his paramount emotion. But then she had been the one who had walked away furious, not him. Her hands were still resting on his shoulders, but there was no warmth to the touch. How to guide the conversation to their future and how his misguided chivalry made no sense? She remembered her father's advice whenever she got into a cultural war with her mother. An apology is always a good start. "I'm sorry for flipping out after speaking with that woman," she began. "I guess I had a small panic attack. What was her husband like?"

Bob continued to sit stiffly, as if he were struggling to resist her. Considering that a sign of weakness, she slowly circled for the kill, waiting patiently for her prey to impale himself.

"Tony?" Bob muttered as if he were taken off guard by the question. "He struck me as a regular kind of guy. Actually apologized for what his wife was telling you."

His last sentence shocked her. Tony apologized for what his wife was saying? How could she not have asked Bob this question while they were waiting to see the doctor? She had fallen for the ranting of a drama queen. "Tony apologized for his wife?" she muttered.

"Yeah, he said she wasn't doing me any favors," Bob chuckled dryly. "But I can't really say how he was mentally. I mean I just met the guy. He seemed normal to me, but you have to live with someone to realize they've changed. I don't have a baseline to compare with."

When Kathy heard this she slipped into sarcasm for a moment. "And you think he was a nuclear physicist on the faculty at Princeton before MS?" she laughed then regretted it immediately. Bob appeared to be on the verge of becoming defensive. It was not a good way to pose the question. She berated herself silently and hoped he would accept the question as a joke.

"No," he sighed. "I think he's just a regular guy with wife problems. What was she like?

Kathy breathed a sigh of relief and then forged ahead. The skeleton of a campaign was beginning to take shape in her mind. Steer the conversation away from Tony's condition and toward Janet's. All she had to do was give an honest assessment and use Dr. Dunn's words to back her up. She was confident this would persuade her beau that he too had overreacted. Then they could put the whole cognitive dysfunction topic to bed and move back to building a life together. "Janet?" Kathy replied. "She seemed to be a bit off. Very anxious, she spent most of the time complaining that no one else saw Tony's deterioration. She talked about how insidious MS was and how cognitive problems were the worst. Thinking about it now, she strikes me as a defeated woman. She has been so consumed by anxiety that there is nothing left for her."

Bob listened quietly. When she finished her description, he did not react immediately, but let the silence allow her words to percolate through his consciousness. She noticed the sound of children playing and the smell of a neighbor's barbeque as a light breeze came through the open window. "I owe you an apology also," he finally admitted. "I overreacted, but there is a reality to be faced."

Kathy could sense his resolve beginning to crumble. She had to play it right to push him over the edge. "Are you referring to the 'what if' game?" she teased.

"The 'what if game?'" was his puzzled response.

"Yes," she chuckled, instinctively knowing to keep him off balance and guessing. "You know. What if this disease gets dramatically worse? What if I can't walk? What if I can't talk? What if my brain is consumed and I become a blithering idiot? What if whatever?"

This seemed to hit him a little harder than she intended, but the idea was to wake him up from his self-induced nightmare.

"Kathy," he began slowly. "I think you're in denial. Things can go wrong quickly and the damage will be permanent."

He was repeating himself, a sure sign that his conviction was weakening. "Who is in denial?" she asked in a calm confident voice. "You just had a renowned doctor who is conducting scientific research on MS tell you that you should just live your life and you're resisting it." She took her hands off his shoulders and ran a finger along his right ear. Then she bent over and kissed his neck. "You just ignored anything he said that implied there was hope," she whispered in his ear.

Bob suddenly stood up, not noticing that his chair pushed Kathy back. "You're denying the reality of my situation," he snapped.

Suddenly his height was annoying. He stood six inches above her and was refusing to turn around to face her, to look down at her eyes. Instead he looked at the opposite wall. She smiled to herself, reading this as the last act of a desperate defense, noting his breathing was a little heavier. Her confidence reinforced, she swooped in for the victory. "I am well aware of our situation," she countered softly. "The only reality is now, and now is love." He was on the verge of capitulation, but had not thrown in the towel quite yet.

"Love is not going to be enough," he insisted.

"No, it won't be," she agreed. "I'm depending on your stubborn streak. You won't back down from fires, why should you back down from MS?" With that she slipped her hand under his shirt and caressed his back.

He took a step back, turned around, and exclaimed, "No! Don't you see? It would be so unfair. You have such a life ahead of you. I'd drag you down."

After all that hard work, he sounded like he was back to square one. She felt a moment of panic then calmed down convincing herself it was just the death rattle of his chivalry. "Drag me down?" she asked. "I need you. Just being with you lifts me up."

The look on his face revealed the pain of a battle being fought inside him. He made a few attempts to speak, but stopped short each time. Finally, he turned away from her and muttered, "You're making this so difficult."

"You're being obstinate," she snapped back

"You'll hate me when my body quits," he assured her.

"Let me decide that if the time ever comes," she retorted. "Right now I love you, just accept that. Didn't you tell me once that acceptance is the beginning of wisdom?"

"So, who should accept, me or you?" he shot back. "You won't accept my new reality."

She saw that this tract was not going anywhere. How could she turn this around to her advantage? "Your little saying is too simplistic. It implies one shouldn't fight. You should change it. Make it more like the serenity prayer. Acceptance of what you cannot change is the beginning of wisdom. So, why don't you just accept that I cannot change my love for you and we're ready to face this together?"

He stood quietly thinking. Kathy could not tell if he was trying to continue the debate or was getting ready to relent. Contradictory thoughts were contending inside him. How to tilt the table her way? She decided to challenge him, confident she knew how he would respond she threw down the gauntlet. Reaching over to him, Kathy gently pulled her beau in and reached up to touch his face. "You want me to surrender? Then tell me to my face, truthfully, that you don't want me in your life anymore."

Bob made a feeble attempt to speak but could only generate a small smile. "Careful, I can see right through you and you know it," she warned.

"You sound like my mother," he chided.

"Women are like that," she informed him. "Guys are too dumb to pick it up."

"You shouldn't have to suffer with me," he insisted.

"My eyes are wide open and see clearer than yours," she told him. She reached up again and ran her fingers through his hair.

"You're trying to distract me," he complained.

"No, I'm trying to help you see more clearly," was her counter, sensing that his last bastion of stubborn male pride was caving in.

"By seducing me?" he accused.

"If it were not for sexuality, women would live with women and men would live with men and the world would be a more peaceful place," she pronounced. Technically it was plagiarism, but Gloria would not mind.

"That sounds rather hard boiled," he observed.

"It's reality," she pointed out. "Weren't you just pushing for me to accept that?" She stood on her toes and kissed him.

"I have to study," he whispered, closing his eyes.

"We're going to put out a fire, then hit the books harder than ever. Just have to remove the distractions."

"Kathy, you're not fighting fairly."

"How does that expression about love and war go?"

"Are we in love or at war?"

"That's always hard to tell when you're referring to men and women."

Bob leaned over and returned her kiss. "Do you realize the pain you're opening yourself up to?" he asked earnestly.

"Do you realize it's already too late?" she said with tears in her eyes. "Love me Bob. I don't intend to give up without a fight and I'm not a good loser."

He picked her up and carried her to the bedroom. She leaned her head on his shoulder and cried in relief, knowing she had won.

Chapter Thirty-eight

Bob sat on a bench at the kitchen table of Six Engine with his back to the wall. He had not felt this good in a long time. The doctor had taken him off prednisone a month before and pronounced him neurologically stable. The weather had cooled considerably as summer eased into autumn and his symptoms had subsided. There was a residual loss of sensation in his hands and feet, but Dr. Bradinsky doubted that would ever go way. Accept it and move on was his mantra. Playing it conservatively, Bob had been driving steadily since returning to duty two months before. Today would be the first time he would pronounce himself strong enough to hang on the side of the rig. Fair warning had been given and everyone was expecting it, but Hector was not happy. If Bob did not drive, it was Hector's turn in the rotation.

"How are you feeling?" Hector asked. It was a moot question. Bob had hung his turnout gear on the side of the rig.

"My boy, I feel great," he gushed, trying not to sound overly enthusiastic.

Hector curse under his breath and went to put his gear in the side compartment and check the rig. The Captain walked in from the watch room after writing up the time blow. "If Hector is going over the rig, I guess you've decided you can handle hanging?" the skipper supposed.

"Yeah, Cap," Bob laughed. "I'm back."

"Well, he would have been driving part of the day anyway," the Captain pointed out.

"Why's that?" Bob asked puzzled.

"The Director wants to see you," was the reply.

Bob suddenly felt nervous. Had the Director heard about his MS and wanted him the transfer out of Six? Would the city force him out on a forty percent disability pension? Everyone assured him it had never happened before. They all said if he was willing to work with the needs of the department, the city would not put him out on disability. That sounded good coming from his friends, but they were not the ones at risk. It is always easier to reassure someone else than it is to reassure yourself. Captain Andrews had over twenty years on the job before he was diagnosed and was already a captain. It would be easy for the department to carry him for a couple of years, especially with all of his experience. Bob only had four years on. Would they force him out on forty percent before he even made captain?

"Why would the Director want to see me?" he queried anxiously. Was headquarters aware of the effort they were all putting in to accommodate him?

"Probably has something to do with acing the captain's test," Jack said as he stepped into the kitchen. Ray came in right behind Jack, tucking his shirt in.

"The Chief's right behind me," Ray informed him. "You could ask him."

Bob looked at the Captain, who simply shrugged his shoulders. He had conveyed the order, but had obviously not been told a reason.

"Don't worry," he advised. "He's probably going to tell you you're getting promoted and ask where you want to go." The Chief walked in on this.

"That might be part of it," he told Bob. "But he has more to talk about. I was told to tell you not to worry. The Director just wants to discuss your future. I'll take you up in the gig. He's at a budget meeting in City Hall until after lunch, so figure about two."

"Okay Chief," Bob agreed, not sure how to take the prospect of discussing his future with the Fire Director. He remembered Captain Andrews' comment about being offered some sort of deal to work straight days. That might be necessary in the future, but not right now. Right now he just wanted to get back to fighting fires. He stood up and slid out from behind the table. Whatever was going to happen that afternoon, this morning he had to help with the house work.

He pulled the first floor with Ray. They gathered the brooms, mops, and bucket from the top of the basement stairs. Bob began sweeping out the kitchen while Ray went to the apparatus floor to fill the bucket with hot water and detergent. By the time Bob had completed sweeping, Ray was rolling the bucket in with his hands grasping two mop handles, the mop heads submerged in sudsy water.

"So, tell me about the ring," Ray said as he dropped a mop head in the bucket wringer.

"The ring?" Bob chuckled. He had sworn Jack to secrecy. Apparently that did not include the firehouse in Jack's mind. "Do me a favor and don't tell Stacey. It's supposed to be a surprise."

Ray laughed. "Jack made me take an oath of silence, although I don't know why. You've been planning your wedding for a couple of months. You went shopping with Kathy for an engagement ring even though she already said yes. The two of you seem to be doing everything ass backwards."

Bob chuckled at his friend's observation. You really could not argue the point, but he felt a need to explain. "I, ah, I never really asked her to marry me," he confessed. "Just told a nurse in the ER that she was my fiancé. I think she would want something a little more romantic than that, don't you?"

"I don't know," Ray said as he lifted the mop head out of the wringer and began dragging it around the floor. "Stacey just pointed at her ring finger and told me to put a ring on it. That seemed to work fine."

Bob dropped the mop into the wringer shaking his head. "You're such a romantic, Ray."

"I leave romance to Jack," was the response. "He was the one schmoozing the ladies until he met his match."

"And he's my advisor," Bob reminded. "So, I'm going to give her a little surprise. She had me swear I wouldn't go out and just buy a ring. We picked this one out together. Then I gave a bogus excuse as to why we couldn't buy it right there. Now it's in Jack's safe deposit box. We'll go pick it up tomorrow and I'll bend a knee and ask."

"It is important that you bend a knee," Ray told him. "Stacey wanted that even after her little ultimatum."

The two of them made quick work of their cleaning duties. As Bob poured the dirty water down the floor drain next to the rig, Jack and Hector came down the stairs. All retreated to the kitchen as soon as the floor was dry.

"What do you want to do for lunch?" Jack asked. "The Captain's doing some paper work. Said he'd be done in fifteen minutes. I figure he'll want to look at some buildings and then we'll pick something up."

"Want to do Italian hotdogs?" Hector suggested. "Been a while since we had an oil change."

"As long as the skipper's up for it," Ray agreed.

With lunch settled, Bob felt compelled to ask the guys their opinions on the Director's summons. "So, why does the Director want to talk to me?" he tossed out to them.

"Maybe he heard you're marrying Kathy Stanley and wants to warn you," Ray laughed. Bob was unsure why the Director would be interested in Kathy. Did he even know her? The puzzled look on his face brought Jack into the conversation.

"There was a press conference after Frank did his hero routine with that stalker thing," he told Bob. "Kathy was at it and asked some hard questions. The Director probably remembers that."

Great, one more thing to worry about, Bob thought. The Director did not like Kathy. His dad and the Director went back a long way, but he did not remember them having anything more than a professional relationship. The entire crew started laughing when they saw Bob's worried look.

477

"Don't worry about it," Ray reassured him. "He just wants to discuss your future remember? I don't know how many times I've heard the old timers say the Director never hurt a fireman."

"He never has," the Captain said as he stepped into the kitchen. "And I've seen so real screw ups on this job." He shook his head and chuckled. Changing subjects, he laid out the battle plan for the morning. "I want to go look at a couple of buildings on Seventeenth Street. The second tour had a job in them the other night."

With that they all began making their way to the rig. Hector hit the button for the overhead door before climbing into the cab. The door was still climbing when the joker circuit on the alarm panel clicked. "That doesn't sound good," the Captain commented as everyone stopped to listen. A round of ten bells came over the circuit, telling them a full assignment was being dispatched. This was quickly followed by groups of one bell, four bells, four bells, and nine bells. Station one-four-four-nine, Bob knew Eleven Engine was first due. Six was next. A full assignment at this time of day usually meant a fire. Hector started the rig while the rest of the crew climbed aboard. Bob noticed Hank and the Chief coming down the stairs as the rig rolled out.

Eleven called in a working fire as Hector swung the rig onto South Orange Avenue. Bob could see the smoke off to the right. The familiar rush of adrenalin pulsed through his system as he pulled his boots up and reached for his mask. More than at any other time in his career, he wanted the tip today. This would be the litmus test. The timing was perfect. Test his strength this morning; see the Director

478

this afternoon knowing if his limits have changed. The past couple of months had been played cautiously. It was time to push and see if he could still do the job as well as he felt he could.

Hector parked the rig in front of a three story frame that was the south exposure. Eleven Engine had a line running into the fire building. Eleven Truck was raising their aerial to the roof. The sounds of Eighteen Engine, Nine Truck, and Seven Engine could be heard in the distance. The front windows of the second and third floor of the fire building had flames blowing out of them. Ray had stayed at the hydrant on the corner. It would take Eighteen a couple more minutes to make their way from Avon Avenue. Captain Pete wanted water quickly. Yellow four inch hose snaked down the street to the back of the rig. Bob jumped down from the bucket seat and reached up for the four lengths. Grabbing the first few lops of hose he pulled it down, turning the load so the top landed on his shoulder. Jack slid in behind him and pulled the rest of the line out while Bob began walking toward the fire building. Before he reached the sidewalk, the Captain shouted, "Bob, go to the exposure."

He stopped to get his bearings and saw heavy smoke had begun to pour out of the exposure's third floor. He made a quick adjustment and headed for the front door of that building. Jack followed, flaking out hose so the folds on Bob's shoulder stayed there. One of the guys from Eleven Truck forced the door open before he reached it, so he continued in without missing a beat. He now regretted stretching the four lengths. The choice had been made with the assumption that he was stretching into the main fire building. Now that he was going into the exposure, he had too much hose. This was the type of mistake he had to avoid as a captain. It would have taken him a few seconds to stop and look at the situation one more time before choosing a line. By grabbing the four lengths, he had complicated Jack's job.

Bob berated himself as he climbed the stairs. He was so desperate to get a piece of the fire that he had not done a proper size up. The adjustment to captain was rarely seamless, but stupid mistakes like this were unforgivable. The sound of Eighteen and Nine arriving came in through the door. The second floor seemed clear, so he was not going to stop to check it. It had been months since he had the tip. The opportunity would not be wasted covering the floor below the fire. Eighteen could cover that. If he ended up above fire, it would not be a sizable volume. The satisfaction of hitting the main fire was well worth the minor risk of passing the second floor. He began to let the line flake off his shoulder as he climbed the stairs. The sounds of the guys from Eighteen and Nine coming in behind reassured him that the third floor was his.

When he reached the bottom of the stairs leading to the third floor, heavy smoke was pouring out of the doorway above. Surveying the situation, Bob knew the apartment door at the top of the stairs had been left open. The advantage to this was he did not have to force the door or wait for the truck to force it. The disadvantage was if he did not move quickly fire would replace the smoke, making it harder to push into the apartment above him. He immediately began flaking out the remaining hose on his shoulder along the hallway. Then he climbed the stairs with the tip in his hand dragging what hose he needed up with him. The smoke was beginning to pulsate onto the landing. As his head came level with the third floor landing heat forced him to crouch. He lied on the stairs, reached back, turned on his air supply, and waited for water. The thought crossed his mind that he could not get hurt. He did not want the Director to think he was no longer capable of fighting fires safely.

The sound of water pushing through the hose came up the stairs along with some truck men. The stairs below him quickly filled with men crouched down holding ceiling hooks in their gloved hands. The room above flashed over as the water reached the tip. Flames were now blowing out of the doorway, the radiant heat forcing Bob to the stair trends. He put his face piece on, confirmed the nozzle was set to straight stream, opened it up, and drove the flames back into the apartment. After cooling the landing down, he tugged at the hose but could not move it.

"Give me more line!" he shouted through his face piece then pulled on the line again. Still nothing. "Lighten up on the line!" he shouted one more time. The truck men must have assumed Bob was shouting past them to Jack who was at the bottom of the stairs. None of the men waiting behind him attempted to push some line up. This was getting very frustrating very quickly. The air below him was still clear, but he could not see Jack because of all the bodies on the stairs. It was too hot for him to stand up and motion to Jack. He shouted for line again, mixing a few expletives into his demand, as he continued to play the stream into the third floor. Captain Pete crawled up past the guys waiting as Bob continued to curse and shout for line.

"Bob!" the Captain shouted clearly from a few steps below, not having bothered to put on his face piece yet. "The Chief wants to know if you can move into the third floor."

With that Bob lost it and began swearing a blue streak. "If you give me some line, I'll put the fire out!" he screamed through his face piece.

The Captain did not respond verbally. Instead he stepped down to the landing. The result was line being pushed up the stairs. Bob crawled unto the landing, playing the line off the ceiling and into the doorway. Along with smoke and heat, the familiar sounds of a working fire filled the air. He crawled into the first room and quickly darkened the flames. This fire was his.

* * * * * * * * * * * * * * * * * * *

"Sorry for yelling at you on the stairs, Cap," Bob apologized as the Captain wrote up the book.

"Don't worry about it Bob," he laughed. "I've been there. That's why the Chief insists on keeping the stairs clear. No need for a bunch of truck men to lie there waiting for you to push in. You did a good job. Feels good to get back into the building doesn't it?"

"Cap, I don't have the words to tell you how good it felt," Bob sighed. "But if you don't do it for a while, you get rusty."

"Oh, how so?" the skipper asked looking up from the journal.

"Made a few stupid mistakes I don't think I would have made six months ago."

The Captain put his pen down and leaned back in the chair. "You did a good job of covering them up," he pointed out. "That's the sign of a professional."

Bob chuckled. Captain Pete was trying to make him feel better. "I'd prefer to avoid the dumb mistakes, Cap," he responded. "I'm going to make enough honest ones without being stupid."

"What are you referring to," the skipper asked.

"Didn't do a proper size-up before I chose the line, so I ended up with enough line for the original fire building, but too much for the exposure,' Bob confessed.

"That's why you're going to make a good captain Bob," was the reply. "Always thinking of how to improve your game, never afraid to criticize yourself. It was a minor mistake and one you recovered from quickly. Now how about you hit the shower, so we can eat lunch. Get yourself squeaky clean. You have to see the Director this afternoon."

After a lunch filled with speculation and banter, Bob found himself in the back seat of the Chevy station wagon that served as the chief's gig.

"I'm going in to speak with the Director ahead of you," the Chief informed him. "I'll try and get him in a good mood. That will be challenging since he dealt with the budget all morning."

This only heightened Bob's anxiety. Budget meetings would highlight the need for efficient use of personnel. Would a fire captain with MS now appear to be too much of a liability? Maybe it was a mistake to have studied for promotion. Right now he was one of five hundred-fifty firefighters. If he were promoted, he would be one of only one hundred thirty captains. His nerves were obvious to the Chief.

"I wouldn't wind myself up too much, Bob," the Chief advised. "Remember, your father and the Director go back a long way. Your dad knows where all the bodies are buried."

Bob laughed at this. He had not considered it. Although he doubted there were any embarrassing secrets between his father and the Director, He was aware they had known and respected each other for decades. Did that give him a cushion? There was no sense in thinking about it now. The job he did this morning should prove he could still fight fires. That was the bottom line. Any questions about his capability could be parried with that.

Hank parked the car in front of fire headquarters. Bob and the Chief stepped out, walked through the front door, and made their way up to the second floor. Bob dropped down in a chair outside the Director's office while the Chief went inside. After a few minutes, the Chief stepped out, gave Bob a reassuring nod, and went to talk with the Director's secretary. Now it was Bob's turn. He inhaled deeply, pushed himself out of the seat, and walked into the office.

He stepped into an elongated space dominated by a conference table in the center and a large desk at the far end. Whether the location of the desk was meant to impress someone walking into the room or not, Bob found it intimidating walking the twenty feet from the door to the chair in front of that desk. Fire Department memorabilia and pictures lined the walls. A large chrome bell from one of the old rigs rested on a shelf behind the Director. John Field sat at his desk with a friendly smile on his face. He rose as Bob approached and extended his hand.

"Hello Bob; how are your parents?" he greeted.

"Hello Director," Bob returned the greeting, a little surprised at the warmth. Even though he had grown up with the Director's son, Bob had not thought he would stand out from any other firefighter. His father had always told him John Fields was an honorable man who did his best for the guys. These thoughts gave him a little reassurance, but they also delayed his reaction. He had been asked a question that required a response.

"My folks?" Bob said. "They're enjoying retirement in Florida. Mom says it too hot in the summer. Dad says he doesn't miss the cold, but overall they sound happy." Talking about his parents calmed him a bit.

"Good, good," Director Fields said as he motioned for Bob to sit in one of the seats facing his desk. "I remember when you father was promoted. You were a little guy at the time and headquarters was in City Hall. You couldn't resist giving a shout under the rotunda to hear the echo. Everyone thought it was cute except your mother."

They both laughed. That was twenty years before, but Bob still remembered his first trip to City Hall. "I wanted to speak with you about your upcoming promotion and your condition," the Director began.

"Yes, sir," was all he could blurt out. The Director picked up on the tension in Bob's voice and shifted the conversation from a personal one to a professional one.

"The Chief told me you did an excellent job at that fire on Eleventh Street this morning," Director Fields informed him. "He also said something about you yelling at your captain." The last sentence was said with a smile.

"I was having difficulty getting the truck guys on the stairs to lighten up the line," Bob explained.

"Communications inside a fire building can be tough," was the response. "Bob, I'm going to ask you a question and I need you to be completely honest with me."

"Yes, sir," Bob promised.

"The Fire Department is like a family," Director Fields began. "Everyone eventually hears of the triumphs and troubles of everyone else. Now I don't need you to tell me exactly what you face, but I do need your word that if and when you can no longer do fire duty you will be upfront with me."

"Yes, sir. You have my word."

"Good, now I'd like you to think about taking classes at the National Fire Academy. You have a good mind and have gained a lot of experience over the past few years. We could use both of them down at our academy. Everyone down there could retire tomorrow if they wanted. I need some young guys down there. Guys who can better relate to the new kids coming on."

Captain Andrews had been right; the Director was offering him a deal. "Director," he replied. "Whatever I can do for the department and the guys; I was honestly afraid you would insist I go out on a forty percent pension."

486

"No, I would never do that," Fields reassured him. "It wouldn't make any sense. It would cost the city a considerable sum to train someone to your level. But before it came to that, there are positions on this job that need to be filled and don't require you to do fire duty on a daily basis. You've earned one of those if you need it."

Bob began to breathe a little easier. His primary concern was partially answered. The Director would not force him off the job. What about the city?

"Director, I appreciate all you're doing for me," he began, but then found he was at a loss for words.

"I'm not giving you a free pass, Bob," the Director informed him. "But I don't get the impression you want one. You still have some concerns?"

Bob was definitely not interested in a free pass. He knew he could do the job and intended to do it for as long as possible. But what if the Law Department heard of his condition and insisted he leave? "I was wondering what would happen if the city became aware of my condition?" he asked.

The Director looked him in the eye and said, "The city knows what I tell them. There are NFPA standards for your condition, but even with those it's my call. If you need a little more assurance, you have the mayor in your corner."

"The mayor?" Bob asked in surprise.

The Director chuckled. "Yes, as I understand it, you and Frank Helms are close. The mayor has never forgotten Frank's help when the city was paralyzed by those shootings. Then, when he left the job,

Frank started a promising business in the city and on top of it all he helped with a trade mission from China. What I say only goes so far. What Frank says? Well the mayor will surely take it into consideration."

Bob was speechless. He was a political in without working for the mayor's campaign or even contributing to it. He did not even live in the city anymore. Before Bob could say anything in response, the Director asked, "I understand you're engaged to Kathy Stanley. Is she the reporter who covered those shootings?"

Just when Bob thought he could relax, the only other concern he had crops up. Was there no relief? Gauging the look on the Director's face, Bob saw no annoyance or anger. In fact, his boss looked a little mischievous. His father had commented once that John Fields had a robust sense of humor. Hoping for the best and knowing that he could not answer otherwise, Bob shook his head yes. "One and the same, Director."

The Director chuckled. "She asked the Police Chief some hard questions about Frank's involvement in bringing Dan O'Brian to the Arson Squad office. But the mayor appreciated the fair coverage she gave throughout the ordeal. Besides, the Police Chief has since retired. Her article on the academy class was great. The mayor and I both welcomed the positive press. She seems like a lovely girl, Bob. Does she know about your health concerns?"

"She's been with me every step of the way," Bob said with relief. "Sometimes relentlessly pushing me to see doctors."

Fields laughed. "That's the way women are. It's good she knows. Always maintain an honest relationship. It's worked for me for forty-two years."

"I intend to Director," Bob assured him. "She's too smart to do otherwise." Both men chuckled.

"I'll call you as soon as the certifications for promotion come back from Trenton," the Director told him as he stood up. Bob interpreted this as a sign their little chat was over and stood up. The Director extended his hand and shook Bob's warmly. "Oh, one other thing. There are a couple of commendations coming out tomorrow. You figure prominently in both. Chief Simmons tells me one was a little unusual. Something about a reluctant citizen and forceful persuasion."

"Oh, God," Bob muttered. "I really didn't want him to write that one up."

Fields laughed. "That's not the first time something like that happened."

Bob walked out of the office feeling confident for the first time since that doctor's visit. The Fire Department takes care of its own whenever possible. He did not intend to disappoint. His life was again his own. It was not going to be easy, but MS would not control his destiny. He thought for a moment that he would control it, but then he remembered Kathy's comment about being part of a team. He would be the center. She would be the point guard call the plays. He would get the glory. Who had it better than him?

Chapter Thirty-nine

Bob followed the instructions of the GPS device given to him by his daughter and eased his Thunderbird off the Garden State Parkway at exit seventy-seven. He had learned the hard way not to second guess his Christmas gift. Even though Millie had inherited Kathy's lack of technical prowess, she was a product of her generation and so very savvy with the latest electronic gadgets. The recently retired Deputy Chief had resisted picking up one, claiming using it was an excuse not to think. His wife called that statement an excuse to get lost. He had to admit there were fewer arguments while driving once he had relented and let the machine direct him. Not that those disagreements occurred in this car. She refused to ride in it, saying it was too cramped. Whenever they traveled as a couple, they drove her Mercedes. The former Commandant of Training turned onto Double Trouble Road, chuckling at the name. He was convinced that the road was given that label because some poor bastard had two girlfriends on either end. The Bayville VFW post was a short distance away. This was the first year he would attend the retired fire picnic as a retiree. The past few years he had come down to see all the old timers with whom he had worked. Now he could officially think of himself as an old timer, although the twenty year olds who passed through the academy must have thought of him as a dinosaur long ago.

Over the past few months, Bob had begun writing about his career and life. At times it was hard putting it down on paper. The frustrations felt from concessions he had to make for MS weighed on him. Even though he was still mobile, waking up each morning feeling the Sword of Damocles was hanging over him took some of the enjoyment out of life. He remembered the woman Kathy had spoken with when they had seen Stacy's professor right after being diagnosed. Now he understood her anxiety. Especially after experiencing his wife's changing personality with the approach of menopause. Their children growing up and leaving the nest did not help matters. Bob, Jr. would be starting Rutgers next month, deciding against his mother's alma mater. It seemed after looking into the engineering colleges at both schools, Rutgers came out on top. Bob was content. It would cost considerably less to attend Rutgers than it would to attend Columbia. An added benefit was the only counter to the females in his life would be a twenty minute drive up Route Eighteen.

He was riding solo today because Kathy had insisted on helping her son begin to organize for the move into the dorms. Hopefully she would not get too teary in front of Bobby. She had done so much better when Millie had gone off to Columbia. He had been the worried one then. Putting it off to each of them knowing what their gender could do to the opposite sex, Bob prayed she would not become overly anxious about their son and college. Anxiety was already eating away at her and their relationship.

Her anxiety had only pushed him away. As it grew over the years, so had the extra time he had spent at work when she was not on assignment in Asia. They each had done their best to be there for the children, but when things got dicey at home Bob preferred the peace of his office after hours. That was where he had begun recording his recollections of life and career. With this review of life he had realized how far they had drifted apart. A question that had crossed his mind had inspired a poem. He reviewed it in his mind as the car slipped past stands of pine trees.

Tell me

Tell me if you dream of me
Tell me what you see
Do I appear as a mature man whose strength is waning?
Or a vibrant youth the way you first saw me?

I can tell you how I dream of you
A vivacious young woman fills my view
She has a heart as large and open as the clear summer sky
Was it not from such a heart that our love grew?

Tell me when I pass through your rest
I need to know if it is filled with suffering and regret
Once we lived for the future and its promise, not in the past with its pain
The sufferance of life has torn at us, robbing you of the man you met

The woman in my dreams is not filled with concerns
She is ready to take on life with all its capricious turns
Able to face fear and push through to find what she seeks
So full of passion and the desire to learn

What became of her?
What became of me?
Did we ever share life and love?
Tell me, was it only a dream?

He intended to give it to her after the picnic. The timing of this presentation was important, dictated by a particularly acrimonious argument during which she accused him of being unable to talk with her. Instead he used poetry as a substitution for verbal communication. Hopefully, after seeing so many of the guys, the magic of poetry would reawaken the woman he had known twenty years before. Maybe that would lead to a discussion about their future.

With retirement, he thought they had a chance to reconnect. Now when her job pulled her away, they could go as a couple. It would depend on the assignment, but on those that did not cover emergent events they could explore the world together after she left work. The kids were grown, so there was an opportunity to re-introduce themselves to each other, to search for common ground beyond child rearing and family obligations. While Kathy worked, he could visit fire departments in whatever country they were in, write stories about similarities and differences, and submit them to fire service magazines back home. He already had friends on the Taipei department after years of visiting her mother's family in Taiwan. With the Mandarin he had picked up working in Frank's office, he could communicate with his buddies on the Taipei Fire Department. How to interview firefighters who did not speak English or Mandarin was a detail that had not been worked out yet. The question of English speakers in foreign countries brought back the memory of that crazy kid on the PATH train. God, that was before he knew of MS. If only the kid had been right and everyone spoke English. Then that little detail would take care of itself. Details, they were for after he persuaded Kathy that his idea was worthy of pursuing. It was only a dream, but it was certainly a viable one.

The pine trees on either side of the road gave way to convenience stores and fishing tackle shops. Traffic was light, but that was to be expected at one o'clock on a summer afternoon. Commuters had made their way to the Parkway hours before and beach goers had long since settled into the sand. He slowed down and eased into the VFW parking lot. It had begun to fill up with cars displaying firefighter union stickers or firefighter license plates. When he was appointed to the job you were lucky to get a decal for your back window. Now there was a choice between decals and different style plates, depending on which state organization your union local belonged to. The Newark firefighters local had gone independent a few years earlier and had their own plates. The officers' union had plates from the state organization to which they were affiliated. Hector knew more about that. He had been on the firefighters' union board of directors before being promoted. Now it appeared he would be president of the officers' union. Bob pulled in next to Ray's truck, stepped out into the sun, and reached for his cane. Thank God there is a breeze and shade in the picnic area, he thought as he walked to the entrance. Otherwise, he would feel miserable in the heat.

Last year he had seen Chief Simmons and Hank. Sadly, Hank had passed away in January. It had been a tough year for the older generation. His dad had passed away from heart failure in February and Kathy's father had succumbed to pancreatic cancer in April. The Fire Department of the World War II generation was leaving. At least Kathy had preserved some of their experiences with her oral history. In the end it had been a labor of love because it certainly was not done for profit. The market for that type of book was limited. After paying for his ticket at the entrance, Bob began looking around the pavilion. Overhead stood a heavy timber gable roof which was supported by metal columns rising from the ground, meeting the roof about twenty feet above. The sides were open, allowing the gentle breeze to cool the area. Even with this breeze, the smell of hamburgers and hot dogs roasting on a grill permeated the air. Groups of men milled about chatting with drinks in their hands. The few wives who made it sat at some of the two dozen tables under the manmade canopy. While only partially through his inspection, Bob spotted a table with Chief Simmons and Captain Pete. Pete must have made a special trip up from North Carolina just for the picnic. If you wanted to see the past legends of the Newark Fire Department, this was the day. He paused at the bar to pick up a soda and strolled over to their table, answering greetings from the guys along the way.

How long was it since he had been in the firehouse? He made battalion chief fifteen years before. When they promoted him, the only opening was in training. Since he had become involved in training at the urging of Director Fields, it was a logical move. Thinking about it now, it was ironic. MS had not removed him from the field. It was a promotion that did it. One of the cardinal rules of the Fire Department was go where the openings are when they promote you. You can fine tune your career later. After that he had spent very little time in the firehouse; keeping his promise to the Director that he would do what was best for the department. When he made deputy, the Director gave him command of training. By that time the daily exhaustion of MS had made the assignment necessary. An advantage to the academy was getting to know all the guys in the field or at least them getting to know you. It was sometimes hard remembering seven hundred names, although he could usually place men by their company. The recognition issue was most prevalent on days like today. But the men at the table ahead of him did not strain his memory. You never forget the guys with whom you shared the firehouse.

"Hey, Pete," Bob shouted. "How's North Carolina?"

"Oh shit, nobody told me the genie was out of the bottle," Captain Pete exclaimed as he shook Bob's hand.

Bob was unsure what his old skipper meant for a second then realized Pete was looking at his cane. "No. no, this isn't from MS," he laughed. "Plantar facititis is what they call it. It's a ligament problem along my arch. Hurts like hell, but they say it will go away with rest and stretching."

"My wife had that a couple of years ago," Pete laughed. "It takes a while and she let me know how much it hurt, believe me. You scared me, for a second I thought the beast had returned. But you asked me about North Carolina, didn't you? Sometimes I feel like I never left Jersey. All the guys who moved down there get together once a month for a beer, so it's not that much different. Only we don't get a lot of snow. Where's your lovely bride? Not in Asia again I hope."

"No, she took some vacation time to help Bobby pack for college," Bob told his old skipper. He had heard quite a few New

Jersey cops and firemen had settled in North Carolina. They were supposed to be content sipping lemonade and playing golf, but Bob doubted it, at least the lemonade part of the tale.

"College? Little Bobby?" Pete moaned. "I am getting old."

"Aren't we all," Bob replied. Noting Pete looked good. A little less hair, a little more grey, a few more wrinkles, but still not bad for someone pushing seventy. "She'll be down later. She wants to see all the guys she interviewed."

"At least the ones who are left," Chief Simmons interjected with a laugh.

"You look great, Chief," Bob said reaching across the table for the Chief's hand. "How do you feel?"

"Oh, the same old aches," the Chief chuckled. "We were just discussing Jack. What can you tell us?"

He had spoken with Jack earlier in the day. The news from that front was not good. Bob had double checked to make sure it could be shared with the old crew. Just because your best friend confided in you did not mean it was public information. Jack had laughed when he heard Bob point that out.

"Secrets? On the Fire Department?" Jack chortled. "Telephone, telegraph, tell a fireman, remember. No need to hide it. Gloria and I are amicably separated. We still have dinner occasionally. Don't worry, just say hello to everyone for me."

"He says hello," Bob began after his mental review. "He and Gloria have been amicably separated for six months. He says they get together for dinner occasionally. But that is an unusual relationship.

497

They've known each other their entire lives, so I guess they're trying to shift from argumentative spouses to close friends. Can you do that?"

"As long as the divorce doesn't get nasty," the Chief supposed. "And they focus on what's best for their kids, I've seen it work."

Ray strolled over as the Chief was commenting. "Sounds like you're discussing Jack and Gloria," he observed. Bob chuckled when he heard this. Jack had called it right. Telephone, telegraph, tell a fireman, although Ray was really part of the inner circle. Stacy would be up on all the latest and the greatest. The ladies used their own network. Their men were not privy to what was said in any of the emails that flew between Kathy, Stacy, Chingli, and Gloria. Bob doubted the exchanges helped Jack's cause.

"What can you tell us about it?" Pete asked.

"You want the he says or the she says?" Ray laughed. There was a collective groan from around the table.

"What does Jack say?" Pete returned.

"Well, basically it boils down to control," Ray informed them. "You can only say 'Yes, dear' so much before you start asking whose life am I living."

The statement resonated with Bob. It did seem that a desire to control their men's lives was common to all women. Since MS was a wild card that Kathy could not really control, she had become obsessed with trying to control every other facet of life that might even remotely affect the disease. Her preoccupation sometimes made him feel she had married MS and he was only along for the ride.

When this was pointed out, she became enraged and called him ungrateful. After twenty-seven years of worrying with no evidence that her suggestions had any impact, he wished she could back off a little and let him live life. The way things were going, that was highly unlikely.

"'Yes, dear' are two of the most important words for any marriage," the Chief advised with a smile. "Of course, the ladies have to give you some room to breathe. It's harder for your generation. Women were raised differently years ago. In our generation a woman was taught to defer to her husband, at least overtly. Of course then she would eventually get what she wanted by covertly manipulating him. That's the way the game was played back then, but it was a different world. There were fewer choices, so they were more dependent and that's what they were raised to expect."

Bob and Ray smiled. It sounded more nostalgic than true to Bob, but there was no doubt his parents' generation played by a different set of rules. Both he and Ray had wives who earned more money and had more formal education than they did. Jack and Gloria were more evenly matched. Then why had their marriage fallen apart while Ray's and Stacy's union was rock solid? No one seemed to have an answer to that question. Could he even compare his relationship with Kathy to that of their friends? His health was too much of a wild card for that. MS permeated every aspect of their relationship, even limiting the number of children they had. The lost dreams added a bitter undercurrent to their daily lives. Was it possible for them to create a dream based on their reality?

The Chief and Pete seemed a little uncomfortable with the drift of their conversation, so Bob tried to guide it in another direction. Turning to Ray, he quizzed jovially, "Has your independent wife adjusted to you not having to go into the firehouse?"

His friend laughed at the question. "The firehouse was more predictable, especially since the fire rate dropped so much," Ray pointed out. "Now it's phone calls throughout the day from angry people who suspect their spouse is having an affair or their business partner is extorting money."

His friend's attempt to trivialize the private investigation business rang hollow to Bob. Ray had done what all the old timers had advised. When he retired, his part time job had morphed into a full time occupation that gave him a reason to get up each morning. He wondered, could writing become a full time gig for him or would he wallow in the past and grow old quickly. The past had haunted him for fifteen years. The yearning to get back to the firehouse and do something that directly affected the lives of others had never left. It was easy to rationalize how teaching others to save lives and fight fires safely was affecting lives, but that was indirect. Nothing replaced the feeling of pulling a child out of a burning building. The immediacy of dealing with emergency situations was gone. There was no rush of adrenaline in training. Then when a firefighter was seriously injured or killed the questions about how they could have been better trained always resurfaced.

Writing might give him a purpose. It would be a way to thank the guys with whom he had shared his career and his life. How often had he tried to convey these thoughts to Kathy? She had once been the biggest supporter of his writing. Now it seemed to only annoy her. At least Ray had found a way to coexist with the woman in his life.

"What are your plans?" Pete asked the preoccupied Bob.

He snapped back from his momentary mental wandering. "I have some thoughts that have to be negotiated with the wife after Bobby settles at Rutgers," Bob began. "Hopefully, write and travel, but we've been too busy dealing with the kids' issues to plan anything in detail."

"You should bring the oral history of the department up to date," the Chief suggested. "It's been a couple of decades since Kathy wrote it. A lot has changed if you believe half of what I've heard. I think you could approach it from a different angle because you've lived the life and not just been part of the family."

"That's a possibility, Chief," Bob replied. "I'd just have to get permission from the original author and she can be hard to pin down."

"It would be good to push for that," Ray said. "The generational changes have been unbelievable. No one keeps track of who is out of service anymore. These kids coming on today just don't seem to have the same feeling for the job. It's just a place to earn a living. They don't seem to care about becoming better firefighters. The firehouse is just a stop between nights out."

The Chief and Pete looked at each other and laughed. "We've heard that before," the Chief said. "When I came on the job it was the old timers saying we thought they owed us a job because we saved the world from Fascism. Don't worry; they'll get into the stride of things."

"I don't know, Chief," Ray sighed. "This is the video game generation."

"When they get married and have kids, they'll change, believe me," Pete said with a chuckle.

"I'd like to cover the changes to the job more than cover any generational divide," Bob said. "I figure people are people, but the situations they face have changed." He had not really given a lot of thought to a project like the Chief suggested although it had crossed his mind over the past decade. It would be interesting. Just the comparison between the present entrance test and the ones Kathy had recorded would be eye opening. Maybe an oral history project could serve as a catalyst for improving his marriage.

In the end, any writing would be his call. There was no need to make money with it, just a need to occupy his mind. If nothing else, he and Kathy had always lived within their means, so they had no pressing debts. Over the years he had paid attention to how guys adjusted to retirement. The one thing those who made a smooth transition had in common was having a purpose in life. Whether it was volunteer work, restoring an old car, or seeing the world, the content retirees kept a busy schedule that stimulated their thoughts. That was his intention. All he needed was his wife's cooperation.

"So how are you feeling?" Pete asked, pushing the banter aside.

Pete may not have realized it, but that was a loaded question with a host of answers. Over time Bob had fallen into the habit of giving the pat answer of "I'm surviving." Now was not the time to use that answer. It was a heartfelt inquiry from an old friend and deserved an appropriate response. "The cardiologist says I have the heart of someone in their thirties. The urologist thinks I live a wretched life, but can do nothing for me. The neurologist is surprised I'm still walking. How do I feel? When I wake up I feel like I just fought a working fire," he sighed. "By the time I go to bed, I feel like I've spent the whole night at a three bagger."

"Kind of like Sixteenth and Littleton?" Pete asked knowingly.

Bob chuckled wryly knowing the reference was to the day his former captain rode the stairs down two stories. The memory of some jobs never seems to fade. "Yeah, Pete, like Sixteenth and Littleton," Bob acknowledged. "That was a hell of a job, wasn't it?"

"Are you taking anything for the MS?" was the next question. "I've heard about these new therapies that are supposed to slow down the progression. Does your doctor have you on any of them?"

Pete seemed a little uncomfortable with the subject, but felt a need to ask and so was blurting out questions as quickly as they came to mind. Even though more than two decades had past, the bond between the two men that had formed at Six Engine had not faded.

"Cap," Bob replied falling into his old habit of addressing Pete. "I just started something called Copaxone. It's supposed to reduce the frequency of flare ups. Been around for a decade, but since I haven't had any trouble in that decade I just didn't bother. Kathy and the kids finally talked me into it. Can't say it does anything except keep them quiet." His cell phone rang as he finished this statement.

Reaching into his pocket, Bob apologized for the interruption. He glanced at the phone to see Kathy was calling. "It's Kathy," he told everyone around the table. "She insisted I get one of these. I call it my leash. Never too far away to be summoned by my bride." With that he answered the phone and told Kathy where on his computer to find the directions to Bayville.

Chapter Forty

Kathy hung up her cell. Why was she pushing to attend a picnic for retired firefighters? One reason was Bob had attended too many fire department wakes over the past year. Another was first his father then her father had passed away during the same time period. The men she had befriended and interviewed were fading. This would be the last opportunity to see some of them. She felt an obligation to say thanks one more time and catch up on how life had treated them in retirement. Maybe they could give her some pointers on how to handle a retired husband.

She walked to Bob's office and stepped into a man cave, but one that did not have quite the testosterone laced ambiance of his bachelor office. Her mind drifted to that first time she had seen his office while picking up things for a hospital stay. There were no guitars or motorcycle helmets here. His hands had gradually lost so much sensation that the pleasure of playing guitar had slipped away. It had taken her quite a bit of persuasion and he nearly dropping his bike for Bob to admit his compromised equilibrium did not allow him on a motorcycle.

It was around the same time he stopped responding to fires from the Training Academy. Up until then, he had driven to daytime fires to look for potential problems in how the guys operated on the fire scene. These would be discussed with the chief running the fire afterwards and safety bulletins or drills would be put together. When he had stopped she asked why. His response was a typical crass firefighter response. He did not want to be on a fire scene because it was like being a priest in a whorehouse. If you cannot partake in the activities, you should not frequent the establishment. She shook her head in exasperation while moving deeper into the room. Firehouse humor no longer amused her.

Books were still the most prominent feature of this office, which was considerably larger than the space he had used twenty-eight years before. Living in a so called McMansion permitted such expansion. How long since she had been in this room? They had somehow formed the habit of her calling his name and he coming to where ever she was. There was no need for her to invade his space.

Bob had told her the directions to Bayville were on his laptop. She really should get a GPS, but doubted she had the time or patience to learn how to use one. In the end it hadn't been necessary since Bob always drove when they went someplace new. Steeping into his room, she spied the laptop sitting on an imposing oak roll top desk in the far corner of the room. She turned the computer on and waited for it to boot up. Her mind wandered as Windows went through its paces. They had let their relationship slip over the past decade. It was now at a crossroads. Either the two of them would find a spark or they would move on to separate lives. Jack and Gloria were attempting to do so in amicable manner. Why not her and Bob? Just thinking that brought an ache up from deep within. When had they stopped appreciating each other? How could they have raised two wonderful children, but lost themselves? Over the past twenty-five years they had evolved from a couple into parents. Was it too late or could they resurrect their passion?

"Mom, I'm heading out," Bobby called from downstairs.

Kathy walked to the door to make sure her son heard her. "Okay, dear," she shouted. "Be safe. I'll see you tonight."

Her mother would have been appalled by what she just did. You never shout goodbye down the stairs. It was not proper. If you want to address someone, have the courtesy to look them in the eye. That adolescent argument had not carried over to the next generation. Only Bob went through the trouble of speaking to his family members face to face. It was not until after this thought that she realized what she had shouted down the stairs. "Be safe." It was a habit she was trying to leave behind. Although there would never be an admission from her, she knew Bob was right. She worried too much. How had she covered the events in Tian An Men square? Age had brought sense and so caution. It used to be "that will never happen." Now it was "it might." That change drove Bob crazy.

The computer completed its boot up and a picture of Bob's old crew at Six Engine appeared as his desktop background. Four young firefighters and a middle aged captain stood in front of the rig outside quarters. All were wearing their blackened turnout coats with orange plastic Fireball gloves. Their helmets were on and their boots were rolled down. Broad smiles creased their faces while a hand painted sign above the overhead door proclaimed to the world that the busiest engine company in the state rolled out of this building. Seeing this picture as the background of her husband's computer bothered her a little. He had always been so romantic. If she had thought about it, her guess of the type of picture he might put on his desktop would have been a picture of the two of them or at least a family picture. Apparently, romance had been trumped by nostalgia. A part of him still clung to those early days before MS. Pushing these thoughts aside, she focused on the computer. Bob had posted the directions on his desktop. One folder caught her eye as she scanned the screen, "Poems." It had been ages since he had read a poem to her. Not since they had a major blowout and she had accused him of being incapable of communicating with her through anything but poetry. Next to the folder was the shortcut to the directions she was looking for. She clicked on it and turned on his printer. After printing them out, curiosity got the better of her and she opened the poetry folder.

She looked over the titles, picking out so many that were warmly familiar. The focus of his poetry had gradually shifted from her and their love to the children. There was a sub-folder entitled "For Submission." These must be the collection he had published when the kids were young. One of the titles she glanced at caught her eye. "Is It Time?" It sounded like a question he would have asked before retiring. He had spent so much time wrestling with the pros and cons before submitting his retirement papers. In the end, the deciding factor had been MS. A casual comment Dr. Bradinsky had made during what had become an annual visit had pushed Bob over the edge. "If I didn't know you," the doctor had commented after looking at his most recent MRI study. "I would think you were in a wheelchair. Your spine is a mess." After that it was, "Do things while you can before you are no longer able to do them." She clicked on the title to see how he had recorded his struggle. The poem she began to read shocked her.

Is It Time

Is it time at last?
The denials ring hollow
Compromise has only brought bitterness
The projection of personal problems onto others has become absurd

The past comes back to scream "It cannot be true!"
Love cannot die in such a slow cruel way
How can something which began so brightly
Simply fade to gray?

How long have I asked
"Why can't I just leave?"
Is it because of yesterday's hardships?
When does today's pain outweigh the suffering of the past?

History beckons, remember when we burned with passion
Remember when we huddled in the rain
Remember when we glowed with ecstasy
Remember when we endured the pain

Changes have ripped through us
Bringing our passion to its knees
Venomous words are angrily thrown about
The smallest annoyance brings swift retribution

What happened to the passion?
Has it burned so fiercely that all fuel has been consumed?
The night held at bay by its glow again encroaches
Can the life we built together collapse in ruins?

You scream I am not who I once was

I return that you are not the same
Why stay together when all we cause is suffering?
Isolated and injured, each dwells on past slights and present
faults

Stark, bitter choices are now faced
Must we part in anger or can we somehow find peace?
Can we accept the failings that have driven us apart?
And somehow find release?

Is it time, or is there still doubt?
Is it time?

Her hands were trembling slightly as a tear slowly slid down her cheek. Was this his view of their relationship? He had seemed so distant over the past few years. Even though the department had taken care of him and MS had not really affected his career, bitterness had set in. He tried not to let it show and would never admit to it, but she saw through his facade. Whatever embittered seeds he had buried in his subconscious decades before began to sprout after the collapse of the World Trade Center. Hundreds of Newark firefighters and officers had responded to help their brothers in New York City the first few days after the terror attack. MS prevented Bob from following. He would have been a liability on the scene. Instead he had watched the drama of his generation unfold from the academy grounds. All he could do was show support by attending the Fire Department funerals. She had been on assignment in Asia and so was not there to listen to his frustrations. A subtle change had come over him after that. He became less accepting of his limitations and more resentful of her reminders about them.

Kathy knew the problems they faced were not his alone. Even though Bob was assigned to a staff position, her nerves had gradually become raw. She had nothing but admiration for the wives of New York firefighters. How they stayed sane after that was incomprehensible to her. She felt overwhelmed and began counting the days to his retirement. None of this helped their relationship. The bickering and arguments became more frequent. Her hope was after his retirement and Bobby moving to the dorms, they would have time for themselves. Did this poem say he had already given up? Determined to hit the question head on, she printed out a copy of the poem and headed for the door.

By the time she reached the Parkway, Kathy had settled down. Bob had not given her the poem, so he was at worst ambivalent about their future. The reporter had spent the last thirty minutes oscillating between anger and sorrow. Her major in college may have been journalism, but she had minored in English. It did not take an in depth analysis to see that if the words "is it" that were the focus of his poem were transposed, a weary question became a harsh statement. The title would then become "It is Time." This thought brought on a wave of nausea. When had he written it? She should have looked at the document's date before shutting down the computer. Now uncertainty filled her mind. Her anger was not directed exclusively at Bob. She was upset with herself as well. How had they degenerated to this state? Each busy with their own career. Both preoccupied with being good parents. Neither she nor Bob concerned with their relationship. Kathy accelerated up the Parkway ramp, the Mercedes responding smoothly to an angry foot.

Traffic was light which gave her an opportunity to look at herself, at her attitude toward her husband, and her willingness to fight for the couple they once were. Deep down Kathy realized she had insecurities that Bob did nothing to calm. He had been pulling away from her emotionally for quite some time. Instinctively she knew this, but his bottled up frustration and rage at what MS had done to his life had turned the man she knew into an enigma. This in turn frustrated her. Where would he find another woman who had the tools to understand him and his world better than she? Even while thinking this question, she knew it would never be about a more appropriate mate. No, Bob would stay with her or go it alone. He would not share what he considered a wretched existence with any other woman. Her only competition was her temper. The most difficult problem to surmount was their disparate views of how he should live his life.

He had made it clear that in his mind she was trying to control his life and so prevented him from living. In her mind he was trying to be reckless and was an ungrateful bastard for not appreciating her efforts to protect him. How could they bridge such a chasm? Had they even tried? Kathy did not want to think about her last question while cruising south in the fast lane of the Garden State Parkway. Those thoughts would only further infuriate and lead to an unscheduled stop which would result in a speeding ticket. Instead her thoughts were channeled into considering a strategy for the upcoming conference with her other half.

The reporter decided she would not bring up the poem during the picnic. This day was for all the old timers who had contributed so much to her oral history those years before. Although not a huge commercial success, it had taught her much and added to her reputation as a good interviewer. She had honed her skills talking with these guys. They deserved an enjoyable day strolling down memory lane.

Not wanting her questions about the poem's meaning to lead to a confrontation, she had to be clear on what her intent was. A need to know exactly what he had meant was eating away at her. Did he really question his desire to stay together? There was no great financial reason for them not to dissolve their union. The physical passion that had melded them together twenty-eight years before had cooled to a memory. Companionship was the most important attribute of their relationship, companionship and parenthood. Being parents had defined them, but now Bobby was going off to college so that aspect of their lives was about to change dramatically. The impetuses outside of themselves for remaining a couple were falling away. How hard did she want to work at rebuilding?

She slowed to negotiate through the E-Z pass lane of a toll plaza then accelerated at a reasonable pace, gliding into the middle lane. For twenty-four years, they had encouraged and supported each other. He had studied harder for promotional exams than the average undergraduate did to earn a bachelor's degree. She had earned an MA in Asian Studies from Frank's alma mater, Seton Hall. It was only over the past three years that things began to unravel. Before then they had made a great team. Although her point guard had received more glory than his center, Bob had never minded. Instead of jealousy, he was proud and would often tell her how much he admired her achievements. Over the last couple of years that admiration had fallen away; gradually replaced by resentment. This was not directed at what she had accomplished, but at her perception of him.

Kathy had never admitted it to Bob, but as she approached menopause her patience had receded while her anxiety had increased. A change had also come over him. Instead of the supportive, understanding gentleman she had married, she found herself in the company of an angry intolerant man. One who could take no criticism and quickly shut down when confronted with the myriad small ways he annoyed people. His anger would fester until he could hold it in no longer. Then it would explode. This passive aggressive nature only added fuel to whatever fire was smoldering between them. Did the changes have something to do with MS? There was no peaceful way of finding out. They could not discuss the subject between themselves and she had stopped accompanying him to Dr. Bradinsky's after it became apparent that the good doctor thought her questions and concerns were unwarranted.

Her mind was jumping from one point to another trying to latch onto something that would give substance to any discussion they might have. When was the last time she had told Bob of her admiration? Life had thrown him so many curve balls that would have robbed others of their will to live. Loss of his music, his athleticism, the camaraderie of the firehouse, the sense of accomplishment from helping people, the satisfaction of living life on the edge, none of this had crushed his spirit. Instead he had built another life. Kathy was not sure she could have pulled that off. Whenever she had told him this, he had made light of it. Was that why she had stopped or was it because life had become overwhelming for her? The cause could also have been his rage. Did his rage come from her impatience and anxiety or was it the other way around? Question, questions, all she could do was come up with questions, but this was not an interview she was seeking. They would be negotiating for, maybe fighting for, their future life together.

What were his wants and needs? No one knew him better than she. To be happy, Bob needed companionship. He seemed to have lost his ability to happily live alone after their children were born. Could she play on that? Did she even want to? Kathy caught herself. She was conducting a hostile interview of herself. They had shared life, love, and had raised two children. Their marriage deserved a concerted effort because, in the end, she knew no matter what happened; she still loved him.

She exited the Parkway; glanced down at the directions she had placed on the seat next to her; and headed for Double Trouble Road. It was fitting that they both should drive on a road with such a name. They had become double trouble. Over the past few years, she had developed a coping mechanism to deal with their troubles. Whenever he did something that infuriated her, she would address him by his middle name, Andrew. Some might say it was living in denial, but it allowed her to rationalize her love for Bob and desire to continue living with him even as he became insufferable. In her mind the man who so infuriated her was not Bob. She called him Andy. This was not conducive to a resolution of any quarrel they had, but it gave her some release of her frustration and anger. Unfortunately for their relationship, her release made him livid. Pulling into the VFW parking lot, she still had no answer as to how they could stop pushing each other's buttons. The car eased to a halt next to Bob's T-bird. Kathy quietly stepped out, still unsure what to say or do. The poem had thrown her for a loop. She was a woman who liked to feel she had some control of a situation, but now found herself without any control at all. She walked to the picnic entrance uneasy about how the day would turn out.

Chapter Forty-one

Bob opened the door to the Bayville Diner; still a little surprised Kathy had agreed to stop for coffee. It was a half-hearted suggestion on his part as they were leaving the picnic, a way to avoid handing her a poem in public. There was no coffee or tea among the picnic offerings, let alone cake. She had agreed readily, which implied a desire to spend time with him alone on neutral turf. That was a good sign. All in all the strategy of putting it off until after the gathering of old friends seemed to have worked perfectly. His wife had a wonderful time catching up with the Chief and the guys who had contributed to her oral history. When she was around old friends, Kathy glowed, reminding him of why he had married her.

A hostess in her fifties who struck him as the matriarch of the family that owed the diner greeted him. He requested a table, differing to his wife's lower back, and was led to a center table where he sat facing the entrance. Kathy should arrive momentarily. She had paused to say goodbye to the Chief as they left the picnic. While waiting, Bob thought about his interaction with her over the course of the day. The morning had been a pressure cooker. Her "to do" list for Bobby seemed to grow exponentially, leaving father and son amazed. How could someone make a simple move to dorms twenty minutes from home so complicated? He felt guilty about leaving Bobby alone to deal with that whirlwind, but it was best that he bow out and leave a little earlier than she. Arguments that arose from raising and dealing with their son were particularly venomous.

At the picnic, she had been her old gregarious self, floating between tables, remembering the names of everyone, chatting, laughing, and listening. She inevitably drifted back to the table with his old crew then wandered off again. Each time she returned she appeared more like her old self. But there was always something else there, just below the surface. Bob knew his wife too well not to sense it. She was carrying a weight which was probably why there was such a quick agreement to stop for coffee. Did she have a blow out with Bobby? He had coached his son before leaving; telling him to tread lightly because mom was still adjusting to the idea of her boy leaving for college. Did she just want to speak with him about Bobby's plans or was there something more ominous just over the horizon that was about to crash through the diner door? The thought of his wife having an emotional meltdown in the middle of a diner gave him hesitation. Maybe he should not present his little poem today. Kathy's car pulled into the diner lot, as if accentuating the wisdom of his last thought.

Bob rose and moved to pull her chair out as Kathy approached the table. She smiled, shook her head no, and requested a booth. This left him with a bad feeling.

* * * * * * * * * * * * * * * * * * * *

Kathy slid into the booth seat and placed her purse so it gave some support to her back. It had been a great day, but also a poignant one. So many of the men she had hoped to see were there. Yet too many could not make it because of health issues or because they had passed away. Tragically, not all the men who had passed away were elderly. Heart disease and cancer had claimed too many in their fifties

518

and sixties. Chief Simmons appeared to be doing well. She hoped the initial shock at how feeble he appeared did not show. It had been a decade since the two had been together so he had aged ten years in an instant. This had happened throughout the afternoon. As many as twenty years had passed since she had seen some of these men, so it was not always easy to recognize them. They had the advantage of watching her when she appeared on the evening news. None had trouble recognizing her or would have been surprised by the effects of time.

Bob sat across from her with a questioning look on his face. "I thought you preferred a chair to these benches," he explained warily while leaning across the table.

"You know I normally do," she assured him. "But today I think we need a little privacy, so I'll prop my back up with my purse and bear with it." He appeared a little confused, but smiled in agreement.

"We haven't done this in a long time," Bob started.

"Done what?"

"Stopped in a diner for coffee and tea with maybe a piece of cheese cake," he reminded her with a smile. "No kids, just the two of us."

There was no arguing the point, especially when he added "no kids." She could not remember the last time they had done it, only the first time. A thought crossed her mind that she should ask *Anjinsan* to write a poem, but she let that pass. He had already written one. She did not want another to complicate matters.

"You seemed a little surprised when you first saw the Chief," Bob informed her.

"Oh? It showed?" she replied with chagrin. "It's been so long since I saw him. I tried to prepare myself, but it was a reflex action."

"The last five years have been hard on him," Bob pointed out. "His mind is still sharp, but after eighty, the body just couldn't keep up."

"Pete looked good," she commented. "Did he fly up or drive up?"

"Flew, then his grandson picked him up," he told her. "After he dropped Pete at the picnic, he went to the beach and hung out until grandpa called."

"Cell phones make things so much easier," Kathy laughed, remembering how much simpler life had become when the kids got cells. She felt the need to move the conversation along. Small talk was a waste of valuable time on neutral turf. If they could discuss touchy subjects away from home there was less chance of a blowout. When she said goodbye to the Chief, he had mentioned that Bob was thinking of updating the oral history. The Chief had presented the subject almost as a request that she encourage Bob to do so. "So now that Bobby is going away, have you thought about your next project?" she asked, knowing it was not the best beginning. His reaction showed the question was unexpected.

He forced a chuckle as the waitress arrived to take their order. The respite appeared to allow him time to organize his thoughts. When the young lady left, Bob rolled right into a reply. "I don't really know how much time I'll have. After all, he's only twenty minutes away, but the guys thought since I talked about writing I should update the oral history."

Kathy tried to strike a balanced between appearing enthusiastic and assessing what should be a new idea. "That sounds interesting," she began. "You would be the perfect person for the job."

"You know the commitment it would take," he pointed out. "And there's not much of a market for it."

She chuckled at his last comment. "Some things you do for money and some you do for love," she reminded him. "You write poetry for love, don't you?" This was the perfect lead into the question that had been haunting her most of the day.

"I write poetry for a release," he answered appearing uneasy with the subject. "There was another idea I had for a project. Since Bobby will be living on campus for nine or ten months out of the year, I will be free to travel with you. I could interview firefighters in whatever city they send you and either submit articles to fire service magazines or put it all together for a book."

Once he had started presenting this idea, his speech had quickened as if he were afraid she would reject it before the complete concept was laid out. It took her a moment to digest his thoughts. It sounded like it had legs. If they could pull it off, traveling together without kids could add a dimension to their lives. It would force them to focus on each other, but what about MS? Could his body stand the rigors of traveling on a tight schedule? When they flew to Taiwan, he always left the plane completely wiped out and with a case of vertigo. Would his health condition just add to her work load? These questions came up instantly and could not be answered without experience, but his suggestion lightened her heart. Andy was not in sight and Bob was working overtime. The waitress returned with their coffee, tea, and cake before she could respond.

"We'll have to see how it will work out, but it sounds like a wonderful idea."

Bob smiled and leaned toward her and began speaking adamantly. "I figured while you are working during the day, I'll check out firehouses and talk with the guys. Then after the evening news, we have the rest of the night to ourselves." His enthusiasm was touching even if his understanding of her work schedule when abroad was not really accurate. But that was for another time. Now was the time to take advantage of the positive momentum and ask the question that had been bothering her.

"I'd love to give it a try," she assured him, before changing subjects. "I have a question to ask you. It concerns one of your poems. When I went on your computer to get the directions, I couldn't help but notice your poem folder. After I printed out the way to Bayville, I opened the folder and just browsed through the titles, so many of them brought back memories. There was one, though, that I hadn't seen before and, well I thought from the title that it was about your decision to retire. It's called 'Is It Time?'" She turned around and reached into her purse. From the look on Bob's face, it was obvious she did not have to read it to him. "Could you tell me when you wrote it?" She felt the emotions rising as she asked the question. The last words came out as a sad whisper.

* * * * * * * * * * * * * * * * * * *

Bob reached across the table to comfort his wife, realizing he should have taken the time to email the directions to her. If he had thought she could possibly stumble across that poem, he would have buried it in a separate file. The day had appeared to be going so well, but the feeling that something was not quite right had never left him. Hopefully, there were no other surprises. He knew exactly when the poem had been written.

"I wrote it after Bobby's prom," he said softly. She did not need more of an explanation. Bobby had been nervous about asking a girl to the prom. The easiest way around the problem was not to ask anyone. Since Millie had gone to her prom with a girl, her brother thought he could do something similar and go with one of his buddies. Then he could ask any of the girls who had not come with a guy to dance without risk or trouble. Bob had reacted negatively to the suggestion, but Kathy had seen no problem with the idea. He still could not understand how such a simple disagreement had spiraled down to a knock down drag out fight. She saw it as a way for her son to avoid the pressure and possible humiliation of being turned down. He saw it as a capitulation. Millie did what she did because there was shortage of guys. Bobby faced no shortage of girls. All he needed to do was get up the gumption to ask. He was a tall, handsome, intelligent young man. The girls loved him, but he tended to be a bit serious and a little shy. To his father it was an opportunity to build character, a rite of passage. To his mother, it was a threat to her son's psyche. By the time the argument had played out hours later, they were both hoarse from shouting and he had retreated to his office. She did not speak to him for days. Ironically, word got back to Kathy that a friend's daughter had a huge crush on Bobby and wanted nothing more in the world than to accompany him to the prom.

"So, at that time, the words rang true?" Kathy stated.

"They were just thoughts," he answered in an attempt to placate her.

"Just thoughts," she replied with a bitter chuckle. "The last time you said something like that, you tried to walk away from me."

It took him a moment to realize what she was talking about. That was close to thirty years before. If nothing else, the woman had one hell of a memory for slights.

"Do you still have the same mind set?" she asked.

Bob considered the question. Over the years he had learned to try and take a moment before answering questions full of possibilities. "I am hoping we can grow past the mind set expressed in it," he answered cautiously.

"Grow past what?" she quizzed.

"Grow past the shouting, the anger, the tantrums," he answered, instantly regretting his choice of words.

"The tantrums," she snapped in a hot whisper. "Whose tantrums? Mine? Can't you control your loss tongue? Why do you always push my buttons? Can't you take my feelings into consideration just once?"

"I do try," he sighed. "It used to be my effort was enough. Now I have to get it right, trying doesn't count." What he said was not new. They had discussed this before without much effect.

"Before you didn't have to try twice," she shot back, looking directly at him. "You got it right the first time."

It was her pat answer to this complaint. When the kids were young and the hormones were flowing, he was an amazing man. Now he was a schmuck. "Kathy, you don't really believe that do you?" he asked with frustration. "I am human. I will make mistakes or misunderstand what you want."

"You didn't misunderstand before," she claimed. "Now you walk around with an underlying rage at life. What happened to acceptance?"

"Couldn't I ask you the same question?" he parried. "What happened to acceptance?"

He was not the only one fighting to accept what life had become. She refused to see her changes, her short fuse and how it affected relationships within their family. How many years had he spent coaching Millie and Bobby, giving mommy reports while driving them back from after-school activities so they knew what to expect?

She looked tired as she responded. "I accepted MS and the effect it had on our lives. What we live now is our normal. I have learned to accept what has happened and move on. Have you? You're frustrated and take it out on me." The last sentence came out as a hiss.

"Please don't, Kath," he pleaded. "There's more than enough blame for the both of us to share." Why did she always want a confrontation? How is it she could not see her changes? He had to somehow guide this conversation away for the edge of this abyss, so they could discuss improving their relationship before it was too late.

"Life has changed both of us," he began. Before he could continue she interjected herself.

"Who changed first?" she snapped.

She just would not let up. He pushed aside his anger once more in an attempt to defuse the situation. "Whether it was me or you doesn't matter if we want to get back to where we were. We've both changed physically, emotionally, philosophically; our expectations have changed."

This seemed to calm her. She sat quietly for a moment, stirring her coffee and thinking. "How did we get here?" she asked without energy.

"One day at a time," he sighed. "Years go by that way. If we don't feed the couple, they become strangers."

"You think we're strangers?" she asked quietly

"Not yet, but we have to work if we're going to avoid it."

* * * * * * * * * * * * * * * * * *

"We have to work," Kathy whispered. He was beginning to sound like a man willing to negotiate. "What about that poem? 'Is it Time?' Sounds like you're ready to give up," she pointed out.

"I wrote it in May," he replied. "But I chose to still be here."

She liked the way he put that, chose, not settled or felt compelled. He chose. It was encouraging. "So why are you still here?" she asked. Would the romantic Bob answer or the combative Andy?

"Because I know that deep down, the girl who squealed on the back of my bike when I rode through that parking lot entrance is still here. Can she come out to play occasionally?"

Kathy laughed at that memory. She was still a girl in so many ways when they went on that ride through west Jersey. What had happened to her?

"Come out to play?" she sighed. That girl grew up, had a couple of children, a few heart breaks, and has dealt with MS for years. All that helped her develop common sense."

"So, she won't come out and play anymore?" he asked mischievously.

"Bob, you can't ride a bike anymore," she reminded him. How many times had he told her that?

"Well, how about roller coasters? You were once a roller coaster queen, right?"

"Roller coasters?" she asked incredulously. "You spent too much time watching Millie ride them last summer."

"Oh, but I didn't just watch," he revealed for the first time. "We rode them together. I laughed so hard my belly hurt."

Rode them together? Millie had not mentioned that to her. His equilibrium could not handle that. What was he trying to prove? Thank God they had not told her. She would have been worried sick.

"First, thank you for not telling me ahead of time," she laughed. "How did you pull that off with your vertigo?"

"Anti-vert from Dr, B," he smiled.

"You are crazy," she declared.

"You knew that when you married me," he reminded her.

Kathy laughed, enjoying his revelation and his company for the first time in a long while.

Bob reached into his back pocket and pulled out a piece of paper. "Since we spent so much time on poems, might as well add this one." He unfolded the paper and tried to smooth out some of the crinkles before handing it to her. It was simply called "Tell me." When she finished, she looked up at him and attempted to do just that, tell him; while struggling to keep her emotions in check.

"No, it was not just a dream," she whispered, taking a moment to regain composure. She finished her coffee and cake before looking up.

After patting her lips with a napkin, Kathy tried to bring the conversation back to reality. "Do you remember what you told me about Mrs. Banks?" she quizzed.

"Janet?" Bob laughed. "That's an old memory. The woman had a rough life."

"But she was still trying to live it, right?" Kathy reminded him. "You said that was the hand life had dealt her, so she played it as best she could. Can't we do the same thing?"

"I'm trying. That's why I take meds to go on roller coasters," he laughed.

She thought he did that because he was still denying his limitations. But for the first time in a while she could see his point. That was a decided step forward.

"Look, I know of your frustrations," she assured him, picking her words carefully. "I'm not going to insult you and say I know your frustration, but I think I have some understanding of it. My husband does have MS after all."

"I'm sorry to hear that," he said with feigned seriousness.

His playful side was showing which gave her even more hope. The fear she had felt after reading that poem was receding. Their life together seemed to have possibilities again. "Oh, Robert," she sighed, trying to get her thoughts back.

"Robert? You haven't called me Robert since our wedding vows," Bob laughed.

Kathy laughed with him. Where had she come up with that? At least it was not Andy. "I was just trying to get your attention," she told him.

He reached across the table and held her hand. "You did that thirty years ago," he assured her. "You haven't lost it yet."

www.ingramcontent.com/pod-product-compliance
Lightning Source LLC
Chambersburg PA
CBHW020245030726
47499CB00001B/61